TRINITY

Clare Davidson

Published by Smudged Ink Press
Copyright © 2012 Clare Davidson
ISBN 978-0-9926113-1-6

Second Paperback Edition: July 2013

For Tom and Eleanor. I love you both.

Acknowledgements

Edited by Ruth Ellen Parlour
Proofread by Megan Payne
Cover Illustration by Bramasta Aji
Cover Layout by Jonny Coole

Thank you to everyone who supported me whilst I was writing 'Trinity': Joel for the plotting session; Mum and Louise for reading the early draft; Tom for putting up with being ignored for hours on end and Dad for all the technical stuff.

A massive thank you to everyone who has bought Trinity since its original release in July 2012.

Chapter One

"Kiana, are you even listening to me?"

Kiana peeked over the top of her drawing board and smiled innocently. "Of course I am, Ducarius."

The old man pursed his lips and peered at Kiana, forcing the young girl to stifle a laugh behind her hand. He always seemed to be annoyed with his pupil.

Kiana looked back down at her artwork: a detailed charcoal castle. It stood on a tall hill, surrounded by a grey stone wall. She had never seen it before, except in her dreams. From her apartments in Blackoak Tower, she had only ever been allowed to see the sky.

"If you *were* listening to me, what was I saying?"

Kiana rolled her eyes, placed the board and charcoal stick on the plush two-seater and stood. "How can I concentrate when I have a new Guardian arriving today?"

"Kiana, we really *must* continue our lesson."

She folded her arms across her chest and stared down at him. "Why, Ducarius? I'll still be here tomorrow. And the day after that. And the day after that. I'm not *going* anywhere."

She was painfully aware of the petulance in her voice. "Besides, what's the point anyway? You fill my head with history, reading, writing, philosophy and art, *every day*. Why?"

Ducarius threw his hands up and stood. "You are the physical embodiment of a *goddess*, Kiana. Those are all things you should know." As he spoke, he glanced at the tapestry of Miale's symbol—a golden chalice—that hung above the oversized fireplace.

"But *why*?" Kiana turned her back on him and looked out of the open doors that led to her balcony. The sky was a deep, endless shade of blue. "I will *never* use any of it!" *Because I'm stuck here.*

She looked round sharply as the door to her chambers clicked open. It was always locked, confining her within three simple rooms.

Marcas, her favourite Guardian, stepped in and gave Kiana a charming wink. "Your new Guardian is on his way up."

She smiled sweetly at Ducarius. "Can we stop our lessons for today? I promise I'll concentrate tomorrow."

Marcas nodded at Ducarius.

The old tutor sighed and muttered something under his breath as he gathered up the pile of heavy books. "Fine, fine. I'll see you in the morning." He touched his fingertips to his forehead and inclined his head ever so slightly towards her.

Kiana returned the gesture. She kept her eyes fixed on Ducarius until the door was closed behind him. She shivered at the heavy clunk of the lock.

"Are you well, Kia?" Marcas said.

Kiana grinned and half-ran, half-skipped the handful of paces to Marcas. She flung her arms around his chest and gave him a hug. "Yes." She tilted her head up so that she could see the amused twinkle in his hazel eyes. "Are you? I hardly get to see you anymore."

Marcas nodded and used his knuckle to tap her lightly under the chin. "My promotion keeps me busy, you know that. Besides, in a few moments you'll have a new Guardian to entertain you."

Kiana released him and wandered across the cold stone floor. She stopped in front of the vast map of Gettryne that hung on the wall. Several copper pins protruded from the map, marking the villages, towns and cities that each of her Guardians had come from.

She plucked a fresh pin from a leather bag that hung from the wall and turned the cool metal around in her fingertips. The tower's blacksmith had crafted each of the pins individually for her. He had obviously put a lot of effort into each one, even though Kiana had never been allowed to meet him. The one that she held was exquisite: the copper curled round into a spiral, creating a nest in which sat a sparkling green stone that she had been told was an emerald.

"I wonder where he's from…"

Kiana looked back at the map. The greatest concentration of pins rested in and around the city of Ironhold, which lay to the southeast of the tower. She tapped the top of the pin to her lips and then dropped it back into the bag.

With a dramatic sigh, Kiana swirled round towards the window, holding the full skirt of her gold surcoat so that she could hear the swish of the crisp fabric. She could see some of her Guardians laughing and chatting gaily outside. Beyond the chatter, she could hear the annoying chirping of the crickets that lived in the forest. Kiana had never seen it, but she knew from the map that was pinned to the wall that it existed.

Without thinking, Kiana strode out onto the balcony and tried to carry on up the ramp that would have allowed her access to the higher level. Two Guardians blocked her path. Kiana wanted to see the forest, touch the bark of the trees with her fingertips and see the birds that sang every morning. She wanted to hear what grass sounded like as she walked across it and how it felt between her toes.

Marcas' hand closed gently around her arm, just above her elbow. "You can ask him where he's from when he arrives." He led her back into her chamber. "Finn is giving him the grand tour of the tower first. He'll be here soon. That's if he isn't too scared to talk to you."

Kiana stared up at him, her eyebrows knotting together in a frown. "Too scared? Why would he be scared of me?"

Marcas laughed, letting go of her arm. "Ever since last summer, Finn has been telling tall tales about you!"

Her frown deepened. "Last summer?" Nothing special had happened the previous summer. Nothing special ever happened.

Marcas scratched the top of his head and looked away from her awkwardly. "Since you… blossomed."

Kiana stared at him for a moment and then her eyes widened as she glanced down at the slender curves of her body. She had watched her handmaid's body change long before hers had, even though they were the same age. Kiana felt her cheeks grow hot and turned away abruptly. "What exactly will Finn be telling my new Guardian?"

"Oh, you know, how terrifying you can be."

Kiana's lips parted into a small o. "Terrifying?"

"How difficult you can be."

Her mouth dropped open a little more. "Difficult?"

Marcas took hold of Kiana's hand and twirled her round. "And how much you like men!" As she came to a stop, Kiana realised her mouth was hanging wide open. Marcas' grin grew so wide she could see his crooked teeth. "*Especially* your Guardians!"

Kiana snapped her mouth shut. "He won't believe any of that, will he?"

She jumped as she heard two sets of approaching footsteps echoing down the hallway.

Quickly, Kiana smoothed out her clothes, brushed a stray strand of blonde hair behind her shoulder and took a deep breath in a failed attempt to calm herself as she waited with a smile for her new Guardian.

As Finn led the smart young man inside, Kiana looked him up and down. Like every Guardian, he wore a jet-black uniform made of finely spun wool. Beneath it, she could see the curves of his strong muscles. He wasn't tall; however, he had an air of confidence about him that seemed to drain away as soon as his dark brown eyes met hers. His face flushed red, which was an unfortunate combination with his straw-coloured hair.

"May I introduce you to the current incarnation of the goddess Miale: the lady Kiana." Marcas gestured towards her and gave a knowing grin.

Kiana rolled her eyes at the needlessly formal title. The new Guardian would know *what* she was. It was only her name that he wouldn't have known.

"Kiana, this is your new Guardian: Nidan Ward."

Nidan. She liked the sound of his name. "Finn hasn't been mean to you, has he?" Kiana greeted him formally by touching her fingertips to her forehead and then holding her clenched fist out towards him. She expected him to complete the greeting by meeting it with his own fist.

Nidan's cheeks flushed an even brighter shade of red as he took a half-step back, struck his hand over his chest and bowed rigidly.

She looked at Finn and narrowed her eyes. "Finn, what *have* you said?"

Finn held up his hands in a placating gesture. "Nothing! I swear." There was a smirk on his lips that told her he was lying.

Kiana shook her head and rolled her eyes. "Of *course* you haven't." She looked back to Nidan. "You mustn't pay any attention to him." *Please don't believe anything he might have said!* "Finn has an odd sense of humour."

Finn and Marcas both laughed as they wandered outside and onto the upper balcony. She watched as they lounged against the railing, searching the horizon with their eyes.

Kiana flashed Nidan a smile, retrieved the pin that she had dropped into the bag below the map and then looped her arm through his. "Where are you from? Please tell me you aren't from Ironhold! I hope it's somewhere new. If it is, you'll have to tell me all about it."

"A village near Lorwick." Nidan's words sounded clumsy as they tumbled out of his mouth.

No other new Guardian had ever acted so nervously around her. *Should I ask him what Finn said about me?* She glanced briefly at Finn, narrowed her eyes and then turned back to Nidan, smiling. "Show me."

Kiana handed him the copper pin, watching as he pressed it into the map just to the west of the city of Lorwick. She smiled. It *was* a new place.

She led him out onto the balcony so that she could feel the breeze on her face. It tousled her neatly brushed hair and playfully rippled through Nidan's short-cropped style.

"You'll have to tell me everything about your home and family. What does your father do? How many brothers and sisters do you have?" She paused as his gaze dipped to the floor. "I'm sorry. Did I say something that offended you?"

Nidan shook his head. "No." His voice was quiet.

"You've lost someone?"

Nodding, he stared up at the sky, avoiding her concerned gaze.

"You don't have to tell me."

Nidan sighed. "My sister. To the last age of Thanatos."

Kiana suddenly felt cold. She *had* said something wrong. She would never live through an age of Thanatos: her birth had ended the last one and her death would start the next. However, Marcas had told tales of the madness that gripped the people of Gettryne and of all the senseless deaths that occurred. Kiana often chose to forget that everyone around her had lived through the last age of Thanatos and most had lost someone dear to them.

"Nidan!"

They both looked up at the sound of Marcas' voice.

"I think she *likes* you." Marcas gave them both a knowing wink.

Kiana felt heat rise in her cheeks.

Marcas turned away to look back over the railing.

"You shouldn't pay any attention to Marcas. In a few days he'll…"

"Sound the…!" Marcas' booming warning died on the air as fire engulfed his body.

Kiana screamed as Marcas' face contorted in pain. The hungry flames devoured his body and charred his flesh. She tried to run forward, but was stopped by Nidan. He spun her round so that she could no longer see the horror behind her. But she could still smell the stench of Marcas' smouldering flesh. She could still hear his agonising screams and the shouts of her Guardians.

The terrible sound of Marcas' cries began to weaken, falling away from her. Kiana tried to turn round, but Nidan's strong grip stopped her. Marcas' screams faded to nothingness. There was a loud splash. Marcas was gone. Kiana tilted her face up to stare at the perfect blue sky and screamed.

*

Skaric stared at the thick walls that surrounded the tower, his brow creased and his eyes narrowed. In the forest behind him, dry twigs snapped under dozens of booted feet belonging to lightly armoured Wolves. They strained against their orders, waiting impatiently for the nyxii to provide a way into the tower. There was so much tension and anticipation in the air that it made the hairs on Skaric's arms rise. Any Guardian visible on the walls had already been dealt with; the rest were hiding like cowards within the tower. With them was the Wolves' quarry.

The sound of heavy feet clomping across the bank to his right drew Skaric's attention. His skin crawled as he watched Berend, the war leader, pace up and down. Fourteen years Skaric's senior, he was a tall and brutally strong man, whose tanned, scarred skin and full beard made him look all the more fierce.

"She must die," Berend said.

Skaric hated him.

They had been searching for seventeen years—ever since the last period of Thanatos had ended. Finally, they had found Miale: thanks to the wagging tongue of a desperate man. He knew that Berend couldn't afford to let her slip through his grasp: the shame would be too great.

"We must avenge Ysia." Berend stopped beside Skaric and folded his arms across his broad chest.

Skaric glanced at the war leader and then took a half-step away; he had always felt uncomfortable in Berend's presence. Hopefully, Berend was too focused to notice the movement.

To their left, Vali, another nyxus, extended his hand towards the wall, his fingers tensed as fire leapt from them towards a Guardian who had dared to survey the scene. The man's screams rang in Skaric's ears. He clenched his teeth; he had never heard so much death.

"The walls are too strong," Vali said. He turned and stared at Berend with sharp green eyes. He had a lean pinched face and hooked nose, making him resemble a hawk.

Skaric could almost feel Berend's rage growing in seething silence. It was the first time in three incarnations of Miale that the Wolves had gotten so close to destroying the Goddess' body and bringing the time of Thanatos early.

"We have to make these bastards pay!" Berend said. "They deserve to suffer."

Do they? Skaric turned his attention back to the tower. His fellow nyxii had sent searing flames hurtling at the walls, but the strong stone had barely been scorched. There was only one entrance into the tower, but an iron portcullis barred the way.

"Our fire cannot destroy stone or iron," Vali said. "There's no way for our men to get inside."

Skaric bit into his lip. The sudden sharp pain helped to calm him. There was a way. He could see it. Fire didn't have to be the only weapon of the nyxii.

"*Nothing* is impenetrable," Berend said. "There has to be a way. Miale *must* die."

Miale must die. They have subjected us to a thousand years of persecution. We must have our revenge. How many times had Skaric heard those words? *Too many, but I have to live by them.*

He forced his mouth to curl into the ghost of a smile. "There isn't a weakness," he said, his voice little more than a whisper.   "Yet."

"Didn't you hear me?" Vali said. "Our fire cannot penetrate the walls."

Skaric rolled his eyes. The true joy of nyxii magic was that it had no limits other than the will of the caster; his mentor, Jakob, had taught him that. There was no *god* to impose rules upon the nyxii. He glanced down at the ground. All the grass in a circle around him had withered and was blanched of colour. A quick glance over his shoulder told him that the closest trees had also shriveled and died; their leaves, crumpled and brown, littered the ground. *I did that.* He looked up and down the bank. Wherever a nyxus stood, there was death.

Bracing himself, he whispered, "There is a way to weaken their walls."

He shivered as Berend's large, powerful hand curled around his shoulder. Vali opened his mouth to say something but was silenced with a look.

"What do you need?" The war leader's voice was teetering on the edge of excitement.

Skaric paused before replying. His plan would cause the deaths of Wolves, including himself. But the rest of their forces would be able to surge into the tower and flush out their quarry.

"Well?"

He squirmed under Berend's angry stare. *Why did I say anything?*

"Think of how proud it would make your father if *your* actions allowed us to capture Miale. *You* would be responsible for our victory."

Skaric balled his hands into fists. He was a Wolf. Cowardice wasn't an option. Nor was compassion. He shrugged away from Berend's grasp and looked him in the eyes. "Sacrifices." He was certain that the war leader would comply.

Berend grinned grimly. He wheeled away from Skaric and cleared his throat, addressing all the Wolves within earshot in a loud, booming voice. "All those willing to lay down their lives for the glory of Ysia, stand forward!"

Skaric fixed his gaze on the tower. He didn't want to know how many Wolves were happy to place victory above themselves and allow him to take their lives. He didn't want to see their faces.

"Your sacrifices await," Berend said as he returned to stand beside Skaric. Then in a more dangerous tone he whispered, "Make sure this works."

Skaric nodded. "You'd best stand back." He didn't allow himself to look at Berend.

Skaric stepped forward onto healthy green grass and waited for a count of ten, long enough for Berend to get out of the range of his magic. He began to concentrate, narrowing his eyes so that he could focus on the portcullis: their only way in.

He slowly exhaled and then began to pull power from the earth. Energy flowed into him, warming from within. It wasn't enough, but he had known it wouldn't be. Skaric gritted his teeth and reached out with his mind, grabbing energy from the men behind him, from the willing sacrifices.

He could feel their life energy throbbing within him— like a dozen hearts beating beside his own. But faster. More desperate. He heard them all scream—sounds of terror that he tried to block out. It was too late to save them. They had *wanted* to die.

Power sizzled beneath Skaric's skin, so intense that he felt his head would burst. He pushed it all towards his hands, readying himself to release it. He just needed a little more. Behind him, the screams died out as the body of each sacrificial Wolf thudded to the ground.

Skaric waited. He waited until he could no longer draw any more power, waited until he couldn't bear the heat beneath his skin. Then, with a cry, he thrust his left hand towards the tower. Pure, deadly, devastating energy darted from his hand, stronger than a tumultuous wind. As it struck, the portcullis shattered into hundreds of lethal pieces that went flying in all directions.

Skaric heard the Wolves cheer, but it was distant, as though he was underwater. For all Berend's strength and physical might, he couldn't match the power that Skaric had just wielded. Not ever.

Unbearable pain coursed beneath Skaric's skin. The sickening stench of smouldering flesh stung his nostrils. His flesh. Pain like he had never known devoured him from within. At the edge of his vision fire leapt hungrily. The price for his arrogance. His death didn't matter. He was a hero. His name would be remembered amongst the Wolves.

The horror of watching Jakob die flooded into Skaric's mind. He heard his mentor's manic laughter, which had quickly turned to tortured screams of despair.

Fear gripped Skaric. It paralysed him. He could hear the rush of water in his ears. The moat. Skaric staggered towards the welcome darkness of the water. He fell, but the icy shock did nothing to quell the fire.

It's too late. I've destroyed myself! For what?

If he could have screamed he would. He was going to die and he was afraid. The water engulfed Skaric, wrapping him in its deadly embrace as it swept him away.

*

"Switch clothes."

Kiana blinked at Finn. It was such a simple order but she couldn't make her arms move to obey him.

"Now!"

Slowly, Kiana turned to look at her handmaid. Erynn's eyes were red and puffy, her face smudged with dirt from the tunnel and her blonde hair dishevelled. The girl's shoulders shook as she pulled the plain brown surcoat over her head and held it out to Kiana. Like Kiana, she also wore an undyed woollen underdress that preserved modesty.

Kiana stared at the surcoat and then at Erynn. Her lower lip trembled and a lump formed in her throat that threatened to choke her.

"Now, Kiana!" Finn kept glancing towards Ciall, who was standing at the tunnel entrance.

Sunlight filtered in, providing enough light to see by deeper in the tunnel. Kiana could hear the sounds of fighting in the distance. Swords clanged against each other, feet thundered over wood and men screamed. She clamped her hands over her ears and sank down so that she was crouching.

Finn was shouting at her. Kiana shook her head and squeezed her eyes tightly shut. She wouldn't listen. How could he ask her to send Erynn out to die?

A pair of hands closed over hers and pulled them away from her ears.

"Kiana."

Kiana couldn't immediately put a name to the gentle voice. Slowly, she opened her eyes. Nidan was crouching in front of her, eyes alert, body tense, but there was a kindness in his face.

"We don't have time to think," he said. "You need to do as Finn says."

"But…"

"Don't think." He was right. "You *have* to live."

Right again. She stood and pulled her surcoat off with numb fingers. Erynn helped her into the rough wool garment. It irritated the nape of her neck. *It doesn't matter!* She watched as Erynn pulled on the golden surcoat. Kiana had always wondered why she and Erynn looked so alike. Now it was clear: Erynn was the perfect decoy. Kiana shivered violently. Her stomach lurched. She turned away and threw up. Once she had recovered, Nidan offered her a scrap of cloth. She cleaned her mouth and then managed to force a grateful smile to her lips.

"We split into two groups," Finn said. "Bran and Coran will take Erynn." He looked at Nidan. "You're with me and Ciall."

Kiana had enough wits to see Nidan's eyebrows raise as his mouth dropped open. Under different circumstances, his expression might have been comical.

"Let's go!"

She forced herself to follow Finn out of the tunnel, expecting to see Wolves at any moment.

Finn must have sensed Kiana's nervousness. He paused and glanced at her. "From what we could see, the Wolves are concentrated around the moat. It's unlikely they'll find this entrance."

Kiana nodded. They had run through the tunnel for what felt like an eternity, and the fighting sounded so distant. Despite Finn's assurances, Kiana stared after the other group as they vanished into the forest. They had to stay safe. They *had* to.

They ran at the edge of the river across wet, slippery pebbles that threatened to send Kiana crashing to her knees. It took all her concentration to stay upright. She kept looking round. Every sound she heard sent shivers of fear through her body.

A burnt body swept past, carried by the fierce current of the river. Kiana paused, trembling, even though she knew it was insane to stop. "Why?" Her eyes felt heavy under the weight of unshed tears.

"Because the Wolves are monsters," Nidan said as he stopped beside her.

"We have to keep running!" Finn said. "We don't know how long it will take the Wolves to realise you're no longer in the tower."

Kiana swallowed back her tears. "It's my fault. Everyone is dead or dying because of me."

Nidan took hold of her hand. His touch felt warm against her cold skin. "No. They are dying because of the insane hatred of the Wolves. It isn't your fault."

Kiana's legs felt like lead. She couldn't control them or make herself move. She started to sink towards the ground.

"What are you doing?" Finn said. His grip tightened on the pommel of his sheathed sword as he glanced up and down the bank.

Gently, Nidan held Kiana by the shoulders, forbidding her from collapsing completely. "We have to escape." He looked her directly in the eyes as he spoke. "*You* have to escape."

She stared at him, blinking to stop her tears from falling.

"If you don't, the Wolves will win." His voice sounded cracked and his hands were trembling on her shoulders. "People have sacrificed themselves for you and for Miale, but that was our choice, not yours. We all chose to become servants of Pios. We chose to become your Guardians."

"Why? Why would you sign up to die?"

"Because defending you prevents the time of Thanatos coming early. That's what matters."

She nodded slowly. "Your sister." She drew in a shuddering breath. "What's happening… what the Wolves are doing… it's so horrible."

"I know. It *is* horrible. We'll have time to grieve when we reach Valgate, I promise you. But not now. Now we have to run."

Kiana nodded again and righted herself. At the same time, she heard the sound of footsteps crashing through the undergrowth. Finn and Ciall both drew their swords, but when Nidan went to draw his own Finn stopped him.

"Take Kiana and run. We'll follow you when we can."

Nidan opened his mouth and then shut it again. Kiana cried out as he grabbed her hand and pulled her away. She'd already lost Marcas and now Finn was going to vanish too. Even though it made her footsteps clumsy, she looked back over her shoulder until Finn and Ciall had vanished out of sight. Soon after that, all she could hear was the ringing sound of steel clashing against steel. Unchecked tears fell down her cheeks.

They ran past more bodies, some still being carried by the current, others trapped on the bank. All were burned. All were dead. Kiana tried not to look, but it was almost impossible not to. She wondered if it would be possible to rid herself of the horror of the burnt corpses and twisted faces.

As they ran, Nidan kept glancing over his shoulder at her. He looked lost and frightened, but every time he caught her gaze, a confident smile broke onto his face.

Suddenly, Kiana pulled him to a halt. He turned round as she dragged her hand free of his and knelt down beside yet another corpse. Except it wasn't a corpse—not yet. She could see the faint rise and fall of the man's chest and hear his ragged breathing. The sight was hideous. Glistening red welts covered his exposed skin, slowly oozing clear fluid. His face had not been burnt as badly. It was a dark shade of red that looked painfully tender, but there were no open wounds. His dark hair, beard and eyebrows were only a little singed. A revoltingly sweet, acrid stench rose up from the burns, so overwhelming that Kiana could almost taste it in the back of her throat. She clapped her hands over her nose and mouth and tried to breathe calmly. Beside her, Nidan gagged as he crouched down on the pebbles.

Kiana forced her hands away from her face, as she looked at Nidan. "Heal him?"

Nidan didn't move. "He's a Wolf."

Nidan was right: he was her enemy. His hands had probably killed her Guardians. Her friends. Her family.

Kiana's mouth quivered. She was sure of one thing: too many people had already lost their lives. "He's dying."

"He's a Wolf. We need to keep going," Nidan said, tugging at her hand.

Kiana pulled away from his touch. "We can't just leave him." She didn't look at Nidan as she disobeyed him.

"Yes we can."

"No! He's in pain! How can you be so cruel?" She breathed in and out heavily. Her throat felt sore from shouting.

Nidan sighed and pulled a dagger from his belt before holding it over the man's throat. Kiana placed her hands over his, forbidding him from delivering the killing blow, even though her hands were trembling violently.

"He's a Wolf! It's no less than he would do to us." Nidan's voice dripped with venom. "Besides, look at him. Killing him is probably a kindness."

"You can't." Kiana's breath caught in her throat. It seemed that it wasn't just the Wolves who were controlled by hatred.

The Wolf made an odd whistling sound as he suddenly sucked in a large gulp of air. Kiana turned her attention back to him, knocking Nidan's hands and the knife aside without resistance.

The Wolf's eyes opened slowly, revealing cold, light eyes that were full of pain and anger. He stared directly at Kiana and his eyes widened slightly.

He knows who I am. "Can you talk?"

He did not respond. Kiana wasn't even sure that he *could* respond. She reached out a hand but hesitated, unable to actually touch him. His mouth twisted into a faint grimace.

She looked up and stared at Nidan. "Please? Please heal him."

"Even though he's a Wolf?"

Kiana dipped her gaze and looked the Wolf in the eyes again. His stare dared her to kill him. "Yes."

"Why?"

"Because it's wrong to leave him in pain. And Pios teaches us that *all* human life is sacred. Even if he is a Wolf, he's still human."

Nidan rubbed his face with his hands. "He would kill us without hesitation."

Did he really think she didn't know that? Fresh tears welled in Kiana's eyes. "I don't want anyone else to die because of me." She drew in a deep breath. "As a Guardian, you have the power to heal him. As a Guardian, you must do as I say and I am *ordering* you to save him." Despite the stern words, she could feel herself trembling.

Nidan looked from her to the Wolf and then back again. "You're so naïve." He shook his head, muttering something under his breath. "Keep watch. If you hear or see anything, I stop and we run, understand? Nothing is more important than keeping you safe."

Kiana nodded and stood. Water had seeped into her clothes, and the woollen cloth clung to her legs, making them feel heavy and cumbersome. She watched as Nidan laid his dagger within reach but away from the injured Wolf. Then he placed both hands over the Wolf's chest and closed his eyes.

At first nothing seemed to happen. Kiana did her best to keep watch. She glanced up and down the bank and tried to gaze into the forest, listening to the distant sounds of fighting; it sounded more like swords clanging in the practise yard than a heated battle. The trees that Kiana had longed to see seemed to be working against her, as their deep shadows provided a multitude of hiding places for the Wolves that wanted her dead. She couldn't see or hear the birds that woke her every morning with their song. Every living animal in the forest seemed to be hiding from the destructive force of the Wolves. Kiana wished she could join them.

She kept finding her gaze drifting back to Nidan and the Wolf. Nidan's brow was furrowed and his fingertips were twitching. Kiana laced her fingers together and glanced around again. Now that she was further away from the Wolf, her stomach was no longer churning at the sight and smell. She heard the sound of a twig snapping behind her and spun round. An animal? A man? She held her breath and stared. *I should tell Nidan.*

Kiana turned back to face Nidan. His face had become slack, peaceful, and all the tension had drained from his shoulders.

There was no more sound from the forest. It had to have been an animal. Ducarius had told her that there were deer in the forest; his books had contained drawings of the timid animals.

Suddenly, Nidan looked up. "He's one of their cursed mages."

She looked at the Wolf. His eyes were still open, staring and unreadable. "How do you know that?"

Nidan twisted so that he could look at her. "The damage started *inside* him. That's the cost of their repulsive magic. Use too much and it kills them." His mouth curled into a snarl. "I should have known."

"How could you?"

Nidan gestured to the Wolf. "He's not carrying any weapons."

Kiana's brow puckered in thought. The Wolf's weapons could have been swept away by the river. However, if Nidan said the Wolf could cast magic, she believed him. A mage had killed Marcas. Countless other Guardians had burst into flames. *I should hate him. I should want him dead.*

"Can you save him?"

Nidan shrugged. "If the damage is too great, no amount of healing will help him." The corners of Nidan's mouth tugged down. "Why hasn't he killed us?"

Kiana looked at him, puzzled. Surely the Wolf was too injured to harm anyone, least of all her.

"I was taught that a Wolf mage could cast their magic no matter how badly injured they are, even if doing so kills them," Nidan said.

Kiana shuddered and regarded the Wolf. It was a good question, but she doubted he would give them an answer.

The Wolf's brow furrowed and he closed his eyes tightly.

Kiana didn't need to know why the Wolf hadn't tried to kill them. "Will you try to heal him?" She expected Nidan to argue.

He didn't. Nidan puffed out his cheeks and closed his eyes again. This time he relaxed almost immediately. Kiana made quick glances around, watching for danger. When she looked back at the Wolf, his eyes were open again and his expression was less pained. Physically, he looked the same.

Eventually, Nidan rocked back onto his heels and looked down at the Wolf. "He won't die."

"But…"

Nidan snapped his head round to look at her. "I've set magic in place so his wounds will heal quickly. There won't even be any scarring. It's a damned sight more than he deserves."

A smile of relief touched Kiana's lips. She had been wrong to doubt Nidan. "Thank you." She looked down at the Wolf. "Try not to get yourself killed." She began to turn away, but paused. "If you want to thank us, then don't kill another soul tonight."

She held a hand out to Nidan. "We should go."

The nervous expression vanished from Nidan's face. He stood and accepted her hand. As they moved away, the Wolf painfully propped himself up on one elbow. Kiana froze and stared at him.

"Run." The Wolf stared directly at her, his eyes were cold and piercing.

Kiana shuddered.

The Wolf's eyes narrowed in an expression of anger. "Run."

Nidan's grip tightened on Kiana's hand and he pulled her away from the Wolf.

Chapter Two

Nidan dipped his flask in the cool river, took a swig and then stood and faced the imposing cliff that towered above them.

"What are you thinking?" Kiana was watching him intently. The shine had gone from her eyes, and her shoulders sagged under the weight of the day's events.

Instead of replying, Nidan looked at the uneven surface of the dark rock, searching.

"Nidan?" Kiana's voice had risen in pitch.

It was the first rest Nidan had allowed them to have since they had fled the tower. Throughout the day, they had heard Wolves in the distance and caught the occasional glimpse of men through the trees, but by Pios' will they had managed to evade detection.

"We need to find somewhere to hide," Nidan said. He could just make out several gashes and fissures gouged into the rock in the gathering darkness.

"Can't we keep running?" Kiana raised her hand to point downstream. Almost immediately she allowed her arm to drop limply by her side.

"You're exhausted. I'm exhausted. Besides, the Wolves will expect us to head for the main road to Valgate," Nidan said.

Arms crossed, hands resting on opposite shoulders, Kiana moved to stand beside him. "They'll send more men there, won't they?"

Nidan nodded. "But if we head north, we can reach Valgate by going across country *and* avoid the main road." He looked down at Kiana's face, which was cast in shadows in the failing light. Her eyes were wide and fearful.

"There isn't anywhere to hide," she said. "I can keep going." She sounded so defiant that Nidan wanted to believe her.

He narrowed his eyes, stepped up to the rock and used his fingertips to explore the tallest fissure; it was longer than the height of an average man. Already, the shadows were making it look smaller and less significant, but Nidan could see that it extended back into the rock face. It was just wide enough for a person to squeeze through; at least he hoped it was wide enough.

"I think there's a cave here." Nidan glanced at Kiana; her expression was doubtful.

"Won't the Wolves see it?"

"It's almost fully dark. *If* they're searching for us by night they'll need to use brands. That will limit their vision. They'll never be able to tell this is a cave entrance."

Kiana tilted her head to the side as she gazed at the entrance. "Can we fit?"

"I hope so!" Nidan forced a grin to his lips.

Kiana paused for a moment. "We'd better get going then," she said bravely. "Before those bastards find us."

Nidan raised his eyebrows.

"What? Haven't you ever heard a girl curse before?"

He shrugged. "Several times. I just haven't heard *you* curse before."

Kiana laughed, though the sound was strangled and forced and the humour didn't reach her eyes. "Even the incarnation of Miale is allowed to use bad language, you know."

Nidan laughed with her; only *his* laughter was real. Despite their desperate situation and everything that had happened, she could still make a joke.

Taking a long deep breath, Nidan pushed himself into the narrow entrance. He had to keep his breathing shallow, and there was a section that was so narrow it felt like he would become trapped. He was glad that Kiana was considerably slimmer than he was. His face scraped against the unforgiving rock, grazing his cheek.

Nidan froze, holding his breath as an unwelcome sound filled the forest: the unmistakable snap of twigs under boots. There was too much noise for it to be Finn and Ciall. Nidan caught his breath and offered a silent prayer to Pios. He made himself carry on. Behind him, Kiana had stopped and he could hear that her breathing had become faster.

"You have to move," Nidan said through gritted teeth.

Kiana didn't respond and seemed to be frozen with fear.

After two more paces, Nidan broke free of the narrow entrance and stepped into a pitch-dark space. He turned round but Kiana was blocking any remaining light from outside the cave. Feeling the wall carefully, he found the entrance and managed to locate her hand. Her soft skin felt cold to the touch.

"You have to move. If you don't, the Wolves will find you. You *have* to move."

Nidan tugged gently and let out a sigh of relief as Kiana responded. As she stepped into the cave beside him, he heard the sound of strangled sobs escaping her control. He pulled Kiana close and gently covered her mouth, willing her to be silent.

He listened. The footsteps were closer. He could hear the sloshing sound of at least two men tromping through water. Three more walked across the rocky ground. Through the narrow entrance, he could just see the flickering orange glow of fire. Briefly, he was able to see Kiana's unusual amber eyes, wide with terror, and the fine features of her pale, untanned face. Then the fire moved away and the cave was once more plunged into darkness.

An age seemed to pass before Nidan heard the footsteps moving away in the direction that he and Kiana had been travelling. His heart thudded against his chest. The Wolves had been too close. If Kiana had dallied any longer, they would have been captured and killed. But they still weren't safe. They had to stay silent so their hiding place wasn't discovered. His tongue suddenly felt like a lead weight. Visions of nyxii fire blazing through the narrow entrance plagued his mind. He could feel the torture of imagined heat on his skin.

Nidan did not let go of Kiana until he was convinced that the Wolves had moved away. As soon as he did, he felt her sink to the ground. He wanted to find some way to reassure her but didn't dare speak. Instead, he explored the cave. It was deeper than he had expected.

"Let's go further in." Nidan kept his voice low.

He helped Kiana to her feet and, stooping, led the way through the dark until his hand hit the back wall of the cave. Exhausted, Nidan dropped down to the ground. He wrinkled his nose against the stale musty smell. The walls and floor were damp. No sunlight was able to filter in to warm the rock, so the cave was cold. It didn't matter. It was somewhere to rest. Somewhere to close his eyes for a few moments.

Nidan was shocked into waking when Kiana spoke.

"The Wolves don't take prisoners, do they?" Her voice sounded miserable. Even though she had spoken quietly, her words echoed softly around the cave.

Nidan shifted uncomfortably. Water had seeped through his clothing, chilling him. "No, they don't." There was no point in lying to her.

"Everyone will be dead. Everyone." Her voice quavered as though she was about to cry again.

"You should get some sleep." He didn't know how to comfort her; words would do little to console her.

"You should sleep too."

"I will, when you're safe." Nidan had to stifle a yawn with the back of his hand. Pios! He was tired.

He felt Kiana shift her position slightly as she affected a cough.

"You said the Wolves wouldn't find us here. Sleep while you can. You're no good to me if you're exhausted."

Nidan raised his eyebrows at her authoritative tone; it was a shame his expression was lost in the darkness. He *was* exhausted, but that didn't mean he was going to obey her. "I'm trained to stay awake. Besides, it's safer if one of us does." *I only hope that I can.*

He felt her become tense.

"Are you trained to *die*?" Kiana drew in a ragged breath. "Were you all trained to *die*… for me? Was Marcas trained to *die*?" An anguished sob escaped her. "Were Finn… or Ciall… or the other Guardians?" She paused to sniff. "Were Erryn… and Ducarius?

What… about… everyone else who lived and… and worked in the tower?" She inhaled sharply.

Nidan hesitated. What could he say or do to ease her grief? Everyone in her life was probably dead. *Except for me and I barely know her.*

When he did speak, his voice came out as a strangled whisper. "Guardians are trained to defend you. We are… were… all prepared to die for Miale."

Kiana grabbed his hand. She was shaking.

"The souls of the Guardians and servants that the Wolves cut down will already be with Pios," Nidan said.

"I wish the Wolves hadn't come." She began to sob bitterly.

"So do I."

Slowly, Nidan pulled his hand away from Kiana's and wrapped his arm around her, drawing her closer. Under the circumstances, it was the only thing he could do. She needed to be comforted. Kiana began to cry more freely. Although she made very little sound, her entire body shuddered violently. She buried her face against Nidan's side, and soon his black tunic was soaked with tears.

Like him, Kiana stank of sweat, smoke and river water, but there was also the faintest scent of lilac in her hair. Nidan's sister had worn a similar perfume. He tightened his grip. He had never been able to comfort Brid; he had only been a child when she had died. *It was my fault. I failed her.* He wouldn't fail Kiana.

Nidan leaned his head against the damp rock and stared into the darkness. With luck, all of the Wolves would pass them in the night. With luck, he would be able to deliver Kiana safely to Valgate.

*

Berend felt the shame of failure burning in the pit of his stomach. It didn't matter that they had defeated the Guardians; Miale had slipped through their grasp. After overrunning the tower and rounding up any survivors, the Wolves had turned the drafty eating hall into a war room. Outside, darkness wrapped around the tower whilst inside, the only light was provided by a dozen flaming brands seated in sconces around the hall.

He hovered at the shoulder of the Alpha, Adalric, as they slowly circled a pack of grim-faced men. Adalric's height and cold blue stare made him look impressive as he prowled around the men. Adalric's arms were folded across his chest; a stern expression lined his face as he listened to the pack's report, or rather their excuses.

Berend was sick of hearing about failure. With every new report, his shoulders got more hunched and his forehead more creased. His brows hooded his eyes and his mouth was tight, hiding clenched teeth. Was it really so difficult to hunt down one naïve girl who had never left the tower before that day?

"We tracked down a fleeing group of Guardians," one of the men said. He stood completely still, head bowed in subjugation.

Berend didn't know the pack leader's name, nor did he care. The pack still wore their leather armour; the proud image of a wolf's head was etched into each breast plate. It was a shame the pack had nothing to be proud of.

"There was a girl with them wearing Miale's colour, but they were obviously a diversion," the man carried on. "If they knew anything about the direction that Miale had gone, they didn't say."

Adalric leaned forward. "You're sure that the girl was *not* Miale?"

The pack leader nodded. "Her eye colour was completely normal. Besides, if she had been Miale, we would have been plunged into the time of Thanatos as soon as we slit her throat."

Berend narrowed his eyes as he remembered the last period of Thanatos and the madness that had gripped people. Alive, Miale balanced people's minds just as Pios balanced the physical body and Ysia *had* provided balance for the dead. The Darkness only knew what happened to the souls of the dead now that Ysia was gone.

"You tortured them?" he asked, though it wasn't really a question.

The man nodded. "But they wouldn't talk. The girl just cried and screamed until we killed her."

"The Guardians are all well trained," Adalric said grimly. "We know that. Thank you for your report, Osgar."

"What should we do now?"

Adalric looked down at the map that was pinned out on the long wooden table in front of him. Berend followed his gaze. The areas that had already been searched and secured had been marked by ugly iron pins.

"Rest for tonight," Adalric said.

"We already have more men resting than we can afford," Berend said. If he were in charge, no one would rest until Miale was found. He was not afraid of exhaustion, suffering or death. He would give anything to avenge Ysia, even the lives of himself and his men. It was in their blood.

Adalric's lips grew taught. "Our men are useless to us if they are fatigued, Berend." He addressed the pack before him again. "In the morning, head north and scout along the main road to Valgate."

Berend scowled. "We already have packs searching that route."

Adalric glanced angrily at the war leader. "I'm well aware of that. I sent them there."

Berend growled in his throat but said nothing. He watched as Osgar and his pack stood to attention and then left the room, their footsteps echoing over the pale flagstones. Another pack stepped forward. More failure. More excuses.

"Raynar, what news?" Adalric said.

After bowing deeply, Raynar opened his mouth to speak. He barely got a word out before the door to the hall opened and one of their chief apothecaries entered.

Adalric immediately held up his hand to silence Raynar. "Brokk?"

"Your son is awake, Alpha," Brokk said from the doorway, where he stood fidgeting.

Adalric nodded and began to walk away from the table.

Berend's mouth briefly relaxed into a smile. He was looking forward to this.

"Alpha, we should hear Raynar's report first," Berend said. Not that he wanted to, but he had to keep up appearances.

"It can wait, can't it, Raynar?"

Raynar bowed his head and nodded. "Of course, Alpha."

Berend followed Adalric out of the hall. The Alpha's shoulders were tense, and Berend hadn't missed the look of concern on Adalric's face. It made him sick.

As they walked across the courtyard, Berend surveyed the devastation. The stonework was blackened, and almost all of the wooden buildings in the courtyard had been burnt. Now only charred skeletons remained. The bodies of horses lay in the ashes of the old stable block. The only outbuilding that was still standing was the barracks, which they had turned into a makeshift infirmary.

Inside, apothecaries were working tirelessly to patch together warriors and those nyxii that could be saved. Bowls of sweet incense were burning, making Berend's nose wrinkle. The incense did little to deter the flies that buzzed irritatingly as they searched for festering wounds to settle on, but it did mask the stench of bitter herbs, blood and death.

Brokk led them to the final bed where Adalric's son lay. His face was turned from them, his breathing brisk and obviously pained.

"His burns are healing far faster than natural," Brokk said without looking at Adalric. "But at the moment, the damage is still deep and he is in considerable pain."

Adalric took a hesitant step closer to the bed. "But he'll live?"

Brokk nodded nervously. "Yes."

"Thank you." Adalric dismissed Brokk with a vague wave of his hand.

The apothecary nodded, bowed and then quickly scuttled off to tend to another patient. The man was a coward. It was obvious what he was thinking: Skaric's burns were being healed by the magic of Pios; there was no other explanation. It would have been better if Skaric *had* died.

"Skaric?" Adalric said, his voice unusually gentle.

Berend curled his upper lip. How could Adalric show his coward of a son any compassion? He watched as Skaric slowly turned his head to look at his father. The boy's face was slightly red with traces of peeling skin on his nose and cheeks. The rest of his body was wrapped in clean bandages, making it impossible to see the true extent of the damage caused by the fire that should have killed him.

"Did we find her?" Skaric's voice was barely more than a whisper.

"No," Adalric said. "But that isn't your fault."

Berend held back a growl. *It was your fault.*

Adalric stepped closer to the bed. "You did well. Without your bravery, we would never have breached the walls."

Bravery? Skaric was a coward. Everyone knew it, yet Adalric wouldn't admit it.

Skaric stared at his father with a blank expression. There was no pride in the young man's face. Berend couldn't wait to see what happened when Skaric owned up to his dishonourable actions.

"But afterwards…" Adalric's voice was hesitant.

Berend suppressed a smile. He waited, hoping.

"…Afterwards you acted like a coward." A coward had no business living, let alone being the Alpha's heir. "Why? Why didn't you accept your death?"

Skaric closed his eyes. "Would you rather I had died?"

Yes, you should have died.

Adalric sighed heavily. He looked like he was about to shake his head.

"Better to die a hero than live a coward," Berend said quickly.

Skaric opened his eyes and stared at Adalric. "I'll accept any punishment you think fitting, father."

Berend looked to the Alpha, waiting to hear the coward's fate. Lashings would be a good start. Serving the women folk would bring shame upon him. Death would be preferable, but Berend knew that wouldn't happen; they had lost too many nyxii in the assault on the tower. That would be the excuse.

"There will be no punishment," Adalric said. "Rest. We can talk again when you are fit and healthy."

Berend gaped open-mouthed as Adalric turned to leave the infirmary. He quickly clenched his teeth and began to follow, but then paused and looked back at Skaric. Adalric had to be shown that he was making a mistake.

"Given what Brokk said, that shouldn't be long. He did say that your wounds are healing unusually fast. Do you know why?"

Skaric didn't deign to give any reply.

"It seems unnatural to me," Berend said. "I'd wondered if you had found some way to make the fire heal rather than destroy. But as we all know, only Pios has any power over healing."

Adalric grasped Berend's arm tightly. "You should watch your tongue. Be careful with your accusations."

"I'm not accusing him of anything, Alpha. I'm simply curious."

Adalric's moustache bristled. "Keep your curiosity to yourself."

Berend bowed his head. "Of course, Alpha." He tugged his arm away from Adalric's grasp and continued to walk towards the exit. The sound of Skaric's weak, pathetic voice stopped him.

"I forced a wounded Guardian to heal me. I promised him his life, and then I killed him." Skaric's voice was flat and expressionless as he spoke.

Liar. "Yet he left you with considerable wounds." Berend glanced back in time to see Skaric grimace.

"He obviously misjudged the strength of a nyxus." Finally there was a hint of emotion creeping into Skaric's voice. "He probably thought that if he left me wounded I wouldn't be a threat. He was wrong."

Adalric laughed. "A mistake the fool will never make again! See," he said, punching Berend lightly in the arm. "There is an explanation for everything. We must go. Raynar will still be waiting."

Berend breathed in and out deeply, but he said nothing as he followed his Alpha. He risked one parting glance at Skaric. If the Alpha of the Wolves had one weakness, it was his compassion for his son. Skaric should have died.

Chapter Three

Everyone within the remains of the tower seemed to have a task to do: looking after the horses, tending the wounded, burning the dead on both sides or readying provisions for the next set of search parties. Everyone except for Skaric.

His wounds were almost fully healed, even though only one night had passed since he had been consumed by fire from within. He stood in the shadow of the tower, watching as his father stood talking to Brokk and Berend in the centre of the courtyard. The apothecary was moving his arms in an animated fashion. Skaric was trying to feign disinterest in their conversation, but the surreptitious glances they took in his direction made it clear they were talking about him. He doubted he would ever be made privy to what they were saying.

Skaric forced himself to look away, turning his attention instead to the jagged remnants of the portcullis. He stared at it, unable to tear his gaze from the destruction. It was suddenly painful to breathe as he took in the damage that *he* had caused. *My magic. Power I dragged out of the earth… and my own people.* The memory made his healing skin itch, and he suddenly felt deathly cold.

Again, he forced himself to turn away and look at the handful of nyxii that hadn't been sent out with packs. They were doing exactly what he should have been: training and honing their talents. He watched as the ground around them died a little more with every spell they cast. All fire. Fire hadn't destroyed the portcullis.

"You should be with them."

Skaric lurched round and came face to face with Vali, who wore a loose-fitting grey woollen shirt and breeches. He wasn't carrying any weapons; the nyxii didn't need knives or swords, and they didn't get close enough to combat to warrant wearing armour.

Skaric pushed the panic from his face and clenched his hands.

"At least you should be helping to deal with the dead. You look fit enough for *that* task." Vali's mouth twisted in disgust as he contemplated the unpleasant task.

There were still plenty of dead bodies that needed to be burned. They were stacked up in piles in the courtyard, and the cloying, stomach-turning odour of burnt flesh hung in the air. Skaric resisted the urge to scratch the scars on his arms. No one in the tower had been spared. Those that hadn't died in the fighting had been rounded up and slaughtered. Wolves didn't take prisoners.

"Why aren't you training?" Skaric hoped his tone sounded casual.

Vali's thin lips relaxed into a grin as he nodded towards a pack that had just returned. "I've been out hunting for Miale since last night." He looked Skaric up and down; his grin melted into a smile. "It's good to see you on your feet."

Is it? Skaric searched Vali's face for a moment; his smile looked genuine enough. He wanted to believe that Vali's words were sincere.

"People are talking about you," Vali said quietly, whilst maintaining a casual expression on his face. "They say you've lost your nerve."

Skaric felt the muscles in his face tense at the accusation. The worst part was, the rumours were right.

"Add to that how quickly you healed…" Vali shook his head. "By the Darkness, Skaric, I thought you would be the last person to bring shame on yourself, let alone your father."

Skaric clenched his teeth. "Just what are people saying?"

"That you made a deal with Pios." Vali's gaze bored into Skaric's eyes as though he would find an answer there.

Skaric forced himself to laugh; it sounded hollow, even to him. "I forced a Guardian to heal me and then I killed him." How many times would he have to repeat the lie before he believed it?

Vali continued to stare at Skaric for a moment longer. He sighed heavily, shrugged and threw his hands up in a submissive gesture.

"Don't blame me. I'm just letting you know what the others are saying. Look, do yourself a favour and get over there, and show everyone that you aren't scared of casting magic."

Skaric couldn't make himself nod and move towards the nyxii. *Vali is right. I am afraid.*

Vali took a step closer, his expression serious. "You know as well as I do that failure isn't an option for us. People should be hailing you as a hero, but instead, they're calling you a coward and insinuating that you might be a traitor."

Skaric ran his hands over his face and shook his head. He didn't understand what was so cowardly about wanting to live, but he knew he would be damned for it. He *should* have killed Miale. That would have saved him from humiliation. She had been right there in his grasp. Skaric pressed his lips together to stop himself from grimacing. He had let her walk away because he was afraid to die. No one knew about his missed opportunity. No one could ever know. He had to find a way to prove himself again. In the meantime, he hoped his father's status would protect him.

"If you don't want to find a knife in your back, you'd better do something to stop their wagging tongues." Vali's expression hadn't changed, but there was concern in his eyes. His words destroyed Skaric's hope.

"What does it matter to you?" Skaric only managed to stare at Vali for a heartbeat before he looked away. Adalric wouldn't protect him; if anything, being the son of the Alpha would bring death on him even faster. He tried not to wonder who would be sent to kill him.

Vali pursed his lips and narrowed his eyes slightly. Then he forced out a laugh and slapped Skaric on the top of his arm. "If you're not around, who else am I going to compete against? There's not one other nyxus that can match either of us in skill and you know it. So stop being a coward!"

Vali wouldn't be the one to kill him.

Skaric didn't watch his friend walk away. He felt torn between anger and gratitude. Eventually, he made himself look back to the nyxii and tried to gather up the courage to stride over to them and show off, as he would have done only days before. He took the first steps but stopped as he left the shadow of the wall. The morning sunlight struck the skin on his face and hands. Fresh pain made his skin tingle and become unbearably itchy. He stared down at the pale pink remains of the burns that covered his hands.

Curse the Guardian that had healed him. Curse Miale. Skaric's chest tightened as a flood of confusion crashed into his mind. It didn't make sense. Nothing made sense. He tugged his sleeves over his hands, bowed his head to shield his face from the sun and strode quickly towards the makeshift infirmary.

*

During the night, Nidan had heard two more groups of Wolves passing by the cave entrance. Eventually, he had fallen into a fitful but necessary sleep. When he woke, his joints were stiff, cold and aching. He had a parched mouth and growling stomach. Light filtered into the cave, though it brought no warmth with it.

They had to get to Valgate quickly.

Nidan glanced down at Kiana. Her face was smudged with grime, but there were clean streaks where tears had washed the dirt away. Asleep, she looked peaceful. Nidan wished she could stay that way for longer, but it was too dangerous. He slowly moved his arm from around her shoulders, disturbing her slumber. He saw her eyelids flutter open, and she stared up at him. Kiana's brow furrowed and her lips parted slightly in an unspoken question. Then she sat up abruptly, letting out a soft cry as her elbow struck rock. Breathing quickly, she stared at the interior of the cave and then at him.

"It wasn't a dream!"

Nidan's lips shrank into a solemn frown. He shook his head.

Kiana wiped her hand across her forehead and then tucked rogue strands of blonde hair behind her ears. "We need to get moving, don't we?"

Nidan hesitated, wondering if she was all right to travel. Not that it mattered: they had to press on if they wanted any hope of escaping the Wolves.

After leaving the safety of the cave, Nidan insisted they walk in the river itself so that they couldn't be tracked. The river didn't hamper their movements too greatly because it was shallower than it had been closer to the tower. They were exposed, but hopefully, the Wolves were satisfied the area had been thoroughly searched during the night and previous day.

At first they walked in silence, keeping up a relatively brisk pace throughout the morning. Nidan tried to watch Kiana and keep a look out for any sign of the Wolves but was hampered by the rock face to his left and the dense trees that lined the river on the opposite bank. The constant babbling of the water tumbling over rocks and pebbles made it hard for Nidan to hear anything more than a stone's throw away. Kiana looked like she was on the verge of tears. She didn't cry. She just clenched her teeth in a determined fashion and stared fixedly ahead.

"Tell me about your family," she said suddenly. "I know about your sister but… I just want to… please tell me about your family."

It was probably close to noon. Nidan was tired, hot and hungry. The desperation behind her question took him by surprise and reminded him of the first time he had met her. Less than a day had gone past. It felt like weeks.

"My father is a messenger for the church of Miale. He taught me about tracking while we travelled together, but that was before I joined the church of Pios." Remembering didn't cheer Nidan up.

Kiana increased her pace. "I don't know what my father's trade is."

Nidan turned his full attention to her and immediately saw that her eyes were red and her face was puffy. Her hands were tightly clenched.

"I don't remember my parents at all," she said in a quieter voice, bowing her head. "The only family I've ever known are dead. Why do the Wolves hate me so much?" She sobbed and stared at him with desperate eyes filled with tears.

Nidan drew in a deep breath and shook his head. He couldn't answer her question. No one knew why a Wolf had killed Miale a thousand years earlier. Since then, the goddess had been trapped in a mortal body. Living. Dying. Being reborn.

"I didn't ask to be the incarnation of Miale." Kiana stopped and pressed her fists to her eyes. "Is it wrong of me to hate the fact that I am?"

Nidan pulled her into an embrace, allowing her to weep into his shoulder. He felt tears soaking through his tunic again. Her sobs were more desperate than they had been the previous night and were completely unrestrained. He hoped that the babbling of the river and the occasional cry of birds would hide the sound of her grief.

Kiana pulled away and used her dirty sleeve to wipe her eyes and cheeks. "I'm sorry." Her tone was oddly formal. She looked away from him. "I shouldn't be ashamed of what I am, much less hate it."

"It's all right…"

Kiana shook her head. "No, it isn't. I have been blessed. I shouldn't be acting like a child."

"Kiana…"

She ignored him and began walking again. "And it isn't my fault that Marcas and the others are dead. The Wolves did that because they are consumed by hate. It wasn't my fault." She drew in a shaky breath. "Besides, this isn't the time to grieve. Not when we're still in so much danger."

Nidan stared after her. *There has to be something I can say.* But no words came to him.

*

Skaric welcomed the dark shadows that were starting to stretch through the forest; they were a welcome relief from the torture of the sun. Was that why Berend had ordered him to go on patrol? Did the war leader want to see him squirm? Throughout the afternoon, Skaric had clenched the horse's reins to stop himself from scratching his itching skin; his need was made worse by Berend's proximity to him. All the time, Berend was watching, scrutinising and silently accusing him.

Several deer trails cut through the forest, making it easy to find routes for the horses. Overhead, the canopy was thick but dappled light still streamed through, creating shimmering pockets of light. It was almost beautiful, almost peaceful.

Until the sounds of other Wolves moving through the forest reached Skaric's ears. None of them were making any effort to be quiet. It was in the moments when he couldn't hear boots breaking twigs that he realised how eerily silent the forest was. There were no birds chirping, no rodents rustling, and the deer had all fled as soon as they had sensed the presence of Wolves the day before. The only sound he heard was the delicate rustle of the breeze disturbing the leaves above his head and the thump thump of two sets of hooves. Sometimes, the horses stumbled over a stone that clicked against their hooves or snapped a twig, but there were no other natural sounds, not even the sound of the river.

They had found no sign of Miale, only the myriad of tracks created by Wolves on foot or on horseback, which had resulted in the forest floor becoming a churned up mess.

"This is hopeless." Skaric frowned and chewed on his lower lip as he realised they were approaching the same twisted tree for the fourth time since setting out from the tower. The thick trunk rose to half a man's height and then split in two. Both sections spread out almost horizontally in opposite directions before curving up again and splitting into branches and leaves. The dark bark had been rubbed off in several places, leaving cream scars; it was probably a favoured scratching post for the elusive deer.

"Yes, it is." Berend jabbed on the left rein to force his horse to turn abruptly so that he was facing Skaric. "But you know we aren't really out here to look for Miale, don't you?"

Skaric's mouth suddenly became dry as Vali's words flooded back into his mind. He tried to dismiss them. Berend could have killed him at any point during the afternoon, but he hadn't.

"It would have been better if father had punished me." Skaric looked up in time to see a thoughtful expression cross Berend's face, but the war leader said nothing. "Anyone else would have been." He had seen men lashed or hung for cowardice.

"Perhaps your father thinks the pain you endured then and the humiliation you are feeling now is punishment enough."

Skaric's hands tensed, causing his horse's head to toss angrily. He quickly dismounted, trusting the well-trained horse to remain close by, nibbling idly on grass and twigs. The twisted tree provided a good leaning post for Skaric. The rough bark pressed through his thin shirt into his back. He stared up at Berend and focused on calming his breathing, attempting to hide his emotions. Skaric didn't want to look more cowardly than he already did. Emotions were for women—or the weak-willed followers of Pios and Miale.

Berend dismounted with a thud. He began to walk towards Skaric, looking down his nose as he spoke. "You must know how much you have disgraced your father."

Skaric hunched his shoulders and bowed his head. Berend began to walk around the tree, never taking his gaze off Skaric. Skaric's breath caught in his throat. He fought against his desire to move; he was already showing enough weakness as it was.

Berend's hand curled around his shoulder. Skaric had to stop himself from shivering and twisting away. His heartbeat increased and he felt slightly light-headed.

"I need you to help me understand something, Skaric."

Skaric curled his hands around the thick branch. Sweat was beginning to make his hands slippery.

"When you were healed..."

"I didn't make a deal with Pios." Skaric closed his eyes briefly. The speed of his response had made him sound guilty.

Berend laughed but at the same time, he tightened his grip on Skaric's shoulder. "I had heard that rumour."

Skaric clenched his teeth and cursed the frailty of his body, compared to the strength of Berend's. His shoulder was aching under the war leader's grasp.

"However..."

Skaric held his breath, waiting.

"The Guardians aren't completely stupid. Certainly not stupid enough to believe that you would let one go in return for healing you."

Skaric couldn't force words into his mouth. No one was stupid enough to expect mercy from a Wolf.

"Did you know that I was the one to find you?"

Skaric's eyes widened. He shook his head.

"Of course, you didn't. You were unconscious. Do you know what else I found?"

Skaric stared directly ahead.

"Two sets of footsteps, leading away from you."

Skaric felt himself shaking. Berend's grip on his shoulder tightened again.

"The tracks belonged to a man and woman. There wasn't the body of a Guardian anywhere near you."

Skaric whimpered softly as Berend's fingertips sunk into the flesh around his shoulder joint. "I dragged myself away… I tried to return to the battle, but my strength failed me and I blacked out." His lie was unraveling and he felt powerless to stop it.

"I think you're lying, Skaric."

Skaric shook his head defiantly. "I'm not."

The memory of the compassion in Miale's amber eyes slipped back into Skaric's mind. He couldn't block it out. There had been more compassion in that one look than he had felt in his entire lifetime. *Curse her.*

He heard the whisper of metal being drawn across leather. He couldn't move or think. Suddenly, he felt Berend's warm breath against his ear and face.

"Despite all your pathetic lies, you are right about one thing. You *should* be punished."

No. Skaric lurched round, wrenching his shoulder from Berend's grasp and swung his clenched fist at the war leader's face. The bones in Skaric's knuckles crunched as his fist impacted against Berend's jaw. Pain flowed through his fist, eclipsed by a sharp throbbing sensation in his side. He choked on pain and glanced down to see a dagger protruding from his torso. The hilt was already slick with blood. His blood.

Berend stumbled back, wrenching the dagger cruelly from Skaric's side as he did so. The war leader used his off-hand to nurse his jaw while he opened his mouth wide, testing the joint.

"There's only one way you can beat me," Berend said, staring at Skaric.

Magic. Skaric bit his lower lip, trying to block out the pain that was smothering his thoughts. He could feel the warmth of blood trickling down his side and leg. He tried to open his left hand, but the broken fingers refused to respond.

Berend began to laugh. Energy flowed around Skaric's body, lending him a strength he had never believed he was capable of. Anger fuelled Skaric's actions as he ignored the pain in his fingers and punched the war leader in the face again. The blow impacted on Berend's nose with a sickening crunch. Blood smeared across the war leader's face. Berend dropped to his knees. Siezing the opportunity, Skaric slammed his foot onto the war leader's hand. Pain tore through his side. He fought through it and applied pressure until Berend released the dagger. Skaric quickly kicked it away.

"Did my father order this, or are you acting alone?"

Berend laughed even harder as he stood. Skaric failed to see the punch until it hit him. Pain slammed into his face, knocking him off his feet. He landed hard on his back, gasping. Loose dirt billowed up in a cloud, making him cough as it settled in his nose and mouth. Winded and with the wound in his side hurting ever more fiercely, Skaric could only stare as the war leader moved with frightening speed. He cried out as Berend's knee thrust into his stomach, robbing him of his breath. Then Berend's hands curled tightly around his throat, slowly squeezing the life from him.

Skaric choked as he clawed desperately at Berend's hands. They were painfully strong and he was pathetically weak in comparison. Berend was still laughing; the sound cut through Skaric's mind like a knife.

"Did… my… father… order… this…?"

Berend responded by tightening his grip on Skaric's throat. He dug his knee deeper into Skaric's gut. Bile rose up into Skaric's mouth. He couldn't breathe. Or choke. Or swallow. He slammed his right palm into Berend's already broken nose and applied as much pressure as he could. The mocking expression on Berend's face was replaced by one of anger, and a hint of the pain he must have been feeling crept into his eyes.

"Why… won't… you… answer… me?" Skaric's voice was barely audible.

With his left hand, he began to grope desperately for the knife. It was his only chance. He managed to force his broken hand to close around the blade. It bit into his skin but he didn't care. He clumsily turned the knife round and took hold of the handle.

Berend loosened his grip slightly and leaned down so that he could whisper in Skaric's ear. "You are a miserable wretch who has brought dishonour on our Alpha. That *cannot* go unpunished."

Black spots were beginning to form before Skaric's eyes. The last of his energy was being choked out of him. His body was becoming numb. Even though his muscles were barely responding, Skaric somehow managed to find the strength to thrust the dagger towards Berend. The blade sank into the soft flesh of the war leader's armpit; it wasn't a deadly blow but it was a painful one. The war leader cried out and fell back, the dagger tearing free from his flesh, his hands pulling away from Skaric's throat. Skaric gulped in precious air quickly, making his body tingle and his head buzz.

Berend closed his left hand over the knife wound and glowered at Skaric. "You little…"

Still gasping for breath, Skaric moved before Berend could finish and plunged the knife into the war leader's right hand. It burst through flesh and bone and became lodged in an exposed tree root that snaked across the forest floor. Despite the sickening light-headedness that plagued him, Skaric staggered to his feet. The forest span and his body swayed. He risked pausing long enough to take a deep breath in an effort to steady his senses and then sprinted towards the horses.

Skaric glanced back in time to see Berend pull the knife from his hand and cast it aside. Fear pulsed through Skaric's veins. Berend didn't need a weapon to kill him. He couldn't let the war leader get close to him again.

Standing, Berend lurched towards him. "It's my duty to ensure that you pay for what you have done."

With violently shaking hands, Skaric grabbed the reins of his horse and pulled it round so that the animal stood between him and Berend.

"Did my father order this?" *I need to know.*

Berend's only response was to continue forward.

Skaric waited, holding tightly onto the horse until Berend was within reach. Then he fought through the ache in his throat to scream as loudly as he could in the animal's ear. Terrified, the horse whinnied and bucked. One of its hooves clipped Berend's knee. There was a loud pop and the war leader collapsed to the ground, writhing in agony, screaming as he gripped his knee.

Skaric's stomach lurched but he wasted no time in mounting the horse, despite the pain tearing through his cut, broken fingers and side. He whipped the reins at Berend's mount, which took fright and galloped deeper into the forest. After urging his horse a safe distance away, Skaric paused and allowed himself to look back. To his alarm, Berend had managed to drag himself upright. The war leader tried to put pressure on his injured leg but howled in pain. Blood poured freely from Berend's nose, drenching his heavy, dark beard and neck with a scarlet river.

"Did my father order this?"

Berend smiled at him, though it quickly turned into a snarl. "What are you going to do, Skaric? Run? Like a coward?"

Skaric gritted his teeth together and urged the horse forward.

Berend's voice roared after Skaric. "That's all you'll ever be! A coward! I'll hunt you down!"

Then the only sound was of hooves pounding on the forest floor, and the only thing Skaric could make himself think through a haze of dizzying pain was that he couldn't go back.

Chapter Four

Nidan lay flat on his belly, listening; it felt like they had spent more time hiding in scrub than walking. He heard nothing except the breeze rustling the leaves above his head. The whinny he had heard moments before hadn't been repeated. Pushing himself up onto his elbows, he surveyed the forest. Nothing looked out of place. Nidan sighed, satisfied the whinny had been another near miss. He averted his eyes and whispered a quick prayer to Pios. He helped Kiana up and then led her towards the edge of the treeline.

The forest had been cut back to make way for farmland, creating an almost regimented tree line that butted up against open ground. *Perfect for being hunted down.* He looked across the fields: those closest had been left fallow, the soil ploughed so that it rose in a series of shallow troughs and peaks like a dark undulating sea. Each field was bordered by a low hedge, creating a giant patch work that led up to the walled city of Valgate.

"There's no other way?" Kiana asked.

"The Wolves will be watching the roads. We could go further north but the longer we're out here the more likely we are to run into Wolves."

Kiana put her hand on his arm. "But surely there will be Guardians looking for us?"

"I doubt it." Nidan sighed. "The only way they would have found out that Blackoak Tower had been attacked is if survivors had reached the city."

He glanced at Kiana as her hand slipped from his arm. She stared down at the ground, blinking fiercely. *I should have kept my mouth shut.* He looked towards the city and the twin flags of Pios and Miale that were flying proudly. No one had any idea that Miale was in so much peril.

Kiana breathed in deeply and then looked at him again. "You've got us this far. I know you'll get us into Valgate safely."

Nidan grimaced. Maybe she was right, but what if they did encounter a group of Wolves? The odds would be stacked against them. He knew that the Wolves normally travelled abroad in packs of at least six. Then there was their cursed mages. There was *nothing* that Nidan could do against fire magic.

He glanced up. It was early evening and the sky was beginning to darken into deep shades of red. Two days had passed since they had escaped the tower. They could wait until nightfall to cross the fields but wouldn't be able to see danger until they blundered into it. Safety had never seemed so close yet at the same time so far away. There was no choice.

"Let's go." Nidan broke out of the forest and headed across the slightly sloping ground in the direction of the city, setting a good pace despite the uneven terrain. The low sun caused their shadows to elongate and stretch out behind them.

They had just climbed through the hedge into the third field when they heard the rhythmic thump, thump of hooves thundering across the fields towards them. Nidan's heart sank. He held his arm out in front of Kiana, barely looking as she turned her fearful eyes towards him. Nidan glanced back over his shoulder. *We can't go back. We've come too far. Pios, help us.*

As Nidan stood rooted to the spot, he saw six riders clear a hedge two fields down. Nidan drew his sword and dropped into a fighting stance, damned if they were going to move any closer to their doom.

The riders approached them at a leisurely pace as though they wanted to play with their prey. Nidan could clearly see the telltale signs that told him they were Wolves—their leather armour, emblazoned with a wolf head, their long unkempt hair and the thick beards that masked the lower halves of their faces. He tightened his grip on the sword and silently begged the frightened pounding of his heart to slow down.

Suddenly, Kiana tugged on his arm. He glanced back at her. She was pointing towards their left at a lone rider that had just vaulted into their field. The rider pulled the horse to a halt.

Nidan narrowed his eyes. "Another Wolf, probably their scout."

Kiana looked up at him, her mouth quivering. "We have to do something! We can't just stand here and wait to die!"

"We can't run either. They'll cut us down before we reach the forest. I'll fight until they kill me." *And they will kill me.* Nidan sighed heavily. He looked at her as the Wolves' horses picked up pace. "I'm sorry. I can't win this fight."

Kiana tugged the dagger from his belt. "I'll fight too." There was a grim expression on her face.

Nidan smiled at her determination and valour. He turned to face the Wolves as they dismounted. In their position, Nidan wouldn't have given up the advantage of being on horseback, but the Wolves had over-confident smirks plastered on their faces. They began to march forwards, drawing their swords.

"Stand behind me. Don't let them get near you." Nidan hoped that the hedge at their backs would prevent them from being circled.

Kiana nodded and obeyed.

Then the Wolves were upon them. Nidan gritted his teeth and engaged the first man, allowing fear and anger to flow through his body, lending him strength and speed. Steel crashed against steel as Nidan blocked blow after blow from first one, then two opponents. Each time their blades struck his, he found his heels digging further into the ground. He wanted to move and dance around their attacks, but Kiana was behind him. *I can't let her die. Pios, help me!*

Block, block, strike. His blade bit into the neck of a Wolf, causing a fountain of blood to spring forth. The man looked surprised and fell, only to be replaced by the next.

They're playing with us.

There was no reason why the five remaining Wolves couldn't just attack as one pack and finish them.

Nidan forced the air out of his lungs in a war cry. He fixed his teeth into a snarl and parried, dodged and weaved, tying the Wolves up in a not-so-merry dance as he struck with a solid kick and then a sweep of his sword.

I'm better than them. He'd win if it was two to one, but the odds were far worse than that. He cut down a second man. Four left, plus the scout. *They know I'm a threat.* He waited for them to stop tormenting him and surge forward. *Is this how Wolves kill?*

He felt Kiana's hand touch his back. "He's coming!"

As all four Wolves swarmed in, Nidan felt the ground shaking beneath his feet as hooves thundered across the field towards them. His sword hand was shaking just as badly.

"Pios!" The tip of a sword sliced through Nidan's tunic, cutting into his skin. The warmth of blood blossomed and soaked the fabric.

There were too many Wolves. But Nidan knew why they were toying with him. *They want me to see Kiana die first. Bastards.*

The rider reached them and didn't stop. The horse charged straight through two of the Wolves, knocking them out of the way. As it reared up, the rider pulled at its mouth, forcing it to wheel round. Its hooves came down, smashing into the head of one of the Wolves. The Wolf dropped to the floor, his skull caved in. Kiana screamed shrilly; the terrified sound sent a shiver down Nidan's spine. He didn't take his eyes off the fight. *Three down; three left.*

From the corner of his eye, Nidan saw the armourless rider gallop away and then circle round to make a return pass. He was hunched over oddly.

"It's the Wolf you healed!" Kiana said; she sounded glad.

Nidan shrugged and blocked another blow. All he knew was that the odds had suddenly changed. He didn't doubt that once all six men had been dispatched, he would also have to fight the mage. Perhaps the bastard wanted all the credit for murdering Kiana to himself. *It doesn't matter. If we survive, I'll kill him then.* Nidan hadn't brought Kiana so far to let her die. He *would* get her to safety. *I have to, for Brid.* The distant memory of his sister sent a surge of energy through Nidan's body.

The mage was upon them again, but this time, the Wolves were not as unprepared. Two continued to engage Nidan whilst the third slashed his sword into the chest of the rider's horse. The horse screamed and continued galloping until all the energy had bled from it. It crashed to the ground, taking its rider with it. The mage was pinned beneath the weight of the horse, helpless. Nidan didn't care. Whether the mage had helped them or not, he was still a Wolf.

He failed to block another blow, which cut into his left shoulder. He cried out in pain. One of the two Wolves tried to lunge around him whilst the other pressed in to attack with fury. They weren't playing anymore. Nidan allowed his attacker to strike him. It was only a glancing blow, but it still stung his arm. It didn't matter. The trick gave him the opportunity to spin round and not only block, but also deliver a fatal blow to the Wolf who was about to bring his sword down upon Kiana.

Quickly, Nidan turned back to the last two Wolves. He blocked another rain of blows, perpetually moving to make himself a human shield for Kiana. He glared at the Wolves. "Run! You can't win. Four of you are dead already; I don't want to make it six." Brave words considering he was still outnumbered.

One of them grinned back. "Only someone about to lose would speak like that."

Nidan bore down upon the Wolf. He blocked a blow and followed it up with a cross-punch to the second attacker's face. Blood gushed from the Wolf's nose and he staggered back with a cry. Nidan brought his sword up to defend against another attack. The he dropped beneath the blow and swept his leg round to pull the Wolf's feet out from under him. The surprised man dropped to the ground hard but quickly tried to right himself. Nidan was faster. He flipped his sword round in his hand and drove it into the man's gut. Blood spilled from the Wolf's mouth. His body convulsed once and then lay still.

The remaining Wolf was on his feet again. Nidan blocked a blow aimed at his head, sprang to his feet and thrust his sword through the Wolf's shoulder. He tugged the blade free. The Wolf staggered, bleeding profusely. Nidan wrapped both hands round the hilt and ran the sword through the Wolf's chest.

Exhaustion swept over Nidan. He leant on his sword. "One left." He looked towards the trapped mage.

Kiana ran past Nidan towards the mage. What was she doing? Even though Nidan had very little energy left, he sprinted to catch up with her. She stopped short of the horse and its pinned rider, clapping her hands to her mouth. Nidan could see that the horse was dead; its rider was attempting to free himself. Nidan gripped his sword tighter.

"Help me," Kiana said as she moved closer.

Nidan pulled her to a halt. "We need to get out of here before anymore Wolves come. We have to get to Valgate." He felt a surge of anger catch in his throat as she ignored him. "Damn it, Kiana! He's a Wolf. Don't let your compassion get us killed."

She stopped and turned her head to look at him. Her eyes were cold. "You're hurt." Her voice was flat.

"Kiana, we can't stay here." *Why won't she see reason?*

"You're hurt."

She was right. With the shock of the fight over, Nidan felt his wounds stinging again. Quickly, he glanced over his injuries as well as he could. His shirt was tattered, mostly slashes on his arms and left shoulder, though he had also been cut across his right hand side. None of the wounds looked dangerously deep, and the black fabric Nidan wore hid the blood stains.

Kiana shook herself from his grasp and turned round to look down at the rider. Nidan followed her gaze. Another Wolf. Not their saviour. Just another Wolf. The mage had succeeded in dragging himself from beneath the dead horse and was beginning to stand. His face was stoically blank even though his shirt was blood-soaked. Nidan quickly took in the Wolf's injuries: the mage had attempted to bandage a side wound; he held his left hand awkwardly with the fingers curled like claws; there were dark bruises around his neck and he wasn't placing any weight on his left leg as he stood. He was a mess.

Nidan stepped forward and readied his sword.

Kiana grabbed hold of his arm. "He helped us!"

Nidan narrowed his eyes; he didn't care.

"He could have helped them kill us," Kiana said. "But he didn't. Maybe he doesn't want us… me… dead at all. You can't kill him in cold blood!"

Yes, I can. Nidan tried to pull away from her, but Kiana clung on with surprising strength. The muscles in Nidan's cheeks flexed, but he made no further attempt to circumvent her.

"I never said I didn't want to kill you," the Wolf said.

Kiana's eyes were wide as she turned round. "But you helped us… because we saved you…"

The Wolf had limped round the horse and was now standing, staring at them both with cold blue eyes. Nidan couldn't read his expression at all.

The Wolf laughed briefly, the sound full of bitterness. "No. For that I should kill you." The Wolf raised his left hand ever so slightly, his fingertips twitching as he tried to uncrumple his hand.

Nidan wasn't going to give him a chance. He rushed at the Wolf.

Kiana grabbed at his shirt but he was too fast for her. "Nidan, don't!"

Nidan seized the Wolf by the neck of his shirt, holding him so their noses were almost touching. "I bet I can kill you before you can work your cursed magic." He stared up at the Wolf, looking him in the eyes.

"If I was going to use magic against you, I would have already."

Annoyingly, the Wolf had a point.

Nidan clenched his teeth. "I should kill you."

"No!" Kiana pushed Nidan away and stepped between them. "Hasn't there been enough killing?"

"There will never be enough killing for the Wolves. It's all they live for. To kill those who worship Miale and Pios. To kill *you*." Nidan could feel his sword hand quivering with held-back anger.

Kiana turned and stared at the Wolf. "What do you want? You obviously helped us for a reason. What is it?"

The Wolf stared at her coldly. "I want answers, Miale." His voice was completely void of passion, but his confused expression told an entirely different tale.

Kiana returned his stare. "Ask me what you want. I don't know if I'll be able to respond."

"Of course you will. You're the incarnation of Miale. If you don't answer, it's because you choose not to."

Kiana sighed.

"Not here; it's too open." Nidan was ready to pick her up and carry her to Valgate if he had to. "We have to get to the city."

Kiana nodded. "We can walk and talk." She peered at the Wolf. "Can you walk?"

Nidan's mouth curled into a snarl. "Does it matter? If he goes within sight of the city guards, they'll kill him."

Kiana sighed. "Then we'll have to finish our conversation before we get that far, won't we?" She smiled at the Wolf. "I'm Kiana." She waved her hand at Nidan. "This is Nidan, my Guardian. What's your name?"

The Wolf's brow became deeply furrowed. Nidan smirked as the Wolf's silence continued. Kiana glanced round and glared at him, her eyes bright as fire. He took a step backwards; it was a stark reminder that he barely knew her.

Feeling chastised, Nidan looked round for the Wolves' horses. They were clumped a short distance away, agitated by the fight but well-trained enough not to flee. "We should ride."

Kiana looked almost embarassed. "I can't ride."

Of course she couldn't; she'd never left Blackoak Tower until the attack.

Nidan smiled at her reassuringly. "I'll ride with you."

The Wolf stayed where he was whilst Nidan took Kiana with him to retrieve the horses. He helped her mount and then swung himself up behind her.

"Nidan…" Kiana's voice quivered in fear.

He looked in the direction she was pointing. Between them and the city, there were more Wolves; Nidan didn't think the pack had spotted them… yet. He felt a sinking feeling in the pit of his stomach. They couldn't win another fight.

"We'll ride north," he said decisively. "Outrun them and hide in the forest. We can approach the city from a different direction once we're sure we've lost them."

Kiana looked over to the Wolf. He was still staring at them.

Nidan sighed heavily. "If you want answers you'd better ride with us, but if you betray us, I'll kill you. Understood?"

The Wolf nodded and limped towards the horses. Once the Wolf was mounted, Nidan leaned down and grabbed the reins of a third horse; he didn't know how far they would need to ride.

"Nidan! They've seen us!"

A quick glance over his shoulder confirmed Kiana's warning. Nidan set his sights to the north and dug his heels into the flank of the horse, urging it straight into a flat out gallop.

*

It was amazing how long it took to walk on a dislocated knee. It didn't help that Berend had led Skaric several leagues from the tower in order to kill him; the irony didn't escape him. Exhausted and in burning pain, he eventually stumbled into a returning search party. With horses. He'd muttered every curse he could think of, wishing all manner of ugly fates on Skaric for scaring his horse away. Skaric thought he was so clever; he always had done. Berend hated him.

He kept his anger and story to himself as he rode back to the tower with the pack. Why hadn't anyone been sent to look for him? By the Darkness, he was the war leader, not some dispensable warrior, and he'd been gone for over a day.

Half a dozen men were on guard when they arrived at the tower.

Berend scowled at them. "I need a healer! And fetch the Alpha. He needs to hear what I have to say."

Two of the men ran off in different directions. Berend rode the commandeered horse into the centre of the courtyard and waited. His hand hurt fiercely where Skaric had stabbed it, and his broken nose made his breathing come out in noisy grunts. Neither wound was anything in comparison to the pain in his knee, which had been made worse by walking. He'd used a stick, of course, but the damage was done. He curled his upper lip into a snarl. What he wouldn't give for a Guardian to be in his clutches now. Damn Pios for forsaking them and siding with Miale. Damn them both.

Brokk was the first to arrive and Berend allowed the sallow-faced man to lead him into the makeshift infirmary and sit him down on one of the beds.

"What happened?" Brokk glanced at the three obvious wounds as though deciding which one he had the best chance of being able to fix.

Berend clenched his teeth together. "Just see to my injuries. Adalric is the first person that will hear *my* story."

Brokk shrugged and used a knife to cut the woollen cloth away from Berend's leg. A quick glance down showed Berend that his knee was a bruised and swollen mess. The joint was twice as big as it should have been, and the knee cap was skewed to one side.

"Would you like something to bite down on?"

Berend shook his head, gritted his teeth and waited. It was all he could do to stop himself from screaming as Brokk's skilled hands popped the joint back into place. All he allowed himself was a low grunt as he clenched the sheet he was laying on in his fists.

"You won't be able to walk on it for a week or two," Brokk said.

He hurried off, returning moments later with a bowl of water, swabs and bandages, just as Adalric burst into the infirmary. The Alpha's eyes fixed on Berend as he strode forward towards his war leader.

"What happened? Where's Skaric?"

Berend twisted his mouth into a grotesque snarl. "Gone. But not before trying to kill me."

He watched as Adalric stared at him. Behind the normally impassioned expression that the Alpha wore he saw a look of confusion, then disbelief.

"Why? Why would he do that?"

Berend winced internally as Brokk began to peel away the bloody strip of cloth that had been wrapped round his hand. He refused to register any pain on his face. He wasn't weak.

"Because he's a traitor. That's why."

Adalric's mouth became taut. "Be careful, Berend."

Berend snorted through his broken nose. Weren't his injuries enough proof? Adalric really was a blind idiot when it came to his son.

"Skaric had Miale in his grasp and he let her go. He told me so himself. He confided in me while we were searching." His words weren't convincing. Everyone knew how much animosity there was between him and Skaric. "Look what Skaric did to me!"

Adalric began to pace up and down in the small space in front of the bed. He clasped his hands behind his back and hunched his shoulders. His expression was dark and brooding.

Fresh pain afflicted Berend as Brokk began to clean the knife wound, readying it to be stitched. "He went wild and attacked me!"

Adalric stopped pacing. "Skaric couldn't hope to win against you."

"Not in even combat. That's why he used his magic against me." Berend motioned to his knee. "Then he tried to finish me off with a knife before taking the horses and fleeing."

"And your face?"

Berend felt a brief flush of heat rise to his cheeks. "I *told* you. He went wild. First he attacked me physically, and when I fought back, he attacked me magically."

Adalric turned round and approached Berend. For a moment, the war leader felt cold as the Alpha stood right over him, staring down at him with anger seething in his pale eyes.

"I see no evidence of burns." Adalric looked at Brokk, who nodded in agreement.

Berend allowed himself to smile. "You saw the magic he used to destroy the portcullis. Was that fire magic?"

Adalric's face drained of colour. "You're accusing my son of treason."

Berend breathed in deeply through his mouth. He had to speak calmly. "Skaric is a coward and a traitor. Why would I lie to you? You know I respect you, as a son respects his father." Just as Adalric had once treated him as a son. Then Skaric had been born. Skaric, who barely had the strength to lift a sword. Skaric the coward.

Adalric's chest heaved as his breathing became heavier.

"If Skaric is innocent, why would he attack me? Why would he have run?"

Adalric let out a growl and slammed his fist down on the bed beside Berend. The wooden base cracked and splintered under the attack. Then he turned away and buried his fist into the nearest wall, cracking the plaster. His entire body was tense with anger. "Isn't it enough that my son acted in a cowardly way? But a traitor?"

Berend stared at Adalric calmly. "He has brought shame on you. He has brought shame on us all."

He watched as Adalric breathed in and out harshly for several moments. There was an angry snarl on the Alpha's face, but in his eyes, Berend saw nothing but hurt and disappointment.

"Brokk, finish patching Berend up." Adalric began to walk away.

Berend forced himself up onto one elbow. "What are you going to do?"

Adalric stopped and turned slowly. "Send men to look for my son."

"To what end?"

Adalric's eyes narrowed. "To bring him back for questioning."

Berend couldn't allow that to happen. "Let me go."

Adalric's lips pressed into a thin line. "You aren't fit." He turned to leave.

"Skaric is like a brother to me." Berend risked a smile as his words halted Adalric. "This madness that has taken him… Perhaps the incarnation of Miale cursed him in some way. Let me find him and bring him back to you. Perhaps his mind can be healed."

Adalric half turned; distrust danced in his eyes. "You called my son a coward and a traitor."

"That is what his actions suggest." Berend had to be careful. "But maybe there is another explanation. Let me find him. I won't let any harm come to him unless he resists too violently." He hoped his words sounded reasonable.

Adalric nodded slowly. "As soon as you are fit, gather men you can trust. Bring Skaric back to me. Alive."

Berend nodded and smiled as Adalric left. There was no way he was going to let Skaric return alive.

*

The evening sky was deepening from red to indigo, just visible through gaps in the canopy above Kiana's head. They had managed to outpace the Wolves. Once in the forest, Nidan had made sure that their tracks became a churned up mess, before setting a relentless pace that had left all three horses lathered in sweat and breathing harshly. Too exhausted to travel further and too far from Valgate to double back under cover of darkness, they had been forced to stop.

The first thing Nidan had done was check what provisions the Wolves had been carrying. It turned out to be enough food for four to five days, if the two of them ate sparingly. They wouldn't be in the wilderness for that long. Nidan would guide them back to Valgate the next day. For the time being, Kiana felt exposed. The only benefit to their current predicament was that she would have time to give the Wolf answers to his questions in payment for his help. Without him, they would have died in that field.

They had propped the Wolf up against a tree. He still wasn't showing any emotion on his face, though his skin was pale and his side wound seemed to be oozing fresh scarlet blood. Not knowing his name was annoying. His animosity was annoying. In fact, everything about him was annoying.

Kiana crouched down in front of him. "You had questions?"

The Wolf looked at her with his cold eyes. He breathed in deeply. "Why did you stop to save me?"

That was easy! "It was wrong to let you die." She shrugged. "All life is sacred, even if the Wolves have forgotten that."

Anger clouded his face, making his gaze seem even brighter and colder as it bore into her.

Shivering, Kiana glanced over her shoulder at Nidan. "You need to heal yourself… and him."

Nidan was looking through one of the saddlebags. He paused and stared at the Wolf and then Kiana. "I'm not healing him again."

Kiana stood and turned to face him, her hands on her hips. "He saved our lives!"

Nidan scowled. "Probably so he could take the glory for killing us himself after he's asked his pointless questions!"

Kiana looked back down at the Wolf. There was so much anger in his eyes, but she didn't believe he wanted to kill her. He'd already had several chances and hadn't taken them. How could she convince Nidan that the Wolf wasn't a threat? "Heal yourself then."

Nidan gave her a lopsided grimace. "I can't. It's impossible to use the magic of Pios to heal yourself."

Kiana wanted to scream. "Then at least clean and dress your wounds. Surely you've been taught how to do that?"

Nidan nodded. It looked like he was going to continue looking through the saddlebags, but instead he paused. "We should tie him up."

Kiana rolled her eyes. "Not now. He's not in a fit state to do anything." *Except cast magic.* She turned her back on Nidan again, crouched down and tried to smile brightly at the Wolf. *If he really wanted us dead, we would be by now.* "Next question."

The Wolf was still staring at her, but he was also trying to open and close the fingers on his left hand. They were all dark with bruises.

The Wolf allowed his hand to slide to the ground where it rested in the crook of a tree root. "Thousands of people have been killed in your name, yet you take the time to save me? It doesn't make sense."

It's all the senseless killing that doesn't make sense. "Most of those deaths occurred before I was even born." She paused, choosing her words carefully. "Recently, it's your people who have brought the war to us. Not the other way around."

He chewed on his lower lip. "Before your current incarnation was born."

Kiana felt like she was being led into a trap but nodded anyway.

"Your soul is immortal. Even if the bodies you are born into are mortal, your soul will carry all of your memories."

Kiana knew very little about the soul. That had been Ysia's domain, her role in the trinity. Kiana wondered if the Wolves had preserved knowledge of Ysia's power and if everyone else had purposefully forgotten. She sat forward onto her knees. "The only memories I have are my own."

The Wolf shook his head as though denying her words. "Why did Pios save you, but do *nothing* to save Ysia?" Every muscle in his face and shoulders was taut.

Kiana returned his stare; her mind raced with questions. "I don't know."

The Wolf's eyes widened; they looked desperate and slightly

less cold. "How could you have condoned so much killing? You and Pios could have brought peace!"

Kiana shook her head. Tears brimmed in her eyes. She couldn't answer his questions. *Why can't I answer his questions?*

"You could have stopped all this!" He staggered to his feet.

Kiana shifted her weight backwards as he stared down at her. Behind, she heard Nidan hurry closer. Without looking at him, Kiana held the flat of her palm up to order him to stop. The Wolf was not a threat. The injured man breathed heavily and tried to walk away, but the leg that had been pinned beneath the horse gave way and he sank to the ground. Kiana couldn't quell her tears as he hunched his shoulders and bowed his head. She clenched her hands into fists, forcing herself to stay still.

"Why did you save me?" The Wolf's voice was almost inaudible. "Why did you and Pios turn your backs on us? You could have saved us."

That was more than Kiana could bear. She felt tears strangling her throat and brimming in her eyes. Crawling forward, she knelt beside the Wolf, ignoring the sting of twigs pressing through her dress. Kiana reached out to the Wolf. She hesitated, knowing he wouldn't welcome her touch. She was aware of Nidan watching her every move; it unnerved her, but she looked to him for help anyway.

"I suppose that's the price for killing a goddess," Nidan said with an uncaring shrug.

Kiana glared at him.

"That was the act of one man!" The Wolf didn't look up as he spoke. "*Not* Ysia. *Not* the rest of our people and *not* me."

"I know." Kiana touched his shoulder. "I don't know why the gods didn't stop the war. I don't know why Pios chose not to save Ysia. I don't know."

"But you should!" The Wolf pulled away from her. His face contorted with pain as his injured hand impacted with the ground.

Kiana felt her body shudder as tears began to overwhelm her. He was right. She should know; she was a god. "Is everything a lie? Am I just a decoy for the true incarnation of Miale?"

"No." Both Nidan and the Wolf spoke in unison.

It almost made Kiana laugh bitterly. "Then why don't I know?" She stared at each of them in turn. Neither one spoke. Her chin trembled as she covered her face with her hands.

She heard Nidan's footsteps walk closer. "You've done this! You've confused and upset her!"

"Stop it!" Kiana lowered her hands.

Nidan was standing over the Wolf, his fists tightly clenched.

"Please, stop it." Kiana's voice had come out as a faint whisper but it was enough to catch Nidan's attention.

He took a step back and turned so that he was standing side on to both Kiana and the Wolf. Tension lined his face and muscles. He was at boiling point and Kiana knew she was about to make him even angrier.

Kiana drew in a deep breath before trusting herself to speak. "I don't want to go into Valgate."

Nidan's mouth dropped open.

"His questions have made me doubt everything I've ever been told about who I am." Kiana stared at Nidan, willing him to stay calm while she explained. "I was told I was the incarnation of Miale and I never questioned that. But the Wolf is right… I should have her memories. I should be more than… than a person. More than just a girl… but I'm not, am I?"

Nidan knelt down beside her, his back to the Wolf. He gripped her shoulders gently. "The power of Miale was greatly weakened by her first death. Imprisoned in the body of a mortal, her power is stretched thin. It's the same reason why no one can channel her power anymore."

Kiana sniffed back tears. "I was told that."

Nidan looked at her hopefully and squeezed her shoulders. "Then that should be enough. That explains everything. Your power is spent on keeping the balance of your domain in order."

Kiana shook her head sadly. "I don't think I can believe that anymore." She felt his grip tighten until her shoulders began to ache. She must have shown a hint of pain on her face because he let go.

"All because of the questions of your enemy?" Nidan said.

Kiana nodded. But she didn't just feel confused. "This has to stop."

"What does?"

She ignored Nidan's question and glanced at the Wolf. He had raised his head and was returning her stare. A look of curiosity played over his face, and she thought the anger in his eyes was thawing a little.

"All this hatred and fighting… it has to stop. The Wolves will keep trying to kill me. No matter how many times Miale is reincarnated, they will try to kill her every time. And we will always retaliate."

"Why shouldn't we?" Nidan said. "They're the ones in the wrong."

Kiana shrugged. Right and wrong seemed like odd concepts all of a sudden. "It can't go on." She pursed her lips as she continued to stare at the Wolf. "Why are your people fighting?"

"To avenge Ysia." His response was impassioned. It sounded like a phrase he had been ordered to believe.

Kiana looked at Nidan. "Why are we fighting?"

"To protect Miale."

Kiana shook her head. She'd asked the wrong question. "A thousand years ago… why did the fighting start?"

Nidan frowned. "To avenge Miale." His mouth became downturned in dismay. "But it's the Wolves who have prolonged the fight!"

She shrugged. It didn't matter. It had to stop.

"Our hatred is justified!" Nidan said. "Miale was killed by the hand of a Wolf."

"One man," Kiana said. "And all of us have been paying ever since. The fighting… the madness during the times of Thanatos… we have to end it all."

"How?"

That time, Kiana did laugh at the joint response. Oddly, the laughter eased the tension in her body. A crazy idea began to form in her mind. "We restore the trinity."

They both looked at her as though she was mad. *Maybe I am.*

"If Pios could have restored Miale's immortality, he would have done," Nidan said.

"Ysia is dead," the Wolf said bitterly.

Kiana refused to believe there was no hope. When they had run from the tower, Nidan had given her hope; he had made her believe she could survive. The Wolf before her, confused and hurting, was proof that the Wolves could think differently, that they could look beyond their hatred. There was always hope.

"Orholt," she said eventually.

Nidan raised his eyebrows. "The first city?"

Kiana nodded. "The trinity was destroyed there. Maybe we can find a way to restore it there."

Nidan clenched his hand in front of his chest. "But no one has been there since Miale was killed!"

"It's the only place that all three gods appeared at the same time in mortal hosts," the Wolf said.

Nidan scowled at him.

Kiana nodded eagerly. "It's the *only* time they took mortal hosts."

"No," Nidan said. "The city was abandoned during the war. There's probably nothing there. We should go to Valgate."

Kiana shook her head. She was *not* going to be shut away again. She grabbed Nidan's hands. "I can't think of anywhere else where we might find answers. Can you?"

Nidan stared at her. Kiana's heartbeat thudded loudly in her chest as she waited for his response. She tried to guess at his thoughts, but his expression gave nothing away.

Finally, he nodded uncertainly. "There's a village. Norlea. It used to be a temple to Miale and Pios but was abandoned during the war. The temple still stands. I visited once with my father." He closed his eyes and his lips moved soundlessly for a few moments. "It's about five days ride from here. You… we might be able to find answers there." His voice sounded weary.

"Why there?" Kiana wasn't ready to thank him.

"It was the main temple in Gettryne until it was abandoned. My father told me they used to keep records through wall paintings. As the temple is still standing, those pictures will still be there, even though there aren't any priests or Guardians there anymore."

Kiana threw her arms around his neck, hugging him briefly. Then she rocked back onto her heels and looked at the Wolf. "Will you come with us?" She pressed her hand to Nidan's lips, cutting off his complaint. "You opened my eyes. I know you want this fighting to stop or you wouldn't be here with us. Help us?"

The Wolf looked away from her.

"We can't trust him," Nidan said.

No. You can't trust him. "We're all tired. We should rest." Kiana edged forward and lightly touched the Wolf's hand. "Think about it?"

The Wolf pulled his hand away and hunched his shoulders.

"If we're going to rest, let me tie him up," Nidan said. "We can't trust him."

Kiana didn't want Nidan to be right, but she wasn't going to risk their lives. She nodded. "But use your magic to make sure he won't die."

Nidan sighed heavily, rolled his eyes and finally nodded. Kiana offered him a smile. How could she restore the trinity if she couldn't heal the rift between two men?

Chapter Five

Skaric woke, gasping for breath. The lingering scent of burning flesh seemed almost real, and the force of Berend's fingers around his neck was almost tangible. The memory of why he was bound and lashed to a tree by a thin leather rein evaded him. He fought against the bonds that had left his fingers and arms aching terribly. Then reality clicked back into place and the knowledge of where he was and who he was with flooded into his mind. Skaric stopped struggling and stared about him, forcing his breathing to calm down.

Grey light filtered down through the tree canopy, and the first rays of the sun were beginning to make the air even warmer. Miale… Kiana—whatever she wanted to be called—was still sleeping. She lay on the ground, huddled up in a black cloak. A Guardian cloak.

Unfortunately, the Guardian was very much awake and watchful. Skaric glared at him and then looked away. The last thing he needed was to look like a fool in front of the man who could decide to kill him at any moment. He tilted his head back against the rough bark of the tree and stared up at the canopy. A myriad of shades of green stretched far above his head. A few days earlier, that same canopy had sheltered the Wolves whilst they prepared to attack the tower.

"Wolf."

Skaric looked round. Nidan was chewing on a strip of dark meat.

"Do you want some?"

Skaric's stomach growled. He hadn't eaten anything since setting out on patrol with Berend. He shook his head.

"It's food, not poison."

Skaric narrowed his eyes. "You got it from the Wolves' provisions?"

Nidan nodded.

"Six men, travelling light. There won't be much left. Save it for yourselves."

He watched as Nidan continued to eat the meat. It didn't matter that he knew the meat would be too chewy and too salty; just looking at food made his stomach hurt and his mouth water.

Skaric tried to take his mind off hunger by sizing up the Guardian. Nidan was shorter than him but much stronger. If it came to a fight, Skaric would lose. But the Guardian *was* injured, whilst the worst of Skaric's wounds—his side, hand and leg—had been healed the night before as a result of Kiana's bizarre sense of compassion.

Nidan had bandaged his own wounds using supplies from the Wolves' packs, but they were sloppy and didn't apply enough pressure. The wounds would get dirty and fester if the Guardian wasn't careful. Skaric bit his lower lip and looked away. He didn't care if the Guardian lived or died. It wasn't his problem.

"Was it easy for you? Killing your own kin? Did you even know the name of the man whose skull you bashed in?" Nidan said.

Skaric stared at the forest floor. "You didn't think twice about killing them."

"They were my enemy. But your kin." Nidan's voice was cold.

Skaric shut his eyes tightly. "Dirk," he said quietly. "His name was Dirk." He recalled the faces of the pack. One by one, he fitted names to them. "Dirk. Erich. Jurgen. Bernt. Konrad. Rikert." Skaric choked on each word as his stomach tightened into knots. He wondered if his father or Berend could have named each member of the pack.

"Leave him alone, Nidan."

Skaric looked up sharply at the sound of Kiana's voice. She was sitting up with Nidan's cloak pulled tightly around her.

Nidan shrugged as he handed her a piece of the salted meat. She took two bites, which took her a long time to chew.

She glanced at Skaric and then at the strip of meat in her hand. "Aren't you hungry?"

Skaric shook his head.

Kiana frowned. "Have you had time to think about coming with us?"

Had he thought about it? Yes. But he had to say no.

"We can't trust him, Kiana," Nidan said in a flat tone. "He killed his kin in cold blood. He doesn't even feel any guilt or remorse about it."

Kiana looked at Skaric thoughtfully. He shifted uncomfortably beneath her gaze, wanting the ground to swallow him up; it was as though she were looking straight through to his soul, even though he knew that was impossible.

"Yes, he does. He just won't admit it."

Of course he felt guilty. He had known every one of those men and they had known him. They had trusted him. Horror gripped Skaric as the realisation of what he had done finally hit him. He wanted to run, to not have to face the strangers before him. All he wanted to do was allow his emotions to spill out. A grim smile touched his lips. Even that was a sign of weakness in the minds of the Wolves.

He wished he could direct his magic to burn through the bonds. If it were possible, there would have been nothing that the Guardian could have done to stop him. Even the thought of such a tiny use of magic made Skaric's skin prickle and his stomach churn with the memory of burning. He hung his head again and bit into his lower lip, forcing down the emotions that were bubbling within him. There was a burst of warmth as blood welled at the fresh wound.

Skaric shivered and tried to pull away as Kiana knelt down before him and placed her soft hand against his cheek. She looked more than a little hurt at his reaction.

"I don't know what's happened to you," she said, her voice kind despite everything. "But I can tell that you're hurting and that you need answers. So I'm offering you the same choice that I did last night: will you help me?"

Skaric stared past her, focusing on nothing but thin air. He shook his head. "Your Guardian is right: you *can't* trust me."

Kiana sighed and shook her head once. "Fine. Carry on feeling sorry for yourself." She threw her hands up. "Curl up and die for all I care!" She pursed her lips thoughtfully. "Is that what you want? To die? Coward."

Skaric clenched his bound hands into fists, digging short nails into his palms. Anger flushed through him. Kiana had no right to brand him a coward. He strained against the bonds that held him pinned against the tree, but only succeeded in hurting his arms and chest with the effort. "Coward? *They* branded me a coward because I didn't want to die. And you call me a coward because you think I do?"

Kiana stood up and stepped away from him.

"I don't!" Skaric didn't bother to lower his voice or hide the anger that was spilling out of him. "But what do you want me to do? Lie? Tell you that you can trust me? Pretend I don't want to see you dead?" *Do I?*

Kiana raised her hands to her mouth whilst Nidan moved to stand in a defensive position. It wasn't as if Skaric could focus or direct his magic; Nidan had made sure of that.

"I'm a traitor." The words cut him as he said them. "Traitors *cannot* be trusted. Do you think I wouldn't kill you as easily as I killed my own people?"

Kiana half turned away from Skaric, which made him feel an even greater sense of anger.

"Isn't that what you wanted to hear?" He strained against the leather again.

"I thought you wanted answers," she whispered.

Skaric closed his eyes and leant his head against the rough bark. "I do. I killed my people to ask you questions. But you couldn't answer them."

Kiana's eyes grew large and her mouth dropped open slightly. "I'm sorry…"

Skaric opened his eyes and stared at her coldly. "*Sorry*? What good does that do anyone? You want me to come with you to search for answers? I could do that. But what do you think will happen after we find them?"

Kiana shook her head. Skaric could see tears sparkling in her eyes. He almost held back his words.

"I'd still want you dead." He looked away from her. "That's all I've ever been taught to want." Those words had probably just got him killed. Skaric strained against his bonds, breathing in harsh rasps—partly in anger, partly in desperation. He didn't want to die.

"Thank you."

Kiana's words made Skaric freeze.

"Thank you for finally being honest with us." She reached out again but didn't actually touch him. "I don't doubt that you hate me and yourself. It's clear that you don't trust yourself. But I want to try to restore the trinity. I can't do that without your help." She glanced at Nidan. "Or yours."

What could I possibly do to help you?

When Kiana looked at Skaric again, her eyes were wide and imploring. "Do we really have to think about what happens after that now?"

She tugged Nidan's dagger from his belt. Despite a gasp of warning from the Guardian, she cut Skaric's bonds.

Skaric rubbed his sore wrists, realising how easy it would be for him to wrest the dagger from Kiana's grasp to stab her before her Guardian could even react. But he didn't. He couldn't. "You are far too trusting."

Kiana smiled. "Maybe. Will you help me?"

Skaric stared at her. Something had to change. Kiana was right. The fighting had to stop. He sighed heavily. "Yes, I'll help you. It's not like I've got anything better to do."

Kiana grinned, and for an awful moment, Skaric thought she was going to embrace him. Thankfully she stayed still, though she did clasp her hands together in her lap. "So… what is your name? It's going to be hard to work together without knowing it." Her eyes sparkled as she spoke.

He sighed. "Skaric." He turned his attention to Nidan to avoid looking at the grin that had spread across Kiana's face. "You won't get far if you don't do a better job of those bandages."

Nidan scowled and folded his arms across his chest. "What do you know about healing?"

Skaric puffed out a sharp breath. There was no sense getting into an argument if they really were going to work together. "Basic field medicine. I can clean and dress a wound."

Nidan narrowed his eyes. "You didn't do a great job of bandaging your side wound."

Skaric did his best to smile. "I think we both know how awkward it is to dress your own wounds, don't we?" *And I had a broken hand. What's your excuse?*

Nidan looked like he was about to argue: his eyes narrowed even further and he parted his lips to speak.

"Nidan." Kiana's voice was quiet but laced with authority.

Nidan rolled his eyes. "Fine. But be quick about it; we need to set off as soon as we can."

Skaric nodded. It wasn't a victory, but it was a first step.

Chapter Six

Nidan winced as he dismounted. His side stung bitterly. The other injuries were faring much better, mainly because the Wolf had changed the bandages every day. The slashes on his arms were knitting together well; there would be scars, but Nidan didn't care. He had earned them defending the incarnation of Miale. Of course, now he was doing the opposite of what he should have been doing: he was taking Kiana away from safety. Nidan had thought about forcing her to go to Valgate, which was still just about the nearest city; then he reminded himself that she was the incarnation of a goddess. He'd take her to the ends of the earth if she commanded him to.

Nidan looped his horse's reins over a tree branch at the edge of the clearing and then lifted his shirt up to inspect the wound. Fresh blood was already beginning to appear through the white bandage, and Nidan could feel a sharp tearing pain along the length of the cut.

He became aware of the Wolf, who was standing a short distance away, watching.

"Will you let me sew it up for you?"

The question *sounded* innocent enough, except it had come from the mouth of a Wolf. Nidan pressed his lips together and shook his head. The same offer had been made every evening. Made and declined. He had to travel with the Wolf; he had to be civil in front of Kiana; he'd even been forced to let the Wolf watch over him while he slept. But that didn't mean that he was going to let an enemy stitch up his wounds: having to allow the Wolf to help with the bandages was degrading enough.

The Wolf stared at Nidan for a moment longer and then rolled his eyes. "I'll get a fire going." He moved away into the forest, collecting fallen branches as he went.

There was no shortage of forests in Gettryne: the twelve Noble Lords all kept large ones for firewood and hunting game.

"You should let Skaric stitch you up." Kiana held a leather saddlebag in her hands. "We're almost out of bandages."

Nidan wasn't worried about himself. He was worried about her. At that moment, sunlight falling through the forest canopy was creating dappled pools of green on her skin and lank hair. Combined with the dust, dirt and muck that were ingrained into her skin, she looked almost inhuman. Her eyes looked larger, her body slightly thinner. It was painfully obvious by the way she walked—slightly bow-legged thanks to saddle sores—that she had no experience of spending long hours riding, or of sleeping on dirt and branches and subsisting on trail rations.

Nidan shook his head and turned his back on her to undo the girth buckles. "We'll reach Norlea tomorrow. We can get bandages there." His voice was unnecessarily gruff.

Kiana appeared beside Nidan as he lifted the saddle off the horse's back. "With what money?"

He grimaced. She was right, of course. They had no money. They had left the tower in too much of a rush, and there had been none in the Wolves' packs—unsurprising as no one in Gettryne would trade or sell anything to a Wolf. Nidan ran his hand over his chin thoughtfully. He could feel the soft covering of a new beard. Wasn't it enough that he was travelling with a Wolf without starting to look like one too?

"What happens if your wound gets dirty, Nidan?"

Nidan moved away from the horse and dumped the saddle on the ground with the others. The Wolf had unsaddled the other two horses as soon as they had stopped; he worked quickly when it came to settling his and Kiana's horses each night. Nidan should have been grateful that he was spared the work.

"I could get sick."

"Could?"

Nidan sighed loudly. "I probably would."

Kiana placed her hand on his cheek. "What good are you to me if you're sick?"

He gritted his teeth. *None. None at all.*

"Don't let your pride put you in danger." Kiana dropped her hand and gazed at him sadly. "Or your hatred."

Nidan growled through his teeth. "He's a *Wolf.*"

"Yes."

"I don't trust him."

Kiana looked away from him and sat down on the floor. She began to pull out some strips of the dried meat that Nidan had come to hate.

"We're running out of food too." She held a strip of meat out to him. "Skaric has had plenty of chances to kill us."

Nidan didn't need reminding of that.

"But he hasn't. Surely he's earned some trust?" She held the meat out to him a moment longer and then began to eat it herself.

Nidan ground his teeth together even harder. He didn't want to trust the Wolf. He wanted to hate the Wolf.

He looked up as the Wolf returned to the clearing, arms laden down with twigs and kindling. On top of the pile of firewood were several tiny star-like white flowers. Each stalk had a dozen of the flowers and narrow green leaves.

Nidan walked over as the Wolf placed the flowers aside and began to build up a fire. "What are the flowers for?" He wrinkled his nose as he breathed in a delicate smell that was both sour and sweet at the same time.

The Wolf glanced up at him. "You boil the leaves up in water and then spread it over the horses; flies hate it."

Nidan could see why. The flowers stank. On the other hand, flies had plagued them each day. He would take smelling badly over being nibbled on by flies.

The Wolf paused, holding a twig just above the thatched pile he had been building. "It's also good for cleaning things: like a needle and thread."

Nidan felt a muscle in his cheek twitch. He glared at the Wolf, knitting his eyebrows together in anger.

The Wolf looked at Kiana, who was still sitting beside the saddles. "Could you look through the saddlebags? I'm sure I saw some cooking equipment in one of them."

Kiana looked at Nidan and then at the Wolf. "A metal bowl?"

The Wolf nodded. Kiana smiled and pushed herself onto her knees so that she could look through the saddlebags.

The Wolf leaned forward, towards Nidan. "Swallow your pride." His voice was little more than a whisper, but there was a hint of anger in it.

Nidan continued to glare at the Wolf who sat back and reached into his pocket for a flint and steel. Why didn't he just use his magic to light the fire?

It took the Wolf three attempts to get a large enough spark to light the curls of bark that he had used as kindling. As the flames began to take hold, the dry wood popped and crackled loudly. Tiny flames curled up into the darkening sky before dissipating in the air. Almost immediately, Nidan felt the warmth of the fire on his skin. It was the first night that they had dared to light a fire, for fear that Wolves would see the smoke. Nidan edged away from the flames slightly. The evening was warm enough.

Kiana smiled at them both as she returned with a metal bowl, a water flask, three metal rods and a ring. "These looked useful," she said as she placed everything down in front of the Wolf. "I'm sure I saw something similar in one of my tutor's books." She dipped her gaze to the ground as her shoulders slumped slightly.

Nidan's heart sank with hers. Her tutor was probably dead, like everyone else who had been in Blackoak Tower.

The Wolf smiled as he picked the rods up and slotted them through the ring, creating a tripod. He placed it over the fire and sat the bowl on top. Nidan couldn't help but smile as a grin slowly spread across Kiana's face. He watched as the Wolf poured water into the bowl and then began to tear the leaves off of the flower stems, ripping each one into several pieces before dropping them into the water.

"That stinks!" Kiana said, her whole face wrinkling comically.

The Wolf smiled. "Better to smell than be eaten alive!"

Nidan looked away and stared at the spongy green moss that covered the ground. Why couldn't the Wolf be more different from himself? Wolves were monsters; he didn't want to have anything in common with one.

"So, shall I fetch a needle and thread or not?" The Wolf's eyebrows were raised expectantly as he stared at Nidan.

Nidan didn't look up. "I don't want your help."

"I know. But you need it."

Nidan ground his teeth together again, his cheek muscles aching with the effort. He had *never* imagined that he would be forced to accept so much help from his enemy.

"Skaric's right, Nidan," Kiana said quietly.

Of course, he was right. That only made it harder for Nidan to carry on refusing. Was it pride or hate? Kiana was probably right in thinking it was a mixture of both. And why shouldn't he hate the Wolf? All Wolves did was murder indiscriminately and destroy *everything* they came into contact with. What made the man in front of him any different?

Nidan lifted his head and glared at them both. "Fine. I need your help. Are you happy now?" He expected to see a look of triumph in the Wolf's eyes. Failing that, anger. But he saw neither. What he saw was sadness.

The Wolf shook his head, stood and headed over to the saddlebags. Nidan stared at the water in the bowl, which was beginning to bubble and spit noisily.

"He's trying to help," Kiana whispered. "You could *try* to be a little nicer."

She was right. Pios, why did she have to be right?

Nidan kept his mouth firmly shut as the Wolf returned with a long length of thick thread, a large metal needle and a swab of cloth. He dropped the cloth into the bowl and then threaded the needle. Holding on to the very end of the thread, the Wolf dipped both into the mixture of boiling water and leaves.

He looked up at Nidan. "Ready?"

No. Nidan tugged his shirt over his head and carefully unwound the bandage around his chest. After a day of travelling in the summer heat, the bandage had become grey and grimy with sweat.

"Kiana, could you hold the thread?" the Wolf asked.

Kiana edged closer to the fire. Once he had given her the thread, the Wolf used the end of a stick to fish the swab back out of the water. Tentatively, he picked it up and moved across to Nidan.

"This might sting."

Nidan looked up at the maze-like canopy and kept his teeth clenched together. He flinched as the hot swab touched the wound and almost knocked the Wolf's hand away as he felt a stinging pain. Instead, he panted against the pain. Nidan glanced down and watched as the Wolf cleaned away the fresh blood and pus before throwing the dirty swab into the fire. A bright orange flame flashed up in a column, briefly making the air even warmer. Next, the Wolf took the end of the thread from Kiana and lifted the needle and the rest of the thread from the water.

He looked Nidan in the eyes. "And this *will* hurt."

Nidan curled his hands into the moss as the needle pierced his skin. He pressed his lips together and stared upwards again, blinking back tears as the Wolf continued to work quickly and methodically. At least they would have a reasonably comfortable night sleeping on a moss mattress.

"We will find answers in Norlea, won't we?" Kiana asked.

Nidan was glad of the diversion her words gave him. "I told you, the original temple still exists."

The Wolf paused, holding the needle and thread slack. He glanced at Kiana and chewed his lower lip. "Is it safe for you to go into the village?"

Kiana blinked quickly and sat up a bit straighter.

Nidan shifted his weight ever so slightly. "He means your eyes." He looked at the Wolf. "Only the Guardians and priests know how to recognise the incarnation of Miale. No one will know who she is."

A small bead of blood formed on the Wolf's lip. "We knew." He averted his eyes.

How had the Wolves known? Who had they tortured and killed

to get such a secret piece of information? Nidan shivered and clenched his teeth again. "No one will recognise Kiana."

The Wolf nodded and carried on. He'd barely completed one stitch before pausing again. "How long do you think you'll need to spend in the village?"

Nidan shrugged and winced in pain.

"Hold still."

"What do you mean?" Kiana asked. "We're all going into the village."

Nidan gasped as the Wolf tugged a little too hard on the thread as he completed a stitch. It was the first mistake he'd made.

"I can't go into that village, Kiana."

"Why not?"

"Because he's a Wolf," Nidan said.

"You mean because he *looks* like a Wolf?" Kiana stared at the Wolf. "We can change that. It's only your hair and your beard."

The Wolf leant forward and snapped the end of the thread with his teeth. Nidan could see the tension in the Wolf's face and shoulders as he rocked back onto his heels.

"I *can't* come with you. I'll wait for you." The Wolf turned his attention back to the bowl of boiling water and leaves. "It's late, we should all get some sleep."

Kiana looked up at Nidan, her brow furrowed. "I suppose I wouldn't want to change the way I look," she said doubtfully. "Would you?"

Nidan looked down at his tattered uniform. He still felt a thrill of pride that he was wearing the Guardian uniform at all; it didn't matter to him that it was wrecked. He shook his head. Nothing would make him want to hide who he was.

He looked down at his side wound. The stitches were small and neat, the wound clean. As part of his training, Nidan had been taught field medicine and how to do stitches. His had never been neat. There had been no point in practising when he could use magic to repair the wounds of others. Apparently, he'd taken a lot for granted.

Chapter Seven

The sun was rising just above the horizon as Berend limped across the camp towards the five men that he had handpicked to travel with him. He had refused the crutch that Brokk had tried to foist upon him; a crutch would have made him look weak. Moisture clung to the stony ground in tiny droplets, shimmering a rainbow of colours as the sunlight struck them. Its beauty was lost on Berend. He had already wasted too much time. Why did Brokk have to treat grown men like snivelling children? As soon as he had been allowed back on his feet, he had been ordered to oversee their withdrawal from the tower. He had led the Wolves north to rocky terrain in the foothills of mountains that were regarded as inhospitable by the people of Gettryne.

"Berend!"

Berend scowled at the tone of Adalric's voice, but he made his expression passive as he turned. Damn the Alpha for waking so early. Berend was forced to lean heavily on his good leg to bow low to Adalric. Away from battle, the Alpha wore a pale leather jerkin trimmed with wolf fur. As Berend stood, he glanced at Vali who was standing just behind Adalric.

"You're ready to leave?" There was no warmth in Adalric's voice or his stare.

When had Berend lost the trust and respect of his Alpha? He ignored Adalric's pointless question. He was wearing his armour, he had weaponry strapped to his waist and back and he was also carrying saddlebags that were full of provisions. It was painfully obvious that he was about to start searching for Skaric.

Berend gestured towards the waiting men. "I want to get as far as possible before nightfall." His quarry was getting further ahead of him with every moment he delayed.

One of the packs had reported that six men had been slaughtered in a field close to Valgate. Skaric's horse—identifiable by its fur-trimmed saddlecloth—had been found in the same field. Judging by the activity of the city's Guardians, the incarnation of Miale had *not* gone there.

"You haven't picked a nyxus to go with you."

Berend hadn't felt the need. Besides, there wasn't a warrior that he hadn't trained; he trusted every one of them with his life. He couldn't say the same for *any* of the nyxii.

"I want you to take Vali."

Berend resisted the urge to roll his eyes. "I have no need of Vali's skills." He had no need of anyone that might possibly sympathise with Skaric. He knew that Skaric and Vali were rivals and friends.

Adalric narrowed his eyes in a slight gesture that Berend almost missed. "Skaric is a nyxus. If he really is a traitor, he could destroy you and your men before you could act."

Berend clamped his teeth together. Skaric didn't have the balls to do that, but Adalric didn't know it. There was no way Berend was going to say or do something that would expose his lies. "Vali is one of our most experienced nyxii. Wouldn't he be more valuable to us if he was sent to search for Miale?"

Adalric's eyes narrowed more noticeably. "Vali and Skaric are evenly matched in skill. You'll need him."

Berend snorted, ignoring the pain that shot through his nose and cheeks. Skaric was better than Vali. He was more creative and adventurous. At least he had been. It wouldn't take a nyxii to catch Skaric now.

"Is there a problem?"

"No. Of course not, Alpha. If you think it's best, I'll take Vali with me."

Adalric hesitated, staring at Berend. "I do think it's best."

Berend quickly shifted his gaze to Vali. He couldn't read the nyxus' expression and that bothered him. "You'd better get a horse ready. Quickly."

Vali gave him a shallow bow. "Of course, war leader." He lingered a moment longer and then headed over to the corral at a brisk pace.

Berend watched him go. "You know he and Skaric are friends, don't you?"

Adalric nodded. Of course he knew.

"And you still think it's a good idea for him to come with me?"

Adalric took a step closer. He was tall enough to look down on Berend with his cold blue eyes. "That's exactly why I want him to go with you. He knows Skaric better than anyone. If *anyone* can help you find my son, it's Vali."

Berend shivered under the Alpha's gaze. "Does he know Skaric better than you?"

Adalric's expression became dark. He clamped his lips together so hard that the colour drained from them. "Just bring my son back. Alive."

Berend bowed low. He didn't move until Adalric had walked away. He curled his mouth into a snarl as he stood tall again. Adalric's confidence in Berend had always been rock solid. He was the war leader for Ysia's sake. He didn't need a nyxus to watch over him, especially not Vali, who was as well known for whining like a spoilt girl as he was for his magical skill. Berend whipped round and limped the rest of the way to his men. His knee—supported by a splint—was as stiff as wood and hurt like fury, fueling his rage.

Annoyingly, Vali joined them just as Berend was about to give the order to leave. Shame. He had hoped to leave the nyxus trailing behind.

As they rode out of the camp, Vali pulled his horse up alongside Berend's.

"You're not happy about me tagging along, are you?"

Berend smiled. At least Vali wasn't stupid. "What are your orders?" He looked across at Vali in time to see the nyxus shrug.

"The same as yours. To bring Skaric back alive." Vali spurred his horse forward, leaving Berend glaring at his back.

*

Kiana and Nidan had arrived at Norlea via a dusty road that cut through open farm land, pregnant with wispy crops. The village itself was surrounded by a sturdy wall made of tree trunks that had been cut lengthways. Two men stood guard. They were well armed but poorly groomed and wore neither a uniform or armour. Kiana and Nidan dismounted, leading their horses as they walked through the gates.

Two dozen single-storey round houses littered the compound. Each one was made from mud bricks with low thatched roofs. A pair of dead rabbits hung outside the closest house, tied by their hind legs. Swarms of incessantly buzzing flies congregated around the dead animals. Each house had a fenced off area at the rear, housing livestock which stood miserably on the dry ground. One household had a pair of plump pigs, another a sheep with a trio of nearly full grown lambs. Chickens waddled about the village freely, clucking as they pecked at the ground searching for food. The village stank of faeces and urine. Straw crunched under Kiana's feet.

A short distance away a small group of children stopped playing with sticks and stones, to stare open-mouthed at the two strangers.

Kiana tugged on Nidan's arm. "Are you sure this village isn't big enough to have a priest or Guardian living here?"

She stared around at the other visible villagers. There were two women filling wooden buckets from a well, their hair tied back and covered with squares of undyed cloth. Another pair of women sat on stools, their legs straddling wide tubs filled with soapy water. Their faces were red as they rubbed clothes over metal scrubbing boards. They had been mid-conversation, but the words had died on their lips.

"Why are they all staring?" She clung even tighter to Nidan's arm.

She had never seen so many people in one place before. The tower had been filled with people, but she had never seen anyone except her Guardians, Erynn and Ducarius.

She glanced at a man who was hammering dents out of an iron pot with a mallet. His arms were as muscled as any Guardian she had ever met, but his expression was cold and distrusting. Opposite him, another man sat carving utensils and further on, there was a scrawny man scraping a dull knife over a dripping wet piece of hide.

Kiana stopped, pulling Nidan as a tall, simply dressed man strode down the road—if it could be called that—towards them. Beside him walked a plump and cheerful-looking woman. The man was looking directly at them; as he drew near, he stopped.

He touched his fingertips to his temple and then extended a closed fist to Nidan. "Welcome to Norlea, Guardian."

Nidan touched the man's fist with his own.

The man's expression was distrusting as he looked at Nidan's face and his dishevelled, tattered clothes. "It's not often that we get travellers here." He wrinkled his nose. "It smells like you haven't had a bath in some time."

Kiana dug her nails into Nidan's arm. She smelt terrible and probably looked worse, though surely she couldn't smell as badly as the village? She had tried to tame her hair and tie it back with the left over thread, but tendrils of it had still snaked loose to curl about her face and shoulders. Her skin felt itchy and her clothes were stiff with filth. She didn't need a stranger telling her how awful she looked.

The plump woman slapped her companion across the chest. "Don't be so rude, Cadman!"

"It's all right," Nidan said. "We haven't slept on a bed in days, let alone had baths! Our home is… was… quite a way from here, further to the west. It was destroyed."

Cadman's expression became dark. "Destroyed? By Wolves?"

The woman beside him drew in a sharp breath and shook her head sadly. Kiana felt Nidan's muscles tense.

"Yes. My companion and I have been travelling ever since. We aim to reach Fairlake."

Cadman stroked his chin. "Fairlake is a long way from here. Wouldn't you be better off heading to Ironhold?"

Nidan gently lifted Kiana's hand from his arm. "I want to deliver my companion to Fairlake first. She is a priestess of Miale."

Kiana's heartbeat quickened. Nidan's words were too close to the truth. What if these villagers had heard about the attack on

Blackoak Tower? What if they guessed who she really was? She took a deep breath. They wouldn't know. They couldn't.

The woman clapped her hands together in excitement. "Poor things! You look exhausted. A Guardian of Pios and a priestess of Miale are more than welcome in our village. It would be an honour to help you. Wouldn't it, Cadman?"

Cadman nodded stiffly. "Of course, Alish. We'll arrange for food, baths and clean clothes for you. You can spend the night here and we'll give you provisions for the next stage of your journey."

Kiana inclined her head in thanks. The thought of warm food, a soothing bath and a comfortable bed filled her with warmth.

After calling someone across to take their horses, Cadman and Alish led them past the houses to the far end of the village. Kiana stopped in her tracks as she saw a building made from grey stone that had been pockmarked by the elements. It consisted of two circular structures that had been joined together in a lopsided manner and a square entrance, which jutted out. The building was obviously ancient with crumbling plaster that had been repaired on more than one occasion. It also looked incomplete, as though there should have been more, and a straight wall had been erected to quickly finish the job. To the side, in the shadow of the village wall, several stone blocks had been neatly stacked.

"The temple," Nidan whispered. "Or it was."

Kiana's chin trembled. It was sad that the building would remain incomplete for eternity. *Except it won't because we're going to fix this. Somehow we'll fix this madness.*

"This is our meeting hall," Cadman said, "but also our home. I am the Elder of this village and Alish is my wife."

"Pleased to meet you," Kiana said quietly, curtseying.

"What are your names, dears?" Alish asked.

Kiana's voice stuck in her throat. What should she say? What if they recognised her name?

"Nye and Brid," Nidan said.

Kiana touched his hand gently, silently thanking him.

"Lovely names! Come inside."

Kiana slipped her hand into Nidan's as they followed Alish inside. Cadman did not follow them.

The entrance hall had no windows but was lit by four brands that rested in iron sconces. The floor was made of flagstones that were cold beneath Kiana's feet: the soles of her slippers were almost completely worn through. At one point, there had been three internal doorways, but the third had been blocked off with stone. Kiana glanced up at Nidan, but he shrugged and pulled her through the left hand doorway into a circular room.

The room had several long and narrow windows that allowed light to flood inside. Faded frescos adorned the once smoothly plastered wall. Wooden chairs stood in concentric circles with space in the centre for a speaker to stand.

"I'll have beds made up in here for you," Alish said. "I'm sorry I can't offer you more privacy. I'll also have a bathtub brought through and fresh clothes."

Kiana felt warmth burning her cheeks. She had slept close to Nidan but bathing in front of him was another matter entirely. Glancing at Nidan, Kiana saw that his face had turned a violent shade of red.

"Sit down. Rest. I'll be back soon." Alish said. She bustled out of the room and closed the door behind her.

"They seem like nice people," Nidan said. "And we could both do with some clean clothes and a good night's sleep."

"So could Skaric."

"We can ask for spare clothes. They'll be only too happy to help us," Nidan said stiffly.

Kiana wrapped her arms about herself and turned away from him to stare at the frescos. It should have been comforting that Miale and Pios were so loved. But the depth of that love was mirrored by equally deep hatred against the Wolves, against Skaric.

The fresco had not been looked after. The red and orange tones were faded and patchy, and in some places, the images they depicted were almost unrecognisable. A solid red border ran around the top and bottom of the wall, whilst the images seemed to grow out of the bottom border. The story seemed to start on the right hand side of the door. There was an image of Miale holding the cup of knowledge. Her hair was flowing and her eyes were blank and unseeing. It was an image that Kiana had seen countless times in her tutor's books. For the first time, she wondered why she looked nothing like Miale.

Kiana slowly turned on the spot, taking in the next section of the fresco. It showed the building of a castle. Her breath caught in her throat: she had seen the castle before in dreams and had drawn a crude image of it over and over.

"Is that Orholt?"

Nidan stood alongside her. "I guess it must be."

Kiana kept looking, her gaze raced over the images: people flocking to the castle, a group of fourteen men with a single crown painted above them, the three gods looking down upon the castle. She covered her mouth with her hands. Ysia's form had been dashed out of the wall, leaving an ugly gash of exposed grey stone.

In the next section, three figures had been painted: two women and a man. Above them were the gods, connected to the figures by strands of red. Once again, Ysia's image had been mutilated.

When she turned her gaze to the next image, Kiana fell to her knees. She saw Miale. Dead. Standing over Miale was a man depicted with the head of a wolf. The wolf's maw was open, its eyes mad and staring. It was inhuman, hideous. Why hadn't they drawn the man with a human face?

In the next image, the wolf-headed man was surrounded by men with swords, one of which had run him through. Even though it was only a painting, Kiana could feel the hatred that had been poured into it. She could see it in the facial expressions of the warriors and the inhuman face of Miale's killer. A thousand years old and the hatred was still so clear.

She covered her face with her hands. "I don't want to see anymore!" But she knew she had to if she was going to get answers.

At that moment, the door opened. Kiana didn't look up. Footsteps walked slowly into the room and there was a metallic clang as something large and heavy was placed on the flagstones. Kiana heard the splash of water being poured. She could look at the fresco later. Get her answers later. After a bath. After food. After rest.

*

It was late afternoon. The shadows in the forest were beginning to deepen, but there was still no sign of Kiana and Nidan returning. Spending the night alone wasn't a problem; if anything, it would be less stressful. From his vantage point in the forest to the east of the village, Skaric could see the tall wooden walls of Norlea. Wisps of light grey smoke rose from within the walls, the only sign of life except for the two guards that stood outside of the gates.

Skaric smiled as his horse ambled closer and used its large face to nudge and nuzzle his hand, searching for something more interesting than brambles and leaves.

"Sorry, girl. No treats." Skaric absently stroked the white star on the horse's otherwise black face. Its hair was short, coarse and smelled musty. It also stank of garlic, but Skaric had gotten so used to the bittersweet scent that he barely noticed it. He used his leg to push away from the tree that he had been leaning against and scooped up the horse's reins. It was best if he headed deeper into the forest before settling down for the night.

Skaric hadn't gone far when the sound of light footsteps caught his attention. He froze. The horse carried on moving, its hoof falls sounding achingly loud as they clattered over loose stones on the ground. The horse bumped into him, knocking him forward a couple of footsteps before it stopped and let out a loud snort. Skaric turned and pressed his hand against the animal's nose. The warmth of its breath was wet against Skaric's hand as he tried to listen. The footsteps were moving parallel to him, and he could also hear a high voice singing, pretty and youthful.

Skaric secured the horse to a solid looking tree branch and ducked behind the cover of a thorny bush. He had no time to get further away or to conceal the horse.

Moments later, the owner of the footsteps—a dark-haired girl of perhaps nine or ten—wandered past his position. She was dressed in simple hand woven clothes and carried a wicker basket. Skaric could just see that it held a small handful of rich red berries. He held his breath as the girl paused a few paces away from him in order to pick berries from a nearby bush. Then she moved on a short way, singing a cheerful ditty to herself, innocently oblivious to the horse that stood through the trees a short distance away.

Move away.

The girl paused at a tree and stared up at it. Her face lit up as she grinned. Skaric followed her gaze and saw a brightly-coloured bird sitting on a high up branch preening itself. Suddenly, the girl set her basket down and began to climb. Surprisingly, she was a swift climber. From where he was, Skaric could watch her quick ascent. The bird cocked its head and looked at her but made no move to fly away.

Skaric's heart hammered as he continued to watch. *Get down!*

The girl began to edge along the branch that the bird was perched on, her arms and legs hugging beneath her. She stopped midway along and reached out to the bird. It looked at her, seemed willing to accept her friendship for the briefest of moments and then stretched its wings in flight. Skaric could clearly hear the girl's sob of annoyance before she began to edge backwards along the branch.

Get down.

There was sickening crack and a scream filled the air. Skaric couldn't breathe. The girl's body hit the ground with a dull thud, followed immediately by the sharp tap of the branch. The girl lay motionless.

Skaric waited. Surely her scream would bring someone running. He counted sixty heartbeats. Nothing. She couldn't be alone… could she? Sixty heartbeats more. The sound of blood rushing through Skaric's veins drowned out the other sounds of the forest. He forced his thoughts to calm, made himself listen. He could hear his horse snuffling through the undergrowth, the creak of branches being tussled by the breeze and the background buzz of insects. No footsteps. No one was coming. The girl was alone.

Cursing under his breath, Skaric left the safety of his hiding place and slowly approached the girl. Her left leg lay at an odd angle to her body, the ground beneath her head was stained with blood and her nose was slowly bleeding. It was only when Skaric was directly beside her, looking down upon her broken form, that he could see she was still breathing.

He knelt beside her and gently patted her cheek. The girl's eyes remained closed, her face completely relaxed. *Walk away.* She wasn't his problem. Skaric stared at her and the blood escaping her injury. *A Wolf would walk away.* He shook his head. He couldn't let her die.

"Why did you come out here alone?" Who was he talking to: an unconscious girl or himself? There was no one to convince that he was about to do the right thing.

Skaric ripped the right sleeve from his shirt and gently lifted her head. The blood was flowing more freely from her skull than he had first thought. He folded the sleeve up and held it tightly against the wound, dismayed that it quickly became drenched. If he did leave her, she would be dead by the time anyone came looking for her. Skaric picked her up and cradled her against his chest. She was surprisingly light.

"You're an idiot, Skaric. A fool."

It didn't matter. He couldn't leave her to die. Not now. Everything had changed.

Skaric carried her towards his horse. Why had things changed? Days ago he wouldn't have cared. She wasn't a Wolf and wasn't his concern. He might have even put her out of her misery.

Why had things changed? Gently, he placed her over the saddle and untied the horse. He began to lead the animal towards the village, walking at its shoulder so that he could keep one hand on the girl's back.

Why *had* things changed? Because his enemy had shown him compassion? Or because he had stared death in the eyes and been afraid? It didn't matter. Letting her die would be callous. He wasn't that person anymore.

As soon as Skaric approached the gates, one of the guards pulled his sword free of its scabbard and held it towards him. The other quickly vanished inside the gate, and less than a heartbeat later, Skaric heard urgent shouting. He grimaced as his gaze dipped to a crossbow that stood propped up against the gate. He couldn't leave the girl and run, not unless he wanted an arrow planted in his back. Were his chances any better if he stayed put?

"She fell," Skaric said in as loud and brave a voice as he could muster. "Do you have a healer inside?"

The gate opened and the guard reappeared followed by several men, all of whom stared at him, their faces twisted into grotesque snarls.

"Wolf!"

"What did you do to her?"

"She fell." Skaric's mouth had become dry, whilst his heart was beating rapidly. At least against Berend the odds had been slightly fairer. "She's bleeding badly. I think her leg is broken. She needs a healer."

None of the men believed him. He was a Wolf. They obviously thought he was stupid. Common sense didn't matter; they only saw one thing—a Wolf standing at their gates. He really was an idiot.

Despite every nerve in his body crying out for him to do something, Skaric stood stock still as the men formed a tight circle around him. He held his hands high to show that he was completely unarmed as the girl was lifted from the horse and carried inside the gate. If they had any sense, they would fetch Nidan. He would heal her. He would make her all right.

Skaric felt the weight of a heavy fist slam into his back, quickly followed by a kick at the back of his right knee. His leg buckled and he dropped to the ground. He could plead for mercy. They weren't Wolves; they would listen. Skaric groaned as a boot struck his cheek.

No, they wouldn't listen.

Their shouts filled the air as more men stepped forward to assault him. Magic. He could use magic. Destroy them all. Take the life from those behind him to kill those in front. Bitter bile rose in Skaric's throat as his stomach somersaulted. His skin had gone cold. He couldn't use magic. He couldn't kill them. *Idiot!*

Skaric was kicked repeatedly in the legs, stomach and face. He took the punishment kneeling down for as long as he could. Their jeers, snarls and attacks grew fiercer, battering his body, wearing down his mind. Skaric allowed himself to collapse. Sharp pain overrode his senses. He drew his knees up to his chest and covered his face with his arms. He didn't make a sound; he simply endured the beating. Gradually his body became numb.

Suddenly, Skaric felt strong hands close around his arms, pulling them roughly behind his back. He was pulled to his feet. Two men held him upright, one on either side. Skaric could just see that there were more people standing outside the gate, mostly men, but there were some women as well. The man immediately in front of Skaric punched him hard in the face. For a while, Skaric stared the man in the eyes; cold hatred stared back at him. The people around him were shouting, cheering the attacker on. The punches became more and more frenzied, harder and harder. Skaric heard his cheekbone crack but oddly, he felt very little pain at all in his body; he just felt a strange numbness as though he wasn't really physical at all. Maybe he deserved what was happening to him.

Skaric's vision was blurred and kept fading in and out. Had another man stepped in front of him? It was hard to tell. One angry face looked like another.

"Bring him inside."

It was a voice he hadn't heard yet. It was authoritative. Why would they take him inside? Couldn't they kill him there?

Skaric was pushed forward. His legs refused to move so the men dragged him instead. Once within the walls, he was pulled fully upright again. Out of the corner of his right eye, he dimly saw Kiana walk out of a twin circular building. The colour drained from her face and her mouth dropped open. She took a few steps forward. *Please don't.* Skaric managed the slightest shake of his head. She stopped. *Thank Ysia.*

"Lock him up." The authoritative voice spoke again. "We'll decide his fate once we know if Innogen is going to live."

Innogen. Skaric would have smiled if any of his muscles had been willing to respond to his commands. There was nothing to decide. They would kill him, but at least he knew the name of the girl he was going to die for.

*

Kiana's muscles twitched as she heard the guard close the heavy lock with a clunk, which was loud even through the wooden door behind her. Or maybe it was because it was so silent inside the storeroom, now a makeshift prison. Kiana was holding a lit torch in her shaking hand. The sweet smell of oil overpowered the room quickly, as did the heat of the flame. She laid the torch down on the earthen ground away from the mudbrick walls. Could mud bricks burn? Kiana didn't want to find out. The flames continued to burn brightly. They danced and guttered, creating eerie moving shapes that lurched around the room in a grotesque dance.

Skaric lay against the back wall, his arms and legs cruelly hogtied behind him. Kiana clenched her trembling hands; her feet wouldn't move. In the ever-shifting light, she could see that Skaric's face was a swollen, bloody and blackened mess. The skin on his arms and hands was equally battered. Kiana's stomach recoiled from the sight.

"Skaric?" Kiana knelt down, keeping her voice quiet. She hadn't heard the guard move away. What if he tried to listen through the door? "Skaric?"

Slowly, his right eye opened halfway. Even that small action sent spasms of pain through Skaric's body. Kiana pressed her fists together at the knuckles, tensing all her muscles. She wouldn't cry or scream. She would stay strong. It seemed to take Skaric a long time to focus on her and then register whom she was; then his face took on an apologetic expression.

"I couldn't let her die." His voice was weak as he spoke through clenched teeth. His words were badly slurred and it took all Kiana's concentration to pick out the sounds.

She edged closer and put her hand on his shoulder. "I know."

Trembling beneath her touch, Skaric whimpered in pain. "Why did they let you in here?"

"They think I'm a priestess of Miale." *Why are you showing pain so clearly? You were so determined to hide it before.*

Skaric's right eye widened and his left eye—gummed shut with liquid—tried to open. "You shouldn't have told them that. Word might get back to the Guardians... or the Wolves."

Kiana pressed her fingertips to her lips as tears edged up her throat. "Don't worry about that. Don't worry about anything, all right?"

Skaric seemed to try to nod but ended up just groaning slightly instead. Kiana swallowed repeatedly. She would not cry. If Skaric couldn't be strong, she had to be. She would be.

"Nidan has healed the girl. Innogen."

"She'll live?" Skaric's voice sounded hopeful.

"He hopes so. She's still unconscious." Kiana forced herself to smile. "But when she wakes, I'll ask her what really happened, and she'll tell them you did nothing wrong. They'll have to let you go."

Skaric moved his head slightly. His neck seemed to be stiff, but Kiana thought he was trying to shake his head.

"They think I'm a priestess of Miale." They'd listen to her. The villagers would do as she said. "Ducarius told me that people accept the word of a priest of Miale as truth."

"That was a long time ago."

The corners of Kiana's lips trembled. She hung her head. They wouldn't listen to her. "When we get you out of here, we need to do something about the way you look." She tried to make her voice sound hopeful.

Skaric stared at her. The silence stretched on, made worse by the ever dancing flames. Kiana wanted to extinguish the brand. She wanted to scream.

"They're going to kill me, Kiana." Skaric's weak voice ruptured the silence.

Kiana shook her head, squeezing her eyes shut. He had to be wrong. She used the back of her hand to gently stroke his face. Even her light touch seemed to make his pain worse. She clenched her hands together in her lap. "How could they do this?"

Skaric half smiled, though the action was rendered ugly by his injuries and the fluttering light of the flames. "I'm a Wolf, Kiana; don't forget that. No one else will."

"But you're not like them…" Kiana stopped as she saw his one-eyed stare become cold and distant.

"You don't know that." His voice was filled with disgust. "You don't know what I've done."

Kiana covered her face with her hands and took several deep

breaths. She would not cry. She would not hate him. When she moved her hands, she realised that his gaze had never left her.

"Don't do that."

His stare didn't waiver.

"Don't try to make me hate you. It didn't work when we first met, and it won't work now. Understand?" It was difficult not to raise her voice. Kiana wanted to shout at him.

Skaric continued staring at her; his right eye glistened in the darkness.

"I'm not going to let them kill you." The emptiness of her words would have echoed around the room to taunt her if they could have. Kiana knew she couldn't save him.

Skaric's right arm strained against the tight ropes. He groaned as his body spasmed and became rigid. What was he trying to do? Reach out to her? Kiana put her arm on his shoulder again and stroked him gently.

"I'm not worth dying over, Kiana. Promise me you won't do anything. Just walk away."

Kiana shook her head so quickly it made the room spin briefly. "I can't..." The fierceness of his gaze made her close her mouth and nod her head.

It made Kiana sick to think that the people who had seemed so kind earlier in the day had turned into monsters before her eyes. Even plump cheerful Alish had screamed and jeered for Skaric to be killed.

"Promise me!" The desperation in his face was too much.

Tears welled in Kiana's eyes. "Why are you suddenly so worried about my safety? I thought you still wanted to kill me..." She tried to make her voice sound light and flippant. The failed joke hung on the air between them, making the hut suddenly seem colder. Kiana shivered. *Why did I say those words?*

Skaric closed his eye, though his body remained tense. His chest shuddered and his breathing became ragged. "I don't." His voice was so weak it was barely audible. "Not any more. Not since you saved my life."

Kiana leaned down to kiss his battered cheek. "You know, Skaric, you are the most trustworthy untrustworthy person I have ever met." She felt him tense beneath her touch.

"Get the answers you need to restore Miale."

Don't say goodbye. "I will. I'll restore the *whole* trinity. I promise." *Please don't say goodbye.*

"You should go."

Kiana shook her head. She couldn't leave him alone. He was in pain, afraid and facing death. He didn't deserve to suffer alone.

Skaric's right eye opened slightly. "They'll get suspicious if you don't go." His voice was insistent, desperate.

Kiana shook her head even more fiercely.

"Please go."

Her hand dropped from his shoulder. She was just making him feel worse. Nodding, Kiana pushed herself back onto the balls of her feet and stood. She began to walk backwards slowly, forcing herself to continue to look at him and memorise every part of his face. Even if he was battered and barely recognisable, she wanted to remember Skaric in that moment. He had stopped looking at her and was just lying as limply as the ropes would let him.

When she reached the door, Kiana bent down to pick up the torch. The flames flickered with dizzying intensity. The shadows in the bottom half of the room became deeper, smothering Skaric. Tears began to trickle down Kiana's face. She brushed them roughly aside, turned and bashed her hand against the door until it was opened for her. She didn't look at the guard as she ran past him into the darkness of the night. She had to get away from the hut. Away from Skaric.

Chapter Eight

Nidan stood outside the old temple, watching as Skaric was dragged out into the sunlight. The Wolf's face was littered with bruises that had darkened into a variety of shades of purple and blue. Nidan clenched his teeth as a shiver ran through his body. He understood why Kiana had spent the night so distraught, but understanding was *not* the same thing as agreeing.

It looked like the entire village was present to watch the serving of justice; even the children were eager to watch alongside the men and women. Some looked curious but most looked angry or stared at the Wolf with disgust; none showed any hint of pity or regret about what had been done to the unarmed man. And why should they?

There was a cheer as the Wolf was thrown to the ground. Both of the men that had held him gave him a kick in the ribs before moving back a few paces. The Wolf didn't move at all; he probably didn't have the strength to.

Nidan folded his arms across his chest, refusing to feel pity. He watched as Cadman stepped forward out of the crowd, followed by a couple who were leading Innogen by the hands. Thanks to Pios' magic, it was now impossible to tell that she had even been hurt.

"Innogen, tell us what this man did to you," Cadman said, his words coated in hatred as he spat them out.

Nidan watched the girl as she stared at the Wolf. What *was* she going to say? Kiana was absolutely convinced that the Wolf was innocent of any wrongdoing. Nidan was less sure. He wanted the Wolf to be guilty. *There, I've admitted it.*

But if the Wolf was guilty why had he tried to save Innogen's life?

Innogen's eyes widened and her mouth dropped open. She reached out and tried to step forward. Her father wrapped his arm over her shoulders and pulled her back.

"What did this man do to you?" Cadman said.

"Nothing. I've never seen him before. I was climbing and I fell." She sniffed loudly. "Why is he hurt?"

The crowd began to whisper amongst themselves.The shrill cry of Innogen's mother instantly silenced them all. "What wickedness is this? What magic have you cast on our child?" She spat at the Wolf.

The Wolf did not respond.

Nidan watched as shouts of agreement ran through the crowd. They had no evidence that the Wolf could even cast magic, but that didn't matter to them. He was a Wolf; it was just another accusation to add more fuel to the fire. Nidan snarled. He had seen firsthand the devastation a Wolf mage could cause. If the Wolf wanted to, he could slaughter them all. Why didn't the villagers stop to ask themselves why the Wolf hadn't done that? Nidan shifted his stance. Why *hadn't* the Wolf used his magic to save himself?

Innogen tried to object as she was led away, but no one was listening to the girl, least of all her parents. She was crying openly, screaming and reaching out to the Wolf.

Nidan felt an odd shift inside himself: his stomach suddenly felt hollow. Innogen didn't see a Wolf. She only saw an injured man. She didn't understand why her family was so angry. Nidan tried to smirk but couldn't force the action upon his lips. She was a child: innocent and naïve. What did she know about the world or Wolves?

"Enough!" Cadman's voice silenced the crowd. "I have seen and heard enough to pass judgement."

The emptiness in Nidan's stomach increased. Cadman had seen nothing except a Wolf returning an injured girl to her home for healing. He had heard nothing more except that same girl proclaiming the Wolf's innocence. Kiana had been right: not just about that but about Nidan as well; he *was* letting anger and hatred drive his feelings towards the Wolf. Skaric. The Wolf had a name.

There was only one judgement that Cadman would pass, and the crowd knew it. They began a unified chant of one word: death. It was a sentence that Cadman could pass because the laws of the twelve Lords didn't apply to Wolves. They killed indiscriminately, so they were killed just as lightly.

Nidan couldn't stand still any more. He pushed his way through the crowd and stood facing Cadman. "What's your judgement?" He spoke loudly so that he could be heard above the chanting.

Slowly the crowd began to hush. Nidan was shaking. His mind was racing. What could he actually do for Skaric?

"Death."

The crowd cheered.

There had to be a way… "How?" He paused purposefully, waiting as Cadman's forehead wrinkled in thought. "Do you often perform executions?"

Cadman's mouth flapped open and closed a few times. "Death by sword!" He looked round at the crowd, raising his arms to elicit another cheer.

Nidan nodded thoughtfully as he waited for the crowd to quieten down. "Will you run him through or sever his head? It can take several blows to do the latter." He began to walk round, catching the gaze of as many people as he could. "What do you intend to do with the body?"

Cadman did not have an immediate answer; his voice stuttered over several failed attempts to speak. "String it up on the walls of the village!"

There was another cheer.

"And go against Pios?" That hushed the crowd. "Pios teaches us that the body is sacred and should be buried." Nidan waited; surely Cadman wouldn't dare to argue.

"He's a Wolf! Pios' edicts do not apply to him."

The crowd agreed with him, cheering and jeering.

Think. Think. Nidan forced himself to laugh. "A body on the wall will turn away any traders that might travel here as summer turns to autumn. What about your children? Do you really want to give them nightmares because they have to see a rotting carcass every day? Not to mention the stench and the rats and birds. Have you seen what happens to a body that's left to fester, rot and be devoured by beasts?" Nidan hadn't and never wanted to.

Cadman's face turned a deep shade of scarlet. "And what would you suggest, Guardian?"

Nidan hesitated. *Let him go?* That still wasn't an option. "I'll take him out into the forest and kill him there."

"I won't have his body buried. Let the beasts devour a beast."

A murmur of approval rose up from the crowd.

Nidan forced his smile to become cruel. "I'll take him now, shall I?" He stepped forward, ready to take charge of Skaric.

Cadman blocked him. "We'll come with you."

Nidan's heart somersaulted. "Don't you trust me?"

Cadman's eyes narrowed. "It's not a matter of trust. You are a Guardian. It's your duty to protect us from the Wolves."

Then why are you so desperate to watch an execution?

"This Wolf tried to murder one of our people. It's our right to watch his death."

There was nothing Nidan could say to that. His vague plan was falling apart because the villagers were determined to watch him execute Skaric. He couldn't do it. "Very well." Nidan forced the words out of his mouth. He had to come up with a new plan. Fast.

Cadman turned to the crowd. "We end this now! The women and children should remain here. Anyone who wants to witness the death of the Wolf should follow the Guardian." He used hand gestures to order the two men who had brought Skaric outside to pick him up once more.

As they did so, Nidan briefly came face to face with Skaric. He kept his expression hard and glared at Skaric angrily. Skaric looked back through his one open eye. It was full of sadness so deep that it swallowed the light of the sun that should have been reflected there. Nidan felt like he had been punched in the gut. He could soften his expression or give Skaric some sort of sign that he'd find a way to save him. Nidan stopped himself. He couldn't; it was too risky. Skaric *had* to believe that he was going to die and that Nidan was the one who was going to kill him.

*

Cocooned within the walls of the temple, Kiana could hear the villagers baying for blood. She covered her ears, squeezed her eyes shut and whispered Miale's name over and over to block out the cheering, fighting the urge to run out of the temple and scream at the villagers.

Kiana forced her eyes open. Skaric's life was out of her hands. She had to concentrate on restoring the trinity. She hesitantly removed her hands from her ears. She could still hear cheering from outside but was able to think past it.

Taking a deep breath, she looked at the worn red shades of the fresco again. She traced her fingertips over the wolf-headed man. Was that all the villagers saw when they looked at Skaric? Had they even bothered to look at the earnest passion in his blue eyes or stopped to think that he had tried to save Innogen's life? Kiana snatched her fingers back. Red powder had flaked off onto her skin. She shuddered. It reminded her of blood.

Clenching her fists to steel herself, she saw a crudely depicted battle. A dozen men represented each side with banners flying over their heads. The banners of the right hand army bore the heads of wolves, teeth barred. Worse, the faces of the warriors had been replaced by vicious, snarling wolf heads. Kiana ground her teeth together. An entire group of people had been vilified because of the actions of one man.

In the sky above the battle, Pios held Miale in his hands. The goddess looked like a broken doll, tiny in comparison to Pios. Tears welled in Kiana's eyes. She brushed them away fiercely with the heels of her hands. She'd cried enough. It was ridiculous that she still had tears left. Kiana gripped her dress in her fists; it had been a gift from the villagers. She wished she didn't have to wear it, but her clothes—Erynn's clothes—had been taken away. She forced herself to look at the fresco again. There had to be answers or a clue that would tell her where to go next.

She saw the castle. It had been hollowed out to reveal a scene completely out of scale. A child had been born and in her hands, she held the cup of knowledge. Miale's first mortal incarnation. For a moment Kiana couldn't breathe. She couldn't move. She couldn't even look away.

She had to stop being silly. It was just a picture, a representation of history. She had to keep searching and finish what they had come to Norlea to do. For Skaric. For those who had died at Blackoak Tower. For Nidan and his sister.

Over the next few scenes the incarnation of Miale grew: first she was a child, next a young woman, then bent with age, until finally she was on her deathbed. Kiana's heartbeat quickened painfully. Her mouth felt unbearably dry and her tongue felt like lead as she turned to face the final image.

The incarnation of Miale was dead.

She stared at the depiction of the first age of Thanatos. The fighting had changed: allies had turned on each other; men leapt to their deaths and women wept, their minds unbalanced, gripped by madness.

Kiana turned away decisively. She didn't need to see any more. She had to go to Orholt.

Everything had gone quiet outside. Why hadn't Nidan come back to her?

She ran out of the temple and into fierce sunlight. Women and children were milling around, talking. When they saw Kiana, they nodded to her. Why weren't they working? Why weren't the children playing? She looked around but couldn't see Nidan anywhere.

Alish broke away from the group she had been talking to and hurried over. "Are you all right, Brid?"

Kiana nodded. "Where's…" She had almost forgotten the false name he had given himself. "…Nye?"

"He'll be back soon, dear."

Kiana stared at Alish. "But where is he?"

"Gone with the men to execute the Wolf."

Air fled Kiana's lungs, robbing her of breath. It couldn't be true. She stepped backwards. It couldn't be true, it just couldn't. Nidan didn't hate Skaric that much, did he?

Alish's brow became puckered. "What's the matter?"

Kiana shook her head, cupped her hands over her mouth and then forced them back down to her sides. "I've seen too much… it's too much…" Tears choked her throat and blinded her eyes. She turned and ran back into the temple, slamming the door of Miale's chamber as she went. The sound echoed around the room and her mind as she crumpled to the floor. Kiana curled into a ball and hugged her knees to her chest. It couldn't be true. Nidan wouldn't. He *wouldn't*. Miale. Pios. He wouldn't.

*

Nidan walked alongside Cadman as the procession of villagers dragged their prisoner through the forest. He didn't speak to any of them or really pay attention; it was the forest and the path they were taking that he needed to commit to memory. A crazy, risky plan had formed in Nidan's mind as they had walked across the fields. It only had a chance *if* he could get back to Skaric quickly. Nidan noticed a bush dotted with strange orange flowers and a tree that had obviously been struck by lightning several years before. A short while later, they crossed a brook that was narrow and shallow enough to splash across.

Finally, they entered a clearing that was littered with the tracks and droppings of animals. Two men dragged Skaric into the centre of the clearing, looping Skaric's arms around their necks to hold him upright.

Cadman moved to stand in front of the Wolf. "Open your eyes."

Slowly, Skaric partially opened his right eye. Nidan could tell from the flex of Skaric's muscles that his companion had tried to open the other eye, but it was gummed shut with blood and puss. Nidan gritted his teeth and focused on keeping a blank, relaxed expression.

"Open your eyes." Cadman signalled to another man who stepped forward to punch Skaric in the gut.

It was interesting that the village elder didn't seem to want to get his own hands dirty. When Skaric still failed to open both eyes, he was gut punched again.

Nidan stepped forward. "I don't think he can." He hoped there was no trace of compassion in his voice, only the cold amusement he had tried to speak with.

Cadman's lips drew taut and his eye muscles twitched. He didn't repeat his order or gesture for another assault. "Wolf, you have been sentenced to death for committing a crime of violence against a member of my village. Do you have anything to say in your defence."

Nidan pressed his lips together, fighting the urge to roll his eyes. It was far too late to offer Skaric a chance to defend himself.

A faint smile touched Skaric's lips. "No." His swollen lips barely moved as he spoke through gritted teeth. "But if this is how you treat someone trying to help, I wonder what you'd do to someone who was *really* your enemy."

Cadman's brow shadowed his eyes as he glowered at Skaric. "You're a Wolf." He spoke slowly as though he was speaking to a naughty child. "You *are* our enemy. You don't deserve to breathe our air." And there it was: an admittance that they didn't need a good reason to kill Skaric.

"And you call *me* a monster." Skaric's voice was reduced to a whisper as he suffered a barrage of kicks and punches: punishment for his glib words.

Cadman accepted a short sword from the man next to him and pressed it into Nidan's hands. "His life is yours to take, Guardian." He stepped away.

The hilt was cold in Nidan's hand. The blade felt far heavier than it really was. It was badly weighted. Nidan tested it by cutting through the air. He had to calm his thoughts. What he was about to attempt was sheer madness, not least because he was trying to save the life of a *Wolf*; his *enemy*. At least he didn't have to use his own sword.

Nidan stepped directly in front of Skaric. There was barely the width of a man between them. He was aware that everyone was watching him, and though his back was turned to almost everyone, the men holding Skaric were able to stare at his face. Nidan forced himself to stare Skaric in the eye. "Are you ready to die?"

A slight smile, full of bitterness, twitched at Skaric's swollen lips. "A Wolf is *always* ready to die."

Maybe. But I know you're not. Nidan drew in a deep breath. In his mind, he offered Pios a quick prayer. Would his god even listen? Pios had allowed Ysia to die despite saving Miale. Were gods just as petty as the humans they watched over? Nidan hoped not. He placed his hand on Skaric's shoulder. His right hand tightened on the hilt of the short sword. Then he looked away from Skaric's face, concentrating on aiming his blow.

Nidan drove the sword point into Skaric's gut. The Wolf didn't make a sound. Nidan felt the resistance of flesh and sinew as he pushed the blade forward until the hilt rested against flesh. Crimson blood oozed over the hilt, making his hand slick and his grip weaker. He looked up and saw pure unbridled pain in Skaric's eye. He gritted his teeth and pulled the blade clear before driving it in again, creating a mirror wound on Skaric's left hand side. His hand was drenched in blood. He watched his companion closely. Skaric was staring forward, his open eye blazing fiercely. Fighting.

Give up!

Nidan pulled the blade free again, slowly; it would cause more pain. Skaric *had* to succumb to the pain. For a moment, the fierce expression remained on Skaric's face, but then the muscles in his face relaxed and the light in his eye was slowly extinguished. Skaric stared at Nidan. Nidan felt his own gut twist and ache as surely as if someone had stabbed *him*. He felt like a traitor.

The drawn out moment passed as Skaric's right eye closed. His entire body slumped in the arms of his captors. Nidan stepped back and drove the sword into the ground. He wanted rid of the vile thing. The men holding Skaric let go, allowing his body to fall unceremoniously to the floor. His blood flowed freely from his wounds, quickly soaking into the moss covered ground.

Cadman peered down at the body. "Is he dead?"

Nidan knelt down beside Skaric's crumpled body. *Don't be dead.* He placed his hand over Skaric's mouth and waited. He could feel his heart thundering in his chest as he waited.

"Is he dead?" Cadman said again.

"How long does it take to check?" another man asked.

"I want to be sure." Nidan felt the slightest feeble breath. He pushed his mouth into a snarl to subdue the tiny smile that crept across his lips. "He's dead."

"Peg out the body," Cadman said. "Make it inviting for the beasts of the forest."

Nidan shivered at the glee in Cadman's voice. He forced himself to stand by passively as Skaric's wrists and ankles were bound to four stakes, which were then hammered into the ground. He watched Skaric closely. *Pios, don't let anyone see that he's breathing. Please.* No one would see: Skaric's breaths were so weak that Nidan could barely be sure that his companion was alive.

As the procession began to move away, Nidan took one last look at Skaric. *Don't die. Pios, don't let him die.*

Chapter Nine

Kiana launched herself at Nidan as soon as he entered Miale's chamber. "How could you do it?" It was difficult to keep quiet as she struck her fists hard against his chest, briefly feeling the tension that had tightened his muscles. "How could you?"

Nidan's teeth were clenched. "I did what had to be done." He spoke quietly and didn't look her in the eyes. "Let's get out of here."

"Why?" Kiana snarled. "You seem to get on so well with these… these monsters!" She slammed her fists into Nidan again and again. Why wasn't he defending his actions? "I knew you didn't trust Skaric. I knew you didn't like him. But did you really hate him so much that you took the first opportunity you had to justify killing him?" She glared at him. *Say something! Defend yourself!*

Nidan stayed silent.

"We wanted to restore the trinity. To bring peace. I thought you did too." She hit him even harder, putting all the weight of her shaking body and anger behind each blow.

Nidan grabbed her wrists. Kiana tried to pull away but her Guardian was too strong.

"Once we're away from here, you can hate me. You can shout, scream, curse or cry. But right now we *have* to go." Nidan released her and stalked past her, grabbing their near empty saddlebags and his cloak.

Kiana watched him, breathing hard. Why was he so desperate to leave? Not that she wanted to stay a moment longer. "I don't want to go anywhere with you."

Nidan paused behind her on his way to the door. "Your behaviour is going to betray us both. Alish stopped me on my way in here. She couldn't understand why you were so upset. You need to bite down your grief. Understood?"

Her bottom lip trembled. Nidan was right; she was acting like a spoiled child and she had to stop.

"Can we go now?" Nidan said, his tone impatient.

Kiana glanced back into the room. "You've forgotten your uniform."

Nidan followed her gaze. His black uniform, cleaned and repaired, sat neatly folded on one of the wooden chairs. Kiana watched as he strode over to it and reached to pick it up. He hesitated for several moments, his fingers falling short of touching it. *Why?* Kiana felt some of her anger ebb away, releasing some of the knotted tension that was making her shoulders ache. He regretted his actions… didn't he?

Nidan sighed, grabbed the black uniform in his fist and stuffed it into a saddlebag. He shouldered both packs. "Let's go."

Kiana followed him silently. She didn't want to go with him but had no choice. For all the knowledge she had been taught, Kiana had no practical skills. Nidan did. *But can I trust him anymore?*

They walked down the road to the gate watched by all of the villagers. The open gate was in sight when Cadman hurried over to them. Kiana held her breath as Nidan offered the village Elder a smile.

Cadman peered at them. "Leaving so soon?"

"We need to get to Fairlake as soon as possible." There was an unmistakable note of impatience in Nidan's voice. "We had planned to leave at dawn but obviously there were more pressing matters to deal with."

Cadman nodded, seemingly accepting the explanation. "Even so, you won't get far before dark. You might as well stay another night and leave in the morning, refreshed."

He was right. It was past noon.

Nidan shook his head. "My companion is distraught that there was a Wolf so near us. I don't think she'll be able to relax until we are several leagues from here."

Kiana didn't think she would be able to relax again, not now that she knew how hideous the world really was. She had lived her life blind; she longed for that blissful ignorance again.

Cadman's eyebrows shot up. "You don't think there are more Wolves close by, do you?"

Nidan shrugged.

Cadman scratched his chin. "I'll send men to the city to warn the Guardians there. Just in case."

Kiana clamped her lips together. They desperately had to get away. She had been able to convince Nidan to go with her, but the rest of the Guardians would take her to 'safety', even if that meant they took her against her will.

"Where are our horses?" she asked.

Cadman frowned. "We were planning a feast for you, Guardian, to thank you for executing the Wolf. Can't we convince you to stay?"

Kiana coughed in an exaggerated manner. "Dust." She feigned more coughing as Nidan turned round and glared at her.

He rolled his eyes and then turned back to face Cadman. "That's very kind but completely unnecessary. Besides, we *must* press on."

Cadman stared at them both in silence for a few moments, the muscles around his mouth twitching in thought. He must have noticed the impatience in Nidan's voice as well. Cadman stroked his chin again. "I'll have your horses made ready and brought over. You must say goodbye to Alish as well. I'm sure you can take the time to say a proper farewell."

Did they have a choice? They wouldn't get far without the horses.

Nidan nodded. "Of course." His voice sounded slightly brighter, but Kiana could see his shoulder muscles twitching beneath the plain brown shirt he was wearing.

Kiana watched the landowner as he walked away. It disgusted her that Nidan was being treated like a hero, but it was odd that he seemed so anxious to leave rather than stay and bask in his glory. Maybe he really did regret what he had done. Regrets wouldn't bring Skaric back. Kiana watched as Nidan glanced towards the gate, up at the sun and then back again. Then he began to pace across the width of the road.

"We need to at least say goodbye." Who was he trying to convince, her or himself? "They can't know that…" he shook his head, pacing even faster.

It was making Kiana dizzy to watch Nidan walk back and forth, back and forth. Suddenly he stopped, placed his hands on her shoulders and drew her into an embrace. His entire body was tense like he was ready to run or fight. Kiana didn't fight against him but didn't return his embrace either. At best, his actions were confusing; at worst, they were insulting.

"Be nice," he said.

Kiana didn't want to be nice. As Cadman and Alish approached, she turned to them and forced a smile to her lips.

"My husband tells me that you're leaving." Alish embraced Kiana warmly.

Kiana shuddered as soon as Alish released her.

"Are you sure you won't reconsider staying another night?" Alish looked at Kiana and then Nidan.

Nidan shook his head. "I think we'll both feel better once we've put some leagues between us and that Wolf."

"But he's dead." Alish frowned. "He can't hurt anyone anymore." Her eyes and face lit up. "Perhaps your Guardian could take you to see the body, dear?"

Kiana clamped her teeth together so that she didn't grimace.

"Then maybe you could see that he's no longer a threat."

From the moment Kiana had made Nidan heal Skaric, he hadn't been a threat to anyone. "I've seen enough death to last me a lifetime. Seeing the Wolf dead won't change that."

Alish cupped Kiana's cheek in her hand. "Of course not, Brid. But sometimes you do have to face the substance of your nightmares."

"I faced him last night. It made my nightmares worse." *Because of what your people had done to him.* "I don't want to see him again, even dead." *Especially not dead.* Kiana stepped back from Alish's touch and turned away from them all.

"Poor thing," she heard Alish say. "She's so damaged because of those bastard Wolves, isn't she?"

No. She was damaged because both sides clung to hatred like a child clings to its mother. What comfort could be found in hatred?

She turned round as she heard the sharp clip clip of shod hooves on the hard earth.

Cadman was grinning. "We took the liberty of giving you some provisions for your journey. They won't last long but hopefully they'll get you part way to Fairlake."

Kiana watched as Nidan reached out and took a firm grip of Cadman's hand. She wanted to scream.

"You and your wife have been very kind to us, but we must go now. We can still make good distance before the sun sets," Nidan said.

"Of course," Cadman's voice was reluctant. "If you really won't reconsider...?"

Nidan shook his head sharply. "We won't. I'm hoping that Brid's nightmares will fade once we reach Fairlake."

Alish nodded and smiled. "She's very lucky to have you."

Nidan was the reason Kiana was still alive, but he wasn't the only one who had saved her life; Skaric had too and now he was dead because of Nidan.

Nidan turned to the larger of the two horses and began to hastily fasten the packs he was carrying to its saddle, alongside another set of bulging saddlebags. The supplies felt like blood money to Kiana.

When he had finished, Nidan turned to their hosts. "Thank you. You've made our journey a little easier." He struck both of their fists with his own.

"And you have shown us the might of the Guardians!" Cadman said.

Nidan smiled but quickly turned away to mount his horse. He looked down at Kiana. "Let's go."

She gave him a cold look and then mounted the second horse.

"May Pios and Miale bless your journey!" Alish called as Kiana and Nidan urged their horses forward.

Nidan glanced over his shoulder. "Thank you!"

Kiana didn't want to hear another word from anyone. She kicked her horse and left the village at a canter—it was as fast as she dared to go, given that she had only sat on a horse for the first time six days ago.

*

Nidan's pulse was racing as they rode down the road that led east from Norlea. He had to pretend they were heading to Fairlake. The land was flat and there was every possibility that the guards were watching. It was a necessary waste of time, but that didn't mean he had to like it. Behind him, Kiana was silent and brooding, which didn't help. He almost told her but bit his tongue and waited.

Finally, Nidan applied slight pressure on the reins. As his horse came to a halt, he glanced back; the village was no more than a blur on the horizon. He breathed out slowly; if he could barely see the village, the guards wouldn't be able to see him. Nidan kicked the horse on once more but turned it sharply towards the forest.

Kiana drew up alongside him. "What are you doing?"

"Going back for Skaric." Now that they were away from the village there was less need for secrecy. The forest was looming ahead of them; as dark and silent as a tomb.

"What's the point? He's dead." Kiana gasped. "You don't agree with Alish do you?" Her voice was shaking. "You don't think I should look... *do you?*"

Does she really think so little of me? "We have to go back." *Why should she think any better of me? She thinks I murdered Skaric in cold blood.* He glanced up at the sky. The afternoon was wearing on; time was running out.

"Why?"

"There's no time to explain." Nidan kicked his horse into a gallop. Too much time had been wasted already.

He was forced to slow down when they entered the forest but quickly managed to locate a path to follow. It had to lead to the landmarks he'd noted that morning. It *had* to.

"Nidan... what's going on?"

The close packed trees made them ride slowly enough to talk.

Nidan glanced at her. "Skaric isn't dead... I hope." He held his breath as he waited for Kiana to barrage him with questions.

She said nothing.

Nidan couldn't even tell if she believed him or not. There was no point in lying, she had to realise that. But what if they were too late? Then she would think it was a ruse. *Pios, don't let him be dead.*

It seemed to take an eternity for him to spot the bush with the odd orange-coloured flowers on. Nidan directed the horses off the track, deeper into the forest. Before long, they passed the tree that had been severed in two by lightning. The two horses splashed through the shallow stream, spraying his legs with water that soaked through his wool breeches. Nidan didn't care.

He pulled his horse to a halt, jumped down and looked up at Kiana. His mouth felt dry. "Wait here… just in case."

Kiana shook her head and dismounted. "I need to go with you. If what you said is true…"

If Nidan ever wanted her to trust him again, he couldn't stop her. Without waiting for Kiana to follow him, Nidan ran into the glade.

Skaric lay as the villagers had left him, staked out on the ground, lifeless. The only difference was that his already filthy shirt was completely soaked in blood. Nidan's pulse raced even faster; his head swam, making his legs feel weak. *Don't let him be dead. Please.*

Nidan stumbled forward, searching for the subtle rise and fall of Skaric's chest. He saw nothing. He swallowed over and over but still felt sick. It couldn't be too late; it just couldn't.

"What did you do?" Kiana's voice was a whisper right behind him.

Nidan twitched; he hadn't realised she had stayed so close. "I stabbed him. Twice." He dropped to his knees and placed a hand on Skaric's chest. *Breathe. Please be breathing.* Nothing. "Use my dagger to cut him loose."

"Is he dead?"

Nidan pressed harder against Skaric's chest and placed his other hand just above Skaric's nose and mouth. *Don't be dead.* His skin felt cold and clammy; his heart pounded.

"Nidan! Is he dead?"

Nidan couldn't feel the warmth of breath on his hand. "Cut him loose." He pressed his fingertips against Skaric's neck, which was as cold as ice. *Don't be dead!* "Cut him loose!"

Nidan watched as Kiana used the dagger to saw through the ropes. As she pulled them away from Skaric's wrist, they saw that his skin was freshly bruised. Nidan felt a surge of energy work up from his stomach into his throat. He tried to feel for a pulse again. Skaric couldn't be dead. Nidan raised his eyes to the sky. Why would Pios listen? Why was he so desperate for Skaric to live? For Kiana? So he wasn't a murderer? It was none of those things. *Pios, let him live.*

There was so much blood. No pulse. No breath. Just blood. Nidan rocked back onto his heels and hung his head. It was too late.

Kiana cut through the second rope, allowing Skaric's body to relax to the ground. "He's dead, isn't he?"

Nidan opened his eyes. He was shaking as he stared down at Skaric. "I tried."

"You stabbed him!"

He glared at her through damp eyes. "To save him! They weren't going to let him live! What choice did I have?"

Nidan hadn't wanted Kiana to see Skaric this way. The sight was terrible. The extra beating the Wolf had received had left its mark, turning his face into a hideous swollen mess. The wounds in his gut were open and ugly.

"I tried."

Kiana moved round to cut through the ropes that tied Skaric's ankles. What was the point? Nidan narrowed his eyes and stared at Skaric's chest. He must have imagined the slight flutter of movement. He held his breath and closed his eyes, concentrating. Pios. Miale. *Ysia.*

Nidan laid his hands over the sword wounds, ignoring the blood that quickly drenched them. He was aware of Kiana coming to kneel beside him; she squeezed his shoulder. The action lent Nidan strength and the moment of calmness that he needed. He felt a great warmth flow through him: the might of Pios' power.

He channelled it into Skaric, targeting the sword wounds.

"He's alive!" Kiana said, her voice much higher in pitch than normal. "Nidan! He's breathing!"

Tension exploded out of Nidan in a sob. He fought to regain

his concentration and continue the healing. If he didn't, Skaric wouldn't survive.

As Nidan had hoped, he had avoided harming any of the Wolf's internal workings. Though the wounds looked ugly, they had only caused pain and blood loss. Nidan grimaced. *Only.* The word made what he had done sound so trivial. Skaric could have died. Should have died. He had already been weak from the beating; he hadn't known Nidan's plan to save his life. He should have given up.

Slowly, the wounds began to close. Skin and sinew began to reform and knit together so that not even a scar would be left at the entry or exit wounds. It would be as though it had never even happened, physically.

Nidan allowed his hands to drop from Skaric's body so that they hung loosely at his sides, then bowed his head and breathed out deeply. There was no energy left in Nidan's body, and his mind felt dull and fuzzy. Sleep. That's what he needed and what he couldn't have. Slowly, he opened his eyes. Skaric was breathing deeply and easily. It was a good sign, but not a guarantee of survival.

Nidan got up wearily. "We need to go."

Kiana stared at Skaric and then at him. "But…"

"Skaric won't die." *I hope.* "But we can't stay here. What if the villagers come back?"

Kiana stood. "Are you *sure* he won't die?"

Nidan nodded, even though he wasn't at all sure.

Kiana pursed her lips as she stared down at Skaric. "Why isn't he awake?"

Nidan sighed; her questions were slowing them down. "He's weak. From the beating… from the blood loss… not even the magic of Pios can restore blood to a body. Only time can do that. Help me?"

Between them they lifted their battered companion and carried him to the horses. With a little effort, they managed to sit Skaric up on the smaller of the two animals. Whilst Nidan held Skaric upright, Kiana used the remnants of the villagers' rope to tie him to the saddle. When Nidan let go, Skaric slumped forward against the horse's neck. The ride wouldn't be comfortable but at least he wouldn't fall off.

"You'll need to double up with me," Nidan said.

The third horse was still in the village. Had Cadman claimed it as a prize? Or would he sell it at the first opportunity? Nidan mounted his horse and leant down to pick up the reins of the other animal. He took his foot out of the stirrup and held it out to Kiana.

She swung up behind him. "Nidan… I'm so sorry."

He didn't need her to apologise.

"I'm sorry I didn't believe in you. I just thought…"

Nidan did his best to look round at her. "Don't apologise. It's what I *wanted* you to believe. I couldn't risk anyone in the village finding out what I'd done."

She rested her cheek against his back. "Even so, I should have had more faith in you."

"It doesn't matter." He meant it. All that mattered was that she was able to believe in him again and that his crazy plan had worked. Nidan kicked his horse forward into a brisk walk, feeling an odd sense of satisfaction as Kiana's arms wrapped around his chest. He had done the right thing. Ten days earlier, if anyone had told him he would save the life of a Wolf—not once, but twice—Nidan would have laughed at them. He was a Guardian; he had sworn to protect the people of Gettryne from the Wolves. He glanced across at Skaric: pale, battered and lifeless. He had done the right thing.

Chapter Ten

Frustrated, Kiana dropped the crude bow and round piece of wood on the ground; Nidan had called it a socket. The spindle, which had been held in place by the socket, also fell to the ground, scattering the tinder beneath it.

"I'm never going to be able to do this!"

Nidan picked up the spindle and socket. "Do you want me to help?"

Kiana looked up at him, scowling. "You shouldn't have to. I should be able to do something to help. How hard can lighting a fire be?"

Apparently much harder without Skaric's flint and steel, just one of the things they had lost along with his horse.

Nidan smiled. "Very, if you haven't done it before."

Kiana sighed and glanced across at Skaric. "When will he wake up?" She didn't really expect an answer. They had put two days distance between them and Norlea, but that made no difference.

Physically, Skaric looked fine. Nidan had healed all of his wounds; the bruises that had marred his face were gone; even the old marks around his neck were now nothing more than a memory. They'd done their best to clean the dried blood from his skin and had changed his shirt. The fresh garment had quickly become dirty from travelling and camping, but at least it wasn't stiff with blood. Despite the improvements, Skaric's skin was deathly pale and he had shown no signs of waking.

Nidan handed her the spindle and socket. "Start again." He smiled at her, encouraging her.

Kiana rolled her eyes, but nonetheless she regrouped the tinder into a neat pile, stood the spindle in the centre and placed the socket firmly on top of it. Nidan had cut a hole into the socket so that the spindle wouldn't slide around. He then helped her to wind the bowstring round the spindle. Next, he held her left hand so that she could apply greater pressure onto the socket and gently took her right hand, helping her to achieve the fast sawing motion required for starting the fire. It was tiring work, even with Nidan's help, but before long, Kiana saw a spark and grinned as the tinder caught light. Nidan quickly placed a pyramid of twigs and logs around the tinder.

"Well done."

"Now I just have to be able to do it myself!" Kiana watched as the dry wood took light quickly. The warmth of the fire danced on her skin, adding to the stifling heat of the evening. She and Nidan didn't need the fire, but Skaric did.

"We should talk about where we're going," Nidan said.

Kiana shook her head. "When Skaric wakes up, we'll all talk about it."

"Kiana…"

She glared at him. "We're still going east, right?"

Nidan sighed and nodded.

"Then we're still travelling towards Orholt. That's where we're going."

Nidan tried to touch her hand but Kiana pulled away. "You haven't explained why."

"I told you…"

"When Skaric wakes up." Nidan stared at the fire, glowering.

Kiana tucked a strand of hair behind her ears. "I'm sorry." She'd done a lot of apologising since Norlea.

"I know."

"I just don't want to explain myself twice."

"I know."

She drew her arms around herself. She wasn't cold; how could she be? The summer heat had grown stronger and stronger and the rain had refused to fall. It felt like Gettryne was gripped by a fever that it couldn't recover from.

A groan behind Kiana made her skin prickle and her heart momentarily stop beating. She exchanged a glance with Nidan before turning to look at Skaric. His eyes were open and he was slowly propping himself up on his elbow.

Kiana grinned. "You're awake! How are you feeling? You must be famished!"

Skaric wasn't looking at her. He was staring at Nidan, his expression dark and his breathing ragged.

"Nidan saved you." Kiana's words seemed to hang on the sudden stillness that pervaded the air.

"I'm sorry…" Nidan began.

"*Sorry?*" Skaric's face was pale, sweat beaded his forehead and his eyelids kept opening and closing.

"They would have killed you…" Nidan said.

"So… what? You thought you'd get in first?"

Nidan stood and took two steps towards Skaric. "I did what I had to… to save you…"

"Stay back." Skaric gritted his teeth. His chest was heaving and the arm that was propping him up was shaking violently.

"They had to believe you were dead." Nidan took another step forward.

"Stay back." Skaric raised his right hand, holding it so the fingers were outstretched towards Nidan.

Heart racing, Kiana hurried to her feet and ran to stand in between them. "Think, Skaric! If Nidan had wanted you dead, you would be!"

Deep lines formed at Skaric's brow as he continued to glare at Nidan.

"I'm sorry," Nidan said.

He tried to move Kiana out of the way, but she resisted by planting her feet firmly on the ground. *Skaric won't hurt me; he won't use his magic against me.* Kiana found herself staring at Skaric's violently shaking hand rather than his face.

"I know how scared you must have been." Nidan raised his hands placatingly. "But I had no way to tell you my plan." He breathed in deeply. "For them to believe… *you* had to believe."

"Listen to him, please!" Kiana could feel the fear strangling her voice. What would have been the point if her companions turned on each other now?

Nidan put a hand on her shoulder. Was he offering her support or trying to gain some himself?

"At the village, your actions made me question everything." Nidan sidestepped Kiana as he spoke.

"Stay back!"

"You could have let the girl die, but you didn't. You could have used your magic against the villagers, but you didn't. Pios help me!" Nidan took two steps closer so that he was staring down at Skaric. "I thought I'd die before I ever wanted to help a Wolf."

Kiana put her hands over her mouth, waiting and watching as Nidan crouched down. *Please, Miale, don't let them hurt each other. Please!*

"I could have killed you. But I chose to save you," Nidan said.

"And now you want me to be grateful?"

Nidan shook his head. "After the pain I caused you? No. I made you face death and I'm so sorry. But I couldn't think of another way. Facing the Darkness must have been horrible."

Skaric dropped his hand to rest on the ground. "You have no idea."

"You're right. I don't." Nidan shifted so that he was sitting down.

Skaric ran his hand over his face. "If you'd really wanted me dead… I would be." He stared at Nidan. "Thank you."

Kiana breathed out slowly. Her chest ached from the effort of holding her breath and her legs were shaking. She allowed herself to sink to the ground. For several moments, she could do nothing except breathe in and out slowly and watch her two companions.

When she felt calm, Kiana looked Skaric in the eyes. "It will be dark soon. You should eat something and then sleep."

Skaric grimaced. "I couldn't eat. Water would be good." He tried to sit up fully, but his arm gave way and he collapsed to the ground, wincing.

Nidan helped him move, propping him up against one of the broad trees.

Kiana fetched one of the water flasks and handed it to Skaric.

"Nidan has been letting me take watches. Short watches." A smile spread across her lips. It felt good to be able to smile.

Skaric glanced at Nidan and then took a sip of water.

"It's given me a chance to rest," Nidan said.

Skaric stared at Nidan. "How long have I…?"

"Two full days."

Skaric nodded and took another longer drink.

Kiana fidgeted with the sleeves of her dress. "Skaric… we need to do something about your appearance…"

He looked away from her.

"You looking so obviously like a Wolf… it's dangerous. Not just for you, but for us as well."

Skaric didn't answer her. Kiana could hear the movement of the water in the flask he was holding as it began to slosh against the hide.

"You could have died!"

"I know." Skaric took a deep breath. "I know that. But it isn't that simple."

Kiana pursed her lips. "I don't see why not. Carrying on looking like that is going to get you killed and possibly us with you. We're not talking much, Skaric. A haircut and a shave…" She paused as Nidan shook his head. It almost stopped her from carrying on but her words had to be said and heard. "Can you go back?"

Skaric stared at her.

"Home… can you ever go back home?"

"After everything I've done?" Skaric shook his head. A sad expression flitted into his eyes. "No. I can't ever go back."

"Then really, what does it matter?" Kiana tried to make her voice sound sympathetic. "Isn't it more important to be safe than to cling onto a past you can never reclaim?"

Skaric continued to stare at her.

At least he had a past to remember. She had been taken from hers as a baby. She'd never known her family; she didn't even know where home was. It would have been easier to shave him and cut his hair while he was sleeping, but that had seemed cruel. "Why is it so important? To your kin, I mean."

Skaric drew his knees up to his chest and stared absently at the campfire. "It's a sign of adulthood." His voice was as distant as his gaze. "When you're old enough to grow a beard, you're old enough to stand in battle and fight or learn the ways of the nyxii."

"Nyxii?"

He briefly glanced at her. "You call us mages."

Kiana shuddered. The memory of seeing her Guardians burn plagued her.

Skaric sighed. "The quicker you're able to grow a beard, the faster you gain recognition amongst the elders. If you're slow to do so, you're more likely to face ridicule." He rested his chin on the tops of his knees. The reflected firelight danced in his eyes. "Some of the older men continue to grow their beards and weave a bead or stone into it for…" He stopped abruptly.

"For what?"

Skaric breathed in deeply before replying. "For every life they take in battle."

Kiana's mouth dropped open. She shut it again firmly. "It's obviously important to the Wolves." It seemed pointless and barbaric to judge a man's worth on something so trivial. Not that she knew how manhood was judged by her people. Perhaps it was something equally silly.

"Yes… for the Wolves." Skaric looked at them both. "But I gave up the right to be a Wolf as soon as I helped you two."

Kiana pressed her lips together, forcing a threatened smile away. "I'd best get to work then before the light fails."

"And while you're at it, we can talk," Nidan said.

Skaric looked at them both blankly.

"About what I saw in Norlea, in the temple," Kiana said.

They didn't speak at first. Kiana used the dagger to cut Skaric's midnight dark hair shorter into a ragged but far more acceptable style. As each clump of hair fell to the ground, Skaric's scowl became deeper and deeper. He didn't look at her once; he just kept his gaze fixed on the fire.

They had been given a shaving knife and a bar of soap by Alish. Kiana hesitated; it seemed wrong. Skaric sat absolutely still, his expression completely blank and his stare almost vacant as she lathered the soap and rubbed it into his beard. She raised the blade to start work.

He flinched away from her. "No offence, but have you ever done this before?"

Kiana could feel Nidan staring at her. "My Guardians taught me how to play dice. I lost a game and had to shave three of them for a week." She moved the blade so that it was resting against Skaric's cheek. "So yes, I know what I'm doing." Kiana saw his cheek muscles flex, heard his sharp intake of breath as she began to shave the hair from his face.

On the other side of the fire, Nidan settled down with his sword and a cloth, cleaning the already shining steel. "The fresco…" he said.

Kiana wiped the frothy soap and shaved hair from the blade with a cloth and began another stroke. She glanced at Nidan before speaking. "It showed the events before and after Miale's immortal death."

"I know that," Nidan said impatiently.

She glared at him. "But you didn't study it."

Nidan paused and glanced up at her apologetically. "I know that something in that fresco convinced you we have to go to Orholt, even though it's been abandoned for a thousand years." He hunched his shoulders. "I'd hoped that going to Norlea would have had the opposite effect on you."

Kiana paused mid stroke, acknowledging how hard Nidan's confession must have been. She half closed her eyes, remembering the images on the fresco. "The first incarnation was born there." Kiana opened her eyes and went back to concentrating on her task. Slowly, she was unveiling soft, untanned skin.

"So? Wasn't that to be expected?" Nidan asked.

"She was born there. She grew up there. Everyone else moved away and she stayed there. She died there."

"I still don't get what's so important about that."

"Orholt was the centre of the battle," Skaric said. "Hardly a safe place for the mortal incarnation of Miale."

Kiana looked at his eyes. He still wasn't looking at her. There was a hard edge to his gaze, turning the blue intensity of his eyes to blocks of ice. She shivered. There hadn't been so much coldness in his eyes since he had agreed to help her.

Looking away, Kiana carried on. "She stayed even though it wasn't safe, even when everyone abandoned the city. There had to be a reason for that. A link… a connection. Something!"

She glanced at Nidan. His hand was resting on the blade of his sword, and he was staring at the flames as though in a trance. "But that was a thousand years ago, Kiana. There's probably nothing left."

Kiana felt her lip tremble. Gently, she used her fingertips to turn Skaric's face towards her, so that she could shave the other side. He still managed to avoid her gaze.

"It's the only lead we have, Nidan. Orholt is where this mess began. Besides…" she puffed out her cheeks, unsure if she should say any more.

"What?"

"The castle in the fresco: Orholt castle… I've dreamt about that place since I was a little girl." Kiana glanced to the sky and then busied herself with cleaning the blade again. "Look up."

Skaric hesitated.

"I won't cut you, I promise."

Skaric pressed his lips tightly together but complied, allowing Kiana to begin to shave his neck. She felt him tremble as she touched the sharp blade to his skin.

"I can't explain it. But I know, in here…" Kiana used her free hand to gesture to her heart. "I know we'll find what we're looking for in Orholt. It's like I'm being drawn there." Her words had to sound crazy.

Kiana heard the pop and crackle of the fire filling the silence.

Finally, she heard Nidan sigh. "All right. I believe you."

A lump formed in Kiana's throat as she smiled.

"But it's a long way," Nidan said. "We have to assume the Wolves are still hunting you, and even if they're not, the Guardians will be. Besides, no one has entered the Fallen Lands in almost a millennium. You know going there is madness, right?"

Kiana cradled both her hands in her lap. She was still holding the shaving knife even though she had just finished her task. "I know. But so is wanting to restore a broken trinity!"

"Did the fresco show how Ysia died?" Skaric said.

Kiana looked back at him. His face was still obscured by the white soap froth, but at least he was finally looking at her.

She shook her head. "No. There was only one image of Ysia, alongside Pios and Miale. Before Miale's death."

Skaric nodded, his eyes sparkling unmistakably in the gathering darkness.

Kiana used a clean corner of the cloth to wipe his face, almost gasping at the change. She had never realised how much difference a beard would make to a man's face. "How old are you?"

Skaric's brow furrowed. "Eighteen summers. Why?"

Kiana's eyes widened. This man, who had faced the Darkness twice and risked everything to save the life of a girl—a stranger— was barely older than her. Would she ever have that much courage? That much strength of heart? She doubted it.

"I… I thought you were older than that. The beard made you… you look younger now." Kiana looked abruptly away from Skaric, willing the heat in her cheeks to subside quickly.

He was handsome. She'd never realised that before. His face was lean but not harsh. His features were strong without being imposing. Somehow, the loss of the beard made the intensity of his eyes more prominent. Kiana felt them watching her and in response, her heartbeat quickened.

"Much better." She wrapped the knife in the cloth and then unwrapped it again. "Sleep. You need sleep. We have a long journey ahead if we're going to get to Orholt."

Kiana tried to stand but Skaric took hold of her wrist. His touch was gentle but there was surprising force behind it, despite his weakened state.

"If I'm not a Wolf anymore, what am I?"

Kiana stared at him, her eyes wide. She couldn't think of an answer to give him. His stare was wide and earnest. She had to say *something*. She *wanted* to comfort him.

"Our companion." Kiana worked her wrist free and took hold

of his hand. She felt tension flood into it and felt a brief tug as he almost pulled away from her. Ignoring the movement, she looked him in the eyes, smiling. "Our friend."

Chapter Eleven

Skaric stared down at the patchwork valley as Kiana and Nidan dismounted. To spare the horses, they had been taking turns to walk, despite Nidan's protests that Skaric was not well enough to do so. The plateau came to a sudden end as the ground dropped away in a steep, rocky slope that was easily as tall as Blackoak Tower. A path had been carved out of the hillside, cutting back and forth in a series of sharp twists. A few leagues away, Skaric could see the town of Linden: the last major settlement between them and the border to the Fallen Lands.

A grey wall surrounded the town, encasing a sprawl of buildings of all manner of shapes and sizes. Despite the distance, he could see that two large buildings stood out from all the rest: a tall, pale building with a spire that rose up into the blue sky and a large grey, squat building. They sat next to each other in the centre of the town. Skaric shuddered. He didn't need Nidan to tell him that he was staring at the temples of Miale and Pios.

"Do we really have to go down there?" Kiana said as she joined him. "I don't think the horses will like it."

The path, steep and uneven, was only just wide enough for the horses to walk single file. The stones and rocks that lay half buried in the dirt, combined with the sharp corners, made the path treacherous to navigate.

"We could go further south," Nidan said. "But that would bring us very close to Fairlake and Ironhold."

Skaric shook his head decisively. "We can lead the horses." He didn't want to go anywhere near Iornhold, the main stronghold of the Guardians, or Fairlake, home to the high temple of Miale.

"Are you fit enough to walk? It's a long way down," Nidan said.

Skaric's mouth twitched in a failed complaint. Nidan's concern was probably justified. Skaric knew his skin was still on the pale side of normal; he got tired far too easily and had suffered several headaches and visual hallucinations. At that moment, it looked like Kiana was surrounded by a white corona—a trick of his weak mind and the fierce sunlight. It was hard to ignore the side effects of the blood loss.

"I'll be fine," Skaric said. He didn't care how well trained the horses were; if one of them spooked, it would be safer if they were all walking.

Kiana turned back towards the horses grazing a short distance away. Suddenly, her pupils contracted into tiny pricks as her eyes grew wide and her mouth dropped open. Raising her hand, she pointed at the road behind them. Skaric's stomach lurched as he saw seven riders moving at a fast pace towards them.

"Wolves?" Nidan said.

Skaric peered at the riders, which were quickly becoming more than dark shapes. Bile rose into his mouth as he recognised Berend's hulking form. "Yes."

"We can't hope to get down into the valley fast enough," Nidan said. "We stand and fight. Your magic will even things out."

Skaric's hands began to shake. He tried to think of another way, but his mind was barraged with the memory of searing pain and sizzling flesh. Instead, he faced Nidan. "My magic… I can't…" Skaric looked down; he should have told them sooner. Guilt twisted in his gut; he should have been able to break past his fear of casting magic. If he didn't, they would die. Just the thought of flames feasting on his body made Skaric's stomach heave. "I can't!"

Nidan's eyes narrowed. "What do you mean you can't?"

Skaric couldn't bring himself to answer.

"You should have told us," Nidan said through clenched teeth.

"Don't argue." Kiana said in an urgent tone. "Please!"

The Wolves were getting closer by the heartbeat, allowing Skaric to see that one of the riders wasn't wearing armour. "They have a nyxus with them." He curled his hands into fists.

Kiana stared at them both with wide eyes. "What are we going to do?"

Nidan's lips curled downwards into a small, angry crescent. "We head south and hope to outrun them."

Skaric shook his head. "We won't be able to. We have to go down there." He pointed to the path. Nidan opened his mouth to object but Skaric cut him off. "Take Kiana and the horses. I'll follow you soon." He grabbed the dagger from Nidan's belt.

Nidan's eyebrows drew down over his eyes. "What are you going to do?" He deliberately spoke slowly.

Skaric winced at Nidan's reaction. Hadn't he earned the Guardian's trust? He looked Nidan directly in the eyes as he answered. "Make it harder for them to follow. Now go!"

As soon as Nidan and Kiana set off leading the horses, Skaric dropped down onto the path behind them. He thrust the point of the dagger into the hillside, wiggling it up and down to free one of the stones lodged there. A pattering of soil dropped to the ground before the stone finally came away and plopped onto the path.

Skaric repeated the painstaking process over and over, ignoring the dull pain in his hands from clutching the hilt so tightly. At first, he only managed to dislodge pebbles, which wouldn't be enough. Even though his body felt weak, Skaric's actions became more desperate as he heard the sound of approaching horses; he managed to free a glut of larger stones. The combination of pebbles and small rocks quickly made the path treacherous for horses.

Skaric dared to lift his head above the edge of the plateau. He could see the faces of the Wolves. Every man was familiar to him, especially Vali. Skaric's skin became cold. *Not you. I didn't want you to be the one who was sent to kill me.* It had been a foolish wish. Vali was the obvious choice. The only choice.

Skaric ducked down again and scanned the winding path for his companions. Nidan and Kiana had travelled at a reckless pace and were several twists below him; better to take risks than die at the hands of the Wolves. Unwilling to waste any more time, Skaric quickly began to lower himself down the steep hillside, using hand and footholds to lower himself down at first, before dropping the rest of the way to the path below.

He had almost reached Kiana and Nidan when a shout caught his attention.

"Skaric?" Berend was standing at the top of the plateau with his men; they had all dismounted. "It is you, isn't it? I almost didn't recognise you without your beard. I knew you were a coward and a traitor, but a woman?" The war leader began to howl with laughter. The other Wolves joined in. Except for Vali.

Skaric knew he was within striking distance of Vali's magic. He glanced over his shoulder at Nidan and Kiana; thankfully, they were just out of range and still moving further away. Skaric expected to see Vali raise his hand and begin to cast, but he didn't. Without taking the time to wonder why, Skaric lowered himself down the slope and ran after his companions.

"Nice work with the rocks," Nidan said as Skaric joined them. "I hope it slows them down enough."

So do I. Skaric looked up again. The Wolves, still on foot, were investigating the path. Skaric paused long enough to peer over the edge. They had to reach level ground so they could mount the horses and gain valuable distance on the Wolves. They had to escape.

Skaric fixed his gaze on the path ahead as they navigated a bend that was so tight they almost doubled back on themselves. Four more bends, almost there. It was a lie Skaric had to believe.

Pebbles began raining from above. The horses reared up and whinnied in protest, their ears twitching and their eyes so wide the whites were clearly visible. Nidan and Kiana fought to hold the horses steady. Skaric peered up. Two of the Wolves were at the top of the path, grinning down at him as they kicked more stones over the edge; the stones *he* had dislodged. He bit his lower lip as guilt made his head spin. Skaric pressed his back against the cliff face and edged past the second horse. He caught hold of the animal's reins, taking the burden away from Kiana. She smiled at him in relief.

Another barrage of gravel fell down. Instinctively, Skaric raised his arm. From the corner of his eyes, he saw Kiana drop to her knees, wrapping her arms over her head.

Nidan glanced back, hunching his shoulders against the attack. "We have to keep moving!"

Skaric helped Kiana to stand and then used all his strength to pull the frightened horse further down the path.

No longer directly beneath the Wolves, they paused at a turn.

"They'll probably do the same again when we pass beneath them," Nidan said. "Damn them. Do Wolves always play with their prey? Why don't they just use magic?"

"We're too far away." Skaric still couldn't work out why Vali hadn't attacked when he'd had the chance.

"Keep moving," Nidan said. "It's just small stones. We'll lead the horses through it."

"There are larger stones too." Why hadn't the Wolves used those first? Skaric knew Nidan was right: Wolves often played with their victims before killing them—often making hapless prey believe they had a chance of escape—especially when packs were confident they couldn't lose.

Nidan led the first horse and Kiana jogged alongside him, hugging the cliff face. The Wolves attacked them again. Skaric bit down a cry as a fist-sized lump of stone struck his shoulder. His horse skittered to the side, its hoof almost slipping from the path. Skaric dragged it forward and looked up in time to see a large rock hurtling towards Nidan. He cried out but it was too late.

The stone struck Nidan's head. The Guardian came to a sudden halt. His grip on the horse's reins relaxed. Nidan swayed and didn't right himself. The weight of his body carried him over the edge of the path.

Kiana screamed. Skaric could do nothing but stare as his companion fell, struck the ground and lay still.

"Keep moving!" Skaric said urgently. They had to keep moving. "Kiana!"

The assault had stopped. Hesitantly, Skaric raised his face. He could just see the expression on Berend's face. The war leader was grinning maliciously. Skaric set his mouth into a snarl and took several heavy breaths as anger boiled in the pit of his stomach. He had to stay calm; he had to save his companions.

After another heartbeat, Kiana roused herself, seized the horse's reins and ran forward at a carelessly fast pace. Skaric's heart hammered against his chest as he followed her, praying that neither of them would slip. The Wolves still weren't following, but that didn't seem to matter. *Ysia, don't let Nidan be dead.*

*

"Run!" Berend's shout echoed down the cliff towards his quarry. "Run like the coward you are, Skaric! But we will catch you, and we will make you and Miale burn!"

His men stared at him with nervous expressions plastered on their faces, waiting for orders.

Berend ignored their anxiety. "Clear the path!" He smiled. *There's nowhere they can hide from me.* Berend clenched his fists and turned on Vali. "You shouldn't have stopped my men from attacking them."

Vali stared at him coldly. "They might have all been killed."

Berend didn't see a problem with that. He searched Vali's expression, looking for outright hostility; all he saw was fierce loyalty burning in the young man's green eyes.

"We can't take Skaric back to Adalric if he's dead, can we?" Vali said.

Berend bit down the growl that threatened to explode out of his throat. No matter how infuriating the nyxus was, he wasn't ready to get rid of Vali. Yet.

"Don't you think it was strange that Skaric didn't attack us?" Vali asked. "He was close enough to us."

Berend snarled. "And you were close enough to him, but you didn't attack either."

Vali waved his hand dismissively. "I didn't want to kill him. I don't see why Skaric would have had the same qualms."

Berend laughed. "Maybe he knew he couldn't beat us."

"I know how skilled Skaric is, and so do you. I know he could have beaten us all." Vali's eyes were narrowed in a thoughtful, almost calculating expression.

"He ran because he's afraid! Magic nearly killed him. He's probably too scared to use it anymore. It's pathetic." The words tumbled out of Berend's mouth before he had thought about them. "That's why he threw his lot in with Miale. Because he knew he would be ridiculed for being such a pitiful coward." He smiled to himself.

Vali's expression became cold. "And yet he used his magic against you, didn't he? That is how he beat you in the forest…isn't it?"

Berend clenched his teeth. That was the problem with lies; they had a habit of tripping you up. "How dare you question the words of your war leader." Berend spat the words out as he used his height to overshadow Vali. Annoyingly, the nyxus showed no obvious sign of fear. "Do your job: hunt Skaric and the Miale bitch down."

He peered over the edge ignoring Vali, who was still staring at him. Skaric and Miale had reached the bottom and were struggling to lift the Guardian onto the back of one of their horses. That meant the Guardian had to be alive. *Shame.*

The distance was a temporary barrier between Berend and his prey. The hunt was part of the game. Once he caught them, the fun would begin. Excitement bubbled at the back of Berend's throat. Nothing would stop him from killing Skaric, especially not Vali.

*

After riding across a wide stream, Skaric pulled up his horse, taking care not to dislodge Nidan's unconscious body, which was slung across the front of the saddle. They needed time to see to Nidan's injuries, especially the head wound that was slowly seeping thick blood.

"What's wrong?" Kiana asked, stopping alongside him.

Skaric looked back towards the path they had descended. The Wolves were heading down it, travelling at a more cautious pace than the companions had done. "They're too close."

"Then we should keep going." Fear crept into Kiana's voice, though she was trying to hide it.

"They'll catch us. We need to slow them down."

"How?"

Skaric examined the ground on the other side of the stream. The hot weather had dried and yellowed the tall grass. "Fire." He dismounted and began to rummage through the saddlebags.

He heard Kiana catch her breath. "Fire? I thought you couldn't use magic?"

Cursing the loss of his flint and steel, Skaric pulled out the crude bow and spindle that Nidan had crafted for lighting fires.

"Skaric!" Kiana leant forward in her saddle to make a grab for his arm as he passed her. She caught the fabric of his shirt in her fingertips and held on tightly. "We should just run."

Skaric looked up, scowling. "We *have* to slow them down, Kiana."

"But a fire… it will take too long to set one of any size."

Skaric held a breath in his throat as he fought down the urge to shout at her. "It hasn't rained in weeks. The grass is bone dry. With the wind, it will only take a spark to start a wildfire." He stared her in the eyes, willing her to have faith in his knowledge of fire.

Her mouth quivered as her lips parted. "A wildfire? Won't that be devastating?"

Skaric shook his head. "The stream will stop it reaching the fields, and the hillside will stop it spreading further west." He paused and tried to smile reassuringly at her. The action failed, hampered by the pervading fear that gripped him. "We don't have time to argue."

When Kiana remained silent, Skaric shrugged away from her and stomped back across the stream. The damp cloth of his trousers stuck to his legs as he squatted down. Whilst they had been arguing, the Wolves had reached the bottom of the path. Skaric placed his hand flat on the ground. He could just feel the vibrations of the Wolves' horses thundering towards them. Skaric concentrated on twisting the spindle as fast as he could, refusing to look up at the approaching danger.

His hands were sore and warmed by friction when small flames ignited at the base of the spindle. Skaric cast the tool aside, leant forwards and shielded the fledgling flames as he blew on them gently, fostering their growth. Sweat erupted in tiny beads on his forehead as the flames grew in intensity. *It's a mundane fire. I shouldn't be afraid.* But he was. The dry grass accepted the fire easily. Flames began to spread from blade to blade, aided by the wind and the intense dry summer heat. Skaric pressed his hands against the ground, pushing backwards to stand and run back to Kiana.

Flames crackled and heat built up behind Skaric as he mounted the horse. He barely managed to swing himself into the saddle before the scared animal started forward. Jabbing the horse hard in the mouth, Skaric pulled it to a halt again, though it kept shifting its weight from hoof to hoof anxiously, the whites of its eyes were visible. Beside him, Kiana was struggling to hold her own horse steady.

"What have you done?" Kiana said as they both stared at the fire.

The flames were spreading fast, fanning out across the grass as the wildfire moved towards the Wolves in a devastating wave.

Skaric's only answer was to relax his grip on the reins. Kiana did the same. Their mounts leapt forward at a flat out gallop. Skaric glanced across at Kiana. She curled her fingertips into the horse's mane and hunched low over its neck; her face drained of colour. She managed to turn her face to look at him.

"Where are we going?" Kiana had to shout above the clatter of hooves.

Skaric drew in a long breath, steadying his nerves. "The only place they can't follow us—Linden."

Chapter Twelve

Wagons thundered overhead, creating a deafening noise that made Kiana wince. The deep shadows beneath the arch of the stone bridge shrouded Kiana as she waited by the river that cut Linden into two halves. She was alone. Clutching Nidan's cumbersome sword tightly in her hands, Kiana peered into the gathering darkness beyond the shelter of the bridge. The sky was gradually turning a deeper shade of blue as the last pink hues of the sunset faded away. Linden seemed no less busy even though the day was drawing to a close.

Mud from the riverbank was slowly seeping through Kiana's shabby slippers. The foul stench of sewage floating in the water made her nose wrinkle, whilst her mouth was downturned in disgust. Whilst travelling, she hadn't seen any stretch of water that was so dark, murky and filthy. It made her feel physically sick.

Skaric had to come back soon.

Not far away, music began to play: the sweet, mellow sound of a lyre. It was the most cheerful sound that Kiana had heard since fleeing Blackoak Tower. She missed the gravely voices of her Guardians and the joyful sound of their laughter as they played tricks on each other and her; they were all gone. Pressure formed behind her eyes. Kiana allowed the merry tune to comfort her. Gradually, the music tugged her lips into a slight smile.

She leant her head and shoulder against the underside of the bridge. The stone was rough, cool and oddly comforting: something physically solid and permanent in a life of flight and fear. Kiana half closed her eyes and allowed the melody to drift over her. She longed to know where the sound was coming from; it had to be somewhere warm and inviting, surrounded by kind faces. But she had to stay where she was. *My first time in a town and I'm hiding.*

The squelch of footsteps in the mud shocked Kiana into movement. She opened her eyes as she pushed away from the wall. Hands shaking, Kiana began to draw Nidan's sword from its scabbard. She halted her actions and sighed heavily as Skaric half slid down the bank to join her under the bridge.

"Are you all right?" Skaric's face was full of concern and guilt.

Kiana knew he hadn't wanted to leave her alone, but they'd had no choice. "I'm fine. What about Nidan?"

Skaric shrugged. "I took him to the temple of Pios. They'll heal him up."

Kiana handed him the sword; it was more use in his hands than hers. "And the horses?"

"The Guardian at the temple let me leave them there." He looked away awkwardly as he spoke.

Kiana gave him a lopsided smile. "At least we know that no one will recognise you as a Wolf."

Skaric looked down at the ground; his stance was tense. He parted his lips as though he was about to speak but frowned instead. Kiana heard footsteps approaching on the bank and then a gruff voice startled her.

"You there! What are you doing?" A man holding a lantern slipped into view and peered down at them. "Get out from under there." He was wearing a metal breastplate with Pios' symbol on it and carried a shortsword at his belt.

Keeping her head down, Kiana followed Skaric out from under the bridge towards the guard. She could see that Skaric's quivering hand was hovering near the pommel of Nidan's sword. *Don't do anything stupid, please.* She stood alongside him.

"We don't take kindly to freeloaders," the man said. "Find yerselves an inn, or move along to the next place. Got it?"

"Yes, sir." Skaric spoke quietly and respectfully, but he didn't look the guard in the eyes. Without waiting for the guard to respond, he scrambled up the bank and then turned to help Kiana. Her slippers slipped, throwing her to her knees. There was a squelch as Skaric pulled her out of the mud and up the bank.

Skaric took a step away from the bank but froze as the guard snapped at them both. "And don't think of coming back! I'll be keeping an eye out. Understand?"

Skaric half turned and nodded to the man before leading Kiana away at a purposeful pace.

They stopped in a dimly lit alley a few streets away.

Skaric pressed his back against the limed wall of a single-storey building. "We have to find somewhere to stay the night." He clenched his teeth together and growled low in his throat. "This town is crawling with guards."

Kiana nodded in agreement. "Where can we go? We don't have any money, and we can't go to the temples of Pios *or* Miale for help."

Skaric, still staring at the ground, remained silent. The golden glow of a lantern spilled into the alley, illuminating his tense shoulders and the inky darkness of his hair.

"Do you remember the graveyard we saw on our way into the town?" Kiana said suddenly.

Skaric tilted his face up just enough to look at her.

"It spread outside the town wall," Kiana said. "It will be dry and I doubt anyone else will be there at night." She paused. Skaric's expression of doubt told her she needed to do more to persuade him. "Ducarius told me that it's bad luck to enter a graveyard at night. Something about it being too close to the Darkness," she waved her hand absently.

Skaric's lips became taught. "We don't know where Berend and his men are."

"Surely they wouldn't come so close to a town?"

Skaric shrugged.

Kiana rolled her eyes upwards and raised her eyebrows. "If you can think of anywhere better…"

"There are a few Guardians marching the streets," Skaric said.

Kiana watched him closely. Fear danced in his eyes. She'd forgotten that he had far more reason to be afraid than she did. *The worst that will happen to me is that I'll be locked away again.*

"I'll keep my head down. As long as the Guardians don't see my eyes, they'll have no cause to stop us." She reached out and gently touched his sleeve. "It will be all right."

Skaric sighed and nodded reluctantly before attaching the scabbard to his belt. He looked down at the sword. Kiana followed his gaze. The scabbard was plain and made from dark leather, but the hilt and pommel of the sword were both ornate. The hilt was a triangular shape with the names of Pios and Miale carved on two of the sides; the third side was blank. The pommel was the same shape with the symbols of Pios and Miale on two sides. *The third side must have been for Ysia.* It seemed odd that the blacksmiths hadn't changed the design. Instead, the blank sides of the hilt and pommel were a sad reminder of the trinity's fate. *Things will change. I'll make sure they do.*

"Do you have anything to cover it with?" Kiana asked.

She'd been so concerned about Nidan that she hadn't considered the consequences of being found with a Guardian's sword. Now Kiana understood why Skaric had left it with her.

Skaric shook his head. He closed his hand over the pommel and tugged the sleeve of his shirt down as far as possible. They grimaced in unison; it wasn't perfect, but it was the best they could do.

Skaric glanced up and down the alley. "Maybe we could stay here?" He looked Kiana in the eyes, searching for the answer he *wanted* to hear, rather than the one he was expecting.

"We can't stay here. There's too great a chance we'll be seen by another guard. Or the same one." Kiana's expression softened into a smile as Skaric continued to hesitate. "This is my first time in a town, too."

Skaric's pupils widened slightly.

"It's really intimidating. Big. Noisy. Smelly. The graveyard will be quieter and there will be less people around. Hopefully none at all!" Kiana grinned and tilted her head to the side. "Come on."

*

Skaric's nerves were frayed. They had evaded three pairs of Guardians before reaching the graveyard. With every footstep, he had waited for someone to shout, "Wolf!" He had expected the town guard to surge on him and arrest him or worse. Nothing had happened but that didn't stop his legs and heart quivering. Reaching the graveyard hadn't made him feel any safer.

The graveyard had outgrown its boundaries inside the town. A gap in the wall marked the border between the oldest and more recent graves outside. The graves rambled up a steep hill overlooking Linden, which provided a good vantage point; it had been the only high point that Skaric had seen on their approach to the town. The wall had not been extended to wrap around the new graveyard, which didn't make Skaric feel any better.

Lanterns on the walls and spikes along the street that led to the graveyard provided a small amount of illumination, allowing them to see the brambles and weeds that strangled the headstones. Several of them were so old, it was impossible to read the worn down engraving.

"This is a depressing place," Kiana said as they paced through the graveyard towards the wall. "Ducarius showed me a drawing of a graveyard once, but the artist didn't make it look this miserable." She hugged herself. "I can see why people wouldn't want to come here at night. Do you think the Darkness really is close?"

Skaric shook his head.

"But how could you know that?" Kiana asked.

Skaric narrowed his eyes as he glanced at her. "I've seen the Darkness, Kiana. Twice. There's nothing here except bones of the dead." He paused in front of a grave and stared thoughtfully at the moss-covered headstone. "I don't get why you have places like this."

"Don't the Wolves bury their dead?" Kiana kept her voice to a low whisper.

Skaric shook his head and spoke equally quietly. "They burn them."

He stopped suddenly as he noticed two guards standing at the gap in the wall. There was no gate, which seemed odd. On the other hand, the Wolves hadn't had the numbers to overrun a walled town in generations; it had taken all of their strength to siege Blackoak Tower.

Kiana glanced at Skaric then to the guard and carried on walking towards them. "We'll be safer outside the town, less prying eyes. Come on."

Skaric rolled his eyes. He didn't have the energy to argue with her.

As they approached, the guards snapped to attention. Like the man that had turfed them out of their original hiding place, the two men wore metal breastplates and scabbarded shortswords. Skaric gritted his teeth and clenched the pommel of Nidan's sword more tightly. He tried to relax his gait, but fear made his movements stiff.

"It's a bit late to be visiting graves, isn't it?" One of the guards said.

There was a lantern suspended on the wall revealing him to be a tall, burly man with a shock of red hair. His companion was slightly smaller and much slimmer.

Skaric suddenly became acutely aware of the day's stubble on his face. He had no idea what to say without looking even more suspicious. He touched Kiana's elbow with the intention of tugging her away.

Kiana stepped forward and smiled broadly at the guards. She nodded towards the hill. "We wanted to look at the stars. Is that a problem?"

The guards looked Skaric and Kiana up and down and then, smirking, exchanged glances.

"Go right ahead," the red headed man said. "Who are we to stand in the way of romance?"

Skaric bit down on his lower lip as heat rose to his face. A surreptitious glance at Kiana revealed that she was blushing too. He doubted she'd understood the connotations of her innocently intended words. *At least they won't worry when we don't come back inside the walls tonight.*

Skaric held his breath until they had passed through the gap in the wall and were almost half way up the hill. He didn't relax. He couldn't. Kiana led the way, picking her way up the hill in increasing darkness; the light from the walls did not reach to the top, forcing them to rely on star and moonlight to guide the way. All too quickly, the sound from the town faded away to nothingness.

Skaric kept glancing around, jumping at every pebble they dislodged and every pocket of impenetrable darkness.

"Will you relax?" Kiana said. "The Wolves won't come this close to the town. They're not insane."

Berend might be. Skaric ran his thumb across the smooth side of the sword's pommel. The metal had been warmed by his hand and was slightly sticky with sweat. *Let Kiana be right.* He didn't want her to find out the hard way that he was no swordsman.

Kiana stopped at the crest of the hill where a gravestone stood, much larger than the rest. Someone had taken the time to cut back the brambles and weeds, revealing the stone even though all the others around it were overrun by nature. It had an intricately sculpted likeness of Miale's face in the centre; her hair flowed out and down either side, forming columns that framed the inscription. Skaric watched as Kiana crouched down and traced her fingertips over the single word.

"Alamea," Kiana said. "She must have been an incarnation of Miale." She bowed her head, clenched her hands in her lap and began to cry.

Skaric stepped back awkwardly, unsure why she was upset or what he should do. He tore his gaze away from her and continued to glance around the graveyard. It bothered him that the ground on the other side of the hill was engulfed in darkness. Kiana snatched his attention away from vigilance.

"I wonder what she was like," Kiana said, lifting her head to look round at him. "All that's left is a name. Is that all that will be left of me? Will anyone remember me?"

"Nidan will." Skaric looked down at the ground. "I will."

Kiana stared at him. Tears tracked their way down her pale cheeks, glistening in the moonlight.

"Let's go back into the town," Skaric said. He was in no rush to be surrounded by strangers that would kill him if they worked out who he was, but he felt too exposed on the hillside.

Kiana stood. "What sort of life do I have?"

Skaric stepped back as she stormed towards him.

She planted her hands on her hips as she stared up at him. "The only people who really knew me were Guardians or servants. And you. I've been shut away from the world and everyone in it and for what? Protection?" She was making no effort to hide the anger in her voice.

Skaric glanced back down at the wall. They were too far away for her words to carry to the guards.

"Being locked in the tower didn't protect me from the wrath of the Wolves, did it?"

Skaric dipped his gaze. The tower should have been strong enough to protect her. *It would have been, if I hadn't acted.*

"All Alamea would ever have known is the same four walls and the same faces. Day in, day out. Every incarnation of Miale has been a prisoner. How can that be right?"

"I'm sorry…" Skaric looked up sharply as he heard the soft scraping of boots on pebbles. He pushed Kiana behind him and clumsily drew the sword from its sheath.

Two dark forms appeared from the dark side of the hill, the glint of drawn weapons in their hands.

"Wolves!" Kiana's voice came out as a high-pitched squeak.

Skaric opened his mouth to order Kiana to run, then thought better of it. The Wolves would split up: one to kill him, the other to chase her down. They either had to stand together or run together. Neither plan seemed like a good option; if they ran, they would be cut down before they reached safety. The sword hilt felt heavy and clumsy in his grasp, more like dead weight than an extension of his arm.

Even though it was dark, Skaric recognised the Wolves: Hagan and Xaver, Berend's lackeys. Both men looked surprised as they set eyes on Skaric and then they both bared their teeth as they grinned.

"You might as well surrender, Skaric," Hagan said. "We all know you can't beat us."

Skaric set his mouth into a snarl. He couldn't beat them in combat, but he did have the power to snuff out both of their lives. His stomach heaved at the thought. Skaric felt his sword arm begin to tremble. "Scream," he said. He heard Kiana gasp, but he didn't look back at her. "Scream as loud as you can, for as long as you can. Then stay behind me." He would shield her until help came, even if it cost him his life.

Kiana didn't scream.

Grinning fiercely, Xaver lunged forward. Blindly, Skaric swung the sword in the way. Both swords smashed together, causing pain to shiver down Skaric's arm and into his shoulder. He swept the sword round to defend against another attack. Xaver's actions were haughtily lazy. It didn't matter; if the Wolf actually tried, he would beat Skaric within a handful of blows. Skaric knew it. Xaver knew it. Kiana obviously didn't.

Xaver's blade screeched down Skaric's and bounced over the hand guard, smashing against Skaric's hand. Skaric bit back a cry as pain radiated out from the wound; his hand quickly became slick with blood, and he could barely find the strength to hold the hilt.

Hagan began to laugh. The sound sent chills down Skaric's spine. His skin became cold as Hagan nonchalantly began to move behind Skaric and Kiana. Skaric switched the sword into his off hand and then raised his left hand, extending it towards Hagan. His hand trembled. His stomach lurched. Nothing happened. Hagan laughed even harder.

"Give in," Hagan said. "The outcome will be the same. We'll kill the girl and drag you back to Berend so he can kill you. The only difference is how beaten up you'll be."

Skaric narrowed his eyes as he transferred the sword back into his aching hand. *They don't want to kill me.* He was eager to take any small advantage he could get.

Skaric half turned, placing himself in Hagan's way whilst still barring Xaver.

"You're really not going to make this easy on yourself, are you?" Xaver curled his upper lip in disgust. "We really thought you'd take the coward's way out."

"That is what you are, isn't it?" Hagan said. "A coward and a traitor."

Anger blazed within Skaric.

"We're trying to put things right!" Kiana said. "We're trying to restore the trinity!"

Both Wolves laughed so hard they almost doubled over. Skaric jabbed forward but Xaver easily swatted his sword away.

"I'm bored," Xaver said. "This act of gallantry… does the Miale whore know how fake it is?" He stepped forward swinging his sword in a wide arc. "Does she know how much of a coward you really are?"

Skaric raised the sword to block; realised too late it was a feint and stumbled backwards to avoid the flat of Xaver's sword. Behind him, Kiana squealed softly. He felt her hand on the small of his back, preventing him from falling.

Xaver surged forward relentlessly, aiming a blow at Skaric's side. Skaric had to twist his arm awkwardly to block it. The effort sent a spasm of pain through his elbow. Xaver didn't pause. He aimed his next blow high, grin wide, eyes sparkling in the near-darkness. Muscle memory jerked Skaric's sword arm up into a sloppy block.

He heard Kiana let out a soft cry. From the corner of his eye, Skaric saw Hagan step towards him with the pommel of his sword raised. Xaver aimed low. Skaric spun to face Hagan. He swiped at the Wolf's hand with his sword. Hagan flipped his blade round and slammed the flat of it onto Skaric's shoulder. At the same time pain whipped against Skaric's leg, buckling it. He half dropped but immediately tried to right himself. Hagan slammed the pommel of his sword into Skaric's face. Sharp pain racked his cheek as the bone cracked; blood oozed down onto his chin. He staggered and almost fell but somehow managed to find the strength to stay standing. It didn't do him any good. Pain blossomed at the back of his skull as Xaver assaulted him from behind.

Skaric dropped to the ground, the sound of the Wolves' laughter ringing in his ears.

He pressed his palm onto the ground and pushed up in an effort to stand. Xaver stamped down on Skaric's sword hand, forcing him to release the hilt. The Wolf kicked the blade, sending it spinning across the grass out of reach. Then Xaver used his foot to push Skaric onto his back.

Kiana dropped to her knees beside him and took hold of his arm. She clung on tightly as tears cascaded down her face. Pain made Skaric's senses hazy; his vision was fuzzy, causing an odd white glow around Kiana.

"Why didn't you scream?" Skaric whispered, trying to stand again.

He struggled as Hagan dragged him to his feet. Kiana tried to hold onto him, but Skaric was dragged away from her, his arms twisted against his back. Neutralised, Skaric could do nothing but watch as Xaver dropped his sword and grabbed Kiana. In the same movement, the Wolf pulled a dagger and pressed it to Kiana's throat. A tiny strand of blood slid down her pale neck.

Skaric could barely breathe. "Let… her… go."

The Wolf laughed haughtily and spat in Skaric's face. "You never did know when to quit, did you?"

Skaric pressed his lips together and stared at Xaver. He was bruised, battered and bloody; his joints ached and pain throbbed in his skull. It didn't matter; he couldn't let Kiana die.

"It didn't do you any good, did it? You're still going to watch the Miale whore die," Xaver said. He used the dagger to tilt Kiana's head upwards, revealing the vulnerable length of her neck.

As Kiana whimpered, Skaric shook his head angrily. "No…" He began to tug the life from the ground beneath him. "I'm…" Energy flowed into him as he felt the grass wither and die. "Not."

"Really? And how are you going to stop us?"

Fire burst into life at Skaric's fingertips, hungrily licking at his sweat-soaked skin. His stomach somersaulted as pain sizzled beneath his flesh and raced up his arm until it found Hagan's hand. The Wolf's scream tore the night sky asunder as he released Skaric and staggered back. There was a thud as Hagan's body hit the ground, then a series of soft thumps as the pitiful man continued to flop and writhe.

Ignoring the man's shrieks, Skaric held his burning hand towards Xaver. Kiana was still between them, but it would only take one slight motion to make the fire bridge the gap. Xaver would let go of Kiana, wouldn't he?

"Run." Skaric shivered at his own icy tone.

Xaver's eyes were wide as he stared open-mouthed at Skaric. "Berend said… he told us… your magic…"

Skaric set his mouth into a snarl. "Berend lied. Now run!" *Please run.*

Bile choked Skaric's throat as the stench of burning flesh filled his nostrils. His legs almost collapsed beneath him. *Run!* Hagan's screaming had faded out to an odd gurgling sound, but even that slowly ebbed away.

"Do you want to die?" Skaric didn't even attempt to keep his voice quiet. The guards would have heard Hagan's screams. Soon, men would pour up the hill. They would kill him but Kiana would live. "Run!"

Xaver released Kiana and fled down the other side of the hill. Skaric watched the Wolf run until he had vanished into the darkness. He looked down at his still burning hand. The external flames were slowly creeping higher. His nerves screamed as the internal blaze spread up to his shoulder and chest. Skaric willed them to stop, but whether it was from fear, pain, or confusion, the magic refused to answer his call.

"Skaric?" Kiana was standing. Her eyes were wide and fearful as she stared at him.

Skaric almost cried as he saw the terror in her eyes. *She's afraid of me. Of what I'm capable of.* "I couldn't let you die." The air rushed out of his lungs as she flung her arms around him and buried her face in his chest.

"It's all right," she whispered. "You can let it go now."

Skaric choked back tears.

"Let it go." Kiana embraced him tightly. "Let it go."

Finally, the flames winked out, leaving pain and charred flesh behind. His energy spent, Skaric's eyes rolled back and he collapsed into Kiana's arms.

Chapter Thirteen

Through eyes blurred with tears, Kiana could see brands gathering at the foot of the hill. The faded whisper of shouts reached her ears. They were running out of time.

"Skaric!" Guilt gripped her as she shook him as hard as she could with one hand. In her other hand, she clutched the hilt of Nidan's sword tightly as though its very presence would protect them.

Skaric's eyes flickered open. Kiana saw his pupils expand and shrink as he struggled to focus on her. She didn't want to think about how much pain he had to be in.

"We have to run," she said urgently. "They'll be coming soon. Can you stand?"

Skaric nodded and pushed himself to his feet. He wavered, almost collapsing. Kiana ducked under his arm to brace him. She looked towards the town wall, her stomach sinking as she saw that the gathering of torches was moving towards them.

Kiana half supported, half dragged Skaric through the rambling graveyard, away from the hideous sight of the charred corpse. All the time, she was aware of the guards pounding up the hill, their shouts filling the still night air. Kiana heard the rough voice of the redheaded guard shouting orders that she couldn't quite make out. The once dark terrain became flooded with light, illuminating Alamea's grave. *And the Wolf's body.* Kiana shuddered at the memory of the man's screams and the sight of the fire.

The pool of light spread out, searching for them. Men fanned out over the hillside, shouting to one another. They had to get away from the graveyard. Kiana forced Skaric to move back down the hill, towards Linden but away from the guardpost.

"By Pios!"

Kiana jumped at how close the voice sounded. She heard at least one man wretch violently. The guttural sound made her stomach heave.

She glanced around, wide-eyed, but they were still beyond the light of the brands.

"Summon the Guardians!"

"Poor bastard."

"There should be a girl out here, too. Keep searching!" the red-headed guard's voice rang out over the cacophony of shouting.

They think the dead Wolf is Skaric. Kiana glanced at Skaric. The moonlight illuminated the whites of his eyes as he stared directly ahead, his expression slack. Tears welled up in her eyes and she began to breathe harshly. She became lightheaded and her hands shook even more. Kiana took several deep breaths until the graveyard stopped spinning. They had to keep moving.

Her heart thumped in her chest as they reached the dark shadows of the wall. She could see that two men guarded the entrance to the town. She swallowed hard; there was no way back inside.

"We have to keep moving," Kiana said, as much to will herself to carry on as anything. Although her words were calm, her voice shook as much as her body. Every time she blinked, she could see the after-image of flames. The acrid stench rising from Skaric's wounds filling her nostrils made her nauseous.

They moved slowly round the wall, staying as close to the stone structure as possible. Gradually, the shouts of the guards and the light of their brands became distant. Even then, Kiana didn't let Skaric stop and rest. She had no idea how far they would have to go to be safe.

Safe.

It suddenly seemed like an odd concept. One of the Wolves was still out there—perhaps the entire pack was—yet she was hiding from the city guards, men who should have sought to protect her. *They will kill Skaric. They'll see his burns and know what he is.*

Skaric slipped through her grasp and dropped to the ground. Kiana sagged down beside him. Fresh sobs wracked her body.

"We have to keep going," she said.

In the glow of the wall's lanterns, Kiana watched as Skaric hugged his burnt arm and curled his knees up to his chest. He laid still, teeth clenched, breathing hard, staring into the darkness with wide, fearful eyes. They couldn't stop. They wouldn't be safe.

Kiana glanced around. A deep ditch ran parallel to the wall. She had no idea what it was and didn't care; it was the best cover they could hope for. Kiana tugged at Skaric, but he didn't respond. Crouching behind him, she used all her strength to roll him into the ditch before sliding down after him. They had gone as far as they could.

Dislodged dust worked its way into her throat and nose, making her cough; Kiana suppressed the sound with her hands. Then she began to cry. "I'm sorry," she said between sobs. "I'm so sorry."

She was relieved when Skaric shifted his gaze to stare at her.

"It was my fault we went to the graveyard at all. I'm so sorry."

"Why didn't you scream?" His voice was hoarse and emotionless.

"Wolves play with their prey," Kiana said, her voice trembling. "They were so confident they could beat you… but if I'd screamed… if guards had come… they would have just finished it." It had made sense to her at the time.

"They were going to kill you!"

She shook her head and pressed her trembling hands to her lips. "But they didn't. Because of you."

He had used his magic for her. Why hadn't he simply let her die? It made no sense that he had done so much to protect her. Kiana's mouth felt dry as she imagined what might have happened if Skaric hadn't been able to use his magic. As it was, he had paid a terrible price in order to save her from the Wolves and her own stupidity. "I'm so sorry."

She looked Skaric over, taking stock of his wounds. His cheek was swollen and bloody but the injury paled in comparison to the ugly, foul-smelling burns on his arm. The flames had destroyed his sleeve, leaving his arm exposed up to the elbow. Tentatively, Kiana undid the cord that laced the neck of Skaric's shirt. He didn't react, not even to pull away. She gently folded the fabric of the shirt to the side and gasped. Skaric's chest was covered in glistening white blisters. Kiana remembered what Nidan had said about the magic of the Wolf mages: that it burnt them from the inside out. Tears filled her eyes again.

"I understand," she whispered, gently lacing his shirt for him again. "I understand why you were so afraid to use your magic." She looked him directly in the eyes. "Promise me you won't again. Promise me you won't hurt yourself like this again?"

Skaric opened his mouth to speak and then closed it as his expression became hopeless. His gaze dropped from hers as he went back to staring at nothingness.

Seeking to comfort and to be comforted, Kiana edged closer to Skaric and lay down beside him, resting her arm across his shoulder.

"I'm not hurting you am I?" she asked.

"No."

Kiana closed her eyes. She tried to remind herself that Skaric's actions had been driven by his own desire to survive; yet somehow she knew that wasn't wholly true. *Please don't walk away from me when all this is over. I couldn't bear it.*

Chapter Fourteen

Nidan woke with a start. He lay staring at the ceiling, trying to piece together the jumble of memories in his mind. He remembered the Wolves; the cliff and then… Nothing. Darkness.

Propping himself up on his elbows, he gazed at his surroundings. There were six neatly made beds down both lengths of the room; a plain wooden door at one end and a tall window at the other, allowing bright sunlight to stream through and illuminate the room. Elaborate candleholders stood at regular intervals, each bearing a dozen unlit candles in varying states of use. The dormitory smelt slightly stale.

Hung on the stone walls were embroidered banners alternating between Pios' cupped hands and Miale's cup of knowledge. Beside each bed there was a chair on which sat neatly folded black uniforms.

Nidan's heartbeat increased. It looked identical to the room he had spent eight years sleeping in whilst training in Ironhold. He expected to hear the familiar knock of wooden training weapons coming from outside the window but heard nothing.

How long had he been asleep?

Nidan cursed and then swung his legs out of the bed, inhaling sharply as his bare feet touched the stone floor. Like in Ironhold, a draft whispered through the chamber, cooling the flagstones that had been worn smooth by thousands of pairs of feet. But Nidan was sure he wasn't in Ironhold; he couldn't be.

The door opened and an elderly Guardian, dressed in the traditional black garb, stepped into the room.

The old man smiled kindly at Nidan. "You're awake."

Nidan nodded hesitantly. "Where am I?" It felt like such a foolish question. What he really wanted to know was where Kiana and Skaric were.

The Guardian moved a few shuffling steps further into the room. "In Pios' temple in Linden. I healed you last night."

Yesterday. Nidan's jaw fell slack as he stared stupidly at the Guardian. "Th… thank you."

"You had a broken leg and a bad head injury. Don't you remember?"

Nidan half shook his head. He remembered racing down the twisting path; he remembered the Wolves and the rocks; then everything went blank.

"Your agitated companion said that you had been injured in a riding accident." The Guardian's grey brow rose questioningly. "Your horses are in our stables; we are a lot cheaper than taverns."

Nidan knew that the temple of Pios didn't charge anyone for anything; donations were gratefully received.

"Is… is my companion still here?"

"No. He said you could find him at the Wheel and Flagon inn."

Nidan exhaled slowly. Skaric was still alive. The fact that he'd bothered to get Nidan to safety suggested that Kiana was too. Nidan needed to know she was safe; that they were *both* safe.

"I… should go."

"You're still weak and your leg will feel tender for a few days. You are more than welcome to stay here and rest. The temple of Pios is always open to those who need his help." The Guardian stopped, paused and then spoke more slowly and less insistently. "What's your name?"

"Nye." The dishonesty hadn't bothered Nidan in Norlea, but he had never lied to a member of his church before.

"My name is Peadar." As the white-haired Guardian smiled again, the skin around his mouth and brown eyes wrinkled.

Nidan nodded his head in response. It was an effort not to bow formally to his elder. *I can't let him know I'm a Guardian. I can't betray Kiana.* He hoped that she and Skaric had found somewhere safe to hide; they couldn't actually be in the tavern, not without money. Nidan breathed in slowly as he debated telling Peadar that Kiana was with him. That would keep her away from the Wolves and the folly of her quest.

"Are you all right?" Peadar said.

Nidan realised that he had been staring blankly ahead. "I'm fine… just…" Kiana would hate him if he betrayed her, but she would be safe. *She would be a prisoner again.* He snapped his mouth shut.

"Just…?"

Nidan forced himself to shrug and smile. "Thank you for your offer of hospitality, but I really should go and find my friend."

Peadar paused, pressing his lips together. "You're not planning on leaving the town today are you?" When Nidan stared at him, Peadar carried on. "It's obvious you're not from Linden."

"We're… travelling to visit family in Fairlake."

"You should delay a few days then."

Nidan frowned. "I'm sure I'll be fine to ride." He made a show of flexing his toes. "I can't even tell I was ever injured."

"A man was attacked just outside the town last night. By Wolves."

Nidan sank back down onto the bed, gripping the sheets tightly in an effort to keep his expression neutral. "Wolves?"

Peadar nodded gravely. "A cursed mage was amongst them."

"Them? How many? Were they caught? Do you know who was killed?"

Peadar held his hands up against Nidan's barrage of questions. Narrowing his eyes, he regarded Nidan carefully for several moments before replying carefully. "Well… Wolves generally travel in groups of six." He studied Nidan. "No, they were not caught. They fled before we got there. We found the burnt corpse of man." He drew in a breath that whistled through his teeth. "We don't know who it was but no one has been reported missing, so we assume it was a beggar or a lone traveller."

Nidan's legs suddenly felt weak. He pushed himself onto the bed and began to weave his fingers together in an agitated fashion. "When exactly did this… attack… happen?"

"Just after dusk."

Would the Wolves have killed Skaric and taken Kiana? Possibly. *I don't know that's what happened; it might have nothing to do with us at all.* Nidan couldn't will his heart to stop racing or his hands to stop trembling. It was too much of a coincidence for him to dismiss.

"Needless to say, we have Guardians patrolling outside the town. What few we have left, anyway."

Nidan looked up sharply. He mulled over what to say. He had to be careful; displaying too much knowledge of the Guardians would betray him and Kiana. Not that it would matter if she were dead. *No, don't think that way. It would be obvious if we were in a time of Thanatos.* "Have you had problems recruiting new Guardians?" Nidan hoped his tone was innocent.

Peadar regarded him closely. "My bothers have other duties to attend to."

Nidan nodded and smiled as though he accepted Peadar's words. He knew what they had to mean: as he had expected, word had spread about the attack on Blackoak Tower. "Away from the town?" Nidan knew he was treading a thin line, but he had to find out how much danger Kiana was in. He gritted his teeth together to avoid grimacing, angered that he had to regard the Guardians as a threat.

The muscles beneath Peadar's eyes had begun to twitch ever so slightly. "Yes. There has been some trouble with Wolves to the west. Nothing to worry about. You're a curious sort, aren't you?"

For the first time in his life Nidan was glad when he felt his cheeks grow hot. He smiled self-consciously. "My apologies if I asked anything inappropriate. My mother always said my curiosity would get me into trouble."

"Has it?"

"Not yet!" Nidan attempted to laugh, but the noise sounded flat and died on the air. "I must go."

He glanced around until he located his boots, which sat neatly at the foot of the bed. He saw no sign of his sword. *Skaric would have kept it, to defend Kiana.* Nidan silently thanked Skaric's sense: the sword would have betrayed them all. As he tugged on his boots, Nidan could feel Peadar's stare upon him. *I said too much;*

asked too many questions. He had never felt uncomfortable in a temple of Pios before. He felt sick.

Once he was ready, Nidan stood and smiled at Peadar. "Thank you again for healing me." His body almost bowed out of habit.

Peadar nodded politely. "Let me escort you outside."

The old man had been right: Nidan's leg was slightly stiff, giving him a small limp. Despite that, he had to force himself to walk at a slow pace beside Peadar as they left the dormitory and headed across a courtyard into the temple. The temple was not as large or grand as its sister in Ironhold, but it was beautiful despite that. Sunlight poured in through tall arched windows, illuminating the lofty ceiling, carved stone pillars and green tapestries. Incense lingered on the air and a sense of peace shrouded the hall, almost making Nidan feel at ease.

Anxiety welled within him again as they reached the entrance hall. Peadar produced a large metal key from a pocket and unlocked the tall door with a clunk. He pushed it open on silent hinges before clasping Nidan's hand in his own. The Guardian's skin felt smooth and leathery.

"The temple of Miale is always open to those who need to talk." Peadar released Nidan's hand.

Nidan blinked fiercely.

"It's obvious that you are troubled," Peadar said. He touched his fingertips to his brow and then extended a fist towards Nidan.

Nidan quickly returned the gesture and then froze. On the wall behind Peadar, there was a painted map.

Peadar noticed Nidan's reaction and glanced round. "It's very old," he said. "One of the last maps that still show what the land was like before the War of Tears."

"It's… beautiful…" Nidan said. He found Linden quickly and then looked east to where Orholt was marked on the map.

"Yes. Exquisite work," Peadar said. "And very old. If we could move it somewhere more secure, we would. Alas, we couldn't remove the bricks without damaging the plaster."

Nidan narrowed his eyes. He tried to block out the sound of Peadar's voice as he traced a path from their current location to Orholt. *What will it matter if Kiana is dead?* Nidan's skin felt cold.

He clenched his hands into fists. He had already lost Brid; he couldn't have failed Kiana too.

"The stables are just to the right," Peadar said. "Your horses were watered and fed last night and again at first light. I wish you good luck with your journey."

Nidan tore his gaze away from the map and smiled faintly at Peadar. "Thank you again."

Peadar laughed. "I don't think I have ever heard someone give thanks quite so many times as you."

Nidan hurried outside and jogged down the steps towards the stables without sparing a final glance at the old Guardian. The guilt and fear that filled him was simply too great.

*

After a fruitless visit to the Wheel and Flagon inn, Nidan found himself pacing the streets, leading the two horses. He had run through countless scenarios in his head about what might have happened to Kiana and Skaric; hardly any of them had good outcomes. The town was abuzz with the story of the Wolf attack, but no one had any firm details except that it had taken place in the graveyard. Almost every street had a patrolling guard, though most looked nervous and green as though they'd just been drafted in from the streets.

Nidan's head pounded with anxiety.

With so many guards, he knew his companions would have found somewhere to hide. Damn Skaric for bringing them to Linden in the first place, for separating Nidan from Kiana. No. He couldn't think that way. The Wolves had been too close. Linden had been the only safe place, but knowing that wouldn't help him find his companions, *if* they were still alive.

Nidan reached for a sword that wasn't there. *I should have been with them.* He raised his eyes skywards. Why hadn't Pios granted the Guardians the ability to heal themselves?

He stopped dead in the middle of the main road that ran parallel to the river. He'd tried everywhere he could think of: the bridge, back alleys; he'd even nosed about in the stable blocks attached to each of the inns. With each dead end he felt more frustrated and panicked. Kiana and Skaric didn't know the city. They would have stayed close to the tavern; otherwise, there would have been no point in the message Skaric had left with Peadar. But they weren't there. They weren't anywhere within the city walls.

Unable to breathe, Nidan stopped abruptly. He was barely aware of the throng of people pushing past him or the heavy scent of cooked meat that flooded his nostrils. What if Skaric was dead? What if the Wolves did have Kiana and were dragging her back to their den in the mountains? Nidan closed his fists around the reins, causing both horses to toss their heads. He wouldn't let the Wolves kill Kiana. Until the time of Thanatos started, she was still alive and there was still hope. He needed answers and there was only one place worth looking for them.

Nidan made his way to the graveyard. A pair of Guardians stood at the gap in the wall alongside the city guard. They barred his way as soon as he approached.

One of the Guardians gestured towards Nidan's horses. "If you want to leave, take another exit." His voice was gruff.

Nidan glanced past the Guardian as he nodded. Even from a distance, he could see the hideous burnt patch on top of the hill and the patch of dead grass that stretched even further. The only thing unscathed was a headstone. Why would Kiana and Skaric have strayed outside of the city walls?

"I said move on," the Guardian said.

Nidan puffed out a breath and took a chance; he *had* to understand what had happened. "Whose grave is that?" He pointed towards the headstone.

"Some priestess of Miale," one of the guards said casually.

Nidan bit his tongue. Both Guardians shot the man a dark look, which was all the answer Nidan needed.

He opened his mouth to speak and then shut it. He knew how secretive the Guardians could be, especially where Miale was concerned. Asking anything would arouse suspicion.

Did that even matter? The Guardians would help Nidan hunt the Wolves down. They would help him save Kiana.

That isn't what Kiana wants.

Nidan turned away. He had never felt more alone.

*

Berend stared out over the flat terrain, his arms folded over his chest. The Guardians were out there, circling the town of Linden. The war leader and his men had been forced to retreat several leagues out of sight of the town, which meant more time wasted. The grass fire had already trapped them for far too long, allowing Skaric and Miale to slip out of his grasp. Berend kicked a plume of dirt up into the air and turned back towards his pack.

"They could have already left the town," he said. "Ysia knows which direction they'll head in."

"We'll pick up their tracks again," Vali said calmly.

Berend glared at him. The nyxus was really beginning to grate on his nerves.

"Besides," Vali said, "Xaver and Hagan are still out scouting. Maybe they will come back with news."

Berend knew they would. His fighters were far more reliable than a nyxus would ever be. "What if they stay in Linden?" he said, snapping the words at Vali. "They'll be out of our grasp forever."

"Skaric *won't* stay in a town. He *will* leave and when he does, we will find him and take him back to the Alpha."

Berend raised both his hands, fingertips tensed as though squeezing the life out of something. "I won't be happy until…" He caught himself and turned away abruptly. He hated having to maintain pretence in front of Vali. He hated that Skaric and Miale were out of his reach.

"Until what?" Vali asked.

Berend looked over his shoulder. The nyxus had moved to stand beside him, close enough to be stabbed. Berend's hand twitched on his sword hilt. "Until I've delivered that coward back to the Alpha."

Vali's taut mouth twitched slightly. He might have said something if the Wolf on watch hadn't shouted out.

"Someone's coming."

Berend looked to where his pack mate was pointing. Sure enough, a lone rider was heading towards them. Despite the distance, it was clear the man was a Wolf. Vali walked away. Berend relaxed slightly. Frowning, he waited for the warrior to reach him.

"Where's Hagan?" Berend asked before Xaver had even had a chance to dismount.

Xaver, pale-faced, slid from his horse's back and bowed deeply to the war leader. "Dead."

The Wolves touched their hands to their chests. "For the glory of the Wolves! For Ysia!" Only Berend kept silent during the unified chant.

He raised an eyebrow as he looked Xaver up and down. Xaver was filthy: dust, grime and sweat covered his clothes and skin. But there was also a fine darkness around his lips and nostrils.

"He scouted too close to Linden's walls and got himself killed," Xaver said, squinting slightly as he looked Berend in the eyes.

"And where were you?"

"Scouting in a different direction. I caught a glimpse of the traitor and Miale. They're definitely inside the town." Xaver's words were smooth but unnaturally hurried.

"So, Hagan's sloppiness got him killed and resulted in a Guardian presence outside the town?" Berend asked.

Xaver nodded.

"It's a wonder you were able to escape." Berend inhaled deeply as he finished. He caught the faintest scent of smoke.

Xaver shrugged. "I was lucky."

Berend turned away as he nodded thoughtfully. Did Xaver really believe that he was so stupid? He curled his top lip into a snarl. No one made him look like a fool, especially not in front of a nyxus. He tapped his fingertips on the top of his pommel. "Did you have an opportunity to kill Miale and capture Skaric?"

"No." Xaver spoke with rehearsed promptness.

There was no need for any more questions. Berend turned and drew his sword in the same action. Xaver's eyes bulged and his mouth dropped open as the sword was thrust through his chest.

"*No one* lies to me," Berend said slowly. "*No one* betrays me."

He pulled his sword free and watched with grim satisfaction as Xaver's body dropped to the ground.

"Was that really necessary?" Vali asked.

Berend swung round and levelled the sword point at Vali's neck. "And *no one* questions me," he said, narrowing his eyes. "Especially… not… you."

To his credit, Vali didn't waver. He folded his arms across his chest with almost unnerving calmness. "Apologies. War leader."

It took all of Berend's willpower not to strike the nyxus down. Why was he staying his hand? *Because I might need him if Skaric finds the balls to use his magic again.* He looked down at Xaver's body, focusing on the dark stains around the man's nose and mouth: smoke stains. Perhaps Skaric had already found that courage.

Berend slowly lowered his sword, allowing Vali to walk away. Berend watched him go. *I'll play nice until we've caught Skaric. Then I'll kill you both.*

Chapter Fifteen

Kiana's anxiety had risen throughout the day as she tried to work out a way to contact Nidan without going back into Linden.

She and Skaric had been forced to move away from the town when the search party had fanned out to hunt the Wolves down. It hadn't been easy to pick their way through the darkness. With every sound, Kiana had been sure that either the remaining Wolf or Guardians would descend upon them. Eventually, they had discovered a disused storehouse. Once inside, Kiana had allowed Skaric to collapse into unconsciousness whilst she clung onto Nidan's sword and kept watch.

As dawn broke, she had realised that the storehouse was at the edge of a field that was bleached of colour, cracked and dry. Nothing grew in it, not even weeds. The town walls were visible, and as the day wore on, Kiana watched a steady stream of people enter and leave through the east gate. Nidan was not amongst those leaving.

Why would he be? He doesn't even know we left Linden!

Desperation tied her stomach into knots. She had briefly considered going back into Linden to search for Nidan herself but had dismissed the idea just as quickly. She didn't want to be alone; she didn't want to leave Skaric alone. His burns would betray him until Nidan had healed them.

If Nidan finds us. Pios, let him find us soon.

Kiana had also watched Guardians moving up and down the road. She had lost count of the number of times she had prayed to

Pios to keep them safe from the Guardians. *They're not my enemy. Are they?*

The worst part was that Kiana knew her predicament was her own fault. Skaric had tried to dissuade her from going to the graveyard and she'd ignored him. *I'm such a fool. I know nothing of this world. I should have listened to him.* But she hadn't and all she could do was continue to pray to Pios that Nidan would find them and the Guardians wouldn't.

The setting sun cast long shadows over the ground, and the travellers had thinned out to occasional stragglers. Kiana paced back and forth in front of the window. She could barely keep her eyes open and knew that she would fall asleep if she dared to sit down. Something caught Kiana's eye. She leaned on the window ledge and stared at a lone traveller. He was riding one horse and leading the other, travelling at a gallop away from Linden. Nidan.

Throwing all caution aside, Kiana ran out of the storehouse. She was still clutching the cumbersome sword as she ran to the roadside, waving frantically.

"Nidan!"

Immediately, he pulled his horse to a halt, turned it round and headed back towards her, then vaulted off whilst it was still moving, drawing the horses to a stop. Kiana was glad to see that he looked fit and healthy and had only the slightest trace of a limp.

"Are you all right?" Nidan stared down at her face, his expression pinched with concern.

Kiana nodded and handed his sword back to him quickly, glad to be rid of it and that she hadn't had to use it.

Nidan embraced her so tightly it made her squeal. Kiana felt the tension melt away from his arms and heard his breathing relax. In the arms of her Guardian, Kiana suddenly felt safe. Nidan stepped away. "What happened?"

"We were attacked by Wolves, in the graveyard."

"Skaric?"

"Inside. He has a head injury." Kiana hesitated. "And he's burnt."

Nidan puffed out a sigh. "I knew there was a mage. But I thought... Thank Pios."

Kiana shook her head. "There was no mage. Skaric had to use his own magic to save us."

"He told us he couldn't." Nidan's eyes narrowed. "He lied to us? Put us in danger?"

"No!" Kiana put her hands on Nidan's chest. "He *had* to, Nidan. We would have been killed."

Nidan's breath calmed and the muscles in his chest relaxed.

"He saved my life, Nidan. But he's badly hurt and must be in agony. Not that he'll admit it."

The threat of anger fled from Nidan's face as he nodded. His lips curled into a faint smile. "I'm sure it's nothing I can't heal."

As they entered the storehouse, Skaric was in the process of shakily standing up. Nidan inhaled sharply as he looked at Skaric. A grizzly crown of blood made Skaric's hair damp. His cheek was swollen and covered in a dark bruise. He was holding his burnt arm against his chest, his fingers tense and bent awkwardly. The ugly red blisters glistened with moisture in the failing light.

Kiana gave Skaric a withering look. "You should be resting."

Surprisingly, he sat back down. "I should have been helping you to keep watch." He looked Nidan up and down. "I'm glad you're back."

Nidan smiled hesitantly. "Thank you… I think." A bemused expression crossed his face as he scratched his head. "I'm sorry I was gone for so long." He knelt down in front of Skaric. "Thank you for protecting Kiana. She told me how you used your magic to save her."

The muscles beneath Skaric's eyes tightened and then relaxed. He returned his gaze to Nidan. "I did what I had to."

Nidan pressed his lips together in a grim smile. "Let me heal you up."

Kiana watched as Nidan laid his hands on Skaric's left arm and bowed his head in concentration. Almost immediately, Skaric drew in a sharp breath and fresh pain flickered across his face.

Nidan glanced up. "Are you all right?"

Skaric nodded. "I'm just getting worse at hiding pain."

Kiana couldn't miss the look of doubt on Nidan's face. He

bowed his head again and became relaxed almost immediately. Skaric's entire body became tense. Kiana moved to sit beside Skaric as he closed his eyes tightly, pain etched on his face as the whisper of a cry broke free of his lips. She took hold of his right hand. He tried to pull away, but Kiana held on tightly. *You don't get a choice in this.*

"Maybe I should heal your wounds a bit at a time?" Nidan said.

Skaric shook his head. "Best to get it over and done with."

"I don't understand," Kiana said.

"What?" It still amused her when her companions—who still didn't always agree—spoke in unison.

"Why anyone would want to cast magic that could hurt them so badly." She stared down at the floor as her cheeks grew hot. "I'm sorry… I didn't mean to offend you."

"It's all right." Skaric's tone told her he was lying.

Kiana's cheeks became even warmer.

"At the start of the war, you had magic and we didn't. So we found a way to create our own." Skaric made it sound so simple. Maybe it was.

"Is that why the Wolves found a way of casting magic that didn't require the gods' blessing?" Kiana asked.

Skaric grimaced and almost tugged his hand away. Eventually, he sighed. "Yes. We change the nature of our souls so that we can draw power from the life around us." He sounded like a guilty child admitting to stealing.

"You corrupt your soul?" Kiana regretted the words instantly.

Skaric succeeded in pulling his hand away. "Corrupt?" His forehead became furrowed as his eyebrows pulled down to meet over his tightly closed eyes.

Kiana pressed her fingertips to her lips. "I'm sorry! That was harsh."

Skaric shook his head and slowly opened his eyes. "No. You're right."

Kiana frowned. "When a cursed mage dies… what happens to their soul?"

Skaric stared at her blankly.

"My tutor told me that the soul is the only immortal part of a human. The body and mind perish but the soul lives on with the gods… with Pios." She paused briefly. "Would Pios accept a corrupt… changed soul?"

Skaric looked away. "The soul is reincarnated."

Nidan half opened his eyes to glance at Skaric. "That's not what we believe."

Skaric gritted his teeth. "Then you were taught wrong." There was no malice or anger in his voice, just bitterness. "The soul is reincarnated. If a soul is linked to a god in one life, it will be in every other incarnation." He stared straight ahead. "Except Ysia is dead. So no souls are linked to her anymore."

Kiana glanced at Nidan. His eyes were closed again. She wondered what he was thinking. Did he believe what Skaric was saying, even though it went against what he believed? *Do I believe him?*

"Why did you choose to become a mage?" Nidan said, his voice distracted.

For a long time, Skaric said nothing. In the silence that passed, Kiana watched as the burns on his skin slowly began to shrink and vanish as fresh pink skin grew rapidly to take their place. His swollen cheek shrank back down to its normal size. Strangely, the pain that was etched on his face became deeper and deeper with every passing moment.

Skaric breathed in slowly. "I was useless with a sword. I was physically weak and fast becoming a laughing stock. Magic was the only path I could take."

Nidan looked up. "Surely you could have done something else. A trade, perhaps?"

Skaric shook his head. "Wolf men fight or wield magic." He glanced at Kiana, a guilty expression on his face. "The women do all the menial tasks."

It amused her that he thought that would offend her; learning how to light a fire and cook a simple meal had made her feel proud. "What about forging weapons?"

Skaric looked at her, his expression oddly distant. "Why create weapons when you already have them?"

"Or healing?" Nidan said. "You're skilled at field medicine."

Skaric's eyes darkened. "That wasn't an option for me." There was finality to his tone that made Kiana shiver.

She stared down at the dusty floor. It was easy for her to see the flaws in his culture. She was an outsider. Now that he was away from his people, the blinkers had obviously been removed from his eyes. It had to hurt.

Nidan rocked back onto his heels. Dark circles had formed around his weary eyes. "How is the pain now?"

Skaric smiled thinly. "A little better, thank you."

Nidan stared at him. "It should have gone completely. There's nothing left to heal." His expression became grave. "I've never known anyone who has had to be healed as often and extensively as you."

"I'll just have to stop getting into trouble, won't I?" Skaric's tone didn't sound even remotely jovial.

"I'm being serious."

Kiana didn't like the tension in the air or the concern on Nidan's face. "What's wrong? Why is Skaric still in pain?"

Nidan shrugged and stared down at his hands. "My guess is that his body is tired. It's been ripped apart and put back together so many times that scars are being left. Scars that even Pios' magic can't heal."

Kiana didn't like the implications of his words and she could tell by the tension in Skaric's body that he didn't like it either. "Will the Wolves follow us into the Fallen Lands?"

Skaric shrugged. "Normally, I'd say no. But Berend is fanatical. I wouldn't be surprised if he did."

Kiana breathed in deeply. "We can't afford to run into him and his companions. We have to get to Orholt quickly." It was an understatement and she knew it.

"I saw a map at the temple," Nidan said. "I tried to memorise as much as I could."

Kiana smiled with relief. "How far away is the border to the Fallen Lands?"

"Five days ride."

Kiana shook her head. "We'll do it in three. We have to. We know Berend is far too close for comfort."

"There's a mass of Guardians searching to the west," Nidan said. "But they might work out which direction we're travelling in at any time."

Kiana grimaced.

"Large groups travel more slowly," Skaric said.

She hoped he was right.

"Our other choice is to be prepared for Berend."

Both Kiana and Nidan looked at Skaric with puzzled expressions on their faces.

Skaric stared down at his hands. "We draw him out. Fight him on our terms." He held his hands up. "I don't like it. He's with five men. I can't reliably use my magic and I'm next to useless with a sword. But maybe if we use our wits…" He sighed. "Or we could just make a run for the border and hope they don't follow."

It seemed like their only plan.

"Three days?" Nidan said.

Kiana nodded. "Can we travel that quickly? If we all ride?"

"We'll cover just as much ground if one of us walks, maybe more." Nidan shrugged. "It'll be tough… on the horses as well as on us. But yes, I think we can."

"If we get some sleep," Kiana said. She looked at Nidan, smiling hopefully. "Could you keep watch?"

Nidan returned her smile and nodded. "Get some good rest," he said gently. "We have a long way to go."

*

Nidan had lost count of the number of times that he had run through basic sword drills since his companions had fallen asleep. He stood a short distance in front of the storehouse, bathed in silver moonlight, concentrating on making sword thrusts, arcs and swings precise. He had succeeded until his sword arm had started quivering. The muscles in his arms, back and chest screamed for him to rest. But he didn't.

Nidan heard the soft thud of the door being closed. Glancing over his shoulder, he saw Skaric walking towards him. Nidan stared forward again and carried on with the sequence of moves. He had just stepped forward into a chest height thrust when Skaric stepped in front of him.

"It must be my turn to take watch."

Nidan allowed his sword hand to drop to his side as he stepped out of the stance. "No offence, but you don't look up to it."

It was true: Skaric looked tired and pale. He needed more sleep, not to feel obliged to take a watch. He owed Skaric a good night's sleep for protecting Kiana.

Skaric shrugged. "You can't keep watch all night; not if we're going to set a hard pace to try and outrun Berend."

He was right. He was always right.

Nidan began to move the hilt of his sword from hand to hand, feeling the perfectly balanced weight in his grip. It was a comforting sensation. Nidan tossed his sword back into his right hand and closed his fist tightly around the hilt. He could feel the metal beneath the leather padding that he was crushing with the strength of his grip. "I wish I had been there."

"It wasn't your fault…" Skaric's expression was fiercely guilt-ridden.

Nidan shook his head and drove the point of the sword into the ground. "It wasn't your fault, either." He let out the growl that had formed in the back of his throat and kicked at the loose stones on the ground. A scattering of pebbles and dust rose up to rain back down on his boot. He drew in a deep breath. "If I was able to heal myself, you wouldn't have had to take me to Linden and the Guardians." He watched as the corner of Skaric's mouth jerked downwards awkwardly. "What?"

Skaric took a step backwards and shook his head. "Nothing. It wasn't your fault, Nidan. It's me you should be angry at, not yourself. *I* made the decision to go to Linden. *I* couldn't find anywhere better to hide than the graveyard."

Nidan narrowed his eyes and tried to close the distance between them but Skaric edged away.

"There's something else you're not telling me…"

"Get some sleep, Nidan."

Nidan pretended to turn away, but at the last moment he swung back and before Skaric could react, Nidan grabbed him by the shirt and held him fast.

"Tell me what you're thinking. *Then* I'll go to sleep."

Skaric shook his head. "Are you always this stubborn?"

"Are you?"

Skaric laughed; the sound was hollow in the stillness of the night.

Nidan frowned, released his companion and stepped backwards. "I'm sorry. I'm tired and annoyed."

Skaric's mouth curled into a smile. "I noticed." He made a vague effort to smooth out his crumpled shirt, which seemed futile.

"Whatever it was that you were thinking… tell me."

Skaric rolled his eyes. "Fine. You keep telling me you can't heal yourself… that Guardians *can't* heal themselves… I just can't work out why you'd think that."

Nidan pursed his lips. "I've already told you: when we use Pios' magic to heal, we become acutely aware of what we're healing. On somebody else, that's fine. But on ourselves? The pain becomes too great to be able to fight through."

He watched as Skaric began to scuff the ground with the toe of his boot. There was a troubled expression on the young man's face.

"What?"

"One of the reasons that the Wolves lost the War of Tears was because they were facing a foe that could heal themselves. It didn't matter how strong the Wolves were: the Guardians just kept on coming."

"Surely the Guardians just healed one another?"

Skaric froze for a couple of heartbeats and then continued to scuff the ground. He didn't look up, even though Nidan was staring at him.

"If you *could* fight through the pain, is there any reason why you couldn't heal yourself?"

Nidan peered up at the shapes of isolated dark grey clouds against the inky sky. It was a question he hadn't considered in years, not since he had started his training. The other Guardians had laughed at him and told him it was impossible. Embarassed by his foolishness, Nidan had banished such thoughts from his mind. "I don't know."

Skaric stared at the dirt.

Yet if it was possible… "You know how to overcome pain. Will you show me how?"

Skaric stopped and finally looked up at Nidan. Was that what he had been waiting for all along? To be asked for his help? *I know I'm proud, but did he think I would have refused his help? Would I?*

Skaric chewed his lower lip, his expression thoughtful. "How do you channel Pios' magic?"

Nidan blinked, unsure what that had to do with overcoming pain.

"Describe it to me. I know how my magic works, but I have no idea how anyone channels the power of a god."

Should I tell him? Nidan felt his gut twist. He had no reason not to trust Skaric. Not anymore. "I have to relax and concentrate until all thoughts of anything but Pios have left my mind. Sometimes it helps me to visualise the statue of Pios at Ironhold where I trained." He paused, weighing up his next words. "I had to do that when Kiana ordered me to heal you that first time."

Skaric winced. "I bet you found it hard to concentrate on *that*."

Nidan nodded; there was no point in lying.

"What else?"

Nidan shrugged. "Once my mind is clear, I ask Pios for his blessing and then I feel the warmth of his magic. From there, I can channel it into my patient and heal their injuries."

Skaric sat down on the ground and crossed his legs loosely. "You could probably use the same technique to push the pain away."

Nidan frowned. "How?"

Skaric motioned for Nidan to sit down. He hesitated for only a moment before he obeyed.

"Can I have your dagger?" Skaric said.

Nidan frowned but tugged the dagger from his belt. Skaric held his hand out for the weapon. Nidan flipped it round so that he was holding the blade and held it out for Skaric to take.

"Sorry." Skaric said.

"For what?" Nidan ground his teeth and snarled as Skaric took hold of the hilt of the dagger and tore the blade across the flesh of his palm, opening up a jagged cut. The blood still looked crimson despite the gloomy light. "What did you do that for?"

Skaric shrugged in a frustratingly nonchalant manner. "So that you'd have something to heal."

The initial shock passed but Nidan's hand still throbbed with pain. He wanted to feel angry, but instead he forced a sharp laugh out of his mouth. *Trust a Wolf to do something so reckless.* "So, what do I do?" He spat the words through gritted teeth.

"Close your eyes."

Nidan's hand hurt like fury and he felt ridiculous.

"Close your eyes."

He *had* asked for Skaric's help, and the cut would either need to be stitched up or healed or he wouldn't be able to hold his sword to defend Kiana. Nidan closed his eyes.

"Concentrate on the pain."

Nidan imagined that he was still staring at his hand and at the blood that was steadily pattering onto the dry ground. The pain throbbed in waves that seemed to become stronger. The pit of his stomach churned and bile rose into his throat. Nidan's heartbeat quickened, and he gulped breaths of the warm air to calm down.

"Breathe slowly. It's only a shallow cut. No need to panic."

"Concentrating on it makes it hurt more."

He heard Skaric chuckle. "Of course, it does. That's the point."

Nidan ground his teeth and kept concentrating. Soon, he could feel nothing except for the pain. Every other sensation faded out: the sharp stones that pressed through his trousers, the stiffness in his knees, the weight of his head on his shoulders and the headache that had formed at his temples.

"Imagine you can put all the physical pain into one place." It was as though Skaric knew exactly how Nidan was feeling. "Can you do that?"

Nidan found that he couldn't even nod his head. *What's happening to me?* His heartbeat should have quickened as he panicked, but it didn't. He couldn't open his eyes or snap himself out of… what?

A trance? Had Skaric somehow put him into a trance? There was nothing he could do except what Skaric had just asked him to do.

Nidan imagined that he was bundling all the pain into a tight ball that rested on his palm.

"Lock it away."

How is he doing that? A strong wooden box stood before Nidan, the lid open. Feeling foolish, Nidan placed the ball of pain into the box and firmly shut the lid. There was no lock, but he still heard the click of a lock in his mind.

"Can you ask Pios for his power?"

It only took Nidan a moment of concentration to focus on Pios and ask for his blessing. Instantly, he felt the warmth of power in his body, which was his to manipulate. Nidan could visualise the cut, but it didn't feel like it belonged to him anymore. It was as though he was healing another person. Although he still felt some pain, it was insignificant to him. In his mind's eye, he could see the cut slowly closing up, knitting together and then vanishing into nothingness. At the same time, the box containing his pain faded away.

Nidan wanted to open his eyes, to wake up.

"Slowly. Imagine that night is passing. You're asleep and you can't wake up until dawn has come."

It was exactly as Skaric described: Nidan felt like he was waking up from a very deep sleep. When he was finally able to open his eyes, Skaric was staring at him. The muscles around the Wolf's eyes twitched slightly as though he were trying to peer beneath Nidan's skin.

"What's wrong?" Nidan regarded Skaric cautiously.

Skaric shrugged and wiped his hand over his eyes. "I think I'm still seeing things... from when I got bashed over the head last night."

Nidan frowned. "Seeing what?"

Skaric squinted and then waved whatever he was thinking away. "It doesn't matter." He nodded towards Nidan's hand. "At least you managed to heal yourself."

Nidan stared down at his palm. Although there was still blood, there was no other sign that he had ever been injured. His breath caught in his throat. It was amazing. He had been able to heal himself. But would he ever be able to do it again?

Chapter Sixteen

Relief bubbled in Kiana's throat as they reached the understated border to the Fallen Lands. They had travelled for three gruelling days, and Kiana had spent most of that time in the saddle. The muscles in her thighs and calves ached and ugly red sores lined her legs; she longed for the soothing relaxation of a bath. Nidan and Skaric had taken turns to ride the second horse. Kiana had offered to walk to shake out her joints, but they had refused. She understood she wasn't as fit as either of them.

The border was indicated by a series of stout flagpoles that had been staked into the ground. Kiana lifted one of the limp flags and saw the symbols of Pios and Miale on one side and a large black skull on the other. A single word accompanied the skull: DANGER.

Ignoring the warning, they crossed the border. *Please don't let Berend follow us.* Kiana was tired of constantly looking over her shoulder and of seeing fear in Skaric's eyes. After a few leagues, when the border flags had long since vanished out of sight, the terrain changed abruptly from lush grassland to a desolate wasteland. Nothingness stretched ahead of them. Kiana could see no trees, buildings, or landmarks of any kind; just land that had withered and died a thousand years earlier. It was an odd juxtaposition against the cheerful blue sky. It was also silent. Nothing lived there anymore. No birds; no animals; Kiana couldn't even see or hear any insects. She hunched her shoulders as her skin broke out in goosebumps.

Walking along beside her, Skaric missed his footing and almost stumbled to the ground. He righted himself and then pressed his fingertips to his temples.

Kiana looked down at him anxiously. "Are you all right? I can take a turn walking."

Skaric glanced up at her and shook his head; the colour of the sky was reflected in his eyes. "Do you feel that?" He moved his fingertips in slow circular motions.

"Feel what?" There was a gentle breeze that was causing a fine mist of dust to rise into the air. Kiana could feel it pressing against her skin, making her feel dirty and itchy.

The dust caked them all, covering their skin and clothes in a brown layer. It worked its way into her boots and under her clothes. It stung her eyes, blocked her nose and whipped into her mouth when she opened it. The dust would provide protection from the sun, but she couldn't think of any other positives. *But that isn't what you mean, is it?*

Skaric shrugged. "It's probably nothing." His brow creased.

"How long has your head been hurting for?"

He squinted at her and shielded his eyes, which was odd as the sun was behind him. "I'm probably just tired."

Stop hiding things from me. "How long?"

Skaric glanced over his shoulder. "Since the land changed."

Nidan slowed his horse down so that he was riding alongside Kiana with Skaric walking in between them. "Could it be the echoes of magic? A lot happened here. The deaths of Miale and Ysia; a fierce magical war. It's not surprising that this area is… scarred."

Kiana pursed her lips. That seemed to make sense, but why didn't Nidan feel it too? Why didn't the horses? Why didn't she? She was Miale's vessel after all.

Skaric stumbled again, barely catching himself in time to avoid crashing to the ground.

Nidan stopped his horse, dismounted and held the reins out towards Skaric. "Your turn to ride."

Skaric didn't argue; he looked almost grateful as he accepted the reins and pulled himself onto the horse's back.

Nidan pulled his cloak out of one of the saddle bags and handed it to Kiana. "It will help against the dust."

Kiana looked down at him as she accepted the cloak. "Please tell me you remember enough of the map to guide us." Clumsily, she managed to toss the cloak over her shoulders without having to let go of the reins completely. She fastened the clasp and pulled the hood up to shield her eyes. Her mouth felt disgustingly gritty.

Nidan shrugged; his expression became tense. "I hope so. From what I remember, if we keep travelling due east, we should reach a river by nightfall."

A river sounded nice. It would be somewhere to camp, fill their water flasks and wash some of the dust from their skin.

"I don't understand why people are so afraid to come here." Kiana glanced across at Skaric as she spoke, but he seemed too preoccupied with his headache to answer her.

"Myths build up about places where bad things have happened," Nidan said. "Besides, why would anyone want to come here?" He kicked at the ground, sending more loose dust into the air. Both of the horses snorted and shook their heads. "The land is useless. Dead."

Dead. *How many people died here?* Kiana shuddered and looked down at the ground, trying to picture a time when it had been anything other than fine dust; she couldn't. All she saw in her mind was acres of fields covered with the dead. The taste of dust in her mouth suddenly made her feel sick. Letting go of the reins with one hand, she grabbed a water flask from the saddle, took a large gulp, swilled her mouth out and spat as much of the dust out as she could.

'Very lady like," Nidan said, smirking.

Kiana wrinkled her nose and mouth at him as she secured the water flask's cap. "Didn't one of the ruling lords live in Orholt before the war?"

Still smirking, Nidan nodded. "Yes, before the war there were thirteen ruling lords. Now there are only twelve."

Kiana half closed her eyes, remembering. "In Norlea, the drawing showed fourteen." She recalled the image: fourteen men standing beneath a single crown.

"The Wolves used to be part of Gettryne. They were one of several clans, united by one ruler." Skaric was staring directly ahead.

The crown. "The gods wanted one ruler for Gettryne." Why hadn't Kiana realised that before? It should have been obvious. "That's why they entered the bodies of mortals and made themselves vulnerable. They were trying to unite us all." She felt a stab of pain in her heart. "They failed."

Nidan patted her hand comfortingly. "In an odd way, they succeeded." He glanced at Skaric. "Everyone united against the Wolves."

Nidan was right. Gettryne *had* been united: by hatred. Kiana watched as Skaric tucked his chin against his chest. His blank expression turned into a dark glower.

She shook her head sadly. "That's not what the gods wanted." *Why would anyone have wanted this? All the hatred; all the death. It's pointless.*

They lapsed into silence and set as brisk a pace as they could manage. Kiana fixed her gaze ahead. She longed to reach Orholt. She knew the answers to all her questions would be there. They *had* to be there. She pulled Nidan's cloak tighter around her shoulders and neck, even though its heavy thickness was making her sweat. She grimaced at the thought of the dust on her body turning into a sticky paste. *I really need a bath!* In Blackoak Tower, every day had started with a hot bath. Afterwards, she would sit by the fire or on the balcony as Erynn combed her hair out. The corners of her mouth dropped at the memory. That life had been destroyed.

The setting sun had stained the sky red by the time they reached the shimmering river. The good omen did little to raise Kiana's spirits. The failing light illuminated the peaks and troughs of the water's surface as it trickled lazily over a myriad of smooth stones. The sound echoed around the emptiness of the Fallen Lands. It was not a comforting sound. Kiana dismounted and knelt down on the bank. She would feel better after washing the grime from her face. A shock of cold ran through her as she plunged her hands into the water. She withdrew them quickly but her teeth continued to chatter insanely.

Beside her, Nidan touched the surface of the water with his fingertips. He snatched his hand back as though it had just been burnt. "It's not natural!"

Kiana nodded in agreement. "Nothing about this place is natural anymore." She stared at the water. It was entirely void of life, like the rest of the Fallen Lands.

They made their camp a short distance away. Even then, the only sound Kiana could hear was the tumbling water, disturbing her as she tried to settle into sleep shrouded in dust.

When Kiana woke, groggy and disorientated, she found herself lying in a comfortable bed, surrounded by grey stone walls. The walls were unadorned, except for a tapestry of the cup of wisdom. Her breath caught in her throat. It wasn't Blackoak tower; it wasn't her room. *Where am I?* Slowly, she turned her head; her neck muscles were stiff and her shoulder blade clicked with the effort.

An elderly servant sat by the bed, and even though Kiana had never seen the woman before, she recognised her. There was an odd sense of familiarity in the deep lines on her face and the way her grey hair was arranged in looped plaits. From where Kiana lay, she was just able to see the doorway to the room. A Guardian stood facing her bed, with his back pushed against the wooden door. His expression was grave.

Kiana tried to sit up but there was no strength in her body at all, so instead she raised her hand. She gasped.

"Rest my lady," the servant said, reaching forward with concern. "You *must* rest."

The hand that Kiana was staring at wasn't her own. It was old, gnarled and withered. Dark blotches covered her paper thin skin, which was almost translucent in the sunlight that poured through a nearby window. She moved her hand to her head and clutched at lank wisps of grey hair.

"My lady, please! You must rest!"

It was hard to breathe. Kiana's heart beat slowed. Her hand flopped onto her breast, and she was unable to summon the strength to even twitch a finger. She couldn't move. Everything was becoming dark. The servant's face began to blur. She felt like she was sinking into darkness. She wanted to scream but no sound escaped from her lungs. She couldn't breathe. No air passed through her lips. She heard the failing beat of her heart. Slower. Slower. Slower. She was sinking and no one could pull her back. She wanted to scream. She wanted to reach out for help. *Help me!* No one answered. No air. The sound of her heart was gone. She felt nothing. She was cold. Alone. Sinking.

Kiana woke screaming. She clutched at her throat and gasped in the warm night air until her lungs hurt with the exertion. Skaric was already next to her, yet not touching her. It was still dark but the moon and stars bathed the landscape in an unnatural glow. Although Skaric's features looked grey in the dim light, his eyes were still unmistakably blue. Just staring into the depths of his eyes made her feel alive again. *I'm not dead. It wasn't me. It wasn't me.*

"Kiana?"

Her chin trembled as she tried to hold back her tears. When she found she couldn't, she launched herself forward and buried her head in his chest. Tension rippled through him but Kiana didn't care. She wrapped her arms tightly around his back and allowed the tears to pour out of her until her entire body shook with the effort. Finally, awkwardly, Skaric's arms wrapped loosely around her. Kiana relaxed deeper against him, smothering her fear in his arms.

"What happened?" Skaric's voice was stiff.

Can't you bring yourself to comfort or be comforted? Was your life so cold before I met you? "A dream…" It hadn't been a dream. It had felt so real. "I was old. I was dying. But it wasn't me." Kiana shook her head and looked up at him through tear soaked eyes. Nothing she was saying was making any sense. "It wasn't me." She pressed her cheeks against the rough wool of his shirt. Dust transferred from his clothes to her skin, making her face feel stiff as it mixed with her tears; she didn't care. He made her feel safe.

Gradually, Kiana's tears became exhausted. Still trembling, she pushed herself far enough back that she could see his face, but not so far that she broke the embrace. She frowned. "Where's Nidan?"

Skaric glanced over his shoulder. "Restless, but asleep."

Kiana eased herself out of Skaric's arms and looked over his shoulder. Nidan was laying close by, his brow furrowed. Every so often his fingertips twitched and his head rocked to the opposite side. Nidan looked afraid. Kiana had never seen anyone look afraid whilst asleep before. "We should wake him."

She crawled away from Skaric, across the dusty ground that seemed to crumble beneath her fingertips. Gently, Kiana reached out and shook Nidan's shoulders. He didn't wake.

She looked back at Skaric. "Did you dream, too?"

He shook his head. "I've been keeping watch."

Kiana looked up at the moon but couldn't gauge how much time had passed. Skaric certainly looked tired: his cheeks were pinched and there were deep lines beneath his eyes. How long had he been watching over her? Had he tried to wake her?

She reached down and shook Nidan again. The Guardian was beginning to toss and fight in his sleep. His teeth were clenched and a frightened murmur kept escaping his lips.

"Help me?" Kiana said.

Skaric joined her by Nidan's side and shook him harder than she had dared. He still didn't wake. "You didn't wake up straight away either."

Her heart missed a beat. He *had* been watching over her. "How did you wake me?"

Skaric's face crumpled with guilt. "I didn't. You woke yourself."

When I died. Oh Miale. "He's going to dream his death." Not his death. She hadn't dreamt her death but someone else's.

Suddenly, Nidan sat bolt upright, pulling away from Skaric's grip. His eyes opened and he stared into the stillness of the night, breathing heavily. In the moonlight, Kiana could see that a cold sweat glistened over all of his exposed skin.

"Nidan? Are you all right?"

It was several moments before Nidan's breathing calmed and he was able to look at her and then Skaric. He put his hands over his face and breathed slowly into them before nodding. "A bad dream. A *really* bad dream."

Kiana put her hand on his arm. She couldn't tell which of them was trembling more. "Did you dream you were dying?"

Nidan frowned and then nodded. "How did you know?"

"I did as well."

"It wasn't me though," Nidan said.

"It's this place," Skaric said quietly.

Kiana knew he was right. She stared eastwards across the dismal landscape. There was just enough light to travel by. She looked at her companions. They looked as exhausted as she felt. "We should go." Guilt tugged at her gut.

Nidan stared at her, his eyebrows raised. "It's the middle of the night!"

It didn't matter. "I couldn't go back to sleep anyway. Not after…" she pressed her lips together and swallowed hard. "I just want to get to Orholt as quickly as possible and then get out of here. How far away are we?"

Nidan's eyebrows knitted together. "Another couple of days… I think." He didn't sound sure.

"We can't stay awake that long," Skaric said.

"I know," Kiana said, nodding. "But right now, I don't want to go to sleep again, so we might as well get moving. Maybe tomorrow I'll be less afraid."

Without another word, Nidan and Skaric gathered their belongings and prepared the horses. Kiana watched them as they worked, threading her fingers together as though it would relieve some of her fear. It didn't. Whenever she blinked, she was back in the room again. She felt the strength in her body ebb and flow, as though she was old and frail one moment and then herself in the next. From the corner of her eyes, she thought she caught a glimpse of the elderly servant, watching her, but when she turned to look there was nothing there but darkness.

A light touch on Kiana's arm made her jump and yelp in fear. She swung round and came face to face with Skaric.

"Are you all right?" His touch solidified on her arm. As he held it loosely, her fear drifted away on the breeze.

"Yes."

Concern etched his eyes as they searched her face.

Kiana forced herself to smile. "I am. Honestly."

Skaric nodded, released her and stepped away. Kiana could feel the lingering warmth of his touch.

"Skaric…" She was glad when her words pulled him back round to look at her. "I know I'll have to sleep again. Will you watch over me when I do?" *I'll feel safer if I know you're there.*

Skaric looked at her sidelong, before staring downwards and scuffing the ground with his boot. When he finally looked at her again, he was chewing his bottom lip nervously. Kiana almost laughed but the fear was creeping back into her body. Eventually, Skaric nodded.

Kiana wanted to hug him but instead, she smiled. "Thank you."

He nodded again, more formally than before. "You should ride."

"What about you? Is your head still hurting?"

"I'm fine." He offered her a faint smile and then returned to the waiting horses.

Chapter Seventeen

Skaric rested his chin on his folded arms as he stared at the castle. It sat brooding in the distance: a dark blot rising above the desolate landscape. It was darker than the inky sky, even though the pale crescent moon hung directly above it. It was a day away from them at most, but it still seemed so far.

He glanced across at Kiana. She hadn't been asleep for long, but already her brow had become furrowed and she was starting to twitch as she dreamed. The gentle moonlight highlighted the angles of her cheeks, made sharper by weeks of travelling, and the curve of her full lips, which were downturned. She looked so sad, caught in her dream of death. Skaric curled his hands into tight fists. There was no point in trying to wake her; it wouldn't work. The dream would grip her and then release her when it had hurt her.

Skaric pressed his chin harder against his arms. The discomfort helped keep him awake. He was achingly tired and his head still pounded with pain; he tried convincing himself it was because he kept watch longer than Kiana and Nidan. He had slept better than them because the deaths he dreamt of paled in comparison to the horrors he had lived through. Besides, he had promised Kiana that he would watch over her, and he *wouldn't* break that promise.

He gnawed on his lower lip. What good would watching over her do? It wouldn't stop her from dreaming—or crying. He'd done a terrible job of comforting her. He had never seen such open displays of emotion and affection before, not even amongst Wolf women and children. Once again he felt useless, more like dead wood than anything else.

Skaric's breath crystallised on the air in front of him. Despite the warmth of the night, he suddenly felt cold. Shuddering, he wrapped his arms around his chest and stood slowly. He breathed out again, but the same thing happened as if it was a winter night. His entire body began to shiver.

As he stared, everything began to change. Silver pathways materialised on the ground, crisscrossing over the desolate landscape like a giant spider's web glistening in the moonlight. Dark shapes, barely recognisable as human trudged along the pathways, all heading in the same direction: towards the castle. Skaric looked up but it was now just a black void. He could see the silver pathways swirling into it like a vortex. Skaric's chest constricted. The darkness spread out covering everything like a blanket until it had swallowed up the ground and sky.

The air was knocked out of Skaric's lungs as one of the shadows brushed past him. His skin felt like ice. Trembling, Skaric dropped to his knees and held himself tighter, fighting to squeeze some warmth into his body. *Where am I?* Cold and fear made his mind sluggish, but oddly, his headache had vanished completely. *Almost as if something wanted me to be here.*

Kiana. Nidan.

Skaric looked around for his companions. It was as though he were looking at them through a black veil. They were still sleeping. Skaric narrowed his eyes. Bright white light emanated from them both, surrounding them like cocoons. At Nidan's chest, a brilliant emerald glow throbbed like a heartbeat, whilst there was a golden glow at Kiana's breast. More than that, around Kiana there was a second aura, the same golden light completely enveloping her own like a protective bubble.

I've seen this before. He shook his head at the recalled memory of the pain caused by his head wound.

As his eyes adjusted to the darkness between the pathways, Skaric saw something else: crouching shadows lurking beside his two companions. He took a step closer, but his instincts stopped him. Glancing down, he saw that he would have stepped off the silvery pathways. *I know I can't step off but I don't know why.*

The shadow beside Kiana reached out and brushed its incorporeal hand across her face. Through the shroud, Skaric saw Kiana frown and heard the echo of her whimper.

Skaric understood the shadows' malevolence. *You're lost.* The shadows looked up at him, their eyes burning malevolently like red-hot coals. *And you're hurting my friends.* He couldn't allow that. But he couldn't reach them either. He needed to create a bridge. *Think.*

His mind carried him back to Blackoak Tower and when he realised he could do so much more with his magic than he had ever thought possible.

Skaric relaxed his arms and held his hands in front of him, staring at the white light that surrounded him. Hesitantly he looked down at his chest. Weak silver light pulsed there. His heart leapt. *Ysia.*

It was hard to think clearly with his teeth chattering in his skull, and his heart hammering in his chest just as quickly. His thoughts were racing, trying to make sense of where he was and how he had got there. *I wanted to help. I wanted to be useful.* He breathed out slowly, closed his eyes and tried to quell his tumultuous thoughts. He had to think.

It was just the same as at Blackoak Tower. He had wanted to cast magic beyond his capabilities; he had *needed* to.

My will is an extension of my soul.

Skaric's realisation awoke a slumbering strength within him. He imagined himself reaching out to the two shadows: not physically with his hand but with his soul. He gasped; he felt stretched thin—weakened. As Skaric opened his eyes, he saw that he had created a new pathway. It was paler than those around it, barely corporeal, but it was there and it ran between the two shadows. They looked at him and then at the pathway he had created to save them. Like greedy children, they reached out and pulled themselves onto it. In the same instant, the anger fled from their eyes and, like the other souls that Skaric could see, they trudged down his path and joined the flow.

Skaric's legs were shaking; his heart was quivering. He willed the pathway to vanish. Air suddenly rushed back into his lungs, unbearably cold and crisp. Tingling energy rushed through his body, and then he felt strong and whole again.

He looked at his companions. They both looked peaceful. Kiana looked peaceful.

A smile flickered across Skaric's lips, and he looked down at his hands again. *I'm not useless after all.* His victory seemed bittersweet. *This is where the dead go. I could only be here if Ysia was alive.*

Skaric frowned as a writhing movement caught his attention. Red tendrils flickered throughout his aura, bleeding out and polluting its purity. He felt his stomach twist into a thousand knots. *What have I done to myself?*

At the edge of his vision, Kiana's aura flickered and became even brighter as she sat up and stared directly ahead. At him. Her eyes were wide, her lips parted slightly. Bathed in the light of her twin aura, she looked… like a goddess. Pain stabbed at Skaric's chest; he crumpled to the ground, curling into a tight ball.

Reality snapped around him. The ground beneath his cheek suddenly felt real again, and the warmth of the night wrapped him tightly in its grip, which slowly seeped into his skin and bones.

"Skaric?" Kiana was right before him, reaching out to him.

Skaric hadn't even seen her move. He could still see the faintest trace of the double aura, though the light did not illuminate the darkness that gathered around her.

Teeth chattering, he forced himself upright. "I'm fine." It was a lie. *How could I be fine, now that I know?*

Kiana's fingertips brushed against his hand. He shivered at her delicate touch and then followed her frightened stare to see a thin powdering of ice on her hand.

She raised her gaze to stare at him. "What happened?"

Skaric looked down. He was covered in frost that was beginning to slowly melt. "Ysia… she isn't dead." The words choked in his throat.

Kiana's eyes widened into a pair of perfect circles. "What? How do you know?"

"I can see… I went…" Skaric shook his head; he couldn't explain any of it. "She's alive."

Kiana took his hands in hers, clutching them as though she were trying to warm them. Instinctively, Skaric tried to pull away but a deeper part of him fought down the urge. That part of him *wanted* to feel Kiana's soft skin against his rough hands. *I shouldn't be feeling this way.*

"What did you see?" Her voice soothed his confusion.

"Your soul. And the dead."

He felt Kiana shudder as she held him. He looked over her shoulder towards Orholt. The castle was visible again, though the shadows that cloaked it seemed to have become even deeper.

Anger welled up inside Skaric, clawing at his insides, fighting to get out. He squeezed his eyes shut. "How can she be alive?" He wanted to scream. "Everything I've done… I spent my whole life being trained to avenge her!"

Skaric choked as bile flooded into his throat. He ripped his hands away from Kiana, staggered to his feet and walked a short distance away so that he could throw up. He spat the remnants of bile onto the ground, walked away from the regurgitated contents of his stomach and forced himself to take several deep breaths. It didn't stop him shaking. Skaric felt the gentle touch of Kiana's hand on the small of his back as she tried to rub his anguish away. *Stop! I don't deserve this! You don't know what I've done!*

He raised his head so that he was staring up at the moon. "How could you do this?" His strangled voice came out as a weak shout. "How could you hide from us? Turn your back on us? Make us think you were dead?"

"Skaric…"

He spun round, breathing harshly as he stared down at Kiana. Behind her, he could sense that Nidan was beginning to stir and wake.

Skaric looked down at his hands again. The frost had gone, leaving his clothes uncomfortably damp. He could still see the faint remnants of his own soul, poisoned by fire. His mouth twisted. "What did I do to myself?" He began to step backwards away from Kiana as he tried to claw at red tendrils that seemed to writhe and bury deeper into his soul before his eyes.

"Skaric… you're scaring me!"

Skaric stopped and stared at Kiana. "Everything was a lie. I seized the magic of the nyxii because I believed Ysia was dead. But she isn't." He looked up at the moon again. "You were right, Kiana… I corrupted my soul." He knew he needed to cleanse it. He had fallen into Ysia's realm by accident; now he needed to get there purposefully. What was it Nidan had said? He had to block out all thoughts except for those of his god.

Kiana took two faltering steps towards him. "Sit down… we can talk this through…"

Skaric ignored her, turned his back on her and blocked out the sound of her voice. He couldn't look at her frightened eyes or pale face. Guilt stabbed at his heart but he ignored that too. He breathed in and out slowly, imagining the silver pathways that he had seen and the darkness. Behind him, Kiana was still talking and Nidan's voice had joined in. He ignored them both; he had to.

Skaric began to tremble from the cold. His breath froze on the air before him. He felt the ghost of a touch at his back and spun round. Everything blurred and then snapped into focus. He was standing on the silver pathway again. Kiana and Nidan were in front of him, separated from him by the black shroud. Nidan was staring at him open mouthed, the palm of his hand still outstretched.

You can't reach me here. You can see me. I can see you. But we're not in the same place anymore.

Kiana raised her hands to her mouth and then sagged. She would have fallen, but Nidan turned in time to catch her.

Skaric shifted his gaze and looked at the embodiment of his soul. The red tendrils were real and tangible. He reached into the white haze and plucked one of the tendrils out. It writhed in his grip like a burning snake, scorching him. Unimaginable pain tore through the core of his being. He flung the snake outwards and watched as the darkness swallowed it up. He repeated the process, but the pain drove him to his knees. *I can't do this!*

He looked up at Kiana. Why had she always had so much faith in him? *I have to do this.*

Skaric tore one red tendril after another out of his soul. He gritted his teeth against the pain, ignored the tears that stung his eyes and the distant echo of Kiana's sobs as she watched but couldn't stop him. *Does she even know what I'm trying to do?* Of course not. He'd been too gripped by insanity to explain anything to her rationally.

After tearing the last tendril from his soul, Skaric collapsed to the ground. His chest heaved with exertion and he shivered uncontrollably. As the world around him shifted again, he saw the shimmering aura of his soul surrounding him—or what was left of it. It was a tattered mess.

Almost instantly, he felt Kiana's presence behind him, placing a hand on his shoulder tenderly. "What did you do?"

What I had to. "I… I removed the nyxii magic from… my… soul."

She gasped. "Why?"

Because I had to.

When Skaric remained silent and still, Kiana lay down behind him and wrapped her arms tightly around his shoulders. Her touch was surprisingly comforting. Slowly, the warmth from Kiana's body began to leech into Skaric's.

I don't deserve your kindness. I don't deserve you. Aching from the agony of cleansing his soul, Skaric raised his hands to his face and for the first time he could remember in years, he allowed his tears to fall.

*

Berend's remaining men had been twitchy even before they had entered the Fallen Lands. Now, two days in and with night closing in, they were all but panicking. *Cowards.* Granted, the previous night had been strange for them as they had all dreamt of dying. But that was nothing to be scared of. They were Wolves.

During the day, Berend had seen flashes at the edge of his vision: phantoms that he could never quite see and obviously weren't real. It was disconcerting but nothing to be scared of. He wasn't going to let a few odd happenings deter him from his goal. Sadly, his men didn't seem to be quite as focused on hunting down Skaric and Miale.

He glared at his warriors as they set up the camp. One tended the horses whilst another laid out the bedrolls. The third got a fire ready and the fourth was readying their cooking equipment. They were all working in silence and glancing around nervously. It was pathetic to see grown men spooked like horses. They were all battle hardened; yet, they were acting like green boys. Only Vali seemed unaffected, which made Berend angrier.

Berend looked eastwards across the moon-drenched landscape. Tracking his quarry had seemed impossible at first. The dusty landscape seemed to shift and change with every breath of wind, covering tracks as quickly as they were made. But then they had found signs to follow, most notably the helpful piles of horse dung. The dust could cover the dark brown mounds, but it couldn't hide them.

Where are you going, Skaric? Berend had been asking himself the same question for days. *What are you hoping to find in this godforsaken place?* Maybe the idiot thought that he would be safe, that no one would follow him. Did he really think that he could keep Miale safe if he hid out in the wasteland for long enough? Berend's mouth curled up into a cruel smile. There was nowhere that Skaric could hide from him. *I will hunt you down.*

His men ate in silence, which did nothing to improve Berend's mood. One of the men spilt more food than he managed to eat because his hand was shaking so much he could barely hold a spoon. Vali kept his thoughts to himself. The nyxus had become increasingly quiet since Xaver's execution; that bothered Berend.

A gust of wind swept through the camp, rattling pans and armour and covering everything in a fresh layer of dust. The Wolf warriors looked around wide-eyed, as though they expected spectres to appear at any moment.

Berend rolled his eyes. He'd handpicked each of the warriors, knowing them all to be fierce fighters and utterly loyal to him. That was the only reason they'd followed him into the Fallen Lands in the first place. What was there to be so scared of? A few dreams at night and hallucinations during the day? It was nothing that a strong mind couldn't overcome.

After deciding which men would take the first watch, Berend settled down to sleep, unconcerned about the dreams. He knew he would have them, just like the previous two nights. It was *nothing* to worry about. Dreams had *never* hurt anyone.

Berend lay awake. The dark sky was cloudless, revealing an endless expanse of winking lights in the black shroud of night. He'd never taken the time to look at them properly before. Their trackers used the stars to navigate if they had to travel at night. The stars, like everything else, were tools. His sword was a tool; his horse was a tool; his men were tools. He was a tool in the war against Miale and Pios, and he *would* avenge Ysia's death. He would catch Skaric and Miale and he would strangle the life out of her. He smiled as he imagined closing his massive hands around her fragile neck. Perhaps he would snap it, like a twig. No. She wouldn't suffer as much. He needed to make her suffer before she died. The more she suffered, the more Skaric would suffer. Berend's smile deepened. They were happy thoughts to fall asleep to.

When Berend did sleep, he dreamt. He was standing in battle. He was facing Wolves. He glanced down and saw that he was wearing the black uniform of the Guardians. He was one of many, standing in a bloody field, fighting a fierce battle. It was hard to be upset that he was losing. The Wolf opposing him was a bigger man, a fiercer man. He knew that he had more skill in his hands, but skill meant nothing in the face of fear. He felt fear. It was an odd sensation: his skin prickled and his hands shook with every blow he blocked. There was a weakness in his knees that made his stance feeble. It disgusted him. How could anyone function if they allowed themselves to feel fear? He tried to fight it down, but he couldn't. His actions and emotions were not his own.

He missed a block and was driven to the ground. The air was knocked out of his lungs as he hit the damp grass. He failed to block another blow. He saw it coming as though time had slowed down. He felt each heartbeat. One, two. Three, four. It was achingly slow. Then the sword slashed down his torso. Time became faster again. Pain ripped through his chest as a gash was opened from his neck to his stomach. He looked down in terror as he saw his entrails spill onto the ground in a steaming heap. He tried not to feel fear or pain. It wasn't his body. It wasn't his death.

Berend woke, appalled that his throat was sore from screaming and that he was covered in a cold sweat. Sitting up slowly, he glanced around and realised he was alone, except for one horse. Even Vali was gone. Berend stood and glared into the darkness. There was no sign of his men and their tracks had already vanished beneath the ever-shifting dust. *Cowards*. He was not a coward. He didn't need pathetic weaklings at his side. He would find Skaric and Miale and he would kill them both.

Chapter Eighteen

Everything was exactly as Skaric remembered.

It was midwinter. The early morning air was crisp and cold. He was crouching on the floor; his arms wrapped tightly around himself. Skaric watched Jakob make the preparations for the ritual that would either change his life or kill him. His breath hung in frosted clouds in the air. He hadn't been allowed to wear anything other than a thin tunic and breeches. Skaric clenched his teeth in a vain attempt to stop them chattering loudly; he didn't want to disturb Jakob.

Skaric shivered violently as he watched Jakob digging a shallow trench in the frozen ground. The circular island of earth within the ditch was just big enough for someone small to sit very still in. Jakob began to carry buckets of water from a nearby trough, tipping them into the trench. Skaric briefly considered offering his help before remembering that Jakob had ordered him to stay where he was and stay silent. He bit his lower lip and watched Jakob cautiously. He had seen the nyxus burn a boy for angering him and didn't want to receive a similar punishment.

Jakob was the oldest living nyxii. Not that it meant much. The nyxii didn't have the luxury of living until old age and Jakob was likely to be no exception to that. He was a tall and wiry man with pitch-black hair and a dark, unfriendly eye. He had lived for a little over twenty-seven summers—positively old for a nyxus—but those relatively few years had not been kind to him. His bare arms bore the scars of repeatedly overcasting magic. He did not walk straight or with an even gait as his right leg had long since been crippled and his back was twisted. Skaric could only imagine the depth of the burns that had caused such disfiguration. However it was Jakob's face that was the most alarming. Half of his face had been burnt and melted so that the dead skin seemed to drip down from the skull it clung to. His right eye was gone, leaving a dark socket. Even though he was horrifically disfigured Jakob was proud of the way that he looked – it proved that he was not a coward and that he had done anything and everything within his power to ensure victory for the Wolves. It was a wonder that Jakob wasn't dead.

Jakob threw the wooden bucket into the trough with a resounding clatter before picking up a small bottle of oil. He stepped over the trench and poured the oil around the edge of the circle of earth. The nyxus paused, looking down at the preparations thoughtfully. Finally he nodded and looked towards Skaric.

"It is time," he said in a gruff voice.

Skaric nodded and, trembling, tried to stand. His legs wouldn't answer him; they felt like they had turned to ice and would melt away. Without waiting, Jakob strode forward and grabbed Skaric by the scruff of his shirt. With surprising ease, the nyxus lifted Skaric over the trench and dropped him into the earth circle.

"Stay within the circle. I will guide you through the rest."

Jakob made a brief gesture with his hand, causing the oil to burst into flames that leapt toward the sky.

Within the circle, Skaric sat with his knees hugged to his chest. The flames were excruciatingly hot, and within moments, he found it difficult to breathe. As the flames leapt and danced, he caught brief glimpses of Jakob standing on the other side of the trench of water. Doubt began to creep into Skaric's mind as he wondered if he truly had the nerve to become a nyxus. The doubt worsened. He didn't know what he was supposed to do.

"Embrace the fire," Jakob said, as though in answer to Skaric's thoughts. His voice was unusually soft and quiet.

Tentatively, Skaric held his left hand out towards the fire. The flames licked at his fingertips, sending sparks of pain running up his arm. He cried out, pulled his hand back and sucked at his charred fingertips. From outside of the circle he heard Jakob laughing.

"Not like that, you fool! Embrace it with your body and you will die. Open up your soul to it, allow it in and take the power."

Jakob made it sound easy but Skaric had no idea how he was supposed to do that.

Smoke from the fire was beginning to coalesce around him. A quick glance upwards told him that the smoke was forbidden from escaping above the height of the flames, though he wasn't sure how; it looked as though the air above him was forming a physical barrier, hemming the acrid smoke in. Skaric's eyes were stinging and though he didn't want to he found his eyes watering; he refused to accept that he was actually crying.

He began to choke as the smoke found its way into his throat and lungs. At first he tried to resist the urge to cough but that only made him retch and almost throw up.

Coughing, crying, hemmed in by unbearable heat, Skaric slowly lowered himself to the floor and curled tightly into a ball. He was going to die. The ritual had been his last chance, his lifeline, and it was going to kill him.

"Embrace it!" Jakob's voice shouted to him.

Skaric closed his eyes tightly against the acrid smoke and tried to use his thin shirt to cover his mouth and nose. It didn't help. Briefly, he thought about removing his tunic and dousing it in the water in the trench, but to do that, he would have to put the tunic and his hand through the flames, which was madness. There was simply nothing he could do apart from accept that he was going to die. He allowed his hands to relax, forced his eyes to open and lay staring at the flames, breathing in the smoke.

Gradually, his fear slipped away from him. There was no point in being afraid. There was no point in feeling anything, only acceptance. As the flames seemed to bend down and reach out to him, Skaric suddenly realised that he was doing exactly what he was supposed to do.

He breathed in deeply, allowing the thick, hot smoke to flood into him, burning him from the inside. The flames began to lick around his prone body, prickling his skin until finally they completely encased him. Pain tore through his body and rippled across his skin. He screamed.

It didn't happen like this!

Skaric tried to move, tried to control the fire but he couldn't.

He was standing on the bank, watching as the portcullis shattered. His entire body became an inferno of flames. He lurched forward but the water was gone. *I'm going to die. I don't want to die!*

Chapter Nineteen

Kiana awoke from a dreamless sleep, her arm still draped around Skaric's chest. Her cheek was pressed against the curve of his shoulder; her body traced the shape of his. It was a closeness that should have felt wrong. Kiana closed her eyes and pushed her cheek harder against Skaric's shoulder, soaking up the warmth of his sleeping body. She could feel the harsh sunlight warming her head and face and the tickle of the grey dust blanketing her skin. It didn't matter.

Why didn't I dream? She felt Skaric breathe in perfect time with her; felt the gentle thud of his heart against the palm of her hand. Kiana smiled. *Because of you.*

She sat up slowly. Nidan was watching her, a half smile on his lips. Heat flushed into Kiana's cheeks. She shuffled away from Skaric and tried to drag her fingers through her matted hair. "Have you been awake all night?"

It was Nidan's turn to blush. He shook his head and tossed a flask of water to her. "No. I tried to, but I was too tired. I fell asleep." He looked refreshed.

"Did you dream of dying?" She twisted the top off the bottle and drank a little. It was barely enough to ease her parched throat but they had very little water left.

Nidan shook his head and looked at Skaric. "Last night…" He hesitated. "Do you think he'll be all right?"

I hope so. Kiana shrugged. "I don't know. Do you think he's right, that Ysia is still alive?"

Nidan nodded. "It's the only explanation for what happened."

Kiana threaded her fingers together.

"It changes everything, Kiana. It means we really can repair the trinity."

I should be happy. I should be relieved. Her chin began to tremble with the threat of tears.

Nidan edged closer to her. "What's wrong? Ysia being alive is a *good* thing."

She pressed her lips together and stared at him. "Is it?"

Nidan's eyebrows knitted together. "Of course. It means the trinity isn't as broken as we thought it was."

"But what about everything the Wolves have done?" She wasn't sure why she couldn't speak above a whisper. "What about everything Skaric has done?"

Nidan's mouth dropped open. She thought he might say something but he just sat staring at her.

"You saw Skaric last night… how he acted… what if this knowledge destroys him, Nidan?" Kiana used the back of her hand to wipe the tears from her eyes.

"It won't."

I'm not so sure.

"We won't let it."

"I wanted to make things better." She laid her hand on Skaric's shoulder. "What if I end up making everything worse?"

As though in answer to her touch, Skaric began to stir. He woke coughing violently; a horrible hacking sound that began deep within his chest. He rolled away from her onto his knees and lent forward onto his hands, still coughing as though trying to expel something vile from his lungs. Kiana moved forward and tried to put her hand on his shoulder again. At the slightest suggestion of her touch, Skaric pulled away and lurched to his feet. He span round to face her, eyes wide and wild, breathing fast and shallow.

"Skaric? Are you all right?" Kiana wanted to help. She held the water flask out to him even though the gesture felt weak.

Ignoring the flask, Skaric dragged his hands over his face, smearing the grey dust that had mingled with his tears during the night. "Just a bad dream."

"About dying?" Nidan asked.

Like a frightened bird Skaric snapped his gaze round to look at Nidan. "No. I... I dealt with *that* problem."

Kiana exchanged a glance with Nidan. "Skaric... we need to talk about what happened last night. About Ysia..."

Skaric's eyes narrowed. "No... we don't." He turned his back on her and faced the distant castle, bathed in sunlight. It looked almost inviting. "What we need to do is keep going."

"Skaric..." Kiana tried to touch him again but he pulled away even faster than before.

"You should be happy. If Ysia is alive, you might actually be able to restore the trinity." Bitterness lent his voice a razor sharp edge.

"Your magic..."

"Is gone." Skaric didn't look at her.

Kiana clenched her hands and stared at his back resolutely. "You need to deal with that and with the fact that Ysia is still alive." *But you won't because you don't deal with anything. You push it down and store it away. Bit by bit, it's all destroying you.*

Skaric folded his arms across his chest. "No. We need to keep going to Orholt. For all we know, Berend is still on our trail."

"I don't think anyone could track us across this wasteland," Nidan said.

Skaric glanced round. "Then you're not a good tracker."

Nidan's lips tightened into a thin line at the insult. He said nothing.

Skaric didn't take the hint to shut up. "We've been leaving plenty of signs that even the ash won't cover."

Ash. Kiana looked down at the dust covered ground, horrified. She'd been right. It wasn't dust at all. She wanted to claw the ash away from her skin, nose and mouth, just as Skaric had done to the magic that had tainted his soul. She breathed in and out deeply. Remembering his frantic, mad actions made her shiver. *And now you're trying to push us away again: taunting Nidan; turning your back on me. It won't work.*

"You fell apart on us last night." Kiana heard Skaric draw in a sharp breath. "We have no idea what we're going to find in Orholt.

I need to know I can depend on you and right now I don't." *I'm not going to let you evade the hurt this time, even if you hate me for it.*

Skaric turned round and glared at her coldly. "That didn't matter to you when you first enlisted me into your crusade. I told you that you couldn't depend on me and you *didn't listen.*"

Because I knew you were wrong.

He began to pace back and forth in front of her. "And I *did* let you down, didn't I?"

No. Kiana watched Skaric in silence and gave Nidan a look that warned him to do the same. She hadn't seen him as angry since they had first met. It scared her but if anger was his way of facing things, she wouldn't stop him.

"I almost got myself killed at Norlea. I didn't bother to tell you that I couldn't use my magic and that nearly got us killed. I couldn't even defend you at the graveyard!" Skaric stopped in his tracks and stared at Kiana again. "I've been nothing but a liability since the moment you convinced me to help you."

Kiana swallowed back tears. "Is that what you really believe?"

He nodded, breathing harshly before speaking. "And the worst part is that you have no idea what I've done. You keep on showing me compassion and I don't deserve any of it. You *should* have let me die."

He turned away from her and kicked at the ground. A torrent of ash billowed up into the air. The restless wind took hold of it and swirled it about the meagre campsite.

Kiana tried not to shiver as whisper thin flakes alighted on her skin. *I hate this place. It's going to destroy us.* She took two faltering steps closer to Skaric. "Then tell us. Tell *me.*" *There is nothing you can say that would make me hate you. Not any more.*

Skaric hunched his shoulders and bowed his head.

Do not close up on me. "You've killed my people to avenge Ysia."

"Yes." His voice was barely audible in the silence of the morning.

Kiana nodded and took a deep breath. "You played a big part in the attack on Blackoak Tower."

Skaric glanced at her briefly. "Yes." His shoulders became even more hunched.

"Skaric... I knew that when I asked Nidan to save your life. It didn't matter then and it doesn't matter now."

"It should."

Kiana stepped in front of him and stood so close that Skaric had to look at her or close his eyes to avoid doing so. "Why? You've more than absolved yourself since then in everyone's eyes but your own. Why should the things you did in your past matter?"

"That's not all I've done! You know nothing about me. If you did you *would* hate me."

"So tell me!" Kiana could hear the desperation in her own voice. It bordered on anger. She wanted to scream at Skaric; hit him; anything that would snap him out of his cocoon of self-loathing. *Can't you see how much you mean to me? Can't you see that nothing else matters?*

"We all have secrets," Nidan said from behind Skaric. "We've all done things we regret." His looked down at the ground, an action that almost hid the glimmer of his damp eyes.

Kiana stepped to the side so that she could look at Nidan.

"But if you let those things destroy you, then you're an idiot." Nidan's voice was gruff. Without waiting for a response, he turned away and began to tack the horses.

Kiana could see the anger on Skaric's face. It manifested through his clenched teeth and blank, staring eyes.

"At the tower... it was *my* magic that broke through the portcullis."

Kiana held her breath.

"The Wolves might not have broken through the defences if..." Skaric drew in a ragged breath. His eyes were bright with moisture. "It took more power than I could leach from the ground or myself. So I... I..." He sank to his knees. "You *should* hate me, Kiana... I'm a monster." He hung his head. "I killed my own people. I used their lives to fuel my magic. I did it so that the Wolves could kill you. You *should* hate me." His chin quivered. "I *need* you to hate me."

Kiana knelt down in front of him. "I don't hate you. I couldn't." *You were a different person then.*

Skaric lifted his head to stare at her. There was a deep sadness in his eyes that cut her to the core. "I killed in cold blood, Kiana."

"To avenge Ysia."

"That's just an excuse!" His breathing became even harsher and Kiana could tell that Skaric was fighting to stop himself from shouting at her. "That's the excuse my people use to condone their actions. Ysia isn't even dead!"

"You didn't know that. You acted in the way you believed was right."

"But it wasn't right." He looked upwards. Unshed tears glistened in his eyes. "I *knew* it wasn't right."

Kiana squeezed his arm gently. "Which is why it's tearing you apart now." She placed her free hand on the nape of his neck and firmly guided his head onto her shoulder. Skaric didn't resist her touch.

Over Skaric's shoulder, she could see that Nidan had finished with the horses, but was keeping his distance. There was no anger on his face, even though he had to have heard Skaric's admission.

Thank you. "I don't know why Ysia hid from everyone but I do know she would have had a reason. I can't believe that she would have wanted to cause so much pain and grief," Kiana said.

Skaric's body shuddered against hers.

"We'll find out the truth in Orholt, I know we will." She held him even more tightly as she felt the cold dampness of his tears seep through her dress. "And you're not useless, you idiot." She tried to make her tone sound light hearted. "Far from it."

Kiana brushed his dark hair away from his temple. There was still so much pain contained within him that she could almost feel it simmering beneath the surface of his mind. *Maybe I can. Miale is a part of me after all.* Feeling it and being able to do anything about it were two different things. *Now I'm the one who feels useless.*

She lifted her head and pressed her cheek against Skaric's. Surprisingly he lent into her embrace a little, and Kiana felt him cry more freely. "Thank you." She spoke in a whisper that only he could hear. "I couldn't ever hate you." *Because I love you.*

Chapter Twenty

Even in bright morning sunlight, Orholt was not a welcoming sight. The outer wall of the city was little more than rubble with the occasional jagged monolith still standing. Beneath hideous scorch marks, Nidan could just make out irregular stripes of red and cream on the sandstone. Once, the city would have looked beautiful, especially on a summer's day with the sun's rays accentuating the colours. Now all the sun brought out was the sharp angles of destruction and the deep shadows of soot. Nidan shivered as he walked through the shattered remains of the gate.

Kiana and Skaric rode on either side of him. Kiana stared about, mesmerised by the scale and devastation of the city. In contrast, Skaric stared directly ahead, quiet and brooding.

The first few streets were almost completely decimated, but the farther into the city they went, the more intact the buildings were. They came to a district that looked as though it could still be inhabited. The buildings were crumbling through age and a lack of care but had sustained no battle damage.

The city was deathly quiet. The horse's hooves echoed on cobbles that were hidden beneath layers of ash blown from the desolate landscape outside the walls. Tattered remnants of heavy fabric hung mournfully in the windows of too many houses. Here and there, a door stood open and, as Nidan peered inside, he could see that belongings waited for owners that had never returned.

A faded rag doll lay just within a doorway. It was obviously handmade with yellow woollen hair and two large button eyes. It wore a red dress that might have been a bright and cheerful shade before the ash and sun had deadened the colour. Nidan remembered Brid having a similar doll. Once it had been loved, but as she had grown older, the doll had been cast aside. Staring at the rag doll, Nidan couldn't help but imagine a child reaching back for it, whilst her father carried her away from their home. He hoped they had made it to safety.

"Do you think they thought they were coming back?" Kiana said.

"I doubt it." Nidan continued looking around the city pensively.

"Why didn't they take anything with them?"

"To travel faster?" Nidan looked at her sadly. "We took nothing except my weapons and a water flask when we escaped Blackoak Tower."

"They probably just wanted to get as far away as possible as quickly as possible," Skaric said in a quiet tone. His voice had a sharp edge to it, but that was better than the silence he had sustained since the previous morning.

Did Kiana push you too far?

Nidan looked towards the castle perched on a hilltop at the far edge of the city. The outer wall was made from a darker type of sandstone and had a vast entrance with narrow windows on either side. It reminded Nidan of a face, staring down at the city ambivalently. *For Kiana's sake, I hope we find answers here.* They had come too far to find nothing.

They carried on through the streets without talking. The clatter of the horses' hooves was so unbearably loud it made Nidan's head ache.

"Skaric, is your head still hurting?" Kiana's sudden question made Nidan jump.

Skaric shook his head. "It stopped when I found my way into Ysia's realm." His reply was matter of fact; he didn't look at Kiana.

She nodded thoughtfully but said nothing. Nidan wondered what she was thinking.

He remembered the first time he had realised he wanted to join the temple of Pios. He had woken from a terrible dream about Brid, his head pounded fiercely. Without getting dressed, he had left his house and ran through the streets to the temple. He had burst past the Guardian at the door, finally falling to his knees at the feet of Pios' statue. The pain in his head had vanished almost immediately, and he had known he had found his home.

Nidan shivered. *Will I ever be able to go back to Pios' temple?* He took a deep breath and pushed the thought to the back of his mind.

There was one thing Nidan was sure of: Ysia had called to Skaric, just as Pios had called to him.

They were travelling on a broad street that ran straight through the centre of the city, leading to the castle hill. Several other tributary roads led off from it into mazes of abandoned buildings. Nidan glanced down them all, chasing the dark shadows that kept flitting menacingly at the edge of his vision. There was no way of knowing if they were real or just his imagination. Skaric had stopped their death dreams but not the daytime spectres. The closer they had got to the city, the more Nidan had seen them. He shivered again but this time he realised it really was cold.

"It's the middle of summer. It shouldn't be cold," he said.

But the temperature was dropping. He could still sense the heat in the air; the closeness of it pressed against his skin and made sweat bead on his back beneath his filthy clothes. Yet he was shivering.

Skaric pulled his horse to a halt and gazed around. He frowned and began to chew on his lower lip. "It's as if Ysia's realm is close enough to touch. And see."

Kiana shuddered so hard that she involuntarily jabbed her horse in the mouth. It tossed its head and let out an indignant snort as it came to a halt. Both the horses were becoming nervous. Even after Kiana had relaxed her grip, her horse continued to toss its head; its ears were twitching and its eyes were wide and staring.

"So the shadows I keep seeing… are they real?" Kiana said.

Skaric turned to look at her. "They aren't shadows. They're the souls of the dead." It was the first time he had held her stare that day. Yet after only a heartbeat, he looked up at the castle.

Nidan followed his gaze. At the edge of his vision the black spectres floated past him.

"They're going to the castle?" Kiana's voice sounded strangled.

Skaric nodded slowly. "I don't know why they would, or why Ysia's realm is so close that we can see traces of it."

Nidan rested his hand on his pommel, rubbing his thumb over Miale's name. He understood. "Miale died here."

The muscles around Skaric's eyes twitched ever so slightly. "Her soul must have crossed into Ysia's realm here. Maybe that's why."

They carried on down the main road. The houses got bigger the closer they got to the castle. Nidan stared through the windows as he walked past, catching glimpses of comfortable armchairs and long oak dining tables.

"Do you think there are beds inside?" Kiana said.

Nidan glanced up in time to see her shudder violently.

"Forget I said anything." Her voice was glum. "I don't want to go inside any of them. Not after…"

"They left, Kiana. I don't think the townspeople were slaughtered here." Nidan didn't think his words were making her feel any better.

His stomach was rumbling and his mouth was parched by the time the road opened out into a large market square. Broken remnants of wooden stalls sat like skeletons on the cobblestones. Ash encrusted bunting lay tattered and discarded on the floor, occasionally flapping in the breeze.

On the other side of the square, the road led up the hill to the castle. A temple stood at the bottom of the castle road. It was identical in construction to the one they had seen in Norlea and just as lopsided. There was a large gaping hole where a circular chamber should have been. Nidan didn't need to go inside to know that it was Ysia's chamber that had been destroyed.

An elaborate well stood at the centre of the market. As they drew closer to it, Nidan saw that it was triangular, like the hilt and pommel of his sword. On one side he could see a relief of Miale's likeness carved into the stone. She was holding the cup of knowledge and looked directly ahead. Once she would have had a happy and peaceful expression on her face, except a millenium of wind and rain had disfigured the carving. Nidan touched his hand to his head reverently.

The second side had Pios' image carved on it. Despite weathering, it was possible to tell that Pios had been depicted as an older man, wise and thoughtful in appearance. Nidan imagined it looked just like the statue in Ironhold. Nidan curled his hand into a loose fist and held it out towards the image.

Kiana dismounted and wandered around to the third side. Her expression became horrified as she stared at the well. Nidan joined her. With dismay he saw that Ysia's form had deep chisel marks gouged into it, completely destroying her features. He wasn't sure why he'd expected anything different. Skaric had dismounted and was standing beside them before Nidan could stop him. With a blank expression, Skaric touched his fingertips to his chest, over his heart.

Kiana placed her hand on Skaric's arm. "Maybe Ysia didn't abandon us. Maybe we abandoned her."

Skaric continued to stare forward.

"It was the same at the temple in Norlea," Kiana said sadly. "Ysia's image had been destroyed. I expect that every image of her across Gettryne has faced similar treatment."

"Why?" Skaric's voice was as stiff and tense as his body.

"Because everyone thought that Ysia had sanctioned Miale's murder," Nidan said.

"But *why*?" Skaric turned to face them both. "It was a Wolf that murdered Miale, *not* Ysia. The whole of Gettryne worshipped the trinity. We didn't claim Ysia as our own until the war began."

Kiana threaded her fingers together. "What if the man who killed Miale was blessed with Ysia's magic?"

Skaric looked down at the ground. "Even if that *was* the case, it seems wrong to blame her for his actions."

Kiana shrugged. "Is it? The Wolves rallied behind Ysia." She breathed in slowly. "Hatred and anger cloud people's judgement. You of all people should know that."

Skaric's eyes hardened to ice.

"You said yourself that the Wolves claimed Ysia, and they stood behind the man who murdered Miale. What else was everyone supposed to think?" Nidan said.

Skaric met Nidan's stare. "What if Ysia was responsible?"

Nidan opened his mouth to answer but couldn't find the words. He had lived his life believing that Ysia had wanted Miale dead. For the first time he found himself doubting that truth. *Strange how I doubt it before Skaric does.* "I don't think Ysia was responsible," he said after a long pause.

Kiana looked up at him.

"Just think about it for a moment. Everyone believes that Ysia was behind Miale's murder and that Pios saved Miale, right?"

She nodded.

"But I don't think that Pios *could* have saved Miale." He smiled wryly, glanced upwards and then breathed out slowly. "Pios looks after the body; Miale the mind and Ysia the soul."

Kiana frowned. "I know all that, Nidan. But I don't see how that proves Ysia's innocence, or that Pios didn't save Miale."

Nidan smiled. The answer was so obvious to him, so simple. Why didn't his companions see it too? "Gods don't have bodies, Kiana. There was nothing for Pios to heal."

Kiana's eyebrows raised as her mouth dropped open. "Miale was in the body of a mortal…"

Nidan shrugged emphatically. "So? The mortal wasn't saved. She died. Miale died with her. If what Skaric believes about souls is true, then maybe their souls were reincarnated together. And if that's the case, there's only one god who could have made sure that happened."

"Ysia…" Kiana glanced round at Skaric.

He was frowning deeply as hope exploded in his eyes. "I think Nidan's right. You and Miale have separate souls, Kiana. I've *seen* it." He breathed out slowly. "But why didn't Ysia just reincarnate Miale's soul on its own? Why leave it connected to a mortal soul?"

Nidan shook his head. "That's not something I know anything about. I was hoping you'd be able to think of a reason." He folded his arms across his chest. "Remember I was taught that my soul would reside with Pios when I died. But now I'm pretty sure that isn't true." He glanced up again.

Kiana smothered a giggle behind her hand. "I don't think Pios is going to strike you down."

Nidan hoped she was right. "Why not? I'm saying fairly blasphemous things, aren't I?"

Kiana's eyebrows raised as her eyes practically doubled in size. "Isn't that half the reason we're here? Because the things we'd been told to believe just didn't add up?"

Nidan nodded, but Skaric's expression was downcast and the muscles beneath his eyes were twitching thoughtfully.

Kiana turned and caught hold of Skaric's hand and stared at him. "We *all* realised that things weren't as simple as everyone wanted us to believe. We came here to find out the truth."

"And to restore Miale," Nidan said, smiling at the stare his companions were sharing.

"We've already found out so much…" Kiana said.

"But every answer comes with a score of questions," Skaric said bitterly.

"And we'll get those answers. I *know* we will," Kiana said.

Skaric's expression was doubtful as he slid his hand away from hers.

Kiana turned away from him and busied herself with staring into the dark depths of the well. Pity stabbed at Nidan's heart as he watched her run her tongue over her cracked lips.

"Do you think the water will be like the river?" Kiana said.

"I doubt we'll be able to find out." Nidan stepped up to the well and began to wind the winch, which whined in complaint. He frowned. "The rope should have rotted away completely after all these years…"

But by some miracle, it hadn't. As he continued to turn the winch round, the rope slowly coiled around it like an endless snake. The entire city was more intact than it should have been after a millennium of abandonment. It made no sense. The wooden bucket rose into sight. It was dripping wet and filled with water. Tentatively Nidan dipped his fingertips into the water. Surprisingly, it felt fine. He scooped a small amount into his hand and sipped it. There was a slight metallic tang to it but it tasted refreshing enough. "It tastes fine." He looked at Skaric. "Maybe the source of the water is too deep to have been affected by Miale's death?"

Skaric shrugged. "How would I know?"

Nidan rolled his eyes in a teasing manner. "You *are* the expert when it comes to magic."

Skaric narrowed his eyes and looked away. "Hardly."

Nidan shook his head slightly. "Whatever the reason, the water seems good. We can drink, fill up our flasks and maybe have a bit of a wash. I'll be glad to get some of this ash and grime off my skin."

Kiana grinned. "So will I." She dipped her hands into the bucket and drank deeply.

As Skaric walked away Kiana's shoulders drooped. She stared at the water droplets as they escaped through her fingertips and splashed back into the bucket.

"He's going to leave, isn't he, once this is all over?" Kiana looked up at Nidan, her eyes dark with regret.

Nidan frowned and scratched his hairline. "Maybe, maybe not." He knew that wasn't the answer she had wanted to hear.

Kiana scowled. "He's become so distant from us suddenly."

Nidan looked at her. "Are you trying to convince yourself that he *is* going to go?"

Kiana looked away, laced her fingers together and ran the toe of her boot through the ash that covered the ground, tracing a spiral.

"He's in a lot of pain and he doesn't know how important he is to you," Nidan said. "If you want him to stay you just have to tell him how you feel. You know that, don't you?"

Her eyes grew wide as her eyebrows slid up her forehead. "I… I don't know what you mean."

Nidan rested the bucket on the edge of the well, took hold of her shoulders gently and turned her to face him properly. "Come off it, Kiana. I'm not blind, but Skaric *is*. If he doesn't know how much he means to you, why should he stay?" He released her.

Kiana hung her head. "Are you angry with me?"

It was Nidan's turn to be shocked. "What? Why would I be?"

"Because he's a Wolf? Because of the things he's done?"

Nidan laughed. "Does any of that matter to you?"

Kiana shook her head.

"Besides, he's not a Wolf anymore." Nidan wondered when he

had made that decision. Had it been in Norlea or later in Linden? It didn't matter. All that mattered was how much Kiana obviously felt for Skaric. "He's the man that's given up everything and risked everything: for *you*." Nidan ruffled Kiana's hair. "Tell him. If you let him walk away, you'll regret it." *Just like I would have regretted forcing you to go to Valgate*. It felt like an eternity had passed since that day.

Kiana sighed heavily. "Do you think he'll stop hating himself?"

Nidan shrugged. "With help." He pondered the ramifications of his next words before allowing them to escape his lips. "I did."

Kiana stared at him. "Why would you have hated yourself?"

Nidan splashed water over his face. He felt grey rivers of ash running down his cheeks and neck.

"It's something to do with your sister, isn't it?"

"That obvious?" He splashed more water on his face. *I opened up this door. I knew she would ask me.*

"You don't have to tell me," Kiana said.

"You're right. I don't." Nidan regretted the shortness of his words instantly, but his only recourse was to continue to clean his face. Eventually he let out a long sigh. "It was my fault she died." It had been a long time since he had said those words.

"How could it have been? You told me she died in the last time of Thanatos. It was no one's fault that she was gripped by madness."

Nidan smiled at her sadly and shook his head. "She wasn't gripped by madness, Kiana. I was."

Kiana stared at him. More than once, she looked like she was on the verge of words, but she never managed to say anything.

Nidan curled his hand over the pommel of his sword. "It's all right. I made my peace with what happened." *Most of the time it's all right, anyway.*

Kiana slid her arms around his waist and squeezed him gently. "Is that why you became a Guardian?"

Nidan nodded. He returned her comforting embrace and then gently pushed her away. The pain hadn't subsided; he doubted it ever would. Nothing would bring Brid back. He looked up at the sky. The sun had climbed to its highest point. "Let's rest down here for the day and go into the castle at first light tomorrow." It was the only thing he could say to change the subject.

Kiana was shaking her head. "What if Berend *is* following us? There's plenty of daylight left. We should go to the castle as soon as we're cleaned up."

Nidan began to laugh, glad that the serious moment had passed.

"What? What's so funny?"

"You! When did you become so practical and sensible?" He smiled at her, pride warming him from within. "You've changed, Kiana. You've grown."

Kiana smiled. "We all have." She looked in the direction of the temple and her smile faded.

"*Tell* him," Nidan said.

She shook her head. "What good would it do? Maybe Skaric is just too broken by his past." She followed Nidan's example and began to clean the ash from her face. "We have to go to the castle today."

Nidan nodded and bowed formally, striking his arm across his chest. He knew his actions looked less convincing due to the grin that had spread across his face. As he stood tall he leaned down so that he could whisper in her ear. "You're wrong about Skaric. Don't give up on him. Life's too short for regrets."

*

They walked up the steep road to the castle in silence, concerned that the massive door was closed. Skaric's skin crawled with coldness although it was the hottest part of the day. It was strange to feel so cold when he had felt nothing but the warmth of fire since he had been ten summers old. At least he was relatively clean. It felt good to have the sun on his skin again without a layer of muck and ash in between.

His companions looked more human as well. Kiana's beauty was evident again in more ways than one. Without really trying, Skaric was able to see the purity of the aura around her, bathing her in radiance despite everything she had been through. *She wouldn't have gone through any of it if it hadn't been for me.* He turned away from her, set his sights on the castle and increased his pace so that he was walking ahead of his companions.

Skaric didn't stop until he reached the top of the road. Up close, he could see that the door was blanketed in green moss. The wall towered above him: dizzyingly tall. It wasn't battle damaged but it was crumbling. The battlements were disfigured by the elements, and in places, the stone was so worn that it was possible to see through to the other side. There were so many spots that would have been perfect for nesting birds but, like the rest of Orholt, there was no life at all. Loneliness clung to Skaric like a shroud, even though he didn't have to be alone.

He turned his back on the castle and looked down at the city below him. Orholt looked oddly small in comparison to the castle that lorded over it. Despite that it was the largest permanent settlement he had ever entered. Briefly, Skaric tried to picture the streets packed with people, carts, wagons and horses, just like Linden had been. And guards. And Guardians. He shuddered. *Maybe I do have to be alone.*

Then Skaric's eyes narrowed and he forgot to breathe.

"What's wrong?" Kiana asked as she reached him. Her cheeks were flushed and she stood slightly bent, hands on hips as she breathed in and out harshly.

Nidan reached the top moments later. They had left the horses tethered in the market square.

"Berend." Skaric had to force the words out of his dry mouth.

Kiana followed his gaze, squinting. "It looks like he's alone."

Skaric couldn't tear his gaze away from the dark rider who was about to be hidden by the city walls. There was no doubt in his mind; it *was* Berend.

"Why would he be alone?" Kiana asked.

Skaric shrugged. It didn't feel right. Even if Berend was really alone it didn't matter.

"If he's unaided, we can beat him," Nidan said.

Skaric shook his head. "Berend is a skilled fighter: fierce, ruthless and *utterly* fanatical." *And he wants to kill Kiana.*

"But he's still just one man," Nidan said.

Skaric managed to look away from Berend's distant form. He turned his gaze on Nidan. "So are you." He looked down at his hands. They had once held the potential to wield power that was only limited by the life force he could feed it. Now, they were useless. He curled his fingertips into his palms. *I chose this.*

"We should get inside, then," Nidan said. "Find… whatever it is that we came here to find."

Skaric turned his back on Nidan. "How?" He pressed his palms hard against the door. They sank through the spongy moist moss until he felt the rough surface of the wood beneath his fingertips. He pushed hard, gritting his teeth together until his jaw ached. They'd come too far to be foiled by something as pathetic as a door. There *had* to be a way in.

Skaric almost fell forward as the wood gave way beneath his hands. It fragmented and crumbled, pattering to the ground on the other side.

Nidan stepped up beside him and began to tug the wood away from the hole that Skaric had made. "One thousand years is a long time. It's not surprising that the wood is rotten."

Skaric helped him and together they made the hole large enough to get through. He kept glancing over his shoulder. For a while he couldn't see Berend at all; then he caught sight of the war leader, galloping down the central road towards them.

Skaric's mind became dull. He *had* to pull himself together. He'd faced Berend and survived, there was no reason why Nidan would lose. *Except Berend underestimated me. He won't make that mistake again.*

After squeezing through the hole, Skaric led the way into the courtyard. It was long, narrow and home to several crumbling stone buildings that lined the left hand side. On his right was the castle, which had one grand entrance and a couple of simple doorways. Skaric walked slowly, gazing at his surroundings, forcing his mind to think.

The roofs looked to have been made of slate but had long since caved in, leaving each of the buildings open to the elements. Skaric ducked inside the first, which he thought might have been a stable block by its height and the oversized doorway. He could just see the remnants of stalls, except the wood had almost completely disintegrated leaving a few soft splinters behind.

"How strong do you think these walls are?" Skaric said as he turned to face Nidan.

Nidan shrugged and tested the stable wall by pushing against it with his arms. His muscles bulged as the wall groaned under the strain. There was a grating sound; one of the bricks moved fractionally and some of the mortar flaked onto the floor. "Pretty strong. It would take some work to collapse one of them." He stared at Skaric thoughtfully. "That *is* what you were thinking, isn't it?"

Kiana stared at them both blankly.

Skaric moved round them to leave the stable block, unable to look Nidan in the face. Guardians were renowned for fighting honourably, something the Wolves had used against them far too often. "I know it's a cowardly plan." *But it's better than facing Berend again.*

"I think it's a pretty sensible idea," Nidan said. His expression became thoughtful. "Was Berend the one that tried to strangle you?"

Skaric stopped and raised his fingertips to his neck. It felt like an age ago that Nidan had healed his wounds, but he could recall the pressure of Berend's hands around his neck, squeezing the life out of him.

He carried on walking through the courtyard looking at each building to see if any of them looked fragile.

Nidan jogged to catch up with him. "Berend wants Kiana dead. I'm not going to let him anywhere near her. Tell me how good he really is with a sword."

Skaric grimaced. "The position of war leader isn't handed down from father to son. It's earned. Only the fiercest fighter who has earned the most glory in battle can become the war leader."

Nidan whistled through his teeth. "Right. So Berend is the best fighter amongst the Wolves?"

Skaric nodded.

"And he tried to kill you?"

Skaric glanced sideways at Nidan.

"But you survived, without using any magic?"

"I was lucky."

Nidan laughed loudly. "Luck seems to be your closest friend!"

Skaric scowled. He didn't feel particularly lucky.

He stopped as they arrived at the last building. Ivy had invaded the gaps between the stones, pushing the crumbling mortar out of its way. Looking up, Skaric could see the wall leaning dangerously over him. He laid a hand against the wall, pushing ever so slightly. The stone shifted as though the entire wall was letting out a deep breath. It wouldn't take much to bring the wall crashing down. "Here. If we're going to trap Berend instead of fighting him, it has to be here."

"You're talking about collapsing a wall on him?" Kiana asked, her face ashen.

Skaric nodded. He felt like an even bigger coward now that he was looking her in the eyes.

"Won't he realise it's a trap as soon as he sees the building?" Kiana said. "How are you going to make him stand right here?"

"Bait," Nidan said looking straight at Skaric.

Skaric looked at the ground and nodded.

Kiana gasped. "No! That's too dangerous!"

She looked around, her eyes growing wider as she saw what Skaric had already realised: there was no obvious way to escape. Although there were several doors leading off the courtyard, none were within reach of where they stood. That was what made it a good spot. Skaric would stand and wait and Berend *would* come to him.

Kiana stared at Skaric. "Do you want to die?"

"No." If there was one thing he was absolutely sure of it was that he wanted to live. *Isn't that what led me to betray my people in the first place?*

"We'll work out a way for Skaric to escape," Nidan said in a confident tone. "But we don't have much time to set this up." He headed inside the remnants of the building.

Kiana placed her fingertips on Skaric's chin and forced him to look at her. "You can't do this!" Her eyes were wide and imploring as she held Skaric's stare.

"We don't have any other choice."

"We can fight him. Nidan is a good fighter. Between the two of you, you defeated six Wolves. Have you forgotten that?"

Skaric shook his head. "I know how good Nidan is. But I also know that Berend is better." Holding his breath he took her hands in his. "Berend is coming. He wants to kill you. You understand that, don't you?"

Kiana nodded but her hands were trembling. Skaric could sense her anxiety as she sniffed back tears.

"This is the best way," he said.

Nidan reappeared. Skaric let go of Kiana's hands and, cheeks hot, turned to face Nidan.

"It will work," Nidan said, grinning a little too widely for Skaric's liking. Then his grin faded. "But I can't see any way for you to escape unless you can manoeuvre Berend to stand next to the wall."

Skaric puffed his cheeks out as he released his held breath. He couldn't rely on making Berend stand anywhere. He stared down at his hands. "There is a way."

"How?"

"When I was in Ysia's realm, you couldn't touch me."

"You can't be serious!" Kiana said.

Nidan scratched his chin. "Are you sure you will be safe there?"

Skaric shrugged. "As sure as I can be."

"No!" Kiana's voice had almost risen to a scream. "You might not even be able to step into Ysia's realm. What if you can't?"

"It's the only way," Skaric said in time with Nidan.

He didn't understand why Kiana let out a bitter laugh before covering her face with her hands. He knew why she was afraid, but it was their best chance of defeating Berend. Kiana's safety made the risk pale in comparison.

*

Berend appeared in the shattered hole in the drawbridge far sooner than Skaric had expected. He wasn't ready. Cold dread seeped into his skin as Berend climbed through the drawbridge and stared at him, grinning. Skaric was halfway down the courtyard, purposefully looking for somewhere to hide. He didn't have to fake the fear that crept into his expression. He stopped dead, unable to move under the weight of Berend's stare.

"You couldn't run far enough could you, Skaric?"

Skaric forced himself to walk backwards slowly. His heart was pounding so hard, he thought it would burst out of his chest. What if Kiana was right and the plan was too risky? *It's too late now.*

"Where are your men, Berend? Did they turn tail and run?" Skaric watched as Berend's cheeks twitched at the taunt.

The war leader's mouth contorted into an angry snarl. "Where's the Miale bitch?"

"You won't find her, Berend."

Berend sneered and then laughed. "Really? Who's going to stop me? You? Her Guardian? I know she's in here somewhere and I will find her. After I've finished with you."

"You're on your own, Berend," Skaric said, forcing courage into his voice.

Berend began to close the gap quickly. Skaric staggered backwards quickly, stumbling on loose bits of stone.

"You're so pathetic! You're even weaker than the last time we met!"

That's exactly what you're meant to think, you bastard. Skaric forced himself to fall. He crashed to the ground, falling onto his hip and wrist. Pain snapped through his hand. He pushed himself back up to his feet, turned and ran down the length of the courtyard.

When he reached the end wall, he stopped and slammed his fists against the brick. Then he turned, pressed his back against the stone and extended his left hand forward, hoping he wasn't overdoing it.

Berend's laughter cut through his mind. "We both know you're not going to use your magic. You can't. You're too scared."

Skaric's skin began to crawl as Berend drew even closer. He narrowed his eyes until he wasn't really looking at Berend at all, but at the air around him. The aura of Berend's soul flickered around the war leader. It was a dirty shade of grey, completely different to Kiana's and Nidan's, even different to his own. It repulsed him and made the pit of his stomach churn. *I've always felt this way around him, I just never knew why.*

Skaric lowered his left hand and stood tall. "Why did you lie about my father?"

Berend's face twisted into a snarl. "I didn't lie. You made a presumption and I didn't correct you. What does it matter now? You're still a traitor. What are you going to do? Run home and tell your father you made a mistake? That you didn't mean to get in bed with the Miale whore?"

Anger boiled inside Skaric.

"Do you think he'll forgive you?"

Skaric trembled with anger, fear and shame. *Don't move.*

"Do you think he'll spare your life?"

Skaric's nose wrinkled as he smelt Berend's stench. He was forced to look up as the war leader towered over him, sword drawn. *Now, Nidan!*

"I hate traitors. I hate weakness. I *hate* you."

Skaric stared Berend in the eyes; he couldn't look at the sword. "You've always hated me."

Berend leaned forward and placed his left hand on the wall beside Skaric's head. "Do you know why?"

Now, Nidan! Skaric shook his head. He could barely breathe.

Berend leaned even closer and whispered in Skaric's ear. "Because you were born." His breath was hot and pungent on the side of Skaric's face. "Your father treated me like his son. I would have been the Alpha after him."

Skaric closed his eyes. *I should have known.* "I never wanted to be the Alpha, Berend. I would have gladly abdicated to you." *That's a lie. You don't deserve to be the Alpha.* Despite the stench, Skaric breathed in deeply and slowly opened his eyes. It was an effort to fight past his fear to stare Berend in the eyes again. "It doesn't matter now. Neither of us is going to go home."

Berend began to laugh, but he stopped abruptly as the far end of the wall beside them groaned and then began to fall. The bricks separated and began to rain down on the ground, turning the path behind them into a deadly assault course. Berend grabbed Skaric's neck and slammed him into the wall. Skaric gasped as the air was knocked from his lungs. He tried to gulp more in but Berend's hand constricted on his neck. *Not again!* It would be a matter of heartbeats before the wall crashed down on them.

"You psychotic bastard!" Berend pulled Skaric from the wall, only to knock him back into it.

Skaric's vision blurred; he fought to clear his mind of all thoughts except Ysia. *Now.* Nothing happened. Panic clouded Skaric's mind. He closed his eyes. *Ysia, help me!*

Skaric's body shivered and his stomach lurched. The pressure on his neck eased but didn't vanish. He opened his eyes. Darkness surrounded him. He wasn't alone.

Berend stood in front of Skaric, staring wildly around. "What magic is this?"

"Ysia's." Skaric hated that his voice came out as a pained croak.

Through the veil between worlds, he could see the shadows of rocks falling. The waterfall of bricks had almost reached their position.

Berend released Skaric's neck. "Liar!" He raised his sword.

Skaric's heart leapt into his throat. Without thinking, he reached out and grabbed Berend's sword hand. Everything shifted.

Berend yelled as a large brick slammed into his back, knocking him to his knees. Skaric flung his arms up to cover his head and face. An explosion of pain tore through him as a dozen or more sizeable fragments rained down on him. He he stood his ground, coughing violently as rock dust filled his lungs. He saw the glint of sunlight on Berend's blade. *Ysia!* From somewhere he summoned up the energy to throw himself to the ground. He felt the heat of sparks litter his face as Berend's blade struck the wall directly above his head.

Berend was standing again, towering over Skaric, about to deliver a killing blow. But Skaric wasn't looking at the war leader. He was looking at the remnants of the wall. In slow motion, the last third of the wall began to topple over as one giant piece. Skaric couldn't breathe. The air whispered as Berend's sword sang through the air towards his gut.

I am not going to die here.

Skaric closed his eyes, welcoming the bite of cold that made his whole body convulse. He heard the echo of a terrible anguished scream. Warm tears trickled down his cheeks. Without opening his eyes, Skaric forced himself to stand. The silver pathway was solid beneath his feet. One shuffling step at a time, he forced himself to walk.

After less than a dozen steps, Skaric's legs buckled and he dropped to the ground. Only then did he open his eyes and look back. Through the veil, he could see the wreckage of the wall—a cold stone tomb that should have claimed him. He saw Berend's limp and bloody hand sticking out from between two rocks. Relief flooded through Skaric, allowing him to forget to feel ashamed that he was crying.

Chapter Twenty-One

Kiana's heart felt like it had sunk into her stomach as she waited for the plume of rock dust to clear. Berend was gone: buried beneath the rubble. Less than a moment later she saw Skaric wink into reality. Her heart leapt from her stomach to her throat. She wasted no time in leaving the safety of her hiding place. She held her skirt in her hand as she ran down the spiral staircase. When Kiana reached the bottom, it took all of her strength to push the iron door open. The door's hinges were completely rusted, and they screamed in a high-pitched tone as they were flexed for the second time in a thousand years.

A smile snuck up on her lips as she saw Skaric sitting in the courtyard, leaning back on his hand. Nidan was already there kneeling beside him, a look of concentration on his face.

"I'm fine," Skaric said as Kiana approached.

She had tried to slow down but in the end she hadn't been able to move at anything less than a sprint.

Nidan scowled. "I'll be the judge of that."

From a distance, Kiana had been able to see that Skaric was covered in melting frost and dust. Up close she could see that the back of his shirt was torn as were his sleeves. Thin traces of blood had seeped through the remaining fabric. But he was alive, upright, and he was smiling. Kiana found that his grin was infectious as she gave up trying to suppress her own.

Skaric's smile became mischievous. "You cut it a bit fine with the wall didn't you, Nidan?"

"It was harder to collapse than I thought it would be." Nidan's scowl became even deeper. "You're alive, aren't you?"

Skaric's smile became roguish. "No thanks to you!"

Kiana began to laugh. After everything that had happened, she had begun to fear that Skaric wouldn't smile again. *You must be relieved now that Berend is gone.* She glanced over to the rubble and saw Berend's limp hand.

"So much for cleaning up earlier," Skaric said as he flicked some of the dust off his shoulder.

Kiana laughed even harder. Her sides began to ache as she sank to her knees. She wanted to hug him. Instead, she wrapped her arms around herself.

"Just cuts and bruises," Nidan rocked back onto his heels. "What's so funny?"

Kiana took a few deep breaths and managed to smother her laughter but not her smile. "Nothing. It's just… this is almost over. We made it and we're all fine." She looked away from them at the castle that loomed over them. "And somewhere in there is the answer to saving Miale."

"You hope," Nidan said.

It was Kiana's turn to scowl; yet, she had to admit that there was a chance Nidan was right. *Not just a chance. No one has been here in a thousand years. Why would anything be left?*

Skaric stood and made a vague attempt at brushing the dust from his clothes. "There's only one way to find out." He held out his hand to Kiana.

She paused before accepting it, allowing him to pull her to her feet. She enjoyed the roughness of his hand during the brief moment of contact.

"I doubt we'll be able to search the whole castle before it gets dark," Nidan said as he stood. He shaded his eyes from the sun's fierce glare as he stared at the castle.

Kiana looked at the castle thoughtfully, pursing her lips. "I don't think we have to search the whole thing." She looked at Skaric. "Can't we follow the souls of the dead?"

They were still at the edge of her vision, shambling into the castle; the souls had no paths to follow or doors to bar them. They were so elusive that she couldn't track them at all. But Skaric could. He parted his lips to speak.

Kiana pre-empted his possible objection. "It's the best lead we have. The dead are drawn to the castle Miale died in. That can't be a coincidence, can it?"

Skaric shook his head and half closing his eyes, led the way inside. He paused in the doorway and peered back at the rubble tomb.

"Shut the door," Nidan said.

Kiana frowned. "Why? Berend was alone and he's dead now." Her frown deepened as Nidan smiled and shook his head.

"That's not the point, Kiana," he said in a gentle tone. "Shut the door, Skaric."

Skaric nodded and firmly slammed it shut, dislodging some loose mortar. Briefly, he leant his head against the dark wood and smiled slightly. Without a word, Skaric pushed away from the door and strode across the entrance vestibule. Still not understanding, Kiana hurried to catch up.

The inside of the castle was dingy. There were no windows only narrow slits that the sunlight fought to squeeze through. A thick musty smell hung in the air, making Kiana's nose wrinkle. She guessed that at one point there had been mats on the floors but over time they had disintegrated into a collection of dull fibres and dust that billowed into the air and choked her throat as they walked. Their footsteps echoed through the narrow hallways as Skaric led them unwaveringly into the heart of the castle.

None of the doors were locked and several stood open. They turned into a corridor that was three times wider than the others. Skaric stopped. Kiana followed his wide-eyed stare down the corridor. Tapestries still hung on the walls, but they were tattered, fraying and so faded that it was impossible to see the once proud images. What Kiana could see was the remnants of the colours. The tapestries facing each other across the corridor looked to have been identical to one another. The closest pair to her had been embroidered with shades of silver and black. The next pair had been embroidered in green and brown, whilst the last pair had been embroidered in tones of gold and red. Ysia. Pios. Miale.

At the other end of the corridor there was a large set of double doors, curved at the top and intricately decorated with the images of the trinity. Although dust had settled in the ridges, the carvings were still clear. Ysia's image had not been defaced. She was beautiful, depicted young yet with sad eyes. Kiana glanced up at Skaric. Tears were tracing their way down his cheeks. They curved around his jaw and then splashed soundlessly to the floor. Then he looked up above the images of the gods. His eyebrows raised as his lips parted slightly.

Kiana tore her gaze away from him. At the top of the door there was a single symbol. At first she thought that it was Miale's cup of knowledge set into a circle. Then she saw the cupped hands of Pios cradling Miale's chalice. In the same heartbeat she realised that the circle was Ysia's eternal ring.

Tears stung Kiana's eyes. "All three of the gods together." Her voice was quiet, soft and almost breathless.

Skaric breathed in deeply and then looked at her, nodding. "That's how it was before the war."

"And hopefully, how it will be again. I take it we need to go in there." Nidan nodded towards the door.

"That's where all the souls are going to," Skaric said.

Nidan led the way. It was obvious from the determined look on his face that he was expecting the doors to be difficult to open. Nidan's mouth curled into a half-moon of surprise when they didn't resist or complain. They swung open easily as though time hadn't affected them at all. Inside they could see a vast hall with lofty windows and at the far end a wooden dais.

Kiana's mouth dropped open in a silent gasp. Within the chamber she could see the silver pathways clearly. She could see the black wispy souls of the dead trudging along them. All of the pathways converged at the dais vanishing into a mesmerising whirlpool of silver light that reached out to her and coaxed her into its embrace. Kiana felt the pressure of Skaric's hand on her shoulder grounding her and holding her back. Beside the silver whirlpool was an identical golden one. It was equally beautiful. Equally compelling.

Nidan moved to stand alongside Kiana. "What are they?"

"The gateway to death." Skaric's voice was a quiet whisper. "You… you can both see them?"

Kiana nodded. "They're beautiful." She watched as souls approached the vortexes, expecting them to get sucked inside; instead, they paused and fluttered apart. The now less-than-human remnant vanished into the silver vortex. The rest of the shadowy form took on the shape of an ethereal bird that flew towards the embrace of the golden vortex.

"Are we safe?" Nidan said, his voice cracking slightly. "Could we get sucked inside?"

"The gateways aren't really here, nor are the pathways." The doubt was clear in Skaric's quiet voice. "Our bodies should anchor us."

Nidan coughed. "*Should*. I'm not sure I like the sound of that!"

Kiana narrowed her eyes, peering at the darkness that seemed to pool at the edge of the vortexes. "There's something else." She shrugged away from Skaric and took a step forward, trying to see the two objects that hung in the darkness more clearly.

The first was an intricate birdcage made of silver light. Kiana took another step forward and felt sadness swamp her. It radiated out from within the birdcage. At the same time Kiana felt sorrow rising up from within her, threatening to drown her. Inside the cage she could see a golden bird. Over the sadness she felt a deep sense of longing that pushed her forward. She raised her quivering hands to cover her mouth.

"Miale." Kiana stared at Skaric and Nidan in turn and pointed towards the cage. "Can you see it? I think… I think it's Miale's mind." She hadn't realised that she was crying again but suddenly the tears on her cheeks froze and tightened against her skin. Her breath crystallised on the air before her. "How is that possible?"

"If it is… it explains why you couldn't answer any of my questions," Skaric said.

It explained so much. At the same time, a multitude of questions sprang into Kiana's mind. She dropped her hands to her sides, digging her nails into her palms to calm herself. Her nails had grown far too long and sharp whilst they had been travelling. Almost immediately Kiana felt her palms stinging and the warmth of thin trickles of blood on her skin.

Kiana looked away from Miale to the second entity. A dark humanoid shape seemed to hang in mid-air, surrounded by a brilliant white cage that hung tantalisingly close to the gateway. Kiana watched as a procession of souls walked beneath it. As each soul fluttered apart and passed into the vortexes, she could feel a stab of bitter pain emanating from the figure.

"It's trapped." Kiana couldn't decide what made her unhappier: the desperate longing of Miale's soul for her mind or the prisoner whose combined mind and soul were held captive.

"Yes. He is." Skaric walked past her.

"Who is he?" Nidan said.

"The man who killed Miale."

Chapter Twenty-Two

Kiana gasped at Skaric's words but instantly knew he was right. "They're both trapped. Miale and…" Kiana wished she knew his name. "We have to free them!"

"Them?" Skaric was staring at her, his mouth twisted in a look of disgust.

"If Skaric's right, that man killed Miale. Why would we want to free him?" Nidan said, his expression equally appalled.

Kiana glared at them both, shaking her head as though she could deny their words. "Can't you feel his pain?" She paused expecting some kind of reaction but their expressions did not soften. "I *can*. It's unbearable. Surely neither of you can believe that a thousand years of… of being caught between life and death isn't long enough? He's been punished for far too long!"

Nidan curled his upper lip and looked pointedly away. Kiana looked at Skaric. *You have to agree with me. You've been held prisoner. You've been close to death!* Skaric's expression was thoughtful, but he didn't say or do anything to give her hope.

Kiana turned away from them and ran her hands over her face. "You believe souls are reincarnated, don't you?" She glanced at Skaric in time to see him nod. "I think the dark birds are people's minds. They have to be."

Skaric chewed on his lower lip. "The soul is reincarnated… but the mind isn't?"

Kiana allowed herself to smile, glad that Skaric was reaching the same conclusions that she was. "The minds must go to…" She wanted to say Miale but that couldn't be right. She looked at the golden vortex radiating comfort and peace. It was a place she knew she would be happy. "…To somewhere they can rest forever." Kiana tapped the tips of her forefingers to her lips. "Miale's soul has been connected to mine for a thousand years but her mind has been here… waiting."

"For what?" Nidan said.

Kiana's hand dropped to her side. *It doesn't make sense.*

"Humans live and die," Skaric said. "Our minds and bodies are mortal. But our souls are immortal."

Kiana began to nod as her mind finally began to feel a little clearer. "But the gods are immortal. They were never meant to die. Why would their souls need to be capable of being reborn?"

Nidan scratched his head. "So… their souls *aren't* immortal?" He frowned. "But Miale's soul has been reincarnated. Over and over again."

"What if it hasn't?" Skaric said. "Kiana's soul has been. Miale's soul is attached to hers. What if it's just been dragged through the process?"

Kiana's heart quivered in her chest. "Miale was killed. Look at what's happening to all the dead… their souls and minds are separating. The same must have happened to Miale… except she *couldn't* be reincarnated." She looked at the beautiful silver birdcage. "You were right, Nidan. All this time, everyone thought Pios saved Miale, but that can't be true. Ysia must have trapped Miale's mind so that it couldn't be sucked away. Then Ysia must have fused Miale's soul to mine to protect it through the reincarnation cycle." She turned her hand in a circle as she spoke. "Ysia *must* have wanted to make Miale whole again!"

Nidan's frown became deeper. "Why didn't Ysia just do it then? We know she's been alive this whole time."

Kiana stared at the floor. She had no answer to that. "Maybe she couldn't." Kiana raised her gaze and pointed at Miale's killer. "Maybe he knows." She breathed in deeply. "And even if he doesn't, he can tell us why he killed Miale. Don't you both want to know why the war was started?"

Nidan shrugged. "I'm not sure that it matters anymore. What difference will knowing make? It won't change what happened. It won't help us restore Miale."

Skaric turned his back on them both and slowly walked closer to the imprisoned soul. "I want to know." He sounded tired. "Because of him, countless people have suffered. Because of him, Ysia turned her back on everyone. Because of him, my people have been vilified and persecuted." He half turned to face them. "And I know the Wolves have done nothing to help themselves. They made the situation worse by using a corrupted form of magic and continuing the fighting. But I still need to know why." His eyes almost seemed to glow with an inner light of desperation. "It's all I've ever wanted to know."

It's why you left your people and helped me. Kiana nodded. "But you're the only person that can ask him. You're the only one that can enter Ysia's realm."

Skaric shook his head. "I can take other people with me."

Kiana's eyes widened. "What? How do you know?"

"Earlier… when the wall was falling… I tried to escape into the pathways whilst Berend was strangling me. He came with me." He stared at her earnestly. "I can take you with me."

"I think you're both forgetting something," Nidan said. "That man's mind and soul have been trapped for a thousand years. What makes you think that he's got enough sanity left to answer your questions? And even if he does, why should he?"

Kiana stared at him open-mouthed.

"Are either of you prepared to *make* him tell you what he knows?"

Kiana shook her head as a dark look crossed Skaric's face. She sucked in a sharp breath and held it. *No. Please don't say that you are. You're not that person anymore.*

Skaric's expression softened. "We can ask. If that doesn't work, we could always bribe him."

"Bribe him?" Kiana asked.

Skaric shrugged. "Pretend that we can release his soul. That we *would* release his soul."

Kiana's mouth twisted in disgust. "That's a horrible trick to play." *Why did you have to suggest it?*

Skaric looked away from her.

"We'll do what we have to," Nidan said quietly. "Saving Miale is the most important thing… isn't it?"

Kiana nodded reluctantly. "Now. We should go now." *Before I lose my nerve.*

*

Kiana's stomach lurched as everything shifted around her, and darkness enveloped the room. The light from the pathways and vortexes could not penetrate the abyss.

"Stay on the pathways," Skaric said.

Kiana tried to adjust to her new surroundings. A sudden coldness gripped her. Her teeth began to chatter and she slipped her hand from Skaric's to wrap her arms around herself. Nidan offered Kiana his cloak immediately. He draped it around her shoulders and she huddled into it; the cold still bit into her bones.

"This is… odd," Nidan said. He blew onto his hands and rubbed them together; his breath fogged like a cloud.

Kiana clamped her hands under her armpits. *I hate this place.* "We should do what we came here to do." She looked at the prisoner; felt his suffering. "Is it safe to go closer?"

Skaric's expression was doubtful as he shrugged.

"We're alive," Nidan said. "Our bodies will anchor us, remember?" He didn't sound any more confident than Skaric looked.

Kiana rolled her eyes. "There's only one way to find out." She walked past them both with fake confidence that hid her fear.

The twin vortexes tugged enticingly at Kiana. She stopped just to make sure that she could; the pull was no greater than it had been before. Step by step, Kiana edged forward. With every inch, her confidence grew until she was standing beneath the prisoner. She looked up and her heart sank as she saw how far above them he was. Even Skaric wouldn't have been able to touch the captive.

"Hello?"

If the prisoner heard her, he chose not to respond; Kiana wasn't even sure that he could. Like the other souls, he looked like a black void, an empty shape. Was there even anything of his mind left?

"Wait a moment." Skaric stepped in front of her and bowed his head in concentration.

For the first time Kiana became aware of his soul glowing around him. She gasped at the pure brilliance of the white aura and then stared in horror as she saw the ugly tears that marred it. She watched as Skaric's soul flowed out and away from him, forming a new path that led upwards and ended just in front of the prisoner's feet. When Skaric raised his head he looked exhausted and pale. Dark rings surrounded his eyes threatening to swallow their brightness. He extended his hand, inviting Kiana and Nidan onto the path.

Nidan glanced at the path and then at Skaric, a nervous expression played across his face. "How long will it last?"

"Long enough." The lack of confidence in Skaric's voice was unnerving.

"Let's do this as quickly as possible," Kiana said. She proceeded up the path, smiling at Skaric as she passed him. It seemed insane to her that he had ever believed he was useless.

As they approached the end of the narrow path, Skaric expanded it into a platform so they could stand three abreast. They were close enough to touch the prisoner; none of them did. Flanked by her two companions, Kiana looked up and stared at what should have been the prisoner's head. She expected to see darkness. She saw his face.

It was as though she was peering at him through a thick, black veil. His features were there, but they were shadowy. Kiana hadn't expected him to have a kind face. He had short hair that was as dark as Skaric's and was clean-shaven. Kiana twisted her fingers together. He looked nothing like a Wolf. *The war changed the Wolves more than I realised.* The prisoner's eyes were firmly closed, his brow was creased: a silent reaction to the taunting parade of souls beneath him. As Kiana regarded him, she realised that she found him attractive, something she instantly chastised herself for. *He murdered Miale.* Kiana had to remember that as compassion for the prisoner threatened to overwhelm her. Deep within Kiana, Miale's soul stirred with recognition. Kiana's own concerns and compassion were almost deafened by the goddess' fear.

"Hello?" She said.

The prisoner made no response at all.

"Maybe he can't hear you," Nidan said.

Kiana pressed her lips together and extended her hand, carefully reaching through a gap in the white light that trapped him. She placed the palm of her hand against his cheek. Kiana hadn't really expected to touch anything solid, but her fingers touched a very real, excruciatingly cold surface. She resisted the urge to pull her hand away. "Hello?"

Slowly, the prisoner's eyes half opened. The dark depths of his pupils swallowed the light and reflected none of it back. He looked at Kiana without really seeing her. His expression became anguished and he tried to flinch away from her. The prison flared brighter and he groaned in pain.

"Please go." His cracked voice was quietly heart breaking.

A whisper of a gasp escaped Kiana's lips. "You can hear me?"

The muscles beneath his eyes twitched slightly as he struggled to focus on her. "Why are you here? Haven't you punished me enough, Mira?"

Kiana narrowed her eyes in confusion. "Who's...?"

Nidan placed his hand on Kiana's shoulder, silencing her. "Maybe he's referring to Miale's first vessel? The woman he killed? Perhaps you should play along."

Kiana's eyes widened. She moved her hand away from the prisoner's face.

"You share the same soul," Skaric said.

"Please go." The prisoner closed his eyes tightly. "Please go." He repeated the phrase over and over, muttering it quietly to himself.

Kiana's chin trembled. "What's happened to him... it's awful."

Nidan's fingertips brushed her arm. "He murdered Miale. He doesn't deserve your pity."

Kiana flinched away from Nidan's touch as she stared at the prisoner. "He doesn't look like a murderer. He doesn't even look like a Wolf!"

"Nor do I. But it doesn't change what I've done, does it?" Skaric said quietly.

Kiana bowed her head. "But the only one punishing you is

yourself." She breathed in deeply. "This man is being punished by a goddess." She looked at Skaric for confirmation. "He's being kept here by Ysia, isn't he?"

Skaric nodded. His skin was blanched of colour.

Kiana bit down her concern for him. "I haven't come this far to walk away without answers." Tears stung her eyes and threatened to freeze before she had shed them.

She put her hand back on the prisoner's face and embraced the chill that numbed her fingers. Almost instantly, he opened his eyes and stared at her again. It was the same as before: he didn't really seem to look at her at all.

"Please go." His voice was quieter and teetered on desperation. "Please go."

"I'm not Mira." Kiana felt him quiver slightly. "We share the same soul but we're different people." She stroked his cheek gently. "Do you know how long you've been here?"

"Too long." He averted his eyes. "Not long enough."

"Who was Mira?"

The prisoner began to repeat his plea, his eyes closing firmly.

Please don't be so lost that you can't help us. Kiana pressed herself against the bars so that she could put her free hand on the other side of the prisoner's face. He opened his eyes slowly. "Look at me. Can't you see that I'm not Mira?" *Can't you see that I'm alive?*

His eyes searched hers with a dark intensity that made Kiana shiver. She almost let him go, almost stepped back.

"What's your name?" She felt that she had to know.

He laughed bitterly. "Everyone knows."

"I don't."

His face muscles twitched. "Hakon."

"Who was Mira?"

Hakon's expression melted. "My hands killed her." He didn't seem to notice the deep frown that creased Kiana's brow. "I loved her. *He* loved her."

Kiana gazed into his eyes. His words didn't make sense. *Of course not; he's insane.* She needed a way in: something that would push past the madness in his tortured mind. "Tell me about Mira."

Hakon shook his head and then immediately convulsed in pain as the white cage seemed to press in on him.

A lump formed in Kiana's throat. "I'm sorry." *Isn't it enough that he's trapped? Why prevent him from moving at all?* Involuntarily, she recalled Skaric, hogtied and unable to move in Norlea. *This is worse. This is neverending torture.* There was no reason for her to feel any pity for Hakon. Nidan didn't. She wasn't sure how Skaric felt, not any more. Kiana closed her eyes. Miale's fear still writhed within her but she had managed to ignore it. She had to speak with Hakon.

Despite the chilling discomfort that radiated through her hands, Kiana imagined calming thoughts were pouring from her into Hakon.

"Did you live in Orholt?" Asking about Mira hadn't got her anywhere.

"No. First time. It was so… big."

"You didn't live in a city because you were a…" she paused as she remembered what Skaric had told her: before the Wolves there had been different clans. "You were part of the Wolf clan?"

Hakon responded with the slightest nod of his head.

"Why were you in Orholt?"

"To see the king crowned… my mother… head priestess of Ysia. She insisted. I knew…" Hakon's voice trailed off as he trembled again.

"What did you know?" Kiana's calming thoughts snapped back into her mind; her head suddenly thrummed with a deep, aching pain.

"Mira. I didn't want to come. I knew Mira would be there. Miale's chosen."

Kiana breathed out slowly. It was hard to gather her thoughts as she tried to piece together the fragments that tumbled out of Hakon's mouth. She could feel despair pooling around him again.

"If you loved her, why didn't you want to see her?"

He shook his head and his body shivered against the cruel punishment that followed.

Kiana pressed her hands harder against his cheeks as he tried to pull away. "Why didn't you want to see her?"

"Because… mother didn't approve. Train. Must train. Mira distracts. *Must* train."

Kiana felt warmth on her bottom lip as she let a deep breath escape her lungs. It didn't help her think. She knew that she was treading on dangerous ground. Already Hakon's answers were becoming more fragmented again. The very mention of Mira seemed to act like a dagger boring into his mind, destroying any shred of sanity that he had left. She had to think.

"Your mother… you said she was the high priestess of Ysia? When the gods took human vessels… was your mother one?"

Hakon made a small noise in his throat, which Kiana could only assume was agreement with her words.

She pulled away from Hakon, her eyes wide. "That's why everyone blamed Ysia: because her vessel was the mother of Miale's killer!" But that wasn't enough. She still didn't know why. Skaric still didn't know why.

Kiana reached through the bars again and took hold of Hakon's hand. "Please… I need to know why you killed Mira." She kept her voice quiet and soothing.

"My hands killed her." Hakon was shaking violently but his voice held no anger, only the hollowness of despair.

What does that even mean? Kiana felt a hand curl around her shoulder again. The lightness of the touch told her it was Skaric.

"Ask him about the other man," Skaric said.

"What?"

"Don't you remember? He said someone else loved Mira as well."

Kiana frowned. She didn't understand the relevance; she simply had to trust that Skaric had picked up on something she hadn't.

"Who else was in love with Mira?"

Hakon wrenched away from her, screaming as the silver bars constricted around his soul. Kiana's heart exploded with shock. Her entire body jolted, knocking her off balance. Nidan caught her arm, preventing her from tumbling from the pathway.

She grabbed Hakon's hand again. "Why did you kill Miale?"

Hakon squeezed his eyes shut. "Please go."

Kiana growled; she was getting nowhere. "My soul—Mira's

soul—has been trapped just as long as you have. Every lifetime has been the same. We're held captive." She paused long enough to gauge Hakon's reaction, but his expression had become unreadable. He was staring at her; his dark eyes made her shiver. "It's through love. It's to protect Miale. I've spent nearly every day of my life confined to a small set of rooms. I've known there was a world beyond it, but I was never allowed to see any part of it. I wasn't even allowed to look over my own balcony."

Kiana could hear her voice rising in anger; she didn't care; she had to make him see. "In some lifetimes, I was hunted down and murdered. My soul has died countless violent deaths. Because of *you*!" She breathed in and out several times, pressing her nails into her palm to anchor her emotions. "This is the only lifetime that I've tasted freedom. But it's so fleeting. If we can't find a way to save Miale… to fix the damage that *you* caused… then I will just be locked away again in every single lifetime."

Light reflected in his tears.

"If you *ever* loved Mira… if you *ever* cared about her at all… how could you do that to her? How could you sentence her soul to an eternity of imprisonment?" Maybe Nidan was right; maybe Hakon did deserve to be trapped in the Darkness forever. He had stolen Kiana's life a thousand years before she had even been born. "Why? Why did you kill Mira? Why did you kill Miale?"

"My hands killed her!" Hakon glared at her. "What's the point?" His entire body slumped forward and convulsed in pain. His lucid eyes stared at the ground. "Anything I say will be treated as a lie. The truth can't change what's happened to you… or me."

Hakon tried to pull his hand away from Kiana; she held on tightly with both hands to counter the surprising strength of his soul.

"No. You don't get let off that easily. I want to know the truth. All of it! Now!"

Hakon's hand suddenly relaxed and went limp in Kiana's grasp. "I loved her. But so did he." His gaze shifted so that he was staring past her, focusing on nothing but blackness. "She didn't want him. He punished us both. Destroyed us both."

"He killed Mira?"

"My hands killed her."

Kiana shook her head. Why did Hakon keep saying that? Why not just admit that he had killed her. "Tell me about him. What was his name?"

"Lord Grayvon."

Her eyes widened. "One of the ruling lords of Gettryne?" She knew the family name from her lessons with Ducarius. He had made her learn the lineage of each of the twelve ruling lords. The Grayvon family had ruled over Aelbank for centuries. Kiana half closed her eyes and remembered the fresco she had seen in Norlea. "He was one of the men whom the gods were going to choose between. He could have been made king."

"He *wanted* to be king. He *wanted* Mira. He *thought* the two went hand in hand." Bitterness laced Hakon's voice. "He destroyed her."

"Lord Grayvon is responsible for Mira's death? Your hands, his doing?" Kiana was certain that was what Hakon's ramblings meant. "But if there was a chance he could become king, why would he have killed Miale?"

"He was *never* going to be king. The trinity despised him."

"What? Why?"

"Greed. No magic. Made his own. Tore power from the earth. Killed the land." He whimpered softly. "Killed Mira. Killed me."

"He's describing Wolf magic," Nidan said quietly.

"But the Grayvon family was never part of the Wolves," Skaric said.

Kiana glanced over her shoulder at Skaric. His expression was slack, lost, as he gazed into the blackness beyond the pathways. Anguish formed a lump in her throat as she saw the glimmer of tears gathering in his eyes. "Maybe… somehow… they learned it from him? Hakon was aware of it. The trinity was aware of it. Maybe other people were too?" she said.

"No." Hakon's sharp tone sliced through her thoughts. "No one else knew. Mira didn't know. Mother didn't know."

"Then how did you know?"

Hakon laughed but the sound quickly turned into a strangled cry. "He used it to destroy me. To make my hands kill Mira."

Kiana glanced back at Skaric again.

He shook his head, his brow crumpled. "The magic of the nyxii *can't* do that."

Kiana arched her eyebrow. "Can't? How many magical rules have you broken?"

Skaric looked away from her abruptly.

"How do we know any of this is even true?" Nidan said. "For all we know, he's lying."

"What would be the point in lying? What could he possibly gain from that now?" *I know he isn't. I know this is the truth.*

Nidan shrugged and hunched his shoulders.

You don't like the idea that Wolf magic was created by one of your own. You don't like the idea that one of the ruling lords killed Miale. Kiana didn't blame him. If Hakon's words were true, it changed everything. But what if the truth caused even more pain than the lies? Learning the truth about Ysia had caused Skaric too much grief.

Kiana turned her attention back to Hakon. "What happened?"

He began to cry freely. "I didn't want to hurt her. I couldn't stop my hands!"

Kiana wanted to pull him into her embrace as his anguish poured out of him, but the bars forbade her from doing so.

"She smiled at me. She didn't know. I couldn't stop my hands."

Kiana began to sob as well. She wanted to take Hakon's pain away.

"I was glad when they killed me. I was glad I couldn't see the terror on her face."

Kiana's blood froze in her veins at his words.

"They killed him straight away," Skaric said. "No questions." He almost spat the words out.

His anger and Hakon's pain were more than Kiana could bear. A thousand years of war because of one man's lust and greed. Anger bubbled inside her and for the first time, she knew that she truly hated someone. She *hated* Lord Grayvon. It didn't matter that he was dead and gone, that his soul had been reborn more than one hundred times. She hated the memory of him and the thought of him.

"How do we fix it?" They had so many answers yet Kiana didn't feel any closer to saving Miale. "Why didn't Ysia save her?"

"She couldn't," Hakon said miserably. "The mind and soul separate at the gateways. Ysia has no power over the mind. She couldn't put Miale back together again. She needed help. But no one listened. They pointed fingers and blamed her. They turned against her. Because of my hands."

Kiana released Hakon. She placed her fingertips underneath his chin, forcing him to look at her. His eyes glistened with tears and his cheeks were damp. *Are they even real tears?* "Because of Lord Grayvon. It wasn't your fault."

"Tell Ysia that."

Kiana sank to the ground and hugged herself tightly. She was glad when she felt Skaric's arms embrace her, however hesitantly. She sank back against his chest, leaned her head against his shoulder and allowed herself to cry. "We should go," she said. "You need to rest. We've learnt what we can."

"No," Skaric said.

Kiana was surprised by the determination in his voice. "Why not?"

Skaric's shoulders were hunched. "We *have* to free Hakon."

Kiana looked up at him, wide-eyed.

"You were right," Skaric said bitterly. "He doesn't deserve this. I can't leave him like this. Not now we know the truth."

Kiana trembled. Skaric was right: Hakon had to be set free. She couldn't help but feel afraid for Skaric. His soul was already damaged, and setting Hakon free would mean going against Ysia's will. Despite her fears, she said nothing to dissuade him. There was no point; he would try anyway and she loved him for it.

*

I don't know what I'm doing. Clenching his fists Skaric stood, leaving Nidan to comfort Kiana. He glanced down at them. He could send them back to the physical world; they'd be safe there. But what if he didn't have enough energy to get back again? He turned to Hakon. Every moment that he remained a prisoner was a moment too long. Skaric's wrists and ankles burned with the memory of his ordeal in Norlea, overriding the shaking weakness in his legs and the nausea in the pit of his stomach. Hakon's eyes were closed again, his face slack and expressionless.

Skaric studied the silver cage. The bars looked thin and potentially fragile, probably deceptively so. He shrugged; there was only one way to find out. He wrapped his hands around a pair of silver columns. Excruciating cold ran up his fingers, encasing his hands and arms, creeping into his chest, robbing him of his breath. He gasped painfully, trying to draw in enough air to breathe.

"Skaric!" Kiana's voice was full of fear.

Skaric refused to look back at her. Narrowing his eyes, he gritted his teeth and tried to prise the bars apart. It resisted his strength. The cold made Skaric's body so numb he could barely feel it. *I'm not doing this right.* He relaxed his grip, realising it wasn't physical strength that he needed.

Skaric breathed in deeply and then released the air slowly as he channelled the tattered remnants of his soul towards the silver bar. It was stretched thin already and Skaric couldn't risk losing control of the pathway beneath their feet. He imagined his soul wrapping around his hands and tried to pull again, not with his physical strength but with his spiritual strength.

He felt the bars pull apart. Pain tore through his soul. It burned with cold fire. Igoring it, Skaric seized the next pair of rods.

Instantly, Hakon's eyes shot open. His spectral hands sought the gap and closed over Skaric's hands. Soothing warmth flowed into Skaric's soul, fending off the chill.

"Stop."

Skaric's eyes grew wide as he stood motionless, staring. Somehow Hakon's voice acted like a barrier to Skaric's own will. He could feel the connection like an itch he couldn't scratch. His head began to pound fiercely. "I have to free you."

Hakon's blank expression crumpled into one of confusion. "My hands killed Miale."

Skaric focused on the cage. Even with Hakon's hands covering his, he tried to pull the bar apart. Again it began to give; again he felt unbearable pain. Skaric ground his teeth together so hard that his jaw ached; at least he wasn't screaming.

"If your soul is destroyed you... will... die."

Skaric let go of the white bar as though it had just turned into a live snake in his hands. Behind him, Kiana whimpered fearfully.

"What good will you be to her if you're dead?"

Her? Did Hakon mean Miale? Skaric followed Hakon's gaze and saw that he was staring directly at Kiana. She was crying, her eyes wide and imploring.

"She said you want to restore Miale."

Skaric nodded slowly.

"You need to make Miale's soul and mind one."

Skaric frowned. "But her soul is linked to Kiana's." He looked down. Azure scars ran through his soul, making it look even more ragged than before. His hands were tinged blue and covered in frost. *If I'm not strong enough to break these bars, how will I be strong enough to separate their souls?*

You won't be. You will die.

Skaric looked up and met Hakon's dark gaze, unsure if he had really heard the prisoner's voice in his mind. He was sure that Hakon hadn't spoken out loud. For a man that had seemed gripped by madness, he now looked and sounded entirely sane. Skaric didn't want to listen to Hakon's words; he didn't want to believe that they had already failed because of his weaknesses.

"Your soul can be restored," Hakon said.

An unspoken question hung in Skaric's mind as he narrowed his eyes. Feeling was beginning to creep back into his limbs as the warming comfort of Hakon's soul radiated against his own.

"I can heal your soul with mine."

"What will happen to you?" Kiana asked.

Hakon smiled sadly.

Skaric breathed in sharply. "I want to free you… not destroy you!"

"I'm already dead."

Skaric shook his head. It didn't matter. Hakon deserved to be freed. He deserved to have his soul reborn and… "What about your mind? Will that be destroyed too?"

"No," Hakon said. "It will go to eternity."

Skaric gazed at the golden whirlpool. Eternity sounded much more comforting than the Darkness.

You need to know that your soul holds your emotions. Hakon's words echoed through Skaric's mind. His eyebrows shuddered as a creaseline ran down the centre of his forehead.

Skaric looked into Hakon's eyes. They were filled with so much pain and remorse that it made his heart ache. But there was also a thin sliver of hope sparkling in the dark depths: the promise of absolution. *That's not enough.*

"My mind will be freed. You will free Mira's soul. Together you will restore Miale. That is enough."

Was it? Skaric wasn't so sure. Despite that he nodded. "What do I need to do?"

A faint smile crossed Hakon's lips. "Brace yourself."

Skaric barely had time to comprehend what Hakon had said, let alone do what he had been told. Hakon's soul began to meld into his own. Skaric couldn't think or breathe. He felt Hakon's pain as the silver cage tried to keep him imprisoned. It constricted around his soul and bit into it. Skaric placed his hands around the closest bar and pulled with all his might: physical, emotional, spiritual. He put all the strength, energy and hope he had left into the task. The bar turned to ice in his hands and shattered. Silver shards sprayed into the darkness, slicing painfully through Skaric's soul before they vanished.

Hakon's spectral form stepped forward into Skaric. Unable to move, Skaric's entire body became limp and lifeless. Strength flooded back into his soul. Time seemed to slow down. He fell backwards agonizingly slowly. Each heartbeat lasted a lifetime. A white bird materialised. It stared at him with Hakon's dark and intense eyes. Then it turned and flew into the golden vortex's embrace.

Skaric's heartbeat quickened. He fell. The warmth of flagstones crashed against his back. *Kiana! Nidan!*

*

"Skaric? What happened?" Kiana's voice was urgent and right beside Skaric.

Thank Ysia.

Kiana and Nidan were both looking down at him, standing in the physical world. Skaric couldn't tear his gaze away from Kiana and the brilliant intensity of her soul. It was so achingly beautiful.

He felt heat rise to his cheeks as he was drawn into her amber gaze. Skaric covered his face with his forearms and clenched his hands together. A moment later he heard the soft scrape of Kiana's slippers on the ground and the rustle of her clothes. Her hand alighted softly on his arm, making Skaric's entire body ache with longing.

"Are you all right?" Kiana said.

Skaric managed to nod without exposing his face.

"Hakon…?"

"He's gone." Skaric cleared his throat, unable to trust himself to continue speaking. Even though he couldn't see his companions he could feel their gaze upon him.

"What Hakon did…" Kiana said. "His sacrifice…"

Thanks to Hakon, Skaric's soul felt strong but his body still felt weak.

Kiana began to stroke his arm. Skaric shivered beneath her touch. He wanted to embrace her and kiss her. *What's happening to me?* He managed to swallow back a groan as he clicked a puzzle piece into place in his mind. *The soul holds your emotions.* Hakon had warned him, but he'd been too drained to realise it at the time. *Has his soul amplified my emotions? Or am I feeling his… for Mira?*

"Are you all right?" Kiana said.

Skaric nodded again, refusing to move his arms from his face. His cheeks felt far hotter than before. Every gentle stroke of her finger sent fresh shivers through his body. "I just need to sleep."

"Sleep sounds like a good idea," Nidan said.

Kiana moved her hand from Skaric's arm. She said nothing more. Skaric listened as Kiana moved a short distance away and settled down. *Come back.* He clenched his fists tighter. He would not act on emotions that probably weren't even his own. Skaric closed his eyes and focused on the things he knew to be true: he had freed Hakon and, by restoring Miale, they would redeem him. That *had* to be enough.

Chapter Twenty-Three

Lying beneath a mountain of stone, Berend felt like a dozen horses had trampled him. His left arm was pinned between two blocks; the back of his head was damp and sticky; crushing pain in his chest made breathing painful, and dust filled his nose and lungs. But he was alive.

At first Berend's vision had been too hazy for him to figure out why. As the dizziness faded his anger rose. Rubble had prevented the wall from crushing him, leaving him trapped in a small space. His life had been saved by fate. Through gaps, he could see that it was becoming dark. Berend knew he had to act quickly; it would be madness to try to shift the rock if he couldn't see and he wasn't prepared to wait until morning to free himself and hunt down his prey.

He began with the block that was trapping his arm. Berend gritted his teeth against the excrutiating pain that tore through the limb and into his shoulder, as he twisted awkwardly to push the heavy block.

How had Skaric escaped? Berend could clearly picture the black nightmare that Skaric had briefly plunged him into. It was no magic that he had ever seen before, but he was sure of one thing: it *wasn't* Ysia's magic. Ysia was dead. Skaric was a liar. Skaric was a coward and a traitor and he was somewhere inside the castle, probably laughing and gloating about his victory with the Miale bitch and her Guardian.

Berend cried out as the block finally moved. There was a sickening grating sound and then a loud crack as it fell to the ground. He pulled his left arm to his side, but it was limp and useless: his fingers were bloody, bent awkwardly and would not move; his sleeve was blood soaked and tattered; large gashes ran up his forearm and Berend could clearly see the white of bone in more than one place. Wrath and adrenaline numbed the pain. The injury didn't matter. Berend didn't need the use of his off hand to defeat Skaric or the Guardian.

What had Skaric hoped to gain by claiming he was using Ysia's magic? Mercy?

Berend pulled his shirt over his head. The clumsy action sent a jolt of piercing pain through his broken arm. It was a hard task in the confined space, but he managed nonetheless. With the use of his right hand and teeth, Berend managed to fashion a crude sling, which he slipped around his neck and pushed his broken arm into. Supporting the limb did nothing to ease the pain that coursed through it: sharp and dull at the same time. He ignored it.

He would never grant Skaric mercy.

Berend shuffled onto his knees and hunched over awkwardly, giving himself more leverage. He chose his next stone and began to push against it with his good shoulder. Slowly, it began to move.

How much glory would he receive when he returned home after destroying Miale on his own? With Skaric dead, no one would be able to deny his claim to become the Alpha, even if Adalric's blood didn't run in his veins.

Sweat beaded on Berend's skin and globs of spittle soaked his beard. He vocalised his struggle with the rock in a low grunting sound. It helped.

When Berend returned to the Wolf encampment, triumphant, he would be hailed as the greatest Wolf warrior of all time. Even Adalric would have to welcome him with open arms.

The stone tumbled to the ground. Berend was pitched forward, his chest heaving painfully as he breathed in fresh air. The breeze brushed sharply against Berend's face. He was almost free.

He spied an open doorway. *They've made it so easy for me. Fools.* His gaze drifted from the doorway to the rest of the castle that rose above him, dark against the blood red sky. Berend smiled. It was a fitting colour. Soon he would bathe the castle in the blood of his enemies.

Chapter Twenty-Four

Skaric jolted awake, disoriented. It took him a moment to register the source of the flames that seemed to hover in front of his eyes. When he was finally able to focus, Skaric found himself staring up at Vali. The nyxus was motionless, his expression unreadable as a small ball of flames danced in his blistered palm.

"Kiana? Nidan?" Skaric glanced around the room, his chest constricting painfully.

"They're fine," Vali said. "I'm not here for *them*."

Vali was telling the truth. Nidan and Kiana were just beginning to stir. As soon as his eyes flickered open, Nidan drew his sword and jumped to his feet. The fire in Vali's palm died, casting them in deep shadows.

Skaric held out his hand to Nidan and shook his head. When he was satisfied that Nidan was grudgingly holding back, Skaric looked back to Vali. "We thought Berend was alone."

Vali smiled icily. "Berend *was* alone. And apparently, now he's dead."

"What do you want?" Nidan said through clenched teeth. His sword hand was shaking with held back rage. "I won't let you harm *either* of my companions."

Vali smirked. "Whilst I would love to be the one to kill Miale, I'm here to take Skaric home."

Skaric drew his eyebrows together into a frown. "Take me home? My father wants me dead."

"If he does, he wants to kill you himself."

Skaric shuddered and then shook his head. It didn't make sense.

"After the tower… after I recovered… he sent Berend to kill me."

Vali laughed drily. "No, he didn't." His gaze searched Skaric's face. "Is that why you left?"

Skaric felt sick. He fixed his gaze on the ground. "Yes."

"Then it's little wonder that Berend was so desperate to kill you. Luckily for you, I take my orders from your father. He wants you home."

Skaric clenched his teeth and looked up to meet Vali's cold stare. "I won't let you take me back. Vali… look around you… can't you see that we've all been lied to?"

Vali didn't look but did narrow his eyes, focusing on nothing but Skaric. "Berend lied to you. But it doesn't matter. You're still a traitor, Skaric."

Skaric shivered at the hissing venom in Vali's voice.

"Did you decide to betray us before or after Berend drove you away?"

Skaric bit his lip and glanced at Kiana; her eyes were wide as she stared at him. "Does it matter?"

"Probably not." Vali shrugged. "But *I* want to know and I'm sure your father does too."

Skaric sighed. "After." He risked looking at Kiana. The hurt in her eyes robbed him of breath. Maybe he should have lied.

"Then you're an idiot, aren't you?" Vali said. "By the Darkness, Skaric, your father didn't punish your cowardice at Blackoak Tower. He would have believed you over Berend. Whatever the quarrel was between you two, your father would have taken your side." Vali shifted his gaze to Kiana. "He still might, if you return with her."

Trembling, Skaric clenched his fist. "That isn't going to happen, Vali. I'm *not* going back."

From the corner of his eyes Skaric saw Kiana take a hesitant step closer.

"Skaric… who is your father?"

Vali laughed out loud. "You haven't told them? Coward… traitor… liar." He looked round at Kiana. "You don't keep good company, do you Miale?"

"Her name is Kiana," Nidan said.

Vali waved his hand nonchalantly. "Skaric is the *only* son of the Alpha of the Wolves."

Skaric winced as he heard his companions gasp. He couldn't bring himself to look at them. "Why weren't you with Berend?" He knew his question sounded like an avoidance of the subject but didn't care.

"You're the future leader of the Wolves?" Kiana asked.

Skaric clenched his teeth. "*Was.* Vali, why weren't you with Berend?"

Vali shrugged. "I didn't want to wait around until he killed me. Are you going to come back with me willingly or do I need to use force?" Skaric began to shake his head. Vali carried on. "Unlike you, I'm capable of using my magic. We both know that I could kill those two before the Guardian gets anywhere near me. So… it's your choice. I'll spare their lives if you come back with me."

"I'd like to see you try." Nidan's voice was a low growl. His entire body was tense, ready to close the distance and strike the nyxus down.

"Are you blind?" Kiana asked. "Can't you see what's around you? Can't you see why we're here?"

Vali still didn't look.

He knows the pathways are there but won't acknowledge what it means.
"We've all been lied to." Skaric spoke slowly. "Ysia is still alive. She wants Miale to be restored… not killed repeatedly."

Vali's jaw trembled as he clenched his teeth. "Liar."

Skaric got to his feet and tried to put a hand on Vali's shoulder. The nyxus flinched away. "What good would lying do me, Vali?"

"You shouldn't have run," Vali said.

Skaric shrugged. "Maybe not. But I did and I don't regret it." He caught Kiana's stare as he spoke; her smile stirred up warmth in the pit of his stomach. "Let us do want Ysia wants us to… let us restore Miale… then I'll come back with you."

"Skaric!" Kiana shook her head fiercely.

He ignored her and searched Vali's face for a hint of what the nyxus was thinking.

"Let you restore our mortal enemy…" Vali said slowly.

"It's not like that… Miale was *never* our enemy." Skaric wiped his hands over his face. He didn't know how to make Vali understand.

Vali looked away from Skaric and gazed around the room. He gestured towards the mirage of the pathways, ghostly souls and the vortexes. "What is all this?"

"The gateway to death. Ysia's realm."

Vali peered at Skaric. "You can *prove* that Ysia isn't dead?"

Skaric nodded hesitantly. "I can take you to the pathways."

Vali's expression became instantly distrusting. "How?"

"I can channel Ysia's magic."

"You're a nyxus."

Skaric shook his head. "Not anymore."

Vali ran his hand through his beard thoughtfully. "This is insane."

"I know." Skaric tried to touch Vali's shoulder a second time, but the nyxus stepped back. Skaric's face became taut with tension as he stared solemnly at Vali. It was too recently that he had been the same, shying away from the slightest touch. *I don't ever want to be like that again.*

"If I let you restore Miale… I'd be a traitor, too."

"It's what Ysia wants." Kiana said.

Vali snapped his head round to stare at her. "Is it? How do I know that?" He looked back to Skaric. "What I do know is that our people want Miale dead."

Skaric chewed his lower lip. "And yet you said you'd let Kiana live, *if* I went with you…"

Vali shook his head and turned away.

"Maybe he was bluffing," Nidan said. "I should end this charade now."

Skaric held his hand out again. "Vali is my friend!"

"Was." Vali swung round again. "You gave up that right when you betrayed us."

"We're going round in circles," Nidan said, moving closer to Vali; the nyxus turned to look at him. "Surrender and I'll let you live. Carry on threatening Kiana or Skaric and I'll kill you. I don't care how powerful you *think* you are, I'm pretty sure I can kill you first."

Taking advantage of the diversion, Skaric put his hand on Vali's shoulder and willed them both into the pathways. The now familiar lurching feeling came and went. Bitter coldness seeped into Skaric's limbs. In the physical world, he could see the shrouded forms of Kiana and Nidan shouting at him, but he couldn't hear them and didn't want to.

He stared at Vali. "*Now* do you believe me?"

Vali was visibly shaking as he stared around. A soul brushed past him and he yelped. Skaric caught hold of Vali before his friend fell from the pathway. Skaric gaped at Vali; he had never seen his friend show any trace of fear before.

"I'll give you two choices," Skaric said in a dangerous tone. "Let me restore Miale, and I swear I'll go with you to my father. I'll accept whatever punishment he chooses, even if that means my death."

Slowly Vali turned his head to stare at Skaric. His cold stare had turned fearful. "Or?"

"I'll leave you here." Skaric hoped that his voice sounded determined enough. He doubted he could actually go through with his threat. "Forever."

Vali dropped to his knees. "This is insane." He buried his face in his hands.

Skaric crouched down. "I know. But I'll have time to explain it all to you on the journey home… if you'll let me."

"Let you…" Vali lowered his hands. The colour drained from his face as his pupils narrowed to pinpricks.

"I know it's a lot to take in…" Skaric's voice trailed off as Vali shook his head.

"This is a trick… it has to be… How can everything we've ever known be a lie?"

Skaric couldn't answer him no matter how much he wanted to.

"That glow around you…"

Skaric looked down at his hands. The brilliance of his soul was almost blinding in the darkness thanks to Hakon. Strangely the silver light in the centre of his chest burned even more fiercely than before. "My soul."

Trembling, Vali nodded slowly. "Make me your prisoner."

Skaric drew in a sharp breath. "What?"

"I can't *let* you restore Miale."

Skaric stared dumbly at his friend.

Vali stood, breathing heavily. He raised his hand. "Take me prisoner so you can restore Miale, or stand there like an idiot and let me kill you."

Skaric grimaced and took hold of Vali. "When we're finished, I'll keep my word. I'll come back with you." He didn't wait for Vali to react before willing them both out of the pathways.

Immediately, Nidan was standing behind Vali, his sword tip at the back of the nyxus' neck.

"Tie his hands so he can't target his magic." Skaric was aware of how weary his voice sounded. He watched in dismay as Vali allowed himself to be bound. Skaric looked away. Perhaps there really was no hope for the Wolves.

Chapter Twenty-Five

It was dark when Kiana woke. The silver pathways leant the hall an eerie half-light. Kiana presumed that Nidan hadn't slept. He was standing, leaning against the wall so that he could see out of the double doors and watch Vali at the same time; he was obviously expecting trouble. Not long before Nidan had watched Skaric with the same distrustful stare. Kiana raised an eyebrow as he glanced over in her direction.

Nidan smiled. "Old habits."

Kiana wrapped his cloak around her shoulders as she stood. She was cold, tired and so hungry her stomach ached. On top of that Vali's presence was making her nervous. She didn't care that his hands were tied: he was still a threat; he was still her enemy. Her body shuddered at the memory of hiding from the Wolves; she could clearly recall the fear clinging to her like a death shroud because of fanatical men like Vali.

Kiana looked at the mage. He was staring at the pathways, his eyes haunted and his expression torn between acceptance and denial. *Skaric looked like that once.* The skin beneath Vali's eyes was dark; it was obvious he hadn't slept. Kiana's gaze dipped to his bound hands. She shivered and forced herself to raise her gaze again, meeting Vali's. There was a malevolent darkness nesting in his eyes that had never been present in Skaric's. Vali had the potential to be dangerous. Kiana didn't trust him or like him.

She began to play with the edge of the cloak, picking at a thread of wool that had worked loose.

"Careful or you'll unravel the whole cloak." Nidan said.

Kiana forced herself to smile before pivoting on her heels to stare at Miale's mind. The golden bird stared at her mournfully from the pathways. "I just want to get this over and done with." Kiana felt colder even though the temperature hadn't changed. She glanced sidelong at Vali, wondering if it was safe to talk freely in front of him. *I have no choice.* "What will happen to me, Nidan?" She didn't look at him; his silence made her shiver. "Miale's soul and mind *have* to be joined… what if I'm dragged into her?" Kiana breathed in, embracing the icy air that filled her lungs, and turned to face Nidan. His lips were taut and drained of colour; he dipped his head so that he was only half looking at her. "I'll die, won't I?"

"No." Skaric's voice was full of determination; Kiana hadn't even realised that he was awake. "I'll separate Miale's soul from yours. That's why Hakon sacrificed his soul." Skaric stood, his expression awkward and his gaze dipped.

Why won't you look at me?

Skaric's chest shuddered as he inhaled deeply. "But we have to make Miale whole *first.*"

Nidan pushed himself away from the wall, shaking his head. "Didn't you hear what Kiana just said, Skaric? If you make Miale whole first she could be absorbed into the goddess."

Kiana's sharp breaths sounded loud in the silence of the vast hall. The souls of the dead stomped past her. Thoughts of joining them flooded into her mind. She clenched her hands. She didn't want Skaric to be right, but he was. "Miale's soul *has* to be joined to her mind first. If not, it will be swept away into the gateway and be lost forever."

Nidan crossed the distance between them and placed his hands on her shoulders. "It's too dangerous, Kiana."

She met Nidan's frightened stare. "It's the only way. I won't let myself get lost. I have too much to hold on for." *I hope.* She glanced past him at Skaric.

Skaric kicked at the dusty floor and turned away. Pressure formed behind Kiana's eyes in response to Skaric's seemingly nonchalant reaction.

Nidan stared at her thoughtfully. "I'm going to… check the castle and make sure we're alone." He turned to Skaric. "Can you keep an eye on *him*?" Nidan jerked his thumb towards Vali.

Skaric looked at Vali for the first time that Kiana had noticed. "He's not a threat. We have an agreement."

If Vali wanted us all dead, then we would be. She narrowed her eyes as realisation gripped her. *You've agreed to go back with him, to die. I won't let that happen.* She frowned at Nidan. "Berend is dead. The Guardians have no idea where we went…"

"The mage found us. Maybe there are more Wolves out there. Besides: old habits!" Nidan winked at her and mouthed, "Tell him." Then he tapped the underside of her chin. "Don't do anything until I get back. All right?"

Kiana nodded and watched him leave the hall. She wasn't sure how Nidan expected her to say anything private to Skaric when Vali was in the room watching their every move. She hated the way he stared at her as though he were sizing her up, wondering how to kill her. Her mouth downturned with the awareness that she was not scared of him. Too many people had wanted her dead for too long. She had spent too much of her life living in fear to let Vali's presence trap her in fear.

Turning her back on the mage, Kiana tried to ignore Vali as she took a faltering step towards Skaric. "Skaric?"

He was still refusing to look at her. "I won't let you down."

She smiled. "I know you won't."

Skaric looked at her from the corner of his eyes. "You need to free Miale's mind." A flush of pink stained his cheeks.

"I know."

He nodded and looked away again.

Kiana took another step forward. "Skaric… I…" Her palms felt foolishly clammy. "Skaric…"

Skaric stepped past her. "I need to talk to Vali."

Disappointment flushed Kiana's cheeks. She wanted to say something to stop Skaric walking away from her; instead, she clamped her mouth shut and said nothing.

She watched as Skaric walked over to Vali and pulled the mage to his feet.

"Have you had time to think?" Skaric said. "Have you had time to realise we're telling the truth about Ysia and Miale?"

Kiana could tell by Skaric's tone that he desperately wanted Vali to believe him. She wondered how close they had been. The mage did not reply. Both men stared at one another—an impasse that neither seemed to want to break. Eventually Skaric turned away. The dismal expression on his face made a lump form in Kiana's throat. Suddenly, she understood: Skaric *needed* Vali's forgiveness.

The sound of footsteps pounding on the flagstones forced Kiana to tear her attention away from Skaric.

Nidan skidded to a halt, turned and slammed the massive doors shut. His chest heaved as he pressed his back against them, bracing his legs. "There's no bar."

A tremor of foreboding rippled through Kiana. "Nidan, what's wrong?"

"Berend! He's alive and he's coming!"

Skaric was instantly alert and visibly trembling.

Vali's eyes had also widened. He held his hands out. "Untie me."

"You must be mad," Nidan said.

The Wolf's lips pressed together into a thin line. "I can help you." His tone was blunt yet insistent.

Nidan shook his head. "You want us dead."

"I want Skaric alive at any cost." Vali's mouth quirked up into a malicious smile. "Even if that means killing the war leader."

There was no more time to argue or act. The double doors crashed open, smashing into the unyielding stone walls. Nidan was catapulted forwards into the room. His sword clattered to the floor.

Berend was far larger than Kiana remembered. The war leader's face contorted with rage. His teeth were barred; his skin was flushed red; the muscles in his neck were rigid and veins pulsed visibly beside his eyes. His right hand was curled around a sword that was longer and wider than Nidan's. His left hand was cradled in a bloody sling. Anger boiled in his eyes. He stretched open his mouth and howled with rage. Dread turned Kiana's skin cold. Berend truly was fanatically insane.

Vali positioned himself between Berend and Skaric; fire sprang to life at his fingertips. Awkwardly, he motioned with his bound hands, flinging the spell forward. If it was meant to hit Berend it failed. Instead the fire struck the stone floor, sizzling into nothingness.

"Skaric, get Kiana into the pathways!" Nidan didn't take his eyes off Berend. He tried to right himself but the war leader kicked him back down to the ground.

Kiana hesitated. She couldn't leave Nidan to face Berend alone.

"Go!" The anxiety in Nidan's voice spurred Kiana into action. There was nothing she could do to help him. She ran to Skaric, who seemed rooted to the spot. Berend marched into the room. Fire danced at Vali's fingertips a second time, and fresh blisters opened up on his skin. The mage began to throw the spell forward. Berend was faster. He closed the gap, raised his sword and struck. Vali's flames died instantly. His arms fell limply. Berend's sword burst through his chest. Kiana screamed. The war leader pulled his sword free.

Everything shifted.

Chapter Twenty-Six

Nidan was alone with Berend. He snatched his sword up and scrambled to his feet. The war leader stormed past him. Berend raised his sword and swung it towards Skaric. Kiana's oddly distant scream echoed through the hall. The blow should have cut right through Skaric. It *should* have killed him, except he wasn't physically there.

"What magic is this? You can't hide from me forever, traitor!"

"It's Ysia's magic." Nidan hoped his voice had sounded calm.

Berend swung round to face him. "Liar!"

Nidan let out a bitter laugh. "Look around you." He gestured towards the painfully obvious echoes of the pathways. "If you're too blind to see that Ysia isn't dead, then you're an idiot."

Berend screamed and lunged at Nidan. Nidan barely ducked the blow. He almost fell but managed to spin away to the side. Berend was blind with fury; it would be Nidan's only advantage. He tightened his grip on the hilt, gritted his teeth and lunged. His sword slashed through the air. It screeched to a halt as it impacted against Berend's blade. Nidan ignored the ache in his arm. He rotated the blade away from Berend's sword, swept it around and sliced again. Berend blocked, stepped in and used the full force of his body to knock Nidan off balance. Nidan hopped into a stagger. His knee cracked as Berend's foot slammed into it. He saw a flash of steel before his eyes, slicing him from shoulder to waist. White-hot pain was carved across Nidan's chest. He screamed. His body slammed into the hard flagstones. Berend's mocking laughter reverberated through his mind. Throbbing darkness obscured his vision, robbing him of his senses as he slowly slipped into oblivion.

*

Skaric heard the distant clang of steel on steel; it was like listening through muddy water. Kiana clung to his arm, trembling so hard it made his own body quiver; at least that's what he wanted to believe. Her face was ashen as she stared at Nidan. Skaric couldn't look at the fighting or spare the time to consider a clumsy attempt at comforting Kiana. Gently, he pulled away from her grip and knelt down on the ice-cold pathway.

Vali was barely breathing. Blood oozed from his wound. Although it dripped onto the pathways, it didn't pool there. Skaric's shoulders shook as he clumsily untied Vali's hands; he would not let his friend die a prisoner.

"Is… this… what… Ysia… really… wants?" Vali said.

Skaric nodded. "I think so."

Kiana crouched down, her hands loosely clenched. "Yes. It is what she wants."

"Why?" Skaric hated that his voice was reduced to a strangled whisper. "Why did you defend me?"

Vali smiled weakly. "Told… you. I… take… *my*… orders… from… Adalric." He placed his hand over Skaric's. "Go… home."

"To die?" Kiana said. Her cheeks reddened.

Vali's smile faded. "Maybe… maybe not." His hand dropped to the ground. "He… would have… believed you." His body shuddered and then became deathly still.

Skaric felt numb as the light of Vali's soul pulled away from his body. For a moment, the nyxus' soul lingered in front of them, staring at Skaric. Then it was tugged away by the inevitable pull of the vortex.

Skaric brushed his forearm across his eyes and then pushed Vali off the pathway. Emptiness gnawed at his gut as Vali's body was swallowed up by the void. *This isn't the time to grieve.*

Skaric stood up. "What now?" He sniffed back tears.

Kiana turned her back on him to stare at the silver birdcage that held Miale's mind. "I'll invite Miale in." It sounded so easy.

Skaric placed his hand lightly on her shoulder. "Nidan was right… Miale's mind will be strong. You might…" He inhaled slowly. "Kiana, *I* might lose you." He blinked hard.

Kiana span round, her eyes suddenly alive with light.

Skaric took hold of her upper arms. "I don't want to lose you." It was the truth. Simply, obviously, the truth. His chest tightened.

"We have to do this, Skaric." Kiana's voice was barely audible.

"I know." Skaric leant his forehead against hers and closed his eyes. "Just promise me you'll hold on."

Kiana touched her fingertips to his lips. "I promise." She turned away from Skaric. She was visibly shaking as she stepped towards the birdcage.

The bird looked at her with eyes that held a millennium of sadness. Kiana stepped forward and placed her fingers on the delicate latch. For a moment she hesitated and glanced back at Skaric. He sank his teeth into his lower lip and nodded. With a single movement, Kiana flicked the latch, allowing the door to swing open. She held her hand out. The bird hopped onto it, her wings beating powerfully against the pull of the golden vortex. Pinpricks of blood welled up where the bird's desperate claws pierced her hand. Skaric stepped forward.

"Stay back." The authority in Kiana's tone halted Skaric. He watched helplessly as Kiana drew the bird to her breast and embraced it. It fought against her, claws and beak tearing at her in a frightened frenzy. "Join with your soul."

Skaric was almost blinded as the light of Miale's soul intensified tenfold. Instinctively he covered his eyes with his arms and flinched away from the light. Kiana's body crumpled and fell. Skaric caught her, holding her in his arms as he dropped to his knees. She looked lifeless and her expression was serenely blank. Skaric blinked back tears and then bent his head so that his lips brushed her ear. "*Fight!* You promised me you'd hold on. So *fight!*"

He'd turned his back on his father. He'd lost Vali. Nidan would probably be killed. He *wasn't* going to lose Kiana too.

He forced his gaze away from Kiana's face so that he could look at the double aura that surrounded her. Her soul seemed so much weaker than before, or perhaps Miale's looked much stronger. *That's a good thing.* Skaric wasn't sure he believed it.

Light erupted into existence above Skaric's head. Blinking, he looked up. In the darkness far above him a silver ring rotated, bathing him in its light. Within it, he could see a spiral of green that rotated in the opposite direction.

The gods were watching, waiting for their sister to return to them.

Tears flooded Skaric's eyes, but his awakened emotions felt as though they were curling up and dying inside him.

Gritting his teeth, Skaric forced his hands between Kiana and Miale's souls. Instantly he felt the bitter cold that gripped them and the strength of Miale's soul corroding his own. Self-preservation screamed at Skaric to pull his hands away. *I can't. Not now.* They had come too far for him to give into cowardice. Skaric ground his teeth together even harder and began to prise the souls apart.

Pain wracked Skaric's body. He didn't stop. He couldn't. Cold sweat covered him, making his clothes cling to his body and his hair stick to his forehead. He was trembling all over. Worse still, Kiana's face showed no sign of life. If it weren't for the shallow rise and fall of her breast, Skaric would have sworn she was dead.

He paused and pulled his hands clear of Miale's soul. Almost free, it fluttered in the darkness like a golden flag blown in an invisible breeze. But it wasn't blowing towards the whirlpool; it was blowing upwards towards Ysia and Pios. *She's whole. Kiana did it.*

All Skaric had to do was finish freeing Miale's soul.

He hesitated. He felt weak. His bones were chilled and he could barely move. It seemed unimportant as he gazed at Kiana's lifeless face.

"I can't have done all this for nothing, Kiana. You *have to fight.*"

Skaric gripped hold of Miale's soul at the last point that joined it to Kiana's. He couldn't let her down. He drew in a deep breath and allowed himself to cry out in pain as he continued to wrench the two souls apart. *Fight, Kiana! Please!*

Pain ripped through him as he tore Miale's soul free. He collapsed over Kiana's body, unable to do anything except tremble and cry as he watched Miale's soul fly upwards. His mind told him the sight was beautiful and that he should rejoice, but he was numb to it. With effort, he raised his hand and stroked Kiana's forehead. "Please fight." Sobbing, he clutched Kiana's body in his arms.

*

"Kiana!"

The warmth of a bed enveloped Kiana's body, pulling her into the embrace of the soft down mattress. She didn't open her eyes. She was deathly tired, and whoever was trying to wake her up could wait.

"Kiana!"

She felt a hand shaking her by the shoulders. Kiana opened her eyelids a tiny crack to see the man who was bothering her. Marcas laughed and batted the pillow away as she tossed it at him half-heartedly.

"Can't you see I'm sleeping?"

"Not any more!" Marcas took hold of Kiana's hand and tugged her upright. "Come on, you have to see the sunrise! It's so beautiful this morning."

She frowned at him and then glanced around her room. It was bathed in brilliant golden light. Other than Marcas, she was alone. Where was Erynn? She allowed Marcas to pull her out of bed. Kiana swung her feet onto the floor; she wiggled her toes against the warm flagstones. She was only wearing a simple white night-dress, but she felt no embarrassment.

The tower was completely silent. Kiana frowned, wondering why she couldn't hear the distant sound of her Guardians training or the chatter of the men standing on her balcony.

Marcas led her into her parlour. A fire blazed in the hearth, il-luminating the banner of the cup of knowledge that hung above. The flickering flames highlighted the pure gold in the thread, making the cup appear more dazzling than Kiana had ever seen it.

The doors to the balcony were wide open, allowing a pleasant breeze to coil into the room. It whispered around Kiana, playing with her hair, tugging her outside and when she looked she had to raise her hand to shield her eyes. She could see nothing but the intense golden glow of the sunrise.

"Come on!" Marcas tugged her towards the balcony. His hand felt cold.

Kiana resisted his touch.

"What's the matter, Kia?"

A frown puckered Kiana's brow as she tilted her head to the side and looked outside. "I'm not allowed."

"You can't miss this, Kia! It's amazing. The most beautiful thing I've ever seen." Marcas grinned at her and winked. "Except you, of course."

Kiana should have blushed at his comment but didn't. She didn't even feel the urge to smile. *Something is wrong.*

Fight, Kiana! Please!

Kiana glanced around, but there was no one else in the room.

"Come on, Kia."

Kiana staggered backwards, staring at Marcas with wide eyes. "You're dead!"

Her Guardian's smile faded as he stared at her sadly.

If I go with you, I'll die too! Memories flooded back into Kiana's mind. She collapsed to the floor as she drowned in the tide of joy and pain, laughter and sadness, safety and fear. The warm embrace of eternity shone even brighter. It would all stop if she went with Marcas. All the pain Kiana had felt and the tears she had shed would fade into obscurity. *No.*

She got to her feet slowly, turned her back on Marcas and walked towards the door that led out of her chambers. It was a door that had always been locked: the door that had marked the boundary of her small world. Kiana expected Marcas to stop her, but when she glanced back he was gone. She breathed in deeply and placed her hand on the handle. It turned easily and the door swung open, revealing nothing but empty blackness.

Fear coiled in the pit of Kiana's stomach as she stepped through the door.

*

Nidan desperately wanted to move, but pain shackled him to the cold stone floor and his life force was ebbing away from him. Berend paced back and forth like a starved beast whilst he waited for Skaric and Kiana to step back into the physical world.

"Come back here, coward!" Berend's voice tore through the silence, but if Skaric heard, he made no effort to respond. "I will kill you! No matter how long you hide for, traitor! I will kill you both."

Nidan struggled to breathe. Why couldn't Berend understand that Ysia was still alive? Why couldn't he let go of his hatred and let Skaric and Kiana live?

Above Nidan, a faint light reflected on the ceiling, bathing him in its radiance. A silver ring and a green glow spiralled around one another as the golden spark of Miale's soul rose up to meet them. Berend looked up too, and for a moment, his sword hand shook.

They did it.

Nidan gritted his teeth together. Was he really just going to let death take him? He closed his eyes tightly and concentrated. He balled the agony that gripped him tightly so that he could seal it away into the imaginary wooden box. There was a design carved into the lid: the combined symbol of the trinity of gods.

Pios' power flowed through Nidan instantly. His wounds were close to killing him, but he took Pios' power and used it to repair the hideous damage. Pain burned in his body as the warm magic tickled its way around his injuries, repairing arteries and knitting skin.

As Nidan worked, Miale's light joined that of her sister and brother. For a moment, all three lights swirled together. With a blinding flash, they were gone.

Berend stared at the ceiling of the hall for several heartbeats. Then the war leader turned his attention back to his quarry. Still hidden in the pathways, Kiana and Skaric remained motionless save for the shuddering of Skaric's shoulders.

Nidan balled his hands into fists. *We didn't come here to die!*

His wounds were not fully healed, but he was no longer in danger of dying.

Nidan stood, careful not to make a sound. He closed his hand around the hilt of his sword. He crept towards Berend. *I never thought I'd stab a man in the back.* But he did so without hesitation.

Chapter Twenty-Seven

The twin vortexes called to Kiana, tugging her in two separate directions. But she had survived. Miale was gone and she was still there: body, mind and soul. She pushed herself into Skaric's chest, snuggling into his warm embrace as she stared up into his clear blue eyes. His brow crumpled.

"What's wrong?"

"Your eyes…" Skaric said. "…They're hazel now." The creases vanished from his brow. He began to stroke her face. "You did it." Then he leant down and gently kissed her lips.

Kiana felt weak and drained as her heart fluttered in her chest, making her breathless. She pressed her lips against Skaric's, returning his kiss with all the energy that was left in her body.

As Skaric's lips parted from hers everything shifted. Kiana's legs pressed against the floor and they felt like lead. She was still cold. Skaric was shivering as he continued to hold her. His face was white, his eyes sunken sapphires glittering within dark rings. They were both covered in a thick layer of frost that weighed down their eyelashes and soaked into their clothes. The pathways were gone. The vortex and eternity were nothing more than a memory.

Nidan came to kneel beside them. His shirt was slashed open and bloody. A jagged slash across his chest was knitting shut. Kiana trembled, holding back tears. She sat up slowly and threw her arms around both their necks. She allowed herself to cry freely, her body shaking with happiness and relief.

Kiana released her companions and brushed her tears away

with her fingertips. "Everyone needs to know what we've done. Everyone needs to know the truth." She stared at Skaric and Nidan.

They both held her gaze. Nidan was the first to nod.

"People won't accept Ysia back that easily," Skaric said.

Kiana grabbed his hand. "I know. But we have to make them. Please, Skaric. Nidan and I can't do this alone." Fear danced in his eyes. Kiana gestured at the space where the pathways had been. "If we don't, everything we've done here will have been for nothing."

Skaric squeezed her hand. "Yes, I'll help you." He grinned mischievously. "It's not like I've got anything better to do."

The End

About The Author

Clare Davidson is a self-motivated, character driven fantasy writer, mother, teacher and all-round creative whizz, from the UK. Clare was born in Northampton, but spent her early years living in Malaysia, before coming home and settling with her family in Leeds. After spending time at Lancaster University where she met her husband, Clare has now returned to Leeds with husband, daughter, new baby son, crazy puppy Rukia and Pirate the white cat in tow. In between being a full-time mother, wife and domestic goddess (in theory) and being plagued by various animals, Clare is the author of the fantasy book Trinity and more recently, the urban fantasy series Hidden. Her aim is to drag you into her fantasy worlds and never let you go. She's evil that way!

Connect With Clare Davidson

Website: http://www.claredavidson.com
Facebook: https://www.facebook.com/ClareMDavidson
Twitter: https://twitter.com/ClareMDavidson
Goodreads: http://www.goodreads.com/ClareDavidson
Mailing List: http://eepurl.com/zpjGf

Also By Clare Davidson

Reaper's Rhythm (Hidden: Book I)

When everyone thinks your sister committed suicide, it's hard to prove she was murdered.

Kim is unable to accept Charley's sudden death. Crippled by an unnatural amnesia, her questions are met with wall after wall. As she doubts her sanity, she realises her investigation is putting those around her in danger.

The only person who seems to know anything is Matthew, an elusive stranger who would rather vanish than talk. Despite his friendly smile, Kim isn't sure she can trust him. But if she wants to protect her family from further danger, Kim must work with Matthew to discover how Charley died – before it's too late.

www.ingramcontent.com/pod-product-compliance
Lightning Source LLC
Chambersburg PA
CBHW032059050726
47590CB00001B/335